THE
FERVOR

THE
FERVOR

A NOVEL

ALMA KATSU

G. P. PUTNAM'S SONS
NEW YORK

PUTNAM
— EST. 1838 —

G. P. Putnam's Sons

Publishers Since 1838

An imprint of Penguin Random House LLC

penguinrandomhouse.com

Copyright © 2022 by Glasstown Entertainment, LLC and Alma Katsu
Penguin supports copyright. Copyright fuels creativity, encourages
diverse voices, promotes free speech, and creates a vibrant culture.
Thank you for buying an authorized edition of this book and for complying
with copyright laws by not reproducing, scanning, or distributing any part
of it in any form without permission. You are supporting writers and
allowing Penguin to continue to publish books for every reader.

Library of Congress Cataloging-in-Publication Data

Names: Katsu, Alma, author.
Title: The fervor : a novel / Alma Katsu.
Description: New York : G. P. Putnam's Sons, [2022]
Identifiers: LCCN 2021055197 (print) | LCCN 2021055198 (ebook) |
ISBN 9780593328330 (hardcover) | ISBN 9780593328347 (ebook)
Subjects: LCSH: World War, 1939–1945—Japanese Americans—Fiction. |
Japanese Americans—Forced removal and internment, 1942–1945—Fiction. |
LCGFT: Historical fiction. | Paranormal fiction. |
Psychological fiction. | Novels.
Classification: LCC PS3611.A7886 F47 2022 (print) |
LCC PS3611.A7886 (ebook) | DDC 813/.6—dc23/eng/20211116
LC record available at https://lccn.loc.gov/2021055197
LC ebook record available at https://lccn.loc.gov/2021055198

Printed in the United States of America
1st Printing

BOOK DESIGN BY KRISTIN DEL ROSARIO

Title page art: Pattern © marukopum / Shutterstock

To my mother, Akiko Souza,
for her stories of childhood in Japan during the war,
and my father-in-law, John Katsu,
for sharing his experience of the internment

THE
FERVOR

WASABURO OISHI'S JOURNAL

MAY 1927

The island is windy and perpetually damp. Nothing but stone and tree and ocean, everywhere you look. Harrowing. You wouldn't know it's right off the coast of Shikotan, a bigger island broken off the northern tip of the country. It's so completely isolated, it feels like the end of the world.

We arrived only yesterday and already the cold sea air has seeped into my bones and softened the pages on which I now write. You shouldn't have come, the locals tell me. You shouldn't have brought your wife and child. It isn't safe.

Yuriko and Meiko have not complained, though this place could hardly be considered a vacation destination. They know the importance of this sabbatical from the Central Meteorological Observatory to further my study of the jet stream. This is my last chance, my superiors said when they approved this research trip. They are not convinced that the winds I have discovered are of any importance. Other scientists have ignored my work. The world has not taken notice of my papers.

It is not too late to take up some other research topic. "You are still a young man," my supervisor told me before I was to leave. "You can find something else with which to make your mark." They want me to stop making my measurements so they can use the money to pay for other work. I ~~*know that my discovery will prove to be important one day. My work on the*~~

jet stream will be my greatest contribution to mankind, I feel the truth of this in my heart.

Shikotan Island is my last chance to prove that there is something to "Wasaburo's Winds."

We have discovered that Shikotan also houses a colony for undesirables, the mad and the deformed, the people that society does not wish to see. They are sent here to this lonely outpost—to be studied and cared for, in theory. In reality, there is no other place for them to go. This is the place they are sent to die.

Because I am a scientist, I was expected to pay a visit to the hospital. But beyond such obligations, I was curious, hoping to understand what afflicts these patients, and how it may connect to the terrible lore of this place. I wanted to see them for myself. All the patients I encountered were distracted or deranged. Many violent. The sounds of their wailing and the rattling of their doors carried on the wind.

The man in charge said that everyone seems to get worse very quickly after arriving. He speculated that it had to do with the isolation. Even the attendants themselves tend to descend into a kind of madness here. For that reason, few leave the hospital alive.

But this year, he told me, things have gotten inexplicably worse. New arrivals have plunged rapidly into madness. He has no idea what is causing it. He advised me to send my family back to the mainland immediately and to stay as briefly as possible myself.

The island, the locals say, is cursed.

1

"Well gosh darnit, wouldn't you just."

Archie Mitchell gripped the gearshift of his 1941 Nash 600 sedan, but he could feel the loose spin of his tires over mud.

The late autumn rains had softened Dairy Creek Road into little more than a dark rivulet woven through the dense ponderosas and junipers blanketing the mountainside. Uncertainty spun in his gut. They should have known better than to take these logging roads this time of year.

"The kids, Arch," Elsie warned from the passenger seat. Her blond waves, her pink lips. Hazel eyes darted to the rearview mirror. In its reflection: an assortment of brown and green plaids and corduroys, jumbled knees and slipping socks. The Patzke kids, Dick and Joan, plus three others—Jay Gifford, Edward Engen, and Sherman Shoemaker—made up the entirety of the field trip. All of them with their hair combed tidy for Sunday. Whispering and humming tunes. Dick Patzke pulled on his teen sister's ponytail in the back seat.

"Are we stuck?" asked Ed.

"Everything's going to be just fine," Elsie assured the kids. "The Lord has brought us a little trial by nature is all."

Trial by nature. Archie smiled. His wife was right. He ought to have watched what he said. It's no wonder she had been the star pupil at Simpson Bible College, unlike him. Somehow, despite his many failings, God saw fit to give him Elsie.

He hit the gas again and this time the car lurched forward, a river of putty-gray slurry slipping out beneath them as the tires regained traction.

"You see, then?" Elsie patted his knee. He tried to feel comforted, but the bad premonition, the nervousness that had been ratcheting through his chest all morning, wouldn't go away.

Which was precisely why they were here. This trip to Gearhart Mountain had been Elsie's idea. She and Archie had been cooped up indoors, him fretting over her well-being all the time; they needed a change of pace. It was too easy to go haywire without a little fresh air, and it wasn't natural for a young, happy couple in their prime. Besides which, she'd heard the Patzkes had just lost their eldest boy overseas. Surely it was the duty of their pastor to step in and offer a kindness to the family in grief. It didn't hurt that a pair of avid fishermen in the congregation had told him the trout were still biting at Leonard Creek.

"My ever-hopeful fisherman," Elsie had teased him later that night, when they were lying in bed together under the yellow glow of their matching bedside lamps. "Wouldn't that be a nice thing to do for the Patzke kids? A little day trip some Sunday? The Patzkes could use some time alone to grieve, don't ya think? And besides, I could use the practice if I'm to be a mama soon."

She was trying to draw him out of his thoughts . . . and it worked. Archie rolled over and kissed his wife's round, taut belly. Five months and counting. This time it would all go perfectly. There was no need to worry. A healthy son was on his way—Archie reassured himself of it by the glow in Elsie's cheeks.

He'd whispered yes into her nightdress, and now *some Sunday* had become today.

The woods thickened around them, the sky a blissful blue. Only a few wisps of cloud lingered from yesterday's storm. Still, as they drove up the ever-steepening road, Archie could feel the knot of tension in his chest coiling tighter. He rolled down his window, taking in the crisp mountain air. It was cold enough to carry the scent of winter—and for a moment, he blinked, thinking he'd just seen a snowflake. An eerie feeling moved through him, as if he was in a room in which a door had suddenly blown open. But it was just a tiny seedling, some minuscule bit of fluff held aloft on the wind.

The kids sang hymns again as Archie maneuvered the Nash onto an even narrower service road. It was bumpier than Dairy Creek and he watched Elsie with a worried eye. She had one hand on her belly as they bounced over ruts.

He braked slowly, not far from an abandoned little cabin the fishermen had told him about. "Maybe it would be better to walk the rest of the way."

Elsie reached for the latch. "How about if I take the kids down to the creek? Maybe you can get a little further in the car. That way you won't have to haul the picnic things as far."

She was right, as usual. "You sure you'll be okay?"

Her smile was like sunshine. It filled him with something more than love, a thing he could not name, for it would insult God to know it. How he worshipped her. How he'd lie down on the mud and let her walk across him like a bridge if she asked. How he sometimes feared God had been too generous in giving him Elsie, feared what lengths he'd be willing to take just to make her smile, just to feel her gentle hands on him in the darkness, her curious little kisses that set him on fire with shameful thoughts. With Elsie, he was powerless.

"Of course," she said now. "You know you must *sometimes* tolerate letting me outta your sight." Another smile, and then he watched as the kids scampered out of the car like baby goats let out of the pen.

"I'm gonna catch the biggest fish," one of the boys crowed.

"No, *I'm* going to . . ."

"I'm gonna catch a whale!"

"That's stupid. There ain't no whales in a creek," the first boy shouted back. The voices reminded Archie of when he was a boy, fishing off a bridge with his friends. Children happy to be children, let loose to play. He wasn't hardly thirty years old but he felt like an old man already.

"Last one down to the creek—"

. . . *is a rotten egg*, Archie finished to himself. Some things never changed.

They ran down the trail, goading each other to run faster. Elsie brought up the rear with the Patzke girl. Joan Patzke really was a good kid, Archie thought. Considerate. She knew enough to stay with Elsie, made sure she had company and a hand to hold.

If only every family in his congregation was as nice as the Patzkes . . . If all the parents in Bly could be as good as these children, everything would be all right, he thought. But still somehow, the thought failed to ease the tightness in his chest.

Once the baby was born, he'd be able to breathe again. The doctors all assured him that five months was well and good enough along to stop worrying—but they had said that the last time, too.

He parked as far off the trail as he could, but the Nash took up most of the road. There was no way around it. The trail was too narrow.

He opened the trunk and was enveloped in the aroma of

chocolate. Elsie had decided that, if they were going on a picnic, they needed a chocolate cake. She baked the layers yesterday, setting them out on racks to cool last night. She'd made the frosting this morning, beating the butter and sugar by hand with a big wooden spoon. Elsie only baked chocolate cake once or twice a year, and the thought of it made his mouth water. He lifted the cake carrier and slung the wooden handles over one forearm, then hefted the picnic basket with the other. Inside were turkey sandwiches. A thermos of coffee for the adults and a jug of cider for the kids.

He put the basket on the ground and was closing the trunk when another tiny white seedling, no bigger than a snowflake, landed near his nose. He brushed it away, oddly unnerved by it. That feeling again: a wind surging right through him. He shivered and slammed the trunk.

A woman stood in front of him.

He jumped in surprise, but she remained perfectly still, observing him. She was a young woman and beautiful. She was dressed in a kimono, a nice one from what he could tell, but she was disheveled. Her shiny black hair was falling down in wisps, the ends of her obi fluttering in the breeze.

Where had she come from? There hadn't been anyone on the trail or in the woods—Archie was positive. He'd been paying extra close attention as he navigated the mud.

Funny for someone to be roaming around the mountain in such fancy dress. Though Archie had seen Japanese wearing traditional garb in Bly—years ago.

No Japanese left in town anymore.

The strangest part was the look on her face, the way she smiled at him. Cunning. Sly. It stopped the questions forming in his throat. Kept him from doing anything except stare.

More of the white seedlings drifted between them, swirling

playfully. She lifted a finger and gestured toward them. *"Kumo,"* she in a voice barely above a whisper. Archie didn't know the word but he was pretty sure that was what she'd said. *Kumo.*

The sound of children yelling broke his concentration, and Archie looked away. Little Edward—or was it Sherman?—was shouting something in the distance. Had to be sure Elsie was okay, that the kids hadn't gotten up to some mischief . . .

And when he turned back, the woman in the kimono was gone.

For a moment, he paused, confused. He looked down at the spot where she had stood, and there were no footprints. The mud was untrampled.

A chill ran down his spine, followed by a tremor of guilt.

But then the boys yelled again, in high-pitched, excited little voices, and Archie was forced to let it go.

"What's going on?" Archie called out, picking up the food items again and beginning his trudge toward the tree line. He got closer, and the voices became louder.

"Whoa!" That was Joan's voice.

"Honey?" That was Elsie now. "We've found something. Come look!"

He could see their forms now, through the trees. The creek in the distance, black and twisty as a snake. Something light and large in a clearing, covering the ground like alien moss.

"What is it?" Archie called out, hurrying.

He wasn't at all sure what to make of the shape in the distance: it could be a piece of a banner come loose from a building or warehouse, or even a bedsheet escaped from a clothesline. It was weathered, grayish, and sprawling—unnatural in all this wilderness.

"Some kind of parachute?" Elsie shouted over her shoulder.

A knife of panic. He dropped the basket and the cake. "Don't touch anything!" There'd been a news story a few months back. Something about a parachute falling out of the sky and catching fire on the power lines at a power plant near Spokane. Whole plant could've gone up in smoke but for the generator cutting off. The newspaper had called it a parachute, but onlookers didn't agree. Some feared it was an unmarked weapon of war.

He ran toward them now. "Did you hear me?" His voice came out ragged, breathless. "I said be careful and don't—"

Archie choked and stopped running. Something drifting on the wind caught in his throat. It looked like snow, but it couldn't be. Too early for snow, though not unheard of this time of year. Another seedling—or maybe something else. Maybe it was ash. He saw loads of it in the air now: bits of white fluff, like dandelion seeds but smaller. *No dandelion seeds in November.* He froze, momentarily mesmerized. He lifted a hand to catch one but the wind carried it away.

His hand was still suspended in the air when another bit of white caught on his eyelashes. It was so close to his eye that at first, it was just a semitransparent orb. A mote.

But then, as his eye attempted to focus on it, it moved.

It moved strangely, like it had arms. The arms wove left and right, up and down. With cold clarity, he knew what it was.

A tiny translucent spider.

His shock was cut through with a thundering boom.

And then: he was blown backward, as if from cannon fire.

When Archie was just a kid, there'd been a terrible accident on his parents' farm. His uncle Ronald had gotten trapped in the grain silo when a fire broke out. It was a nightmare, the inside of the silo a whirling tornado of flame. No one had been able to get to his uncle and drag him out, no way to get water in to douse the flames. He remembers his parents' panic, the shock of it, farm hands running and shouting, everyone helpless.

It was a terrible accident. Everybody said so.

Later, when neighbors came over to console Archie's parents, Archie supposedly in bed but listening on the stairs, he remembered how his father had insisted that his brother had brought it on himself. "He was probably drunk," he'd said bitterly before Archie's mother had shushed him. But in that moment, it all made sense to Archie (or maybe he was just grasping at straws): how Uncle Ronald had just shown up on the doorstep one day, no mention of where his wife was. How he slept on the couch and Archie would find him in the morning reeking of alcohol. "He was a sinner. And believe you me, those who sin will meet the fire of Hell in the end," his father had said that night.

And the terrible feeling Archie had had, feeling that he was somehow responsible for it. His mother dismissed it as Christian sympathy. *Because you are such a good boy. A good Christian soul.*

Archie sometimes looked back on that night as the start of something. A fire lit inside him. For years he tried to be good. He would refuse temptation, not give in to sin. He would be above reproach.

All the while, however, he carried a terrible secret. A guilt that he couldn't allow himself to acknowledge and snuffed out as soon as it came creeping back to him.

And then, at last, he found Elsie. Because she was so virtuous, so clean, he found it easy to be good around her. The mistakes of the past were behind him forever, he thought.

But he was wrong.

In trembling shock, Archie climbed up from the roots and mud, staggered to his feet, lumbered toward a thick and billowing smoke. It was as if the spot where everyone had been standing had suddenly opened up, gone volcanic. He choked; smoke burned his eyes. Where was everyone?

The colorful shapes he'd seen just a minute earlier—Elsie's

white cardigan, the Patzke girl's blue dress, the Shoemaker boy's plaid shirt—were gone from his field of vision. Or no, not gone. Strewn across the ground. Like laundry thrown carelessly in the air.

Writhing.

Screaming. Had the sound ripped from his own throat?

He was running again, climbing over two of the clothes piles—one flailing and shrieking, one eerily still. He would trample a hundred burning children to get to Elsie. It was his greatest sin, this worship of her. It was the bit of Hell that burned inside him.

She was screaming. Thrashing. Inhuman.

The next thing he knew was that he was kneeling in the mud beside her—this creature who was his wife transformed. Transmuted by fire and chaos into something else. He whipped off his coat and tried to smother the flames, holding her down. *Let me help you,* he screamed.

But her face was no face, it was all gash: red and pulpy, an open wound, skin seared off flesh. Her lips moved but he couldn't make out what she was saying.

There was moaning all around him. He was paralyzed by shock. This wasn't real. He had plunged backward through time to the night of that fire, only this time, it wasn't his uncle but Archie himself, at the center of the flames, burning alive.

He didn't know how long he knelt there, panting, choking, screams tearing his throat raw. Coughing up smoke and blood, flapping in vain at his wife's burning body, even when she had begun to go still.

Finally, hands fell on his shoulders—dimly, he was aware of two road workers they'd passed on the way up Dairy Creek Road. The strong hands dragged Archie along the forest floor, away from the blast, away from the still-burning pyre the mysterious parachute had become. Away from the children.

Away from her—his life, his future, his everything.

Just before losing consciousness, a thought came to him. *This is my fate. My punishment.*

For the terrible thing he did.

He'd thought he'd outrun it, but all this time Hell had been waiting for him with its mouth wide open.

2

CAMP MINIDOKA, IDAHO

The big truck lumbered slowly through the camp gates, the ruts in the dirt road making its wide body roll like a swaybacked cow. Something unusual about it caught Meiko Briggs's eye. Trucks came to the internment camp all the time to make deliveries, but they were always civilian. This one was painted a dull olive green and tattooed with U.S. ARMY and strings of white numbers all over its flanks. The cargo bed was tented.

Meiko had been walking her daughter Aiko to school that morning when the truck arrived. Her eye followed it down one of the rarely used roads toward a big barn. NO INTERNEES BEYOND THIS POINT, the sign read. Most of the buildings at Minidoka were used by camp residents, but that one was the domain of the administrators. Lately, there had been a padlock on the doors. Guards stood waiting to close those doors as soon as the truck pulled in. They didn't want anyone to see what was inside.

She could not help but wonder what that was about. The military had not bothered with the camp before.

The gate to the camp swung shut, too, though Meiko could barely see the need. It might as well stand open, and it wasn't as though it was ever locked. The executive order that had forced her and the other ten thousand residents to Minidoka two years ago was on the verge of being rescinded. That the residents would be freed from their prison was the talk of the camp lately. A few residents were making plans to leave—prematurely, some grumbled—but most were not. Even as they followed the drama being played out in the Supreme Court, the residents of Minidoka were quiescent. What kept them in the bare-board dormitories, overstuffed in tiny, dust-filled, lice-infested rooms, was more powerful than guards with rifles.

It was fear of what was beyond the fence: the hatred of their fellow American citizens.

They'd all heard stories of Japanese returning to their hometowns only to be threatened, then beaten if they didn't leave. Not to mention finding their homes and businesses bought out from under them. There were cases where neighbors with whom they'd left belongings, neighbors who had promised to save it all until this had blown over, had instead sold out, deciding that the rightful owners would never return.

Friends and neighbors had turned their backs on them, in three short years. The change was chilling.

The appearance of the truck was unusual enough for Aiko to notice, too. She watched with her whole body, it seemed, even rising to her tiptoes to get a better look as it disappeared.

This was not a good sign. The girl had been acting more and more strange lately, seemingly frightened by everything. Not unexpected for a child who had been through as much as Aiko had—living two years in what was no better than a concentration camp, her father off fighting in a war. Lately, however, it had gotten almost too much to deal with. Nightmares, bizarre stories. Claiming to hear voices and see apparitions. "Nothing to worry about. All kids go through it," Mrs. Tanaka had told Meiko one afternoon, as they had been hanging their wash on the line. "It's a phase. You'll see."

Meiko hoped her neighbor was right.

"What are you looking at?" The voice beside them was as sharp as the point of a bayonet. With a pang of concern, Meiko recognized the speaker. He was called Wallaby, or something like that: as a rule, the guards didn't share their names. None of the residents liked this one. He would pull his eyelids sideways and throw slurs at them in a singsong voice, called them "little yellow men." He plainly thought the residents were inferior, not just different from whites but altogether lacking somehow.

Since coming to America, Meiko had come to see that this notion was pure nonsense. It wasn't as though the belief that one race was superior to all others was alien to her—it wasn't, because Japanese were raised to believe that they were better than others. But in Japan, where there was effectively only one race, one people, you could at least see how that notion had happened. Whereas America was made up of so many different kinds of people, you'd think they'd have gotten used to each other by now. How exhausting it must be here to hate everyone who was different.

She knew better than to say this to this guard, however. "We're going." She noticed that guards were prodding other residents who had stopped to look at the army truck, too, telling them to move along.

What made the truck more notable was that there had been an influx of government people lately, too. They'd started arriving at the camp a few weeks earlier. And it was obvious that these men weren't locals. They seemed more sophisticated. They dressed better than the Idahoans, were better spoken. They came in fancy new cars at a time when it was hard to get one because production had been halted for the war effort. If they'd made the trip special, then obviously they had come to Minidoka for a reason, but that was a mystery. They avoided the residents and were escorted by camp officials, who, when asked, said the men were just accountants sent to make sure that the camp was being run efficiently.

How would they explain that truck? Meiko wondered.

The makeshift school wasn't so far from their dormitory block but Meiko walked her daughter there whenever possible. At Minidoka, the school was nothing more than homemade tables set up in an outbuilding. A couple of the residents had been teachers before internment, but most of their instructors were camp residents pitching in to teach whatever they could remember from their own days as students: English, history, math, science. The parents worried that their children were falling behind in their educations, that they would never be able to make up these lost years. Education was important to Japanese parents. They feared their kids wouldn't be able to get into college. That there'd be an invisible asterisk in their records for their years in the camps.

Her daughter had mentioned once that she always walked to class alone whereas most of the children walked together in little groups, and that tugged at Meiko's heart. There were a lot of perfectly ordinary reasons why this might be—her daughter was naturally shy—but Meiko could think of a couple unkind ones, too. Her daughter was only half Japanese, whereas, for most of the kids in camp, both parents were of Japanese descent. Japanese could be very snooty about racial purity. Aiko also didn't like the things that other kids liked—comic books and radio shows, for example. She wasn't fixated on movie starlets and crooners.

Then there was her incessant drawing. Even Meiko had to admit Aiko drew pictures like a child possessed. It was hard to get her to stop, even for meals. And the creatures Aiko drew! Meiko could only imagine what the teachers must think. Aiko had started out with animals and fairies and princesses from whichever fairy tale her father had read to her that night. The usual stuff. But since coming to the camp, she'd started drawing creatures from the bedtime stories Meiko had told her, the ones Meiko had learned from her father back in Japan.

The drawings were getting scarier and scarier. Anyone who saw them would question whether these were unnatural subjects for a child.

Meiko crouched so she was eye level with her daughter. She straightened Aiko's collar, which had gotten twisted. "Have a good day. Study hard. And"—she hesitated over whether she should add the next part—"try not to draw too much. It makes the teachers think you're not paying attention to them."

"I am paying attention. But the demons . . ." Aiko trailed off.

Meiko knew what her daughter was going to say. *But the demons want me to pay attention to them, too.*

Her daughter said the demons followed her. They sat in the corner and giggled at things the teacher said. They told her which residents did bad things when no one was watching, which children stole coins from their mother's purse, and which parents waited until everyone else had gone to bed to beat their children.

The demons, Aiko said, knew everything.

Aiko looked at her mother, stricken. "Mama, I know you don't want me to talk about the demons but . . ." She wriggled, bound by conscience.

She is trying. She really is a good kid. With a sigh, Meiko said, "What is it?"

"Mama, that truck we saw on our way here? The demons say we have to stay away from it. They say there's something bad inside it."

This was new. Aiko had never exhibited any anxiety about the camp, the guards, or the administrators, the others who ruled their lives but generally—blessedly—left the children alone. No, Aiko's stories had all been about the other Japanese and her social anxieties, the kinds of things that made sense for a child to be worried about.

"What do they say is inside it?" Meiko asked. She couldn't imagine it was anything out of the ordinary: surplus office equipment, maybe, or run-of-the-mill supplies. Maybe getting Aiko to explore her anxieties would help.

"They didn't tell me, they just said we shouldn't go near it. That whatever's inside can make you very, very sick." Her voice dropped to a whisper. "They told me things are going to get worse soon. They said we won't be able to escape because they're going to make us stay inside the camp. Because they want us to be trapped."

Meiko's stomach twisted. "Who wants to trap us inside the camp?"

But Aiko's expression begged not to make her say any more.

Meiko felt the color drain from her face. She could hardly believe it was her child, her normally cheerful and obedient daughter. In Japan, her father had told her scary stories once upon a time, when he was trying good-naturedly to frighten her. But then he'd tickle her, or do something to break the tension, and she would know that it was all make-believe.

Here, there was no one to help with her daughter. She did not even have her husband, Jamie, the one who normally dispensed the tickles and kisses and reassurances.

At that moment, one of the teachers stepped out, ringing the big silver bell, calling the children to class. Aiko ran off to join the other children before Meiko could think what to say to her.

Meiko went to the kitchen next. She had a shift that day. She went to her usual station, where someone had already deposited a load of vegetables from the garden to be prepped. Potatoes, turnips, and carrots. How they managed to grow anything in the hard prairie soil was a testament to the skill of the farmers among them, men and women who'd run big commercial farms in Oregon and Washington State. It was a miracle they were able to coax anything to grow on a couple rocky, arid acres.

"What's wrong, Meiko? You look like you saw a ghost." Mayumi Seiko was chopping radish to make pickles. She was the most plainspoken of the kitchen crew, uncharacteristically blunt for Japanese. But then, Meiko had to constantly remind herself that most of these people were Nisei, born in America, not Japanese natives, Issei, like herself.

She slid the carrots in a bucket of water. "An army truck just arrived at the camp." She didn't mention what Aiko had said. A few of them already thought she was a little strange.

"Maybe they're sending soldiers." Patsy Otsuka pushed back a curl that had fallen over her forehead. Every morning she carefully curled her hair to look like Betty Grable's. "Or it could be medical staff to help with the outbreak."

The outbreak. That was the only name they had for the illness that was sweeping through the camp the past couple weeks. No one knew what it was, though the best guess was some kind of flu or ague. It hit people differently—some had fever, some had chills and sweating, others complained of headaches so debilitating that they couldn't stand noise or light—but it was undeniably virulent. Entire dormitories seemingly came down with it overnight. An entire dorm block would get sick and then it would spread to the blocks on either side in just a matter of days. Mostly, people took to their beds shivering and vomiting, but it had affected tempers, with some turning belligerent and argumentative, then violent. Fights were starting to break out among residents, sometimes even with guards. Heads were cracked by truncheons, men dragged to the makeshift jail.

Before the outbreak, they hadn't needed one.

People were frightened by the mystery illness. No one wanted to catch it.

No wonder Aiko said the demons were warning her that people were going to become very ill. No one had died from the outbreak yet—not that Meiko had heard—but it was all around them. The kids probably talked among themselves, scared to death that their parents might be taken from them. It was probably all they could think about.

The poor kid was probably overwhelmed. Swamped with fear.

"If they've sent medical help—well, hallelujah. It's about time," Hiroji Kubo muttered. He was butchering chickens at a table in the back, out of sight. The cleaver came down on the chopping block with a decisive *thwack*. "The camp doctor, he's been useless. No help at all. They don't care if we get sick because we're Japanese."

"They act like it's our fault." It was Mayumi again. "I actually heard one of the guards say, 'What else do you expect from a bunch of dirty Japanese?'" They'd all heard such things said about them, even back in Seattle. Even though you could eat off the floors in most Japanese homes.

Not that people outside used the term "Japanese." None of the internees could bring themselves to say the word "Japs."

"It's not like the guards haven't gotten sick, too," Patsy muttered. She was cubing turnips, eyes trained on the knife as she made perfect little squares. "But they whisk them away, as soon as they start showing symptoms."

"It's to keep from spreading disease." It was Rei Sugimoto. She had been standing in the back, quietly salting fish fillets. Rei was an appeaser, like many of the Japanese women. She never spoke badly of another person. She'd been trained to seem, at least, that she only thought the best of other people.

"Oh, please." Mayumi rolled her eyes. "When it's one of their own, they take care of them. When it's one of us—tough luck."

Meiko picked up a paring knife and began peeling carrots. "I'll ask Ken about it. Maybe he knows something."

The room fell silent, and Meiko knew she'd made a mistake. A couple of the women snuck sideways glances at her. Kenzo Nishi was one of the leaders inside the camp, elected to represent them to the administrators. She could argue that it only made sense to go to him, but everyone guessed there was something more between her and Ken. Even though they both were married to other people, Ken's wife with him here at Minidoka, Meiko's husband, Jamie, flying with the U.S. Army Air Forces in the Far East.

If they knew the real connection between her and Ken . . . Ken, at least, was a respected figure in camp. She, on the other hand, was already despised for being married to a white man. There were people who gave her a wide berth whenever they saw her coming. Shot her dirty looks in church. They assumed she thought herself better than the rest of them. If they knew what had really transpired between her and Ken, they would hate her even more.

In the afternoon, once all the prep work had been done for the evening meal, Meiko left to meet Aiko at home after school.

It was late, with the sun starting to sink on the horizon, when she crossed the road that led to the barn with the army truck. People were starting their evening routines, heading indoors. Many of the administrators had already left for the day, returning to their homes in nearby Jerome. There was almost nobody about—including guards. The few people still outside were hard to make out in the gathering dusk. If she were to sneak over to the barn to take a look around, she doubted she would be seen.

All afternoon, she'd been thinking about sneaking a peek at whatever was in the truck. Then she could reassure Aiko with au-thority that the demons were wrong—and, really, that there were no demons, that these anxieties only existed in her mind. They were all her own. The residents were getting sick, yes, but it was a perfectly natural course of events and that didn't mean anyone was going to die. Maybe that would help the poor girl with her nerves.

At the moment, it was the only comfort she could give her daughter.

The door was padlocked, but the building had windows. She picked one on the north side. She peered in first to make sure there was no one inside, but there were no lights on, either, so she felt pretty sure that it was empty. She tried to lift the sash. It budged slightly but stopped after an inch. She almost gave up but decided she shouldn't throw in the towel so easily. She would try a second time. If it had moved that much, it probably wasn't locked on the inside, only jammed, perfectly understandable given the harsh cold. After a few minutes prying, she was able to lift it high enough to squeeze through.

There wasn't a lot inside the big building besides the truck. There were shelves along one wall stacked with metal cases and wooden crates. The crates were nailed shut and the lids painted with the warning DANGEROUS GOODS. It made her wonder what was inside. Poison? Explosives? What dangerous materials would they send to a camp with children?

The metal cases weren't locked but kept shut with simple latches. She opened one to find gas masks. *Gas masks.* Maybe poison wasn't so far off, after all. A second one was packed with surgical clothing and pair after pair of white cotton gloves. Others held gauze and cotton wool, bottles of rubbing alcohol and ether. Medical supplies, for the most part. Maybe it *was* medical help. But if that were the case, why hadn't they distributed supplies already? Why hadn't they set up additional hospital units? And why would they send gas masks?

Maybe there *was* a reason they didn't want the residents to see what they were bringing into camp, a reason for guards and padlocks.

She went to the truck next. It had California license plates and U.S. ARMY and serial numbers spray-painted in white on its side. It was dusty and looked like it had been driven a long way. The bed was high off the ground and Meiko was not able to pull herself up, so she dragged a box over so she could climb up over the tailgate.

It was fairly dark inside the barn, so she threw the tenting back as much as possible so that she could see what she was doing. Surprisingly, the cargo bed was mostly empty, with only what appeared to be a tarp spread out on the floor. She dropped to her knees to examine it. Feeling the fabric, she knew right away that it wasn't a tarp. It wasn't made of canvas. It reminded her of something from her childhood, something she'd used all the time in Japan: washi paper. Only it was stiffer and heavier than the stuff she'd used to make cards or fashion kimonos for dolls. It felt cruder, too. She had no idea what paper like this would be used for.

It was weatherworn. She couldn't see well because there were few windows in the barn and the light was fading fast, but she could tell it had been exposed to the elements. It also was charred in places, as though it had caught fire. This big piece of washi paper, bigger than any she'd ever seen, seemed to have survived a contradiction of conditions. She racked her mind to think how that possibly could have happened. She was about to climb down from the truck when she saw what looked like writing on the underside of the paper. It was too dark to make out what it said but she thought it looked like Japanese characters. The formal block printing reminded her of official government documents she'd seen among her father's things. They had the same distinctive, square shape.

A troubling feeling passed over Meiko. *It's just seeing the lettering,* she told herself, seeing something that reminded her of Japan. But she felt, too, like she'd forgotten something and this thing on the floor, whatever it was, was reminding her of it. It tugged, trying to unearth something in the back of her mind, but all she had was the ghost of a memory.

And it was bad, this feeling. Just like the demons had said.

She tried to shake it off. There were no demons, only a little girl's shattered nerves.

If this did belong to the Japanese government, how had the U.S. military gotten hold of it? It could've come from the war zone, of course, but if that were the case, why bring it to an internment camp in the middle of the prairie? Wouldn't they keep it on one of the dozens of army bases along the coast? It made far more sense that they would keep it somewhere secure, somewhere they had the people trained to analyze such things.

She left the mystery inside the truck reluctantly, climbing through the window and dropping to the ground. She knew she couldn't stay any longer: Aiko would be home from school. She didn't want her daughter to be left on her own any longer than was absolutely necessary.

She found Aiko sitting on her bed, a notebook open before her. Luckily, the girl was good on her own. Maybe it was the by-product of being an only child.

"How was school today?" Meiko asked as she hung up her jacket, her exploration in the barn put out of mind.

"Fine. We worked on multiplication tables." Math wasn't Aiko's favorite subject but she was good at it. Then again, the girl was good at many things. Languages, for instance: she'd picked up Japanese, a hard language to master. And art: fantastic Japanese demons not-withstanding, Aiko could reproduce any photo or painting from memory. As proud as Meiko was of her daughter's talents, however, she wanted the girl to push herself. Drawing would not pay the bills when she got older. Meiko wanted her daughter to be employable, to be able to support herself and not depend on a man to put a roof over her head.

That was how Meiko had been raised, and look what it got her.

"Do you need to get started on your homework?" They had a few hours until dinner in the mess hall. A Japanese meal and an American one, for the Nisei children who didn't like the weird things their parents ate.

"I have a chapter to read for history." American history was, ironically, the only history they taught in the camp's makeshift school. Not world history and, God forbid, nothing about the country of their ancestors, of Aiko's grandparents. *The country we are at war with.* Meiko pushed the last thought away: she was tired of struggling with this reality, the unfortunate turn her life had taken. Never did she guess, when her father had sent her away years ago to marry in America, that the two countries would be at war.

"Get started now, while the light is good." The illumination here wasn't good for reading: bare bulbs suspended from the ceiling. When they were being rousted from their homes and herded into railcars and buses years ago, no one had thought to bring lamps with them.

Meiko did her housekeeping while Aiko read. It was an endless battle in the camp against the dust blown in from the prairie. It crept through cracks in the hastily built walls, constantly depositing a fresh coat of fine, pale sand all over everything. Meiko methodically moved through their room, shaking out the neatly folded clothing and dusting shelves made of board and cinder block.

While she dusted, she asked herself for the thousandth time: how had she ended up here? The military should've kept them from sending her to an internment camp. You would think the fact that her husband was a serviceman—and a pilot to boot, an important job to judge from the fuss made over them—meant *something*. To be treated with so little honor was insulting. She had heard that white aviators' wives lived in nice houses on military bases. No such offer had been made to her, of course. It was a constant reminder that she was worth less than white women.

Now that the executive order had been lifted, she and Aiko could leave the camp if they could find someone to sponsor them. Jamie knew this yet had not offered to ask his parents. They lived somewhere in Washington State. She had never so much as seen a photo of them, let alone met them. There was bad blood there, she knew. Jamie had left home as soon as he was out of high school, but he had never shared the details with her. Aiko clung to some hope—a child's fantasy—that her grandparents would rescue them one day, that they would suddenly appear at Minidoka, bundle her up in their arms, and whisk her off to a house with a white picket fence. Meiko understood what it was really about: the child craved security, a place where she would always feel safe. But Meiko knew instinctively that the Briggses were not coming, that they would never help them. Ironically, this security was exactly what Aiko's grandfather in Japan would give her. He would love to meet his granddaughter, the only daughter of his only daughter. But between the war and the thousands of miles of ocean separating them, that was impossible and, in all likelihood, would never happen.

After dinner in the mess hall, Meiko shepherded Aiko along a different path back to the dormitory. She said she wanted to take in the night air, but the truth was that she wanted to check on something. To satisfy her curiosity.

They ambled slowly down the trail that led to the camp entrance, past the administrative buildings, and then on to the gatehouse. The gatehouse was closed at this hour, of course, though the floodlights were on, as always. They illuminated the road from town even though no one ever visited the camp at night. Meiko assumed they did this in case of an emergency that, so far, had never happened. Thank goodness.

But in the bright light, Meiko saw—for the first time she could ever remember—there was now a chain. It was looped between the bars of the gates, two fat coils of link on link.

And completing the picture, leaving no doubt as to the intent, was a huge, solid-looking padlock.

3

Fran Gurstwold woke in the dark, suddenly cold. Her head was hazy; she was not in her apartment. Dread tickled her throat. The air felt different, smelled of burnt leaves, smoke. For a moment, she wondered if she'd been abducted, or was in some kind of eerie, waking dream.

Then she turned and saw the shape of Richard's sleeping body beside her, one leg strewn out from beneath the sheet. She let out a sigh. His muscled back rose and fell. Beyond him, a near-gone bottle of bottom-shelf Merlot stood uncorked, two empty glasses ringed in darkness beside it. *Right.* Lake Ogallala. The ramshackle old cabin they'd borrowed from a friend of a friend. Far enough out that no one they knew would hear about it. Far enough that it wouldn't get back to Winnie.

That accounted for the the unpleasant stillness. She lay back on the lumpy, feather-stuffed pillow and breathed slowly, steadying her heart, as the earlier part of the night returned to her: the restless unzipping, the sheen of sweat, the hungry, frantic way she and Richard always fucked as though the world were about to end. They were calling this the *second* world war, after all. She hadn't known the world could sustain more than one. Maybe it wouldn't.

Her head hurt. Forget sleeping. She rolled over and reached for the flannel jacket she'd brought with her—Richard had warned her it would be cold at the lake—and threw it on over her bra, the new double-A cup with the silk lacing. She dragged a hand through her snarled hair.

Fran always thought she could have been pretty except that she had the kind of face that, as she'd been told by a foster parent once, made men want to hit it. It was the kind of thing that got said to orphans. Unremarkable eyes, a wide jaw, and an upper lip that always wanted to curl softly into a snarl. She had the most unladylike ratty hair. But the far worse liability than her face was her mind. All its morbid curiosity, its rabid focus on details. Her inability to forget anything, good or bad. Especially the bad.

And she had a bad feeling in her gut now. An empty feeling. Restless, she tiptoed through the still cabin, stopping by her purse to retrieve her cigarettes and lighter, and then went out on the porch.

She tapped out a cigarette and lit it up. It was freezing outside, away from the woodstove, and her bare legs instantly broke out in goose bumps, but Richard didn't care for cigarette smoke, the way it clung to his clothes and tipped off his wife later. It wasn't often they got to play house like this. Usually they met at a hotel a couple blocks away from the newspaper, but that was a huge risk. Once or twice they'd made do with the back seat of his big car, a Chevrolet Fleetline Richard had bought in 1941, right before production was halted because of the war effort.

They never met at her place: he refused to come to her apartment and it was just as well. She spent as little time home as possible, hated its forever backed-up drains, its hovering scent of emptied soup cans, the knotty array of strewn papers and clothes across the floor. Her cat, Marcel, had gone practically feral from his long days alone in that place. She felt guilty for leaving him on his own so much but liked to think he shared her preference for solitude.

She took a drag on the cigarette and leaned against the railing, still trying to calm the anxious rustle in her chest. The darkness out here was complete, full of a fresh, wintery sting, unlike back home, where there were streetlights and puffs of exhaust chugging out the backs of passing cars. The night felt alive, in a way that stirred and unnerved her. She scanned the bumpy line of trees, hardly a ripple of black against black. Anyone could burst out of the forest—would she hear the crackle of twigs before it was too late?

But she was being paranoid. The lake was deserted this time of year. On Saturday, they'd walked around the lake's edge for a while but the wind over the water had been bitterly cold and they'd given up after fifteen minutes. Being the off-season, it was hard finding places to eat, and Fran was a miserable cook. Mostly they snacked on crackers and cheese and salami, and drank beers they kept on the porch in a cooler. He'd held his beer in one hand and brushed a stray hair out of her face with the other. He'd laughed as she ranted about some inconsistency in *The Chicago Manual of Style*. When darkness came, she'd prayed that the trash wouldn't draw bears out from the woods.

She flicked ash over the railing and took another drag. Her mind flitted ahead: it would be a long run over the next couple months. Thanksgiving, then Christmas, capped off by New Year's Eve. Everyone would be talking about what they were going to do for the holidays, where they were going to go. They'd grumble about the bother of driving for days to see relatives back east or having the house full of visiting family. Complaining in the smug, oblivious way that people do.

Winnie was a good little cook, or so she'd overheard Richard say. Her turkey was probably a point of pride with its perfectly crisped skin, the homemade roasted chestnut stuffing. At the table, their two children, girl Cissy and boy Brian, spit-polished and in their Sunday best. The four Hansons would bow their heads as they said grace. The perfect family, all of it a perfect lie.

That wasn't what she wanted, though, was it? A family, two kids? So why did the idea fill her with so much anger?

She dropped the butt over the railing and lit a second one.

The flick of her lighter seemed to ignite the sky, and she blinked, startled, as a bright orange fireball flared over the treetops, filling the night's stillness with a noisy *boom*.

She nearly dropped the second cigarette as she backed off the railing and squinted.

All the crickets had gone silent.

"Oh shit." What was that? Fireworks? It was the wrong time of year for that, and who would be shooting off fireworks out here in the middle of nowhere, at this hour? She watched the streaks of flame fall from the sky, watched them go out just as quickly.

She stood there, staring at the ashy trail left behind. She'd had a fleeting boyfriend as a teenager, Gary Ry—crooked teeth, crummy manners, thick-handed but sweet—and Gary'd seen one too many pictures. He believed in extraterrestrials, was always ready at the drop of a hat with some piece of trivia or another: a sighting in Arizona, an abduction in Vermont. She'd thought of it as an embarrassing fetish. A bit pervy, really, all those stories of probings. She hadn't thought of Gary in ages but a funny thought possessed her now. A thought that whatever she'd just witnessed was not of this earth.

A strange instinctive worry squirmed through her stomach. She ran back into the cabin, heedless of the way the screen door slammed. She shook Richard, hard. "Hey, Rich. Hey. Get up. Something's going on."

He barely raised his head off the pillow. "What?" She recalled how much of that bottle he'd put back, and the whiskey before it. *Antifreeze*, he'd joked, rattling the flask.

"Didn't you hear it?" she said over her shoulder as she slipped her frozen legs into a pair of trousers, threw on a waffled long-sleeved shirt, and put the jacket back on. She started lacing her boots. "It was so loud, Rich." A thought came to her. "Maybe we're under attack."

That seemed to wake him up. He pushed back the blankets. "What are you doing?"

"I'm getting dressed, obviously. We're going to investigate." She grabbed the flashlight she'd brought in from the car.

He grumbled but he got out of bed and put on his clothes, clearly still in a daze. He came up behind her and ran his warm hand up beneath her shirt. "You're cold," he whispered, his voice still thick with sleep. "Let me warm you up under the sheets."

She caught his big, deep brown eyes in the spotted mirror. "Later." She pulled away and went to the door. He groaned but followed her.

As soon as they were outside, she headed in the direction where she thought the fireball might've landed, though she wasn't feeling confident now that they were surrounded by darkness. If it'd been a bomb, she told herself, it would've been louder. They'd see trees aflame.

Then again, she was no expert on weaponry. She looked up into the darkness. Would another fall from the sky at any moment? The beam of her flashlight bounced across the indifferent trees. They had to hurry. They had to find it.

Distance over wide, open spaces was notoriously hard to judge, especially at night. It seemed like the explosive, whatever it had been, had fallen just over the ridgeline . . . but it could be miles away, and even if they found it, how would they find their way back?

The surrounding forest was a bewildering mass of leafless black trunks and branches, the ground a thick carpet of dead branches and brown leaves. There was no light to be had outside the thin beam from the flashlight. What if the batteries suddenly died? She tried to push the thought from her mind as she trudged along, concentrated on putting one foot in front of the other. But there really was no light: not one speck from any of the other cabins they'd passed earlier in the day, not one stray headlight from a car taking the access road through the woods. Not even much by way of moonlight.

She remembered the smirk on the waitress's face last night when she told her where they were staying. *This time of year we only get hunters, and you don't look like no hunters.* The ridicule in her voice hadn't been lost on Fran. This woman could see it all over them: a couple city folk running off for a tryst in the woods. What a cliché. *Just be careful to look out for bears,* the waitress added. *You got a gun, don't you?*

She was fairly sure that Richard Hanson, the man who was normally prepared for anything, had not brought a gun with them to Lake Ogallala.

When it came to doing battle with his fellow man, Richard would say that words, not bullets, were his weapon of choice.

Words would not be of much use against a bear . . . or much else you might come across in the woods.

There was a loud crack to her right. She froze. "What was that?"

"I can't see a thing," Richard said behind her. He sounded irritated. "I think I just stepped on something."

Fran pictured a wild animal, preparing to lunge. But there was more to fear in the woods than bears and coyotes. Axe-wielding maniacs; she'd heard enough in her career as a reporter to know it wasn't as uncommon as you might think. Men who stalked their neighbors, looking to slake a long-suppressed desire. "I hope you're right. Come the fuck on, then, and quit making so much damned noise."

"You're nothing but a dirty sailor," he said. His typical response to her habit of rolling curses off her tongue.

"And you fucking love it," she sent back. She was pretty sure Winnie never said a bad word, even if Richard begged for it.

She clutched the flashlight harder.

She estimated that they'd been walking maybe fifteen minutes when she smelled something peculiar. Smoke, but not wood smoke. It was chemical. An odor from a factory or plant. She was sure of it.

She started to walk faster, following the scent, chest hammering. Richard murmured behind her. "Slow down, sweetheart."

"Don't you smell that? I told you I saw a fire . . ."

They practically tripped over it. Wisps of some kind of material scattered over the ground. The material was white and stood out against the dark forest floor. The burnt smell hung heavy in the air.

She crouched, shining the flashlight beam directly on the material. "Jesus! What do you think it is?"

Richard leaned over, reaching for it.

"Hey, be careful! This could be a crime scene."

"That's your problem, Fran. Always so melodramatic." The accusation hurt more than he knew. As the mistress, you weren't allowed to create drama. Emotions were the property of marriages. When the wreckage was your own fault, you didn't get to pout about it.

"What crime do you see?" he went on, clearly trying to calm her. He rubbed her back. "We're in the middle of nowhere." He picked up a scrap of the material and brought it close to his face, squinting. "Hey, shine that light over here so I can get a better look."

She did. He rubbed the scrap between his fingers, even gave it a sniff, then recoiled. "I think it's some kind of paper." No wonder it had gone up so quickly. "I wonder where it came from. Do you see any writing on it anywhere?"

Her breath knocked in her chest. She cast the beam over the

tatters on the ground. "I can see a few fragments . . . parts of a letter or a number, maybe." Nothing more than a smudge of black here and there. Honestly, it didn't look like any writing she was familiar with. "And I don't think you should be handling that. We should leave it for the police."

"What do you mean, police? We're not going to bring the police into this."

"There's a story here, Richard."

He made a face. "Kids probably made a campfire so they could neck in the woods."

"I saw fire in the sky." It was obvious that this wasn't a campfire. The war had been going on for a few years now, mostly taking place across foreign skies, on fronts Fran would never see firsthand. And yet . . . had it come for them at last?

"Ah, damnit!" He dropped the fragment to the ground, shaking his fingers as if they'd all of a sudden been scalded.

She lunged toward him. "You okay?"

He didn't answer, only looked at her with concern. "Think, Fran. If we report this, we'll have to explain why we're here. I'm not going to lie to the police. You're not putting me in that position."

Winnie. It always came back to Winnie.

"Sweetheart, you've been in compromising *positions* all weekend," she shot back, more offended than she meant to be.

"Come on, Fran. Don't be like that. Don't worry so much, alright?" He squeezed her shoulder.

It was easy to believe things Richard Hanson said. It's what made him such a strong, charismatic leader. That confidence. The invisible power that rolled off him, the ease of it, like a stretching lion.

And yet. She looked at the smoldering heap, which still billowed and heaved in the night air, like a breathing creature, tentacled and ashen. The whole thing gave her the creeps, made her body go unnaturally cold. It almost felt like the thing was calling her toward it, beckoning, though probably that feeling was just her own morbid curiosity. Once again, she thought of old Gary Ry and his *sightings*.

Richard had already turned his back on the smoky debris and started walking in the direction of the cabin. "There's no story, Fran." He turned back and took the flashlight from her hand. For just a second, he looked remorseful. Or possibly, even, afraid? "Probably some trash that caught fire and got picked up by the wind."

"We'll never know if we don't look into it." Were those Japanese letters on the papery fabric? "What if this is some kind of weapon of war?"

"It's out now. The fire's out."

But it wasn't. There was a fire flaring now, he just couldn't see it. The heat of curiosity.

He wrapped an arm around her and together they made their way back to the cabin through the darkness. He didn't say anything more, but she could swear she felt the tremble of his arm on her shoulder. He was shaken, too. He knew she was right; he just couldn't say it.

Her mind had already leapt ahead. As soon as it got light, she would come back and collect some of the debris to take to the police. She didn't want to use her bare hands—she'd seen Richard's hands turn red after he'd handled that scrap. His right hand had looked inflamed. She'd boil water and make him scrub well once they were back at the cabin. In the morning she'd come back with that pair of thick utility gloves in the trunk.

Her instincts were good, she knew. They were what had kept her alive this long.

Tomorrow. She'd go after the story at first light.

Today I met with the oldest man on this speck of an island. He told me he was over 120 years old, which of course cannot be true, but there is no doubting that he is very, very old. Everyone says he knows the old ways on this island the best.

The old grandfather welcomed me to his hovel, which clings to the end of a rock peninsula that juts over the ocean. As his great-granddaughter served us tea made from nettles, he explained to me that this island is the home of three of the fiercest kami *in the panoply of deities: Fujin, the god of wind; Raijin, his brother, the god of lightning and storms; and Raijin's son, Raitaro, the god of thunder. He said these three gods live here, and if you go about the island during a storm you may see them.*

Then he asked if I believed in the gods. He figured that, because I was a scientist, I probably didn't.

I told him that all Japanese believe in the gods at least a little, no matter how modern they are, and even though I am a scientist, I am also an old friend of Fujin, the god of wind. Then I told him with a wink that I had come for us to be reacquainted. This made the old man smile.

I asked him if there was a god or demon responsible for the madness spreading at the hospital. Of course, he said. That would be the demon jorogumo.

This was a name I hadn't heard before. When I asked him to tell me more about this demon, he said that the island was a kind of nest, particularly the area where the hospital is located. It is here, he claimed, the jorogumo lays her eggs.

I asked if this jorogumo was a bird demon of some sort, and the old man laughed.

Not birds, he shook his head. Spiders.

4

CAMP MINIDOKA, IDAHO

Meiko walked a little faster when she saw the delivery truck pulled alongside the kitchen's supply shed. That truck was her only regular contact with the outside world. Old Mr. Samuelson made the delivery himself, as though he didn't trust anyone who worked for him to do it right. Or perhaps no one who worked for him liked to talk to Japanese. Meiko wanted to think it wasn't the latter.

She ran up to the shed, joining the other kitchen workers. There was Mr. Samuelson in his butcher's apron, clipboard in hand, checking off crates and wrapped slabs of beef and hog as Meiko's coworkers toted them off the truck. Oddly, the grocer seemed to keep his distance from them, something he never did before.

"Mr. Samuelson was just telling us that the people in town have heard about the illness out here," Hiroji said as he walked by Meiko, a big chunk of hog carcass balanced on his shoulder. His expression said it all: *Here we go.*

"Sure, they're a little alarmed. You can't blame them, can you?" Mr. Samuelson called out, pen poised over his clipboard. "We hear it spreads like wildfire and lays you out for weeks. The mayor said the camp administrators won't tell him anything. We have to go by what we hear from the guards, you know. Gossip's out of control. It spreads through the town like wildfire."

"They say it's just the flu," Hiroji said over his shoulder.

"Doesn't sound like any kind of flu I heard of," Mr. Samuelson grumbled back.

"It's not like we know any more than you do," Patsy said. She lugged a sack of flour to the kitchen's wagon. "They won't tell us anything, either. We have to piece it together for ourselves."

Mr. Samuelson shrugged. "They're scared stiff in town of catching it. My wife didn't want me to come out here. It's not just for our health, mind you. She's afraid of what the neighbors will say, that they'll boycott my shop."

That sent a chill through the group. What would happen if the townspeople refused to have anything to do with the camp? They depended on Mr. Samuelson for so much, all the things they couldn't grow in their vegetable patches. Rice and wheat, oil and dairy. They kept no cattle or hogs, had no access to a river or lake for fish.

"Right—they'd rather see us starve," Mayumi grumbled.

Everyone in the camp knew that was why they were kept in a place like this, far away from the public. It was easier for the public to forget about the inhumane thing that was being done in their name. Out of sight, out of mind.

"We heard people are going mad here, attacking one another. That people are like rabid dogs, foaming at the mouth." Meiko and the others looked at each other sheepishly. Things had taken a turn for the worse shortly after that truck had appeared. It seemed things got worse every day and there was no end in sight. Just last night there had been a fistfight in one of the dormitories. Two neighbors who hadn't had a cross word between them in all their time at Minidoka suddenly lunged at each other, bloodlust in their eyes. The guards had to separate them and eventually took both away. There was gossip that one had died overnight, but there was no confirmation yet. Rumors flew like wasps through the camp, each story more outrageous than the last. It was impossible to know what was true with all the lies, many of them coming from the guards.

No one was going to tell Mr. Samuelson that he was close to the truth. "The fighting—it's only been isolated cases," Hiroji said finally. "It's not as bad as they're making out."

"Well, maybe someone ought to tell that to the guards," Mr. Samuelson grumbled.

Meiko stood with the others to wave goodbye to the grocer. Meiko had wanted to warn him not to listen to the guards, and not to let the people in town pay them any mind, either. Few of the residents trusted them anymore. Meiko remembered that, in the early days, the guards were like neighborhood policemen. You could go to them when you had a question or needed help sorting out a misunderstanding. There had only been a handful of them in the beginning, and if you didn't know who they were you wouldn't have been able to guess their job. They dressed in everyday work clothes. They wore no insignia. You could tell who they were because they were the only young white men in the camp.

Now the guards were different. There were more of them. They wore an informal uniform of khaki pants and beige work shirts. They carried truncheons and walked in a kind of formation meant to intimidate. They glared at the residents, even grandmothers and mothers escorting their children to school. It reminded Meiko of little boys playing at being soldiers. She couldn't understand why the guards had become more militaristic when the camps hadn't changed. They were still peaceable and, all things considered, remarkably relaxed. It made no sense.

Well, she supposed it was not quite so peaceful now, not with the disease rampaging through the camp. Everyone was tense and on edge, especially the guards. They barked at the residents and often seemed to barely stop themselves from breaking into violence.

Lights-out was moved up an hour. Residents were told to keep to their dormitories, no socializing allowed between blocks. Seatings were staggered in the mess hall, as though they were afraid of letting them congregate, though Rei insisted it was to slow down the spread of the disease. There was even talk of discontinuing school, which only worried parents more, knowing their children were already at a disadvantage after being yanked out of school back home.

Hiroji stepped to the front of the kitchen wagon, slipping on the harness so that he could pull it like a plow horse. Several of the women went to the back to push. Meiko picked up a heavy sack of rice to lighten the load and began trudging to the kitchen with the rest of them.

Patsy fell into step beside her. "I went to see Stan Goda last night. Stan got sick over a week ago and he's still sick as a dog. He told me last night that he'd seen a ghost. A woman in a kimono holding a baby. She told him that her baby was sick and she begged him to look at it. Can you believe it?"

Meiko felt a little buzz of familiarity behind her eyes. Where had she heard this before?

"You know Stan, right? A pretty tough customer. He's a welder, used to work at the shipyard . . . Not the superstitious type, in other words. Said he never believed in ghosts but what he saw changed his mind."

"Oh, I don't know . . ." There was something about the story that made Meiko uneasy, made her want to push it away. "If you get a fever, if it's bad enough, your mind can play tricks . . ."

"He's not the only one, okay?" Patsy dropped her voice to a whisper. "The Yamadas told me the same thing. A woman in a kimono with a baby. Saw their dead grandparents, too, even though they've been gone twenty years. People are starting to worry there's something supernatural going on."

"Supernatural?" Meiko's first reaction was to scoff.

"That's the Japanese way, isn't it? They have a ghost or demon for every tree or crossroads or temple over there, to hear my father tell it. I don't know what's going on . . . But if it's not the illness, why would their dead relatives come visit them? It's like we're cursed . . ."

Meiko had to stop herself before she let Aiko's warning slip out. *The dead are coming to warn us.* But it was too fantastical, bizarre. It couldn't be true. And anyway, how could her daughter know? It had to be her imagination—*everyone's* imagination running away with them. Looking to the fantastical for answers because nothing made sense anymore, not when your government could lock you up without reason and your neighbors, people you thought were your friends, stood by and did nothing to stop them.

There was nothing to do for her anger, her fury. Hadn't they been through enough, made to suffer unjustly, and now they were being ravaged by a strange, terrible disease for which there appeared to be no cure. And they were helpless to do anything about it, to save themselves.

What bothered her the most, of course, was that she could do nothing for her daughter.

Aiko had done well under the circumstances. The most troubling factor, aside from living in a prison camp, was that her father was gone. At first, there had been plenty of able-bodied men in the camps because, after Pearl Harbor, they stopped allowing Japanese Americans to join the military. That changed in 1943 when the government decided that Nisei would be allowed to enlist. It kicked off a bitter debate in the camps over whether the men should serve the government. While arguments raged during Minidoka's town hall events, they'd heard that ten thousand Nisei had volunteered in Hawaii, where there had been no internment.

Now there were fewer men to be seen at Minidoka—a small

number had volunteered, joining the segregated 442nd Regimental Combat Team—but by then, Aiko's story was known throughout the camp. The other children didn't know what to make of the half-breed daughter of an Issei and a white man. Half-breeds were not common among Japanese Americans, with Nisei children strongly encouraged to marry within their own race. Issei still told their children in private that Japanese blood was superior. Too, interracial marriage was still illegal in many states, if unevenly enforced. More realistically, Nisei knew that half-breed children would not be as accepted as full-blooded Japanese children were. They would be regarded as curiosities at best, inferior mongrels at worst. If Meiko had known how prejudiced Americans could be—Nisei as well as whites—she might've thought twice before agreeing to marry Jamie Briggs.

It had only been four blocks from the house where she had lived in Seattle to the boardinghouse that held everything in the world that mattered to her now. Even though there were plenty of Asian faces in this part of town, Meiko still felt self-conscious walking by herself. While her English was good, she knew her accent was thick: even the people she was staying with could barely understand her.

These four blocks had become her world. Across them, once or twice a week, she transformed from the younger, more innocent girl her family remembered to the conflicted woman she had become.

A flutter in her gut: there was the boardinghouse, straight ahead. Kenzo would not be home and she'd planned it this way. He'd be at the farm in the valley, overseeing the care of his crops, cabbages and peppers and string beans, vegetables he sold to the Japanese stores in town. In Japan, she had never even stepped foot onto a farm. She'd lived in a city. She'd never had the slightest interest in farming. Her mother had told her that farmers were crude and uneducated. Not like their people, scientists and teachers.

Back then, there had been no talk of Meiko marrying into a farming family. At some point, however, Wasaburo's dream of seeing his oldest daughter married to a scientist or diplomat vanished. It was around the same time that the invitations for her father to speak at conferences started to dry up. Her parents began meeting with matchmakers representing families in America. When her father decided to accept an offer from Kenzo Nishi's family, he had tried to assure Meiko that it was a wise decision. It's different in America, *he'd said.* There, it will be good to have a husband who works the land. There is a lot of land in America. It would be good to own a part of it.

She climbed the steps to the boardinghouse's whitewashed porch and rang the doorbell. The proprietor, a widow in her sixties, answered the door. "Mr. Nishi isn't here right now, Miss Oishi."

Meiko looked down, cowed by the older woman's stare. Her cheeks were so hot she was afraid they would burst into flame. "I'm not here to see Mr. Nishi. I'm here to see Mr. Briggs."

They walked side by side on the sidewalk, not touching. She longed to hold his hand like the other couples they passed, but that was impossible. As it was, they were taking a risk that someone would see them together and mention it to Kenzo. Jamie had explained that it was perfectly plausible for a guy's girl to be seen with the guy's good friend. Nothing suspicious there.

Except there was good reason for Kenzo to be suspicious. If he knew.

*S*he remembered the day she met Jamie Briggs on Kenzo's farm. He *was showing her around the place when Jamie touched down in his Stearman Kaydet, a former training aircraft for the navy, modified to do agricultural work. He dusted crops for Kenzo Nishi. Kenzo ran the Japanese farmers consortium in Seattle, helped them sell their goods to grocery stores and restaurants in the city.*

Jamie seemed to Meiko like a god alighting from the sky, stepping down from the aircraft.

Meiko hadn't known many gaijin—foreigners—in Japan; she'd never gone gaga over the few she'd seen in movies or postcards, so when her heart fluttered at the sight of him, she trusted it wasn't because of his features.

Kenzo introduced them, embarrassing Meiko by explaining why his family had gone to a matchmaker. "There are over thirty Japanese men for every Japanese woman in Seattle. This was the only way to find a mate, to marry, and have children. Having children is important for farmers. The bigger the family, the better." It made her feel like a broodmare, her only value in her ability to produce children.

She admitted to Jamie that she'd never been in an airplane, having come by ship to America. "We can change that anytime you want," he'd said. "I'd be happy to take you up. Just say the word." She surprised him—and herself—by volunteering on the spot. Kenzo had been surprised, too, but didn't discourage her. He even helped her climb into the tandem cockpit next to Jamie, waving as they taxied down the mown strip of grass and took off.

She was terrified the whole time, but exhilarated, too, as they glided over the fields and skirted the treetops. He later told her it was the most thrilling ride he'd ever had in a plane, and it was because Meiko was sitting next to him, her leg pressing against his, her hands digging into his forearm. He'd been enchanted by the look of sheer delight on her face, impressed by this young woman who had sailed across an ocean without family to marry a stranger and embark on a new life in another country. She seemed impossibly brave to him.

She did not feel brave today. She feared Jamie would lose all respect for her after she'd said what she'd come to tell him today.

They stopped at the drugstore and got drinks at the soda fountain, then took them to a picnic table in a courtyard surrounded by brick walls on three sides. Even a brush of his hand made her feel better. That was why she was drawn to Jamie: he was strong and calm. He looked at her with the utmost respect. Nothing else existed for him when she was around. She had known from the moment she'd met him that she could depend on him, no matter what.

She couldn't look at him when she told him why she'd come. Her shame was too great. "I am afraid we have made a terrible mistake. I'm—late."

He reached for her hand, twining their fingers together. "What will you do, if you are pregnant?"

She knew what she wanted, but it was impossible, given her situation.

He didn't wait for her reply. "Marry me, Meiko."

She laughed because it was what she wanted to hear, even if she could never, ever accept.

A look of confusion passed over his face. "What's so funny? I'm serious."

There were a million reasons why they could not marry. They barely knew each other. He was estranged from his family, but she didn't know why. For Japanese, it was practically unthinkable to cut off your family like that. Of all the things that worried her about Jamie, that worried her the most.

And then there was her own situation. She was promised to Kenzo. If she didn't go through with it, she would be ostracized for shaming her family. And her family would certainly renounce her if she married a gaijin. As much as her father admired all things Western, he was proud of his Japanese heritage. She could well imagine her mother's reaction: her grandchildren would be mongrels. She'd never accept that. She'd renounce them first.

"It is impossible . . ."

"It's legal here in Washington State." He thought she was talking about the law. The law was the least of her worries.

He seized both her hands. "We love each other, Meiko. That's all that matters. We'll make it work."

She wanted to believe him, but she hadn't been born with his confidence. She had her father's and mother's voices in her head, telling her to be smart. Practical. Obedient. Following your heart was foolish. Following your head was wise.

And honor. Always do the honorable thing.

What about love? Shouldn't we honor love? It was such a rare gift, and how lucky was she to have found it? There was a child to think about, a love child.

Everything in my life has always been decided for me. *It was how she'd ended up here, in a foreign land, living a life she'd never, ever imagined. Something good had to come from all this upheaval. There had to be a reason that this was her fate.*

It is time I make decisions for myself. *She opened her eyes.* "Yes, Jamie. Yes, I will marry you." *She was so flooded with happiness at that moment that she could barely speak. Behind the happiness, though, was a knot in the pit of her stomach because she knew she was betraying Kenzo, a man who had never harmed her, a man who had shown her only kindness. Kenzo Nishi was an honorable man, as noble as any man she had known in Japan. Her parents had chosen well. He was losing not only the woman he was supposed to marry but also Jamie, a business acquaintance who had become a friend. Kenzo, the innocent, would be the one to suffer.*

Even as Jamie gathered her in his arms and crushed her to his chest, the two of them laughing and crying at once, she knew she would be punished for this one day. Punished for this terrible betrayal. Honor was everything, and she had broken it.

5

It took hours to rush all the bodies down the mountainside. By then, evening had fallen and all but one—Joan Patzke—had been pronounced dead.

Archie Mitchell put his hand on the metal door handle to the morgue and gave it a slight push.

It had been little more than a day since the blast that tore through the center of Archie Mitchell's world, destroying his future, his happiness, his ability to hope. Destroying his sense of reason . . . his sense of God. *The Lord works in mysterious ways.* It was a phrase he had offered to others time and again. But this . . . this was no deed of God's. This was—sure as anything—the Devil's work.

Archie's eyes ached; his ears still rang. They'd tried to keep him in for observation that day, until he convinced the doctors he wasn't injured and was taking them away from the ones who could use their help. Still, then, he'd paced the glaringly bright halls, making righteous, impossible demands. Shouting at the startled nurses and then bursting into tears.

He couldn't understand how he was still living, witness to the wreckage. The world spun. Nothing made sense. Everywhere was

Hell, but a new kind—a bright white Hell made not of flames and fear and pain but of silence, anguish, disbelief.

He knew he shouldn't be there—it wasn't authorized without clearance—but the whole hospital basement appeared to be empty at this hour, and the metal doorknob gave at his touch. He stepped inside the morgue. One of the overhead lights had been left on and a radio played somewhere. The refrigerated vaults were full to overflowing—too many deaths for a town this small—so one of the boys lay on a metal table, covered by a sheet.

Archie stared at the small lump for a moment, two moments, unable to unfreeze. Then he carefully circumvented the table. He knew which vault held his wife.

He headed for it instinctively, grabbed the big metal handle, gave it a jerk. There was a moment of pneumatic suction, then release. A hiss like a lover's sigh. He pulled out the tray holding Elsie's body.

Elsie, who had been laughing in the bright sunshine, telling him to stop worrying about a little mud under the tires. Perfect Elsie. Elsie who was his everything.

For whom he would do anything—and had. Had made one of the ugliest, most regrettable decisions of his life, just to appease her, to keep her safe. And yet here she was, like this. Lost to him. Despite what he had done. What *they* had done.

Or maybe . . . *because of it.*

A woman's face—Meiko—appeared before him, ravaged by tears. Begging, pleading for help. *Think of Aiko, if not me.*

His heart sank. *Oh God.* He was surely damned.

Before his eyes, Meiko disappeared, replaced by the kimonoed woman in the woods. Her sly smile mocking him, as though she knew every bad thing the preacher had ever done.

She stretched a finger toward him. Fear knifed through him.

Don't let her touch you. He didn't know what it would do or what it meant, only that he wouldn't be able to bear her touch.

He stumbled backward a step and she disappeared. *Thank God. Thank the Lord.*

Satisfied that the apparition was gone, he moved toward the body before him. Toward his Elsie—or what was left of her. After one moment of hesitation, he folded back the sheet, uncovering her face. He had seen it twice now, and knew that was not the sort of thing a husband should see. It was not the last memory he should have of Elsie. But—again—he couldn't help himself.

Her loveliness had been ruined by the explosion. Her skin was gone in places, leaving a red and pink angry landscape behind. The only part intact was her eyes. Maybe she'd thrown her hands in front of them at the last minute, sparing them the worst damage.

All his dreams had gone up in that instant.

He remembered telling Jamie Briggs about the day he met Elsie. He had become friends with Jamie at the apartment building where Jamie and Meiko lived in Seattle, where he had a room in the basement. Elsie had sat next to him in a class at the seminary. They had talked for over an hour after class that first day, pretending to be thrilled by the syllabus when really, they had been thrilled at finding each other. He knew as soon as he'd met her that he was going to marry her. Jamie had congratulated him and said it had been the same way with Meiko. That he'd known the instant their eyes met that she was the one for him. Both he and Jamie had gone through a lot together, though Jamie was a few years older. Both had been lost, had cut off ties from their families back home. Archie had sought salvation through God. Both felt, though, back in those days, like the only thing that could ever possibly save them were these women.

He looked down at his wife now. The demon she'd become. A wild thought came to him: had she been this all along? A monster, made-up in the shape of a beautiful human? But no, his mind was falling apart. He had been traumatized. He wasn't thinking straight.

He stared at her. Decay was already setting in. He saw the signs. The skin was putrefying. *All is corruption.* The army asked if he would hold off on burial so they might have a little time to study the body. He said yes, of course, stunned that a representative of the army came all the way out here to Bly just to pay respects and investigate the accident, rather than the local authorities.

The colonel had grabbed Archie's arm at the end of their talk, grabbed him and held him firmly. "You're to talk to no one about what happened here today, do you understand? Don't talk to the press, don't talk to your neighbors. Any leak would only benefit the enemy . . ."

"The enemy?" Archie was confused. "Are you saying this has something to do with the Japanese?"

The colonel released Archie, giving him a strained look. "I'm not saying anything of the sort. But . . . they can't know where we're weak. I'm not asking you: that's an order. If we catch you talking to anyone, it's off to jail."

As though he wanted to tell anyone that he'd let his wife and these children die.

He should be here in the morgue with them.

He bent down to kiss Elsie's cold forehead, patched together with medical tape. Something dusted her closed eyes. A white powder, like the remnants of ashes. Like the little fluffs he saw in the mountain wind, tiny things that looked like minuscule spiders.

With shaking fingers, he brushed the stuff gently away from her eyes.

At that moment, the doors swung open and an attendant walked in. He did a double take when he saw it was Archie. "You shouldn't be in here, Reverend," he said softly.

Archie nodded as he pulled the sheet up over his wife's face. It wasn't Elsie anymore, anyway. Not really. Elsie existed now only in his mind. In his memory. In the plans they'd made that would never come to be.

He trudged back up the stairs and made his way to the ICU. There was a stillness to the intensive care unit that unnerved him now, unraveled him to the core. The nurses moved around in a kind of hush. Everyone spoke in whispers.

"Why don't you go home and rest," one of the nurses urged. He found his way to the doors of the ICU, though he'd been told repeatedly he was not authorized to pass through them.

"Why can't you let me see Joan? I have to see Joan," Archie said, hearing the high whine of his voice as if it was someone else's. But the desperation had made him out of control. All he knew was that he had to get a look at her. The one survivor. Maybe she would live. He had to believe that. Maybe she would remember something, some detail that would unlock the horror of what had happened. It had been impossible to get to see her, however. Mr. and Mrs. Patzke didn't seem to want him around; he'd seen the way they cast dirty looks at him. The Patzkes blamed him, of course. Why shouldn't they? He was alive and their children were dead, or nearly dead.

The nurse looked at him with a mix of pity and exhaustion that made him briefly wonder what all she'd seen in her lifetime. "If you need a ride back home, you just let me know," the woman said kindly. Women were always kind to Archie; that was the trouble, wasn't it? "Doris's shift ends soon and she'd drive you, sweetheart."

Archie didn't go home, though. How could he? How could he ever return to the sweet little house—to Elsie's kitchen, still smelling of chocolate. To the tiny room where they'd started stockpiling baby clothes. A new rocker.

He paced the waiting area. Finally, he found a moment. They moved Joan into an OR and then moved her back into the ICU.

During the transition, the parents had been sent out of the way, and he had an in.

He approached her bed and stared at the teenage girl, lying quietly, sedated now. The scene of the explosion came back to him—how wild and thrashing she'd been, not still at all. Not quiet then. The road workers who'd come at the sound of the explosion had tried to put out the fires eating up her clothes, her flesh. She had been screaming and—strangest of all—scratching at herself.

He'd asked the doctors about that and they'd looked at him like he'd lost his mind. Maybe he had: his wife had just died, after all. Joan's struggles were normal for a burn victim, they told him. *She wasn't scratching, she was trying to put out the flames*, they told him, but none of it looked right to him. And the victims—as horribly as they'd suffered—did not look like normal burn victims.

He remembered the smell released by the flames. Strangely chemical.

He willed Joan to wake up. She was so still that it didn't even look like she was breathing. He found himself, despite everything, despite the complete abandonment of everything he'd ever believed in—the absence of God, the absence of reason—beginning to pray.

The prayers, one after another, tumbled soothingly across his lips.

The Patzke girl twitched, and Archie startled, the words dying on his lips. He leaned closer. "Joan? Can you hear me?" He kept his voice low; he didn't want anyone in the hall to overhear him. "Joan, you forgive me for what happened, don't you? You understand that it wasn't my fault . . ." *I should've insisted that they wait and we could all walk together down to the stream. I would've stopped them from touching that thing on the ground. I would've saved them.*

The young girl's head swiveled toward him like a thing on a wire. A movement that was inhuman and uncanny. Her eyes, slightly open, looked dead, white and watery, like a fish's. Yes, that's how she seemed to him: she was already dead. Cold, clammy, pale, bloodless.

But she was moving. How could that be? Her head canted toward him; her lips moved. He couldn't hear what she was saying. Did he want to hear?

Of course not, but he could not resist. He leaned a little closer to her, careful not to touch her anywhere. He could not bear to touch that cold flesh, that much he knew.

Her mouth opened wider. But instead of speaking, she made a horrific gurgling sound as something tumbled out. Bubbles. Tiny white bubbles, rolling off her tongue and over her lips, cascading down the sheets.

Archie's stomach churned as he bolted backward.

They weren't bubbles—but spiders. More of those same minuscule spiders he had seen floating in the air right before the explosion. Hundreds, thousands of tiny white baby spiders spilling from her mouth and crawling toward him.

This couldn't be happening. His mind had fastened onto the idea of spiders. And yet . . .

Before he knew it, he was at the door and screaming. Blood-curdling, terrified screams. It brought doctors and nurses—and the Patzkes, too. A swarm of people, all alarmed, checking on Joan and trying to calm him, trying to reassure him that there were no spiders, that it was all his imagination and to be expected, given what he'd gone through . . . Though he saw the skeptical looks on some of their faces and heard Mrs. Patzke say, under her breath to one of the orderlies, "I want him out of my daughter's room . . ."

Then he heard the thing that he already knew: one of the nurses at the bedside cried out, "There's no pulse on the patient—we're losing her . . ." And all hell broke loose, Archie's scene forgotten; they swarmed around the bedside, Mr. and Mrs. Patzke and the older daughter, Betty, shoved to the side as they tried to resuscitate.

Which would be fruitless, Archie already knew.

A wail broke from Mrs. Patzke and she crumpled into her husband's arms. She cried and cried, Mr. Patzke trying to comfort her when it looked like he only wanted to join her.

And then Mrs. Patzke raised her head and pinned Archie with a look of cold hate. "What did you do to our daughter? What did you *do*?"

Behind her, Betty flashed him a forgiving look. A touch of kindness he would remember for as long as he lived. She moved away from her parents and Joan and the loud beep of machines, ushering Archie gently out of the room.

He stumbled into the hall. The nurses and doctors were already comforting Mrs. Patzke—*you're just upset, he's a man of the cloth, he was only trying to help*—but Archie knew they were wrong to try.

Joan's mother was right. Archie knew he was to blame. For this whole unholy mess, he alone was to blame. *Those who sin will meet the fire of Hell in the end.*

I n the end, it was Betty Patzke, the older sister of Joan, who gave him a ride home. He sat in the dark for a long time, not even taking off his coat or his dirty clothes. Wanting to let the day go, but unable to.

Finally, he broke down and drank two beers from the icebox. Then a third and fourth.

Somehow, on the fifth, his favorite picture of Elsie was clenched in his hand, the one in the big brass frame. Behind that, a second, smaller photograph he'd kept hidden there. Elsie hadn't wanted to see it anymore, not after what happened, but for some reason Archie couldn't make himself throw it away.

Now it was the last picture he had left of his friend Jamie. As well as Meiko and Aiko, gathered beside him.

It had been taken a few years ago, the three Briggses standing on the lawn right here in front of this house. Jamie had escorted his wife and child to Bly, where Archie, the newly ordained minister, had been posted: the idea was they'd stay with Archie and Elsie while Jamie did his part for the war. Cute little Aiko, looking in Archie's direction with trust in her eyes; they'd formed a bond from their Seattle days, the little girl practically had grown up at their kitchen table. Meiko, the mother, looking distant and hard. Like she knew what was coming. Like she knew he was going to betray them.

A wave of nauseous guilt moved through him.

The room tilted.

He tucked the photograph back under the frame, and let the darkness come.

6

CAMP MINIDOKA, IDAHO

Meiko stopped at a table in the mess hall. Two women looked up at her, clipboards and pens at the ready.

She pulled down the bandana she'd tied over her nose and mouth as a makeshift mask. She had found two more dead this morning while making her rounds delivering soup to the sick. "Dormitory block H, the third building. Shiro Takahashi, in the first room on the left. And a woman in the Fukudas' room. I'm not sure who she is."

The two women nodded as they wrote down the information. "We'll send stretchers."

Meiko headed for the kitchen, pail rattling at her side. Rather than panic when the outbreak took a turn for the worse and people started dying, the residents had taken matters into their own hands. What else were they to do, since the camp administrators seemed to be totally overwhelmed? Space had run out days ago in the tiny, under-resourced hospital. Volunteers used stretchers to fetch patients to the overflow hospital tent set up by the vegetable gardens, while one of the storage sheds had been cleared out to hold the dead.

If there was one thing the camp residents were good at, it was organizing. They'd been organizing for the common good since the day they arrived. They'd formed committees and boards, drew up rosters, assigned duties, created clubs. They organized dances for the teenagers and sports teams for the children. Men like Ken Nishi were elected to steering committees; women like Ken's wife organized sewing bees and made sure there were enough blankets for the sick and elderly. It was their way of pretending that they still had an ounce of control over their lives.

And so, when the illness tore its way through the camp, they did the same thing. If the administrators weren't going to do anything about it, then it was just one more thing that the residents would take care of themselves.

By the end of the first week, the emergency committee reported its observations to a gathering in the dining hall. Once the illness got a foothold in a dormitory, it would sweep through in a matter of days. It affected men, even the strong and healthy ones, more than women. It favored adults but spared children. Some people seemed immune to it, but it was impossible to predict who that might be. Meiko hadn't yet caught it. If she had some kind of immunity, she was glad for it: there was no one else to take care of her daughter, Aiko. And she needed to stay well because Jamie would be coming home from the war any day now. He'd written to say as much.

Meiko delivered soup from the kitchen to the afflicted all over the camp, and she used the opportunity to make her own observations, a habit ingrained in her by her father, the scientist. She saw patterns. It had a sinister effect on the victims' minds. Cups of broth were hurled across rooms. The afflicted invariably became suspicious, even paranoid. Sometimes, they didn't recognize her and would accuse her of trying to steal from them. Or cheat them, spy on them. The elderly would fall into a trance, unable to remember where they were or what was happening to them. Thinking they were back in Japan, calling to absent family members.

And everywhere, whispers of ghosts. Of a woman in a kimono holding a baby, who disappeared after saying one word, a word no one had been able to make out.

With the ghost sightings, there were rumors and guesses. That they had been cursed by the dead for disgracing their heritage by not fighting the executive order when it had first been enacted (that by the contingent who wanted to sue). That they were being experimented on by the military (that by the small but fervent contingent who saw conspiracies everywhere). That it was divine retribution, and they were paying the price for the attack on Pearl Harbor (that from the contingent who had wholeheartedly embraced Christianity).

Meiko could do nothing to disprove any of these theories, but she had noticed more practical things. As she hustled daily across the camp with her tin pail full of soup, she noted for instance that there were fewer guards and administrators about. Maybe that was normal procedure when there was an outbreak, to protect them from getting sick, too. Others said it was cowardice. It wasn't like the residents of the camp were going to do anything to take advantage of the situation, riot or try to leave the camp. They could've done that at any time but hadn't. The elders were always telling them they had to be good, that they had to be model citizens—stay in the camps, distance themselves from the rest of America—to prove that the terrible things said about them were not true. That they were good American citizens, their loyalties undivided. Meiko chafed at this the most: as though she hadn't done enough to prove herself, letting her husband go to war and leave her to fend for herself with no family, no friends, no one to help. But she shut down these bitter thoughts as soon as they came to her, as she always did. Bitter thoughts were of no use.

And then there were the unexplained visitors from outside. The first wave had recently been joined by three more. She only saw the men who had arrived in the cars for a minute or two, as they were hustled between buildings with the camp doctor trotting at their side. The cars had remained lined up outside the camp director's office building, the huge vehicles with flaring fenders bristling like an imperial guard. Hopeful residents believed they were experts brought in to consult on the illness. People had taken to calling them "doctors" but no one knew who they really were.

Everyone wanted to believe that they were here to help, but Meiko knew it wasn't the case. They'd first started coming here *before* the outbreak had begun. Before the army truck had arrived with its mysterious cargo.

And yet, Meiko wasn't one to panic. She was extremely pragmatic; her father had always praised her for that. She'd told herself this was like any other disease and believed it to be true.

Until one night.

Meiko woke to the feeling that something had brushed her face. Like something small had scurried across it.

Was she awake? It felt like she was still asleep. She blinked away the heaviness in her eyes as she glanced around the room. The first thing she looked for was Aiko, of course, and there her daughter lay in bed, chest rising and falling slowly, reassuringly. She widened her view to other parts of the room, captured in blacks and grays like a painting. But it was unnaturally quiet, not even the ever-present howl of wind outside the building to remind her where she was.

Could it have been a ghost? The thought popped into her head, unwelcome. She didn't believe in ghosts, not while the sun shined, but it was hard to feel as certain at night. Especially with the stories flying around camp, the afflicted screaming in terror at seeing long-dead relatives trying to talk to them. Her own daughter telling her there were spirits and ghosts among them all the time, trying to get their attention.

It can't be a ghost. There are no such things as ghosts or demons. Those are only stories. Folktales.

The man at the window gave away his presence by moving, like an animal breaking cover. She was so startled that she drew the blankets to her chin (a childish reflex, she later chided herself, childishness a luxury she could not afford). But the face still hovered, pale and demonic, predatory eyes like a hawk's.

The ease of his stare unnerved her, though she wasn't unused to the fact that men felt they had permission, always, to look at a woman. For a moment, she thought of closing her eyes and pretending to sleep, hoping he'd vanish. But that would be cowardly. Besides, he might try to come inside. He might be looking for a woman on her own, easy prey, or . . . She looked over at her daughter, asleep, defenseless. Was he one of *those* men, the kind every mother fears?

She blinked, and just as suddenly, the face was gone. He'd either left, or would be approaching the door to the dormitory in seconds . . .

Shakily, she threw back the blankets, reached for her overcoat to cover her thin nightdress, and tugged on her boots. She listened. No footsteps. No turn of the knob.

Her heart raced—had she dreamed him?—but she had to find out what this man was up to. If he was a guard . . . well, the guards were not supposed to roam freely throughout the barracks at night. The internees were allowed to have some privacy in their topsy-turvy lives. She wanted to find the man who was peering through windows to look at little girls. She'd confront him. No: once she figured out who he was, she'd *report* him.

Where had he gone? He seemed to have vanished, but she kept looking, the darkness nudging at her on all sides like a sentient force. Meiko shivered inside her coat (the prairie was bitterly cold at night, as ever) as she jogged between the dormitories, trying to keep to the shadows. The moon hovered, as the face in the window had, watching to see what she would do. But the moon, she knew, was not her protector. It would not react if you cried out.

Again, a flicker of movement gave him away. Was he luring her?

It was at the door to the kitchen. No one would be working at this hour, though. Roy Onagi was the first one to arrive in the morning to start the fires in the big ovens, but that was still hours away.

It could be the man who had been at her window.

She found him at the back, facing the shelves where they kept food. Bins of the last of the produce to come from the fields, dirt still clinging to skins. Tubs of milky water, cakes of tofu floating inside. She could only see his back. His arms moved subtly, as if the darkness had tentacles. She couldn't tell what he was up to. He seemed to be . . . running his hands over the turnips and greens, cabbages and carrots. Fondling them, touching them.

Quietly, she stepped closer. Drawn to the strange intimacy of it.

A thought came to her: *Maybe he's hungry. Maybe he's looking for something to eat.* Her heart, a mother's heart, softened.

Still, it made no sense. The guards had plenty of food. They were well-fed.

No, he was *rubbing something on the food.* A shudder of disgust ran through her.

Growing up, she had been taught that women were not supposed to speak. It was unbecoming to be loud, to demand attention. Yet everything about this moment was unnatural—the fact that she was alone in this normally lively camp, the camp itself quiet like it had been drugged. Finding this strange man sneaking about. Knowing it was her duty to confront him. She had to fight her every instinct in order to find her voice. "What are you doing?" she said as loudly as she could. "You're not supposed to be here."

The man whirled around. She didn't recognize him; he wasn't one of the guards, after all. He was probably one of *them*, the strangers who'd arrived, who'd been watching them. One of the new "doctors."

She could tell she had caught him by the flash of anger in his eyes. He bristled like a wolf at first, but that look was quickly suppressed. "What are you doing up at this hour? Curfew was hours ago. It's not safe—especially not for a little dark-eyed beauty like you."

The camp administrators spoke like this to the internees rarely. It made her all the more unsure who this man was, who the strangers were. He didn't seem like a guard. The guards tended to work in bunches. A pair, at the very least. She had developed a special dislike for the guards, of late: they reminded her of the pictures of the *Sturmabteilung* she'd seen in the newspapers in Japan. Her father had told her that these men brought Hitler to power. They liked to be called the Storm Detachment, but they weren't real military, they were men who liked to dress up in brown shirts and terrorize their neighbors. The guards here had become exactly like that.

She stuck out her chin, defiant, though she was aware of how small she was next to him and that there was no one else around. "What are you doing with our food? I saw you—"

"And what do you think you saw?" He grinned, and there was something sickening in it. An excess of saliva. A strange way his eyes seemed to bore into her and then skitter away. *There is something wrong with him.* "You know what I think: I think you saw me and wanted me. Came looking for a little fun. But it's dangerous out here at this hour. Didn't they warn you? Naughty, naughty."

A disturbing chill moved through her, that she shouldn't be out here alone with this man. If it came down to her word against his, there was no doubt whom they would believe. Not the geisha, the porcelain doll, the temptress. She'd seen it in Seattle, whenever there'd been an attack. White men claiming it wasn't like that: she wanted it. Wanted a white man.

But she wasn't going to give in, not this time. "It's *you* who isn't supposed to be here. When I tell the administrators—"

He waved his hands, shushing her like you might silence a child. "No reason to get the administrators involved. They know what I'm doing. They've got their orders. Besides, it's not like they're going to listen to your kind anyway." He grinned when she took a clumsy step backward.

"I was only checking for vermin. We wouldn't want an infestation here at the camp. Vermin might even be responsible for this outbreak." He spoke calmly but his expression was contorted, his scowl an angry gash cut across his face, like the scary faces of demons she had seen in old woodcut prints. Like a Noh mask. "It's our job to find out what's going on here. To understand why you're all getting sick. To find the root of the problem. My bet is that it's rats. And you know what we'll do if it is?"

He was whispering hoarsely. And what was that? Long foamy threads had formed at the corners of his mouth, like a rabid dog. But this spittle was bright red.

Meiko checked around her, panicky. She worked in this kitchen and knew her way around, even in the dark. He had backed her up, step by step, until she was almost boxed into a corner.

"We'll *exterminate them*," he hissed.

He dove at her, thinking he had her trapped, but she knew there was a space no wider than the span of her two hands between the tall shelves. She had squeezed through there whenever the aisle was blocked by another kitchen worker.

She squeaked through the opening now, just as he reached for her. She felt like a mouse, squeezing into a crack, then disappearing. His frustrated curses rose behind her. *Jap whore. I'll tell them you're a spy. They'll never take your word over mine.*

The door was right in front of her. She'd stand a better chance of getting away from him if she could just get outside. Six strides, five . . . As she threw the door open and felt the rush of frigid night air hit her in the face, there was a jerk on her arm. It was like a dog coming to the end of its tether. He yanked her backward, then trapped her in a bear hug. He forced her to the ground and knelt on top of her, pinning her with his weight.

She tried to throw him off, but he was twice her size. *I can't breathe. Let me go. I can't let you kill me. My daughter needs me.*

Inexplicably, he was trying to steady her head, but she twisted left and right, trying to escape his grasp. He grabbed her jaw roughly in exasperation, like he wanted to break it off, and she felt her mouth being forced open and *something deposited in it.* Then he held her mouth shut and covered her nose until she was forced to gulp . . . to swallow whatever it was he gave her, no doubt the same thing he had been spreading on their food . . . It was fine and gritty like sand, but that made no sense . . . Why would he want her to swallow sand?

She was still wondering this when everything went black.

When Meiko woke up the next morning, she was in her own bed, snug under the blankets. Her coat hung from a peg by the entrance. Aiko was still asleep, her face serene and undisturbed. The frights of last night—a man with a face like a Noh mask, dripping blood, wrestling her to the ground—seemed impossible. It seemed like the culmination of the horrors she'd endured the past two years, all her fears finally coagulating in her mind.

And yet, she knew it hadn't been a dream. For one thing, she ached like she'd never ached before except for childbirth. Under her nightgown she found huge ugly bruises all over her arms, legs, and back. And there were traces of grit in her mouth, which she tried to spit out. The thought that this man had brought her back to this room, had taken off her coat and put her in bed, in the same room where Aiko had been sleeping, made her feel violently ill.

She dressed and went straight to Stanley Drabroski, the camp official responsible for the kitchens, the only one of the administrators she felt comfortable talking to. The only one she felt she could take a chance on.

"I was attacked last night by one of the men visiting the camp." She doctored her story a little, deciding it would be better if she told Mr. Drabroski she found the man when she'd gotten up to use the latrine. He'd think her hysterical if she told him she'd seen the man at her window like a Peeping Tom.

Mr. Drabroski was normally a nice man, big and soft and white like a Parker House roll. He listened sympathetically, peering at her over the top of his black-rimmed glasses. He didn't react the way she hoped he would, however. No outraged outburst, no apology. Maybe she'd misjudged him. Maybe you couldn't expect anyone as soft as a Parker House roll to be strong enough to stand up for one of *them*.

When she'd finished, he frowned thoughtfully. "That's a pretty serious accusation, Mrs. Briggs—now, don't get me wrong. I believe you. I know you're not the kind to tell stories." He pursed his mouth. "I need to take this to the camp director. Those men—if it was one of them—they're on a special mission, you see. They're not in our sphere of control. Still, they shouldn't be interfering with the residents. Between you and me"—he leaned across the desk like he was taking a risk sharing this with her—"we heard this morning that one of them had been taken away. There had been some kind of problem, I'm not at liberty to say what exactly, but perhaps this was your man. I'll find out and get back to you. In the meantime, you shouldn't worry too much. They're only going to be here for a few more days and then you won't see them again."

She went back to her room, angry with herself for bothering to go to Mr. Drabroski. All she'd done was let him know she could make trouble. She had put herself and, more important, her daughter in danger, instead of playing it smart.

Not that she could see any smart move left to her. She'd never felt so powerless.

Her dormitory room was empty. Aiko had left for school already. Her bed was neatly made, her few toys put away. Their home looked like a hotel room made up for the next guest. Stools pushed under the small square table. Two bowls, two cups lined up on a linen tea towel. Meiko walked around, running her hand over the furniture, looking for—what? More proof that she'd lost her mind, she fretted.

Dust, so much dust. It came from the Idaho plains, fine as talcum powder, soft like down. Like the other housewives, Meiko dusted assiduously, but could not hold it at bay. It came back the next day.

Still, Meiko had *just* dusted yesterday afternoon. It shouldn't be back already.

She looked at the dust on her fingers, rubbed them together to feel the fine fur ball up on her fingertips.

But there was something different mixed in with the dust, something unexpected. Grit. Like sand on the beach where Meiko used to vacation with her family in Japan, her father the scientist, the naturalist, forever poking about tidal pools and picking lichen and barnacles off rocks.

This wasn't like the usual dust at Minidoka. It was hard and—if she squinted, standing at the window—it seemed to be translucent and shiny. Like an opal.

She went around the room looking for more. She found it was in some places, not in others. Not like dust that floated freely on the air. It was in the bed, under the covers. In the tea towel where the eating utensils rested. Sprinkled in their neatly folded clothing.

She remembered the feeling of the grit forced into her mouth.

And then she saw it: a tiny translucent spider running up her sleeve. Then a ripple of movement on the folded towels as a line of spiders ran, looking to hide in another stack of cloths.

They looked familiar, these spiders. Where had she seen them before?

She had just turned to run and find the nearest neighbor, to warn the others, when everything suddenly spun out of control. Down was up and up was down. She felt like she was being flipped like a giant omelet and now she was lying on the floor and the room was still spinning violently, in a way she'd never felt before. In a way that felt like it would never stop.

Save my daughter. She must not spend the night in this room.

But there was no one there to tell. To warn.

7

Marcel had been missing for nine days, the longest run yet. Fran knew the cat had never much liked her and losing him had always been a distinct possibility. Several times during this stretch, she could swear she heard his cry, thin and plaintive, making her think he'd gotten trapped in the walls again. That had happened once before, when a bit of plaster below the leaky kitchen sink had crumbled and he'd walked right through the hole. He'd been gone four days that time before turning up in a neighbor's apartment.

That morning, she left a saucer with his favorite niblets on a window ledge before leaving for work. She tried not to think of him outside, freezing, waiting for her to get home.

The newspaper offices were at the end of a twenty-minute walk. Standing at her desk, Fran pulled off her wool gloves and dropped them in her purse. She blew on her fingers, trying to breathe warmth into them. It felt like winter out there, alright. The streets were covered in a thick, icy slush and the wind cut right through her coat. An early harbinger of what would be a bad winter, she had no doubt. If Marcel hadn't made it home by now, the chances of his faring on his own through a brutal Nebraska winter were slim to none.

THE FERVOR

Thanksgiving had only just ended but both desks were already strewn with Christmas decorations. The entire newsroom had been sprinkled with tinsel and paper chains, like Santa's elves had come in and decorated the place overnight. No mystery there: the elf was Natalie Perkins, Fred Seacrest's secretary. Fred Seacrest was one of two brothers who'd inherited the newspaper after their father's death, and he loved the holidays. The call would soon go out for holiday stories.

Fran went over the lines in her notebook, written the day before. She'd been working out ideas but most were retreads, stories she'd written before, one way or another: what the boys at St. Thomas's orphanage want under the tree, the governor's wife's favorite cookie recipes. Fran had even gone to the huge books they kept in the back of the newsroom, every issue they'd printed bound for reference. *The old stories graveyard* is how she thought of the forgotten alcove. The more recent volumes—the last few months' worth—were kept out on a long table, but Fran had to go digging in the stacks for the volume with last December's stories.

Fran sat, tapping the handwritten lines with the worn eraser on her pencil, but her mind was on that weekend in the woods and the fireball in the sky over Ogallala. She longed to break out of the women's pages, and this was the kind of story that could get her in the right section of the newspaper, the section that mattered.

That last morning by the lake, before Richard woke up, she'd gotten up with the gray dawn light, grabbed the garden gloves as well as a discarded paper bag, and retraced her steps through the woods. The site of the explosion had been easier to find by morning, though some of the material of the mysterious object had drifted into the nearby trees overnight. She'd been able to separate a few large swaths of grayish fabric, papery but dense, almost like bark, and wedge it into the paper bag. There were dark cords, and she'd gathered some of those, too.

Whatever it was—maybe a parachute?—it had been designed to float on the air, she thought. But parachutes didn't explode.

Crusted along the gray material was a white dusting, like a mold. With the gloves, she was able to scrape some of it off, and watched it float into the air around her. She remembered again how Richard's hands had turned red that night. Probably the material had been hot to the touch. By now it was cold.

She'd collected her evidence, made a mental map of the location, and then trudged back to the cabin. She put the samples in the trunk before going inside. Richard didn't have to know. He'd only protest. And besides, this wasn't his story.

It was hers.

Since their return, she'd taken to scanning the wire stories with more vigor. Looking for something—anything—that resembled what she'd seen. Her voice low, she'd made an anonymous call into the Ogallala station. She'd looked up the local news outlet there and dialed them, too. No one had reported anything unusual the weekend before Thanksgiving. No one had seen an explosion at two or three in the morning. If it had been four or five, maybe some hunters would've been out, but no such luck.

And something *was* wrong, though she couldn't put her finger on it. Ever since she'd gotten back to her apartment in Lincoln, Fran had felt different. Changed, somehow. She'd convinced herself it was this story. She'd be restless until she had an answer.

Which was why she'd begun dogging the wires.

Two teletype machines sat at the back of the newsroom, AP and UPI. The wire stories came in all day, every day, typed onto a continuous roll of paper. The job of distributing the wire stories fell to Richard's assistant, Tommy McShea. A couple times a day, he would tear the stories off and drop them in the desk editors' mailboxes: world news, national, regional, sports. It was up to the desk editors to decide if they'd use the wire story for filler in their section, but sometimes they would assign one of their reporters to follow up on a wire story, treating it like a tip.

Good wire stories for the women's section of the newspaper were rare occurrences. But Fran got a thrill coming down here before Tommy to read stories from Washington, D.C., and New York City, where things were happening all the time. Important things that affected the future of the nation.

She looked around carefully: Tommy was nowhere in sight. Tommy was a nice kid, only recently graduated from high school. Richard kept him running errands all day long, including personal ones like getting prescriptions from the pharmacy, fetching his lunch, and feeding the parking meter. The poor kid might be any-where, but Fran suspected he might be out with a couple of the copyboys, sneaking the first cigarette of the morning on the roof. Fran went over to the teletype machines, tore off the long sheet of paper with an evening's worth of stories, and took it to the card table they kept for this express purpose: sorting the stories. She leaned over the paper, scanning each story, then used a metal straight edge to tear it off in a strip. Read, rip, read, rip—until she had a pile of neatly torn strips. Then it would be a matter of separating them into piles for each of the desk editors.

Depressing news from the internment camps. Not one but *two* stories of some kind of skirmish, fighting among the internees. Which struck Fran as strange: when was the last time there'd been *any* story out of the camps? The internees were known for being law-abiding, downright polite given their situation, protesting through the proper legal channels. Never any ruckus. She slowed down to read the stories more closely. A brawl in Manzanar, the camp near Los Angeles, and—holy Toledo—a shooting at Topaz, a camp in Utah. One of the internees had been killed. The stories said the people in the camps had been violent, fighting each other, trying to tear down the facilities. Maybe there'd been violence, but the reason behind it? That seemed off. False. It seemed, to Fran's trained eye, less like news reporting and more like propaganda. Dirty, slanted words conceived by a dirty, slanted mind.

She was so completely absorbed in her reading that she didn't notice Marjorie Elling peering over her shoulder. Marjorie Elling sat at the desk next to Fran's. Her mainstay was the agony aunt column. Three times a week, she answered questions from readers. *How do I get my mother-in-law to stop criticizing me? Why won't the neighbors let their children play with mine?* If readers could hear the scathing replies Marjorie made up for the amusement of the rest of the reporters, they wouldn't be so fast to write to her with their problems.

"Panning for gold?" she asked, handing Fran a cup of coffee. The agony aunt column made you into something of a cynic.

"Oh, thank God," Fran said, taking a grateful gulp of the black sludge. She tore off the top story. "If I write one more piece on the governor's wife's Christmas cookies, I'm going to scream."

"Amen to that, sister." Marjorie nodded toward the newsroom, most of the desks occupied by men in white shirts and narrow black ties. Cheap plastic-framed eyeglasses on fat middle-aged faces. "They'll have to let you in the boys' club one day. Just gotta find a subtle way to slip in. Bake a little politics into that cookie dough."

Fran smirked. "Is that auntie's official advice?"

"Don't quote me, girl. That one was off the record." Marjorie raised an eyebrow and sauntered off. All the women on staff, all five of them, that is, had a kind of understanding. They backed each other up. Gave each other tips when the boss was in a mood. Found subtle ways to pass a tissue if someone left the editor's office in tears or tuck a tube of concealer in a desk drawer if someone's husband had had a bad night and taken it out on the wife.

Fran turned back to the reel. Every day since that night in

Ogallala, she'd waded through these wire stories, looking, looking, looking.

Which was why, today, when she read about the explosion in Kalispell, it took her a second—and a few rereads—to comprehend it. Right here, in front of her. A lead. A clue.

At last.

It was like lightning had hit her square in the chest. She bent down and read it a third time:

> DECEMBER 1, 1944, KALISPELL, MONTANA: The remains of a gigantic parachute were found by loggers in Flathead County, according to local officials. Authorities were hesitant to link it to a mysterious event in Thermopolis, Wyoming, which had occurred five nights earlier, in which a glowing red light was seen in the sky, and the discovered charred remains of what was described as a large parachute. No further details have been provided for either of these incidents.

Her pulse burned in her veins, and she was right back on that frigid porch, staring at the night sky over Ogallala in shock.

It was time to move.

Richard was in his office. She saw him through the big window that looked out on the newsroom floor, the portal through which he summoned reporters, knocking on the glass. He had been hunched over his desk, pencil in hand, working away at some poor writer's piece. The door was closed, which meant he didn't want to be disturbed.

She went in after a quick rap on the door. He jerked his head up angrily, the reprimand dying on his lips when he saw who it was.

His appearance took her aback. She hadn't seen him since they'd gotten back to town, him being caught up in his family's Thanksgiving festivities and all. He'd had the full week off.

"Are you feeling okay? You look terrible." The first thing that came to mind was that he'd had a hard night of drinking. His face was bright pink like he had a fever, and he had dark rings under his eyes like he hadn't slept. Even his clothes were disheveled, and that wasn't like him. Richard rarely had a hair out of place; he liked to give the impression he had everything under control. Always.

"It's nothing, just a head cold. Something I probably caught from one of the kids." It didn't sound like a cold. "What do you want? Can't you see I'm busy?"

"Have you heard about this?" She shoved the newswire article under his nose.

He barely scanned it before he pushed it back at her. "So what?"

"*So what?*" This wasn't like him. Richard had been dismissive that night, perhaps focused on covering his own ass. But he was a brilliant journalist. He got just as excited about a lead as she did.

"The last night at the cabin—and now this?" she went on. "Three sightings in a handful of days." She picked up the scrap of paper, afraid he might hold it hostage. "I've got to go back to Ogallala, or, or—"

"Damnit, Fran," he said, hitting the desk. Once again, she was so startled by his behavior she took a step backward. In a more hushed tone he continued. "Do *not* mention that place here. I was at a conference that weekend and I don't know what you're talking about."

"Richard. Come on. This isn't about . . . *that*. This is something bigger. Montana? *Wyoming?*" Her mind raced. What could connect all these disparate places? "There's a story here . . . It's . . . it's bigger than I even thought." Three states. Three states *so far.*

Mysterious explosions.

Parachutes.

This was major. This was a fucking *world war* they were in, after all. And even though folks in Nebraska were worn out from the war effort, even though those stories had declined in the past year, this was something happening on *domestic turf.*

That fiery thing, that undying curiosity in her, was already racing way ahead, burning through the stagnancy of this tiny office. She'd heard about German prisoner of war camps scattered around the States, hidden in remote spots where the average civilian wouldn't even know about it. Nazis, housed on American land, sometimes even working American farms. She'd heard rumors of an escape here or there. Enemies on home soil. In her mind, she was spinning out all the possibilities: a second Japanese sneak attack, spies and sympathizers, a secret agent feeding instructions to German prisoners of war. This could be big.

Richard was talking to her, saying something soothing, and dimly, she noticed he had a bandage on his hand—the one that had touched the explosive—but the words weren't penetrating through the hot rush of blood in her head.

Someone walked by close to the window. Marjorie. She glanced in as she walked past.

That was enough to shut Richard down. "Freddie's. Tonight," he muttered.

Before he could change his mind, she slipped back out. He was wound up—first day back on the job after the lull of wife and kids and tryptophan. He was just out of sorts, she told herself. He'd be his old smooth self, the brilliant man she couldn't get enough of, later. Tonight, when they were alone.

Richard had deemed Freddie's a safe spot for them to meet, perhaps because it was in a part of town that most people would consider dangerous. She didn't especially like going there by herself at night. She picked a booth in the back and had a martini while she waited, resolving to pace herself on the drinks, that she'd been hitting the bottle a little too hard lately, but she'd barely taken the first sip when Richard slid into the booth opposite her. To her concern, he looked worse than he had that morning. His face glistened with a sheen of sweat. A stab of worry went through her.

When he reached for her martini, she saw that his hand was trembling. "Do you mind? I'm parched."

She watched him drain the glass. "Maybe you should be drinking water."

He waved for the waiter, signaling for two more. "Look, I can't stay. I promised Winnie I'd get home on time. Her sister Linda's in town still. Linda's a hawk. I think she suspects something. We might have to lay low for a bit—"

"Richard, we haven't seen each other, not like this, since that weekend."

"That's because she's on to me, watching me. I can see it in her eyes, Fran. Like I said, we have to lay low." He was acting as if they'd robbed a bank, or killed someone.

"I'm not here to talk about all that anyway, so you can cool it." Did men have any idea how it felt to be a woman? They seemed to have no read whatsoever on whether you were in the mood for some fun or ready to cut their dick off. "I want to talk about the story." She'd been mapping out ideas and theories in her head. She just needed someone with whom she could talk it through.

He patted his sweaty face with the cocktail napkin. What was wrong with him? "We've been through this, Fran. I have to tell you, it's not just the discretionary issues. I don't . . . I don't *like* this story. Something ugly about it."

Ugly. The word lingered like a slap in the face. Fran had been told she was ugly, in more ways than one, many times.

He scratched his neck. "I say we just leave it be. Gives me a really bad feeling."

"Leave it be?" The notion was impossible—had been impossible since she'd first witnessed that blast, showering the night sky in streaks of wild orange light. "Where's your ambition, Richard?"

"Ambition?" He paused, staring at her. She realized, too late, that no man likes to have his ambition questioned. "What are you getting at? Is that a threat?"

She was taken aback. "What? No."

"Because if you're trying to threaten my job, threatening to go public about . . . about *us* . . . about *this* . . . well good luck to you, Frances Gurstwold. You think the world believes you, a woman who purposefully leaves the top button of her blouse undone, a woman with no family, a woman who lives alone in the wrong part of town and who is widely known to drink too much . . . You think they'd listen to *you* over *me*? You come from nothing, sweetheart. You're nothing."

Now the repulsion, and shock, were in full force. This conversation had taken a sudden turn. She hadn't been threatening Richard, but he was acting so paranoid, so defensive. *He* was the one threatening *her*.

This man. This man who, up until today, she'd considered closer to her than anyone else in the world. This man who'd taken her under his wing. Who lifted her out of the typesetting pool and made her a reporter, who laughed at her grammar jokes and taught her everything she knew about good journalism. This man who had the ability to make her entire body tremble with pleasure.

The martini squirmed in her stomach and she thought she'd be sick. She'd been punched by a man before. She'd been betrayed before, too. But she had been young. This was different, wasn't it? Richard was a mature adult, and so was she. Maybe he never loved her, but there'd been a mutual respect. She was tempted to storm out but couldn't leave things like this. Something was clearly wrong.

The round of drinks showed up and he sloshed his back unceremoniously.

"Richard." She kept her voice calm. She knew how to steady him. The skill grew stronger the worse a situation got. "I'm not telling anyone anything. I promise you that." She put her hand on his. She noticed his was hot. "Baby, calm down. Rich. It's okay." She didn't know why she rushed to soothe him, even after he'd just berated her, wounded her. But there it was. Fran didn't question why she felt the urgent need to de-escalate a heated confrontation. It was like she was a fireman, and he was a blazing inferno, her only thought to *put it out*. She'd been doing it on and off since as long as she could remember. It was how you survived.

He seemed to soften, letting out a ragged breath.

"That's right. That's right. You wouldn't. You need this job. It's all you got. You're right. I'm sorry I overreacted." His eyes seemed to flash, as if returning from a daydream back into the present. "I've got to get going. It was good to see you, though. I'm glad we could clear the air."

She simply stared at him. What was wrong with him? They'd just fought. An ugly, brutal fight. He'd just lost his mind at her over nothing, and here he was acting like nothing had happened.

"You're like a dog after a scent," he went on, "and I've always enjoyed that about you. It's what makes you so sexy." He stood up and left a few bills on the table. "That blouse suits you, by the way," he added, and then he was gone.

The next morning, Fran, wrapped in a patchy chenille bathrobe, stood over the kitchen sink while she had a cigarette. The sky was thick and gray. It was winter in Lincoln alright. There'd probably be another snowfall tonight. Outside, two stories down, she heard the tires cutting through slush piled in the street. Horns echoed off brick buildings. The streets were filling with people as another workday started.

There was still no sign of her cat, dead or alive.

She resolved to call in sick. They owed it to her. She never took a day off and often spent her weekends following up on leads or fine-tuning a story to hand in on Monday. She was nauseous with disappointment and something worse. *Hurt.* She couldn't call it heartbreak, not really. She didn't love him. And yet the feeling was the same anyway, as if she had.

Something had happened to Richard to make him change practically overnight. He wasn't himself, either physically or mentally. The inflammation on his hand. The bags under his eyes. The redness in his cheeks. Had he come down with something over the long weekend, out in the woods?

She reheated yesterday's coffee in the cheap aluminum pot and carried it with her to the bedroom. She'd lived in a two-room apartment on the third floor for the past two years but she looked around her now as if seeing it for the first time. When had it become such a rat-trap? No wonder the cat had bolted at the earliest opportunity. Every surface in the little bedroom was heaped with stuff. Clothing worn days before, never put away. Shoes kicked off, lying on the floor next to each other like drunken partners. Tottering towers of half-read newspapers piled on the nightstand, the floor, on top of the chest of drawers. Notebooks she'd used for stories filed long ago, notes for stories she'd never gotten around to writing.

She flicked ash into the only empty ashtray she could find. Maybe Marcel had had the right idea. She had to do something, to get out. She had to change her life. She didn't want to be the second-string writer for the women's pages in Lincoln, Nebraska, for the rest of her life. Destined to become an alcoholic, to hear Richard tell it. She wanted more, and no one was going to hand it to her. She'd have to fight for what she wanted, and she'd always known this.

Something was going on, not too far away. *Wyoming, Montana.*

She pulled her suitcase out of the closet and started throwing things into it. Clean underwear, a couple cardigan sweaters, a tangled pair of sheer hose, stained at the toes.

The last thing she packed was the paper bag containing the mysterious scraps she'd found at the site in Ogallala. She tucked it into a pocket on the inside lid of her suitcase.

She threw on her good winter coat—nice and thick, even if it was starting to bald at the elbows—stepped into a pair of boots, set out a big pile of catnip, just in case, and then locked the door to her apartment and descended the stairs.

Outside, the first flakes of a new snow drifted past the windows.

8

Meiko's subconscious showed her where she had heard the story of the woman in the kimono before.

The memory came to her in her sleep, of a drawing in a book her father had shown her when they returned from Shikotan. The drawing was of a beautiful woman in a fine, fancy kimono, holding a baby in her arms. Crying at a man as he passed by, *Please save my baby.*

This is the jorogumo, her father had told her. *The old man of Shikotan told me that the island was its home.*

You could tell by the way the woman was drawn—the way she floated, the way her kimono seemed to be carried on the wind—that she was a demon.

We barely escaped her grasp, her father had said. *We are lucky to be alive.*

Why does she need the man to save her baby? Meiko had asked. She'd been very young and all she could think about was the infant—not so much younger than her—being imperiled. Fear clawed at her heart. What kind of world allowed an infant to be in mortal danger?

There is no baby, her father had said. *It is a trick.*

A nother memory.

I'm sorry I put you in danger, her father had said that day, as he put the picture book away. He'd looked so sad. *I'll never do that again. I promise.*

But here she was, dying of a mysterious illness, because her father had sent her away to make a new life in America.

She finally stopped drifting through old memories and woke.

Where am I?

She tried to open her eyes, but they felt like they were welded shut. With effort, she finally was able to open them a crack.

She was in her room, lying in her bed. That was good. She was afraid they would've taken her away by now.

She tried to get up but found she could not move. The ache was so much worse than before. She was racked by pain. It went through her like a knife. The slightest move and she was on fire. And she was so weak, she couldn't fight through the pain. The pain was so strong she could barely think.

It had to be the grit, the sand—whatever it was that man had forced her to ingest.

She thought about her neighbors, the ones who had come down with the illness. Would that happen to her? The mad gibbering, incoherence, then finally, attacking everyone who came close? Would she lose her mind, be unable to tell right from wrong, friend from foe? Be lost in a world she could no longer make sense of?

Tears sprung to her eyes. Why were they doing this—those men in the fancy cars, because she had no doubt they were behind this? She wouldn't spare the camp officials from blame: they were complicit, because even if they couldn't stop the outsiders, they could let the world know what was going on inside the camp. They didn't because they were afraid for themselves, because their comfort and security mattered more than the lives of thousands of Japanese.

The part she couldn't figure out was *why*. Why were they going through all this trouble, infecting them, putting them through such torture? The residents were already their prisoners. If they wanted them dead, there had to be easier ways to kill them. Though Meiko thought of the stories she'd heard of the Nazis, how they'd rounded up their enemies and kept them in camps, slowly starved and tortured them to death. Maybe it was harder to kill a lot of people all at once than it seemed.

Her mind rebelled. *That's ridiculous.* She'd been living in America for a long time now. America was not Nazi Germany. Rounding up citizens in camps in order to kill them: it was impossible. It went against everything America stood for—everything Americans *said* they stood for.

Yet here she was, dying in an internment camp.

It had taken months and months after the Nazis first started gassing their prisoners for word to get out, for the world to know of the horror. If everyone in Minidoka died, the world would not know what was going on in time to save them. What was being done to them.

If everyone in Minidoka died—that meant Aiko would be killed, too.

Her eyes snapped open. She searched, nearly blind, for her daughter.

But the room was empty.

Now that I have been looking for the tiny, translucent spiders, I see them everywhere. Hanging from the tree in front of our cottage. Spinning a web in a corner of the ceiling in Meiko's bedroom. Scuttling among our dishes in the cupboard. I told the housekeeper to kill them, that I don't want to see any of these spiders in the house, but she is aghast. She says they are the children of Fujin, the wind god. She says that he brought them to this island and that most islanders consider them to be lucky.

The old man had said they were confined to the area around the hospital, but we are on the other side of the island. It can only mean that they are spreading.

I packed several of these spiders in cotton wool and sent them to an old friend who is an entomologist at Meiji University to see if he can identify the species. I have heard Japan has no poisonous spiders, but I would like to be certain.

9

Her dad was coming.

It was this thought that kept Aiko Briggs squirming in her seat, a simple wooden stool, unable to concentrate on her history home-work. Jenny and Rebecca had bragged this morning that they had already finished the whole chapter, and Aiko didn't want to fall behind. She wished she were Sansei, like them, the children of Nisei with their American names and white-skinned dolls. The girls traded candy wrappers like a currency and shared paperback mysteries, always leaving Aiko for last. She knew it was because her mother was Issei, and those born in Japan were distrusted, seen as most likely to be spies. Which struck Aiko as funny. She tried to imagine her mother as a spy, but couldn't do it. Her mother, who spent so much of her time caring for the sick and tending to her home.

But she knew the real reason Jenny and Rebecca and some of the others looked sideways at Aiko was not that she was Nisei. It was because her father was white, and they knew it. Everyone seemed to know, without being told, as if it were written across Aiko's face, coded in the faint freckles on her pale brown cheeks or the six inches of height she had on them. They saw how Aiko and her mother were given a compartment with a little extra space, how Meiko was assigned one of the more coveted jobs in the kitchen, and thought it was unfair.

It *was* unfair. Just not for the reasons they said. Aiko would have happily given up some of their private space for just one friendship like the kind Jenny and Rebecca had with each other. Someone to whisper about boys with. Someone who would make her feel less alone.

Meiko had said the others would warm to her once they got to know her, but things had only gotten worse at the camp, not better. One of the girls had seen her odd little drawings in the corner of her notebook and asked Aiko about them: loosely sketched ghosts and demons sometimes occupied more space on her pages than schoolwork. Some that looked human but had fangs the size of tree trunks. Others that resembled birds or snakes. Demons in beautiful kimonos, demons dressed as samurai. Demons lurking in the ruins of old palaces, or tiptoeing through the forest.

Excitedly, Aiko had told them all about the demons and fairies, *yokai* and *yurei,* in the stories her mother had told her from her Japanese childhood. The tales passed down from *her* father, Wasaburo Oishi, whom Aiko had never met. She'd thought the other kids her age would find them as darkly intriguing as she did, as vividly real, but they recoiled from her. They saw how she believed a little too much in the stories. How she spoke of them as if they were more than myths.

Her mother understood: the other girls didn't need the folk stories the same way Aiko did. Aiko wanted to believe in demons and spirits because she needed them. Because—except for her mother— she was alone. And as important as her mother was to her, even Aiko could see that here in the camp, her mother was powerless.

They needed protection. Especially now that the demons had arrived at the camps.

It had all started when a few of the people in Block H had mysteriously taken ill. The Hanamuras, and then the Ogabes. American doctors arrived right away, almost as if they'd expected this to happen—though Aiko's mother had told her these men weren't doctors. Once her mother had said that, Aiko could see for herself what these new men, the visitors, were.

They might've been in Western clothing, but these were demons.

You felt it in their eyes. In the way the air shivered around them. They brought evil with them. They dispensed it in the air and made everything in the camp go bad.

She knew this because the spirits had told her. She'd already told her mother about the spirits who visited her, and her mother hadn't told her that it was all in her head, no, but she also told Aiko she mustn't share this with anyone else because they wouldn't understand.

Aiko understood: her mother didn't believe her.

Last night, the camp awoke to screaming. Hiro Hanamura had attacked and killed his wife and by the time everyone had run out to witness what was going on, they only saw him being dragged away in darkness, blood and foam pouring from his mouth. A covered stretcher followed.

By dawn, all that was left of the formerly well-liked Hanamuras was a torn bit of Mrs. Hanamura's nightdress, having snagged in the rough wood of the doorway, waving limply like a white flag.

Even Aiko had heard the whispers by morning. People said Hanamura had torn apart his wife's throat with his teeth. That the "doctors" had to anesthetize the old man, he had gotten so uncontrollable, but the cyclopropane ended up killing him. *Put him down like a dog*, people muttered.

Two had been killed the day before—Sam Kikuchi and Bob Ueno. Taken out behind the administrative buildings by the guards followed by the sound of gunfire echoing between the barracks. The camp director had explained that it was because they had been trying to get to town. They would've infected everybody, caused an *outbreak*, and they couldn't allow that. Stopping them had been the responsible thing to do, surely everyone understood that.

People were in a panic.

Town people had begun to appear at the entrance to the camp, carrying signs. Aiko had mentioned seeing them on her way to school, early in the morning. People so angry that they got up extra early to shout at children. They kept their distance, but they clamored at anyone who passed through the gate, the camp workers who went home to their families in town at quitting time, the olive-green cars of military men arriving for unexplained visits.

They shouted frightful things about the residents, how they should be put down to save the "greater population." How the lives of the people in town were more important than the lives of those inside the camp. "They're responsible for the Jap disease!" one man had screamed until he was bright red in the face. "It's a Jap scheme! The emperor is using them to kill us!"

"It's Pearl Harbor all over again!" another woman wailed dramatically. She kept shouting it adamantly, but Aiko didn't think what she'd said made sense.

There were rumored to be reporters in the crowd, though it seemed like the camp guards sent them packing quickly enough.

And now, the worst thing had happened, the thing Aiko had feared the most.

Her mother was ill. She couldn't speak, couldn't move. Couldn't hold her daughter's hand or tell her to be brave.

But she would be brave. Her mother would hang on and get

better because her father was coming. This thought kept Aiko from breaking down, from following the urge to run and run and never look back. Her dad was coming. They had his letter to prove it. She knew he'd make everything alright. And even more than the excitement of seeing him after too many years, of being swung aloft by those strong arms and warmed by his hearty laugh, of showing off all the crafts she had made in their art class and watching as he beamed with pride—more than all of that was the sheer bliss of knowing what the effect would be on *everyone else.* He was more than their rescuer. Jamie Briggs was a uniformed pilot with a smile like a lit marquee. He walked into a room and ladies crossed their legs and twittered, while children scampered over to beg for funny stories. Everyone loved Aiko's dad.

And soon, she'd be able to hold his hand and flee from this place, escape, before the bad demons got her, too.

Her mother was still sleeping, and Aiko felt restless. She listened to her mother's labored breathing. The weather turned really cold a few weeks earlier, and that did not help matters. The barracks had been hastily built and did little to keep out the cold. Wind whistled through cracks between the boards. Neither of them had enough warm clothes. No one had known, when they'd been rounded up, where the government was taking them or that they'd need their winter clothing.

Aiko had piled both their blankets on top of her mother, along with her winter coat and shawl, but still her mother shivered and her teeth chattered. Aiko had even borrowed another blanket, a thick one, from one of the neighbors. That helped a little but was not enough. It seemed to Aiko that her mother was getting worse. She was delirious most of the time, whenever she wasn't asleep.

There was a noise at the threshold. All they had for a door was a length of cloth hanging down like a curtain. *Noren,* her mother called it. It was Mrs. Tanaka, their neighbor. She also worked in the camp kitchen. She had a pail with her, with a tin pie plate on top for a lid. She had taken over soup delivery to the sick since her mother could not. "I've brought some soup for your mother, Aiko." She set the pail on the table and reached for two small bowls on the shelf. She poured soup into one of the bowls.

"I bet you haven't eaten lunch yet." A cloud of savory, salty aromas rose into the air. Miso soup. Fat chunks of tofu bobbed in the opaque broth, and Aiko's mouth watered. Mrs. Tanaka offered it to Aiko before pouring a second bowl for Meiko. She stood over Aiko's sleeping mother for a moment, pressing a hand to her forehead. Then she turned to Aiko. "Why don't you join the other children in the dining hall once you finish that bowl? You're only twelve, you're still a child. You should be playing. They're making Christmas decorations. It will be fun."

Aiko hated when people called her a child. With her father gone, she felt as though she'd grown up faster than most. She looked up from the bowl she'd already begun sipping, basking in its steam, to the cot. "I can't leave my mother."

"I'll come back when I finish delivering soup and stay with your mother. I'll make sure she eats something. You should get out for a little while. Go on. It will be okay."

Something about the way Mrs. Tanaka spoke made Aiko think it was important that she go. There was a hint in it: *fit in with the others.* She didn't want to go, but honestly, she was afraid of what might happen if she refused. She didn't want the "doctors" to come poking around.

"Alright. Thank you very much." Aiko put on her coat, boiled wool with wooden toggle buttons. She hated to leave her mother's side, but then again, she thought maybe she could squirrel away some materials to make a present for her dad. And, though Jenny insisted it was childish, making crafts always soothed Aiko—she could daydream while her hands moved rapidly and beautiful creations issued forth, as if arriving out of some other dimension.

Perhaps her dad would like a pop-up card, with little buildings and people cut out by hand. The way a neighbor had taught her back in Seattle. She'd make it wintery and beautiful. He loved every holiday, but especially Christmas, and the family had celebrated it every winter in the apartment in Seattle, stringing up lights together. He'd taught Aiko his favorite carols.

But her mother had not had the heart to celebrate in the camp.

Aiko kissed her mother's forehead. As she looked up, she gasped: in the corner, watching them, was a *yurei*, a ghost. This one was new. She hadn't seen it before.

The figure was a young woman, younger than her mother, dressed in a *kyokatabira*, the white kimono worn by the dead.

Kumo, the ghost mouthed, pointing to Aiko's mother. Spider.

Aiko stood up and quickly checked the corner of the room, but the *yurei*, if it had been there at all, had dissolved into the dark shadows. She wanted to get her book of Japanese folktales, which had belonged to her grandfather, and look up the *yurei*, see if she could identify it. But—no, not in front of Mrs. Tanaka. Her mother wouldn't want her to do that.

Instead, she buttoned up her coat and kissed her mother again on the forehead. Then she made her way slowly to the dining hall, stepping carefully through the mud so as to do the least damage to her only pair of shoes. The lights in the mess hall twinkled at her, harshly cheerful. Inside, many children and teens she recognized had gathered at the long tables where they usually took their meals. The center of each table was piled with supplies, strips of colored paper and pots of paste. She saw Tamiko Sato with Susie Yamada and Chibi Kasa, the girls who were always the kindest to her. They waved her over but Aiko hesitated. She knew she didn't want to be distracted, to relax too much and forget about the time. She wanted to hurry back and be with her mother again. Until her mother was well, life would be disturbingly unsettled. She felt adrift, like that time she'd gone to the beach and gotten preoccupied building a sandcastle close to the water, and then forgotten where her parents were. It had been frightening and dizzying, searching the crowd for their faces. She'd been about to look for a policeman when her father came running and scooped her up in his arms.

Time passed quickly as Aiko worked. She knew what she wanted to make for her father: something to remind them of their home back in Seattle. They'd had another home briefly, staying with a friend of her father's in Oregon for a very short time, but the house in Seattle was the home they would be going back to, she was sure of it. She ignored the instructions from the chaperones—"now thread one strip of paper through the loop you just made, and paste it closed to make a link"—and the whispers of the other girls, all gossiping about what presents they wanted for Christmas. She took a piece of blue construction paper and started cutting. *Snip, snip, snip.* Slivers of blue paper flew. "Where did you learn to do that?" Chibi said, stopping what she was working on to watch.

"A friend of my father taught me." Aiko took her paper and folded it in a couple places, so it could stand. She placed it on the table in front of her: it was the skyline of their block in Seattle. The line of the roofs, the outline of trees. Windows cut out in the houses, chimneys standing tall. There was a candle burning by the pot of paste and bits of art supplies, supplementing the dim light in the dining hall, and Aiko placed it behind the scrim so that it threw house-shaped shadows on the table. It looked cheery and warm.

Tamiko clapped. "I recognize that—it's our old neighborhood."

"It's so pretty," Susie said. Aiko had to agree. *The dream city.* Because it was her mother's dream to go back home.

The girls began chattering again, but their voices had turned sharp and needling.

"Did you hear about the fight in Block M? I heard Mr. Tashigowa broke Mr. Hanza's jaw."

"I heard Jason Kitamata scratched his own eyes out! That's why he's in the hospital tent."

Their murmurs were thick with morbid delight. Aiko thought of her mother, wondered what the girls whispered about her.

She picked up her paper scrim and folded it carefully. "I'm going to check on my mother," she told the others.

The walk back to the barracks was lonely. It was too early for the sky to be so dark, and an icy wind had begun to roll through the camp. A storm was coming.

Their room was dark. Mrs. Tanaka had turned off the oil lamp. That meant her mother was probably still asleep. Aiko relit the lamp, hoping it wouldn't wake her.

The cot was empty. Her mother was gone.

Aiko put a hand to the thin, lumpy mattress. It was cold.

Aiko tried to remember where the Tanakas lived. There were twelve barracks per block, six compartments per barrack, and they all looked the same. It was easy to get lost. But she found Mrs. Tanaka in the hall in her overcoat and a scarf wrapped around her hair, sweeping dust out into the courtyard.

"Mrs. Tanaka! Do you know where my mother is? I went back to our room . . ."

The pitying look in the neighbor's eyes stopped Aiko cold. "Aiko, your mother . . . I got one of the doctors to look at her while you were away."

One of the demons. She brought one of the demons into our room.

". . . and he thought it would be best . . ." Mrs. Tanaka stopped, took a deep breath, and looked Aiko squarely in the eye. "They took her to the infirmary."

The infirmary. It stood by itself, near the building that housed the military police. That's where the visitors were, the men they called doctors.

Her mother had seen them for what they were: bad. Maybe not demons themselves, but just as bad.

And now they had her.

10

The blank sheet of paper stared up at Archie stubbornly. He'd been holding his pencil for the better part of an hour and his hand had started to cramp.

It was Saturday afternoon. The sermon for tomorrow's service was due but the words were not coming to him. He'd never been this late writing his sermon, ever. The only thoughts that came to him were dark, flickering ones, flames at the edges of his consciousness, turning everything in their path to ash. Thoughts he could hardly share with his congregation. He couldn't stand up and tell them all that every time he closed his eyes, he saw the children's bodies, like burnt rag dolls strewn across the forest floor. What he'd witnessed—or had he?—in Joan Patzke's hospital room. The nightmares that shook him awake sometimes with visions of a world in which everything was as Elsie had been—a false illusion. Beautiful until you touched it. Then it all became a kind of demonic dust.

He feared his soul had died up there in the mountains that day. That to speak would be to spread the soul-death to anyone who would listen.

It was hard not to give up. Let God go.

But the beers in the icebox ran out eventually, and even the dark, torturous visions billowed and swayed, sometimes clearing from his mind for whole hours at a time before returning with a vengeance. This morning he forced himself to stand in the shower, to shave his face. He looked himself in the mirror: a young man, recently twenty-nine. Handsome, if ragged. Eyes that said, *I forgive you your sins, for how could I not? How could I, of all sinners, not believe in second chances?*

But the real question remained curled inside him: could *he* ever be forgiven?

Now Archie clenched and unclenched his hands, trying to work out stiffness. His fingers were puffy and sore. Not from arthritis or overwork; no, he'd been out in the shed night after night, punching the beams until his knuckles were bloody. It was one of the things he did when he fell into despair. When he woke up in the morning and Elsie was not lying next to him in bed. When he stood over the sink, brushing his teeth, and caught sight of her pink toothbrush in the cup. When he realized the house was so empty and still that he could hear himself breathe.

The loss of his wife was incomprehensible, and so, too, was his own weakness. *He* was the one others were supposed to turn to when they suffered unimaginable loss. *He* was supposed to have the answers, to be the one to bring comfort and solace. He was supposed to believe.

It was not too much of an exaggeration to say that he didn't know what to believe anymore.

He rose from the spindle-backed chair and walked out of his tiny study (a pretentious name for the small room where he kept his books from seminary) and out the front door. Hoping none of the neighbors were watching, he stood under one of the pines and took some deep breaths, the only thing he could think of to clear the black cloud in his head.

The minister from Sprague River had dropped by out of the

blue two days earlier. Archie tried to listen as the man did his best to comfort him, but it was impossible to pay attention for more than a word or two. A nice enough man but bland and utterly forgettable—borne out by the fact that Archie couldn't remember his name. *Spend time with family,* he'd said.

How would he define family? Elsie had been his family, and now she was gone. He had family to the east but had left them behind when he decided to go to seminary.

And then there were the people who became like family, the people who accepted you for who you were and didn't try to make you be something you weren't.

He put Jamie Briggs in that category.

His thoughts led him again to Meiko and Aiko, the day they'd been forced to pack their bags and leave for the camp. They'd been like family, too.

The guilt of what he'd done was a demon in itself, strangling him from the inside.

And people were always praising Archie's kindness. Didn't that just make what he'd done worse?

Just as Archie's agitation was peaking, he heard the sound of a car pulling up behind him. He turned to see an old pickup truck easing up to the curb. It belonged to William Voorhees, a farmer from down in the valley. The driver's door squeaked as Voorhees climbed out.

Archie tried to smile but it would not remain in place. "What can I do for you, William?"

Voorhees held out a dish covered with a tea towel. "My Nina made you a casserole. Thought you might not feel much like cooking."

The icebox was filled with untouched casseroles.

He lifted the tea towel to a landscape of melted orange cheese, exactly how he imagined the surface of Mars might look. It didn't matter what was under that cheese, pasta or mashed potatoes, hamburger or tuna. He had no appetite. He lowered the towel and forced a smile at Voorhees. "It looks delicious. Give Nina my thanks. I'll be thinking of her tonight when I sit down to supper."

Archie hoped the man would head back to the truck, his good deed for the day done, but Voorhees showed no sign of leaving. "You look kinda down, padre. Need someone to talk to?"

The last thing Archie wanted to do was show his vulnerabilities to a member of his congregation. It was bad enough they all pitied him: he didn't need to show them how weak he was, too. But Archie couldn't think of what to say in that moment, his mind a gray fog of unhappiness and unrelenting anger.

Voorhees squinted up at him. "Maybe it would do you good to have some company. Take your mind off things. Some of the guys get together evenings at the Moose Lodge out on Route 140. You know the place?"

He'd driven past it a few times. A quiet building, an unpopular spot or so it seemed, but then Archie would've driven past it during the day when it was likely empty. It might be lively in the evenings with cards and beer, maybe bingo games or some local fellow with a fiddle.

Still, seeking out company and distraction struck him as unseemly. "I don't know, William. I'm not a member—"

"You don't have to be. You'll be my guest. I'll leave your name at the door." Voorhees gave Archie a weak tap on the arm. "Stop by anytime. It'll do you a world of good."

Archie stumbled through his sermon that Sunday on autopilot, inwardly hating himself, knowing he couldn't hide the deadness in his heart from the congregation. He endured their well-wishes after the service was over, accepted another deluge of casseroles as well as fried donuts and cupcakes. The cupcakes only reminded him of Elsie's chocolate cake. How it had fallen to the ground during the explosion, chunks of brown cake like handfuls of flesh and shards of white china like bone, embedded in the dirt. By the time he got home, he felt like an animal that had been chased by predators, his heart pounding. Grateful to have made his escape.

By Thursday night, he was beside himself with agitation. It wasn't right to avoid other people, he knew that, but he didn't think he could endure one more knowing look or well-meaning platitude. He considered getting in his car and driving, heading east until he found himself back at his parents' home. Knowing the folly of that—did he need any more evidence that he hated himself, to subject himself to that punishment?—he headed west, and within twenty minutes pulled into the parking lot at the Moose Lodge.

It looked welcoming in the twilight. Lights over the entrance twinkled at him, beckoning. The parking lot was half-filled with pickup trucks and station wagons. With his window rolled down, Archie could hear the muted sound of men's voices and something being played on a jukebox. As much as he hated to admit it— because it seemed like a betrayal of Elsie—something inside him twitched. His body responded, like a man in the desert smelling water on the air.

Once through the front door, he looked for William Voorhees but he wasn't there. No matter: he recognized a number of men in the room from church. For a brief moment he felt relief, but then had to fight the urge to turn around and go home. They wouldn't understand why he was there so soon after his wife's death.

A man waved him over to a table of about six or seven men huddled close together. Archie answered the summons even as he racked his brain to remember who the man was. Oh yes, he owned the garage in town. Had a funny name—Dutch. Dutch Talbert. Archie didn't know the others.

"Fellas, this is Archie Mitchell," Dutch said, gesturing to Archie, and was answered by grunts of acknowledgment. "Take a seat. Join us." One of the men pulled an empty chair over.

It wasn't until Archie was sitting that Dutch added, "You heard about that explosion over on Gearhart? Archie was there. He lost his wife." They looked at him with pity and curiosity, which he was sick of.

One man to Archie's left—their shoulders jostling, there was so little room to move; why did they need to sit so close?—poured beer from a pitcher and pushed it to him. "That was you? Terrible thing that . . . And the Patzke family? To lose two of their kids like that, and another in the war, too . . ."

A short man next to Dutch eyed Archie sharply, like he was judging a cow at the state fair. "So, tell us what happened."

Up to this moment, it hadn't been hard to respect the army colonel's edict not to talk about it. Aside from the police, no one had had the nerve to ask him directly about the incident. His neighbors and congregants tiptoed around it like mice sniffing around a loaded trap. He had replayed the scene over and over in his mind, of course, a movie on a loop that he was helpless to stop. He wondered if talking about it would expel these terrible pictures from his tormented mind. If it might be like an exorcism. And if he were going to release some inner demon, maybe it would be safest among strangers.

Besides, the colonel's warning seemed overblown. It wasn't like any of the men at this table were spies for the Japanese. They were all patriots, like him.

He took a deep breath. "We decided to go for a picnic and some fishing on Gearhart Mountain . . ."

He described the memories as they came to him: the kids jostling and playing in the back seat, how the road up the mountain was thick with mud, forcing them onto a little-used access road. How he'd seen the thing lying on the ground—broad and flat and white—and known there was something alien and strange about it, but he was dealing with the picnic things, getting them out of the trunk of the car . . . Why had he done that? All that could've waited, the important thing was Elsie and those kids . . . And then *BOOM*, the explosion rocked the ground under his feet. He told them how his ears had rung and smothered out the sound of his wife and those children screaming. He was about to describe what he saw when he got to his wife, how the skin melted off her face—and the spiders at the hospital, should he tell them about that? Did he still believe that was what he'd seen?—when Dutch Talbert leaned over to put a hand on his arm and said that was enough and there was something about his expression that made Archie stop. He blinked and saw the men around him had grown ashen and leaned back in their seats. Keeping their distance, disquieted by what he'd said. Words could be like a contagion, too, and now he'd contaminated them with what he'd seen, what he knew.

After a minute of uncomfortable silence, the man who'd poured beer for Archie said, "Maybe you can confirm something for us . . . We heard it was a Japanese bomb. Is that true?"

Archie opened his mouth to answer but . . . he hadn't seen it himself, knew only what the police had said and bits and pieces he'd overheard at the hospital. Something about writing, and what the paper was made of . . . but nobody knew for sure. They were guessing.

Plus, it strayed dangerously close to what the colonel had said.

Archie took a drink to give himself time to think. "Well, I don't rightly know . . ."

"Don't ask the padre such nonsense." Dutch shot a look of disgust at the man who'd asked the question. "Everyone knows we're too far away for the Japs to bomb us."

"Look at what happened at Pearl Harbor—"

"We're a lot farther out than Hawaii, aren't we? Besides, if they could send bombs, don't you think they would've bombed our asses to oblivion by now? Naw . . . whatever it was couldn't have come all the way from Japan."

"Then what do you think it was?"

Dutch snorted. "We all know who was responsible for that explosion. Sympathizers. Spies."

At those words, the group fell silent. Spies and sympathizers, the silent threat—they were told—was always hovering in the background. Archie thought of the posters at the post office and town hall, of slant-eyed Emperor Hirohito with fearsome front teeth like a giant rat. DON'T FEED THE JAPS INFORMATION . . . KEEP YOUR TRAP SHUT. CARELESS TALK MAY COST AMERICAN LIVES . . .

"The Japs got spies all over the West Coast. Everybody knows that." Heads nodded. "They're probably testing their bombs and booby traps in the woods where they think nobody will find them and you"—Dutch nodded in Archie's direction—"were unlucky enough to come across one."

Archie's stomach tightened. Did any of this sound remotely plausible? And yet . . . it was comforting, too, to think there might be an explanation for Elsie's death. That it hadn't been his fault. That the men sitting around the table didn't blame him or think him a coward.

"This area is crawling with Jap sympathizers," the man to Archie's right said, to mutters of agreement. "Softheaded idiots. We're at war, or have they forgotten?"

Archie thought of the editorials in the newspapers and radio programs reminding everyone to be on the lookout for suspicious behavior. Warning everyone that their neighbors could be spies. Suspect anyone who admired Japanese culture. Look for telltale signs: chinoiserie displayed in their homes, books about samurai, bonsai plants on the windowsill. Did they like Chinese dumplings and egg foo young?

There was a time—Archie burned with shame to remember—when this could've been said about him. When he lived in Seattle and was going to seminary. There were a lot of Japanese there. You'd have to be living under a rock not to know some. His best friend, Jamie Briggs, had even fallen in love with a Japanese woman.

He pictured them together, Jamie and Meiko, with their daughter, Aiko. This was not a pleasant memory, and he shut it down quickly. He refused to think about it.

He assumed everyone in Bly was like him, basically tolerant. As he looked around the table, he realized his assumption might be wrong. Maybe his neighbors didn't like their Asian neighbors. They just didn't go around talking about it, kept their feelings smoldering inside. Did they think *he* was a softheaded idiot?

Maybe he was, and it took his wife being murdered to open his eyes.

He felt like his world had been suddenly turned upside down and shaken like a snow globe.

That was when Archie noticed the man sitting next to Dutch was shaking. He was a bundle of nerves, like one of those fellows who come back from the service shell-shocked. One of his legs constantly jittered, and his free hand kept tapping the table. He obviously spent a lot of time outdoors, his face tanned and wrinkled like cowhide, though he only looked to be in his twenties.

Dutch noticed Archie staring. "This is Gus Wallaby, a nephew of the Samsons. You probably heard about Barney Samson getting hurt on the combine last month, so Gus came down from Idaho to help."

It seemed a long way to come to help out on a place as small as the Samsons', but everyone knew there was a shortage of able-bodied farmhands. Wallaby extended a hand to Archie. His palm was damp and left Archie's hand feeling itchy. "Sorry about your wife."

"So, you're from Idaho? Do you work on a farm out there, too?" Archie asked, but only to seem sociable. Honestly, he didn't care what the man did.

One of the others jumped in. "He was a guard at one of the Jap internment camps."

Jap. A familiar mix of shame and guilt ran along Archie's spine. "You don't say?"

"He was just telling us what it's like," the man who'd poured Archie the beer said.

"Things are bad." Wallaby took a swig of beer, then dabbed the corners of his mouth with the back of his hand. "Worse than the ghettos in New York. There've been more fights lately, but what do you expect from people like that—"

Locked up in a barren camp in the middle of nowhere for years.

Archie pushed the thought away. That was the minister talking.

Maybe they deserved to be in a camp.

"I'm glad to be leaving, after being cooped up with all those Japs," Wallaby continued, warming to the topic. "They're not humans, not like you and me. They're animals. A young man beat up on a grandmother. Gangs roam the camp. They attack each other like rats. The way they live, packed together like vermin, it was only a matter of time before things would go to hell . . ." He scratched absently at his forearms, as though triggered by the thought of brushing up against them.

Archie thought of the stories he'd heard from missionaries who'd gone to China and Japan, writing back to tell of families piled on top of one another in huts, living in squalor. But he'd been trained at seminary to think they were no different from the tenements in New York City and San Francisco packed to the roof with Italians, Irish, Polish.

But maybe his teachers had been wrong. Maybe they'd been softheaded. Too tolerant. *We're talking about the Japanese, the people who killed Elsie. They're different. That's why they're the enemy. You have every right to hate them.* Nobody had more of a right than he.

"We heard there's some kind of disease sweeping through the camp. It's been in the newspapers."

"Bad cold. Maybe the flu." Wallaby reached for his glass when a phlegmy cough rumbled up from deep within his chest. All eyes turned to the outsider.

"What kind of disease did you say it was, out in this camp of yours?" Dutch asked.

Wallaby ignored him. "If every American could *see* what it's like in the camps, you can bet there'd be no Jap sympathizers. They hate us and they can't wait to get out and come after us. They're going to take what's ours. Americans everywhere should run every Jap outta this country—if we don't shoot their asses first . . ."

He was cut off by another cough, this one almost painful to hear. Wallaby brought a hand to his mouth to cover it, but not quickly enough. A spray of fine red drops splattered across the table. A mist seemed to hang in the air.

Blood.

Dutch lifted his arms, as though in surrender. "You don't have the tuberculosis, do you?"

A few of the men scrambled back from the table, abandoning chairs. Nobody went to the local Moose Lodge expecting to bring a disease like that back to their homes and families.

They wouldn't let this guard leave the camp if there was a chance he had TB, would they? If there was any disease blossoming inside the close quarters of a camp or prison, it would be TB. Archie wanted to believe that the government had plans for that sort of thing and knew how to protect the rest of the country from contagion.

"I told you, it's nothing." Wallaby stuffed the handkerchief he'd used to dab his mouth hastily into a pocket, but it was obvious he was no longer welcome. He shoved his chair back as he got to his feet. "You'll see . . . They want your women, your businesses, your homes, your livelihoods. Everything you've worked hard for. There'll be nothing left for your children. This won't be a white country anymore. It's up to you. If we don't do something about the Japs—if we don't keep them in their place—they'll be coming for you next."

Wallaby stormed off, his rancor hanging in the air. Rancor so strong that Archie could swear he felt it crawling all over him, so strong that he wanted to scrub it off. Archie and the others looked at each other, unsure of what had just happened. They wanted to believe it was just talk, but this man had been inside the camps, had seen what was going on with his own eyes. Surely, he knew.

Archie downed the rest of the beer. It was watery, but his head spun all the same.

Dutch picked the upended chair off the floor and set it right. Then he looked over his shoulder before speaking. "Look, I'd say that bomb the padre found in the woods is *proof* that not all our enemies are locked up in the camps. We got Jap spies living among us. The softheaded liberals would have you believe there's no threat, but we know better. We know they're wrong. The question is, what are we going to do about it?" He turned to Archie. "We could use you, padre, if you want to join us. People should hear what you got to say." *Archie Mitchell, you are a witness. You must testify.*

But then there was that hard glint in Dutch's eyes. It was a look Archie had seen before and knew to be afraid of.

It wasn't until that second that he remembered the woman in the kimono. Could she have caused the explosion? Was she a sympathizer, setting traps in the woods?

He flushed with embarrassment. He couldn't tell anyone about what he'd seen: it was preposterous. If you were a spy behind enemy lines, the last thing you'd do is dress in a flaming-red kimono while doing your dirty work.

No, that had been his imagination. His guilty conscience.

At the same time, though, his head spun and his blood pounded in his ears, and he knew this anger in his heart wasn't going to go away on its own. He hadn't gone looking for a fight, but when the fight came to your door, sometimes you couldn't turn the other cheek. If he shirked his responsibility, other people could die.

What would Elsie want him to do?

But he knew what she'd want—she'd asked him once already, hadn't she?

He met Dutch's eyes, and nodded.

A grin broke out over the mechanic's face. "Glad you're with us, Archie. We get together Wednesday nights at my garage. Eight thirty. Don't be late."

11

The crunch of gravel. The glare of early-winter sun. Fran squinted through the dashboard as she pulled up in front of the Polson news office, the *Flathead Courier*. She braced herself against a heavy gust of cold wind as she shoved open the door of the old Rambler and stepped out. A small tumble of cigarette butts drifted off her coat. She slammed the door and shook her legs; she'd been behind the wheel for three solid hours since her last stop someplace outside Missoula.

Beside the newspaper's office sat Flathead Lake, winking in the windy sunlight, an immense blue body of water, beautifully clear, and behind it rose a line of purple mountains, the peaks all dusted white, like something on a postcard. *I'm here, in beautiful nowhere. Thinking of you!*

The air was so crisp it actually hurt her lungs to breathe. She'd need another cigarette just to bring the warmth back to her blood. She felt in her pockets, then reopened the Rambler to grab her pack, which was half-empty already and lay strewn on the passenger seat.

She had initially planned on taking the bus, but then thought better of it; there were a lot of wide-open spaces in Montana, places not reached by bus. There were countless ways to become lost, and countless reasons doing so might be deadly.

Thank God she managed to talk her friend Oscar—a car nut, always working on one or another in the cinder-block garage behind his house—into lending her some wheels. It was hard to find someone who would trust you with an automobile, not when there hadn't been any passenger cars made for almost a few years now on account of the war effort. Usable tires were hard to come by, gasoline rationed. Oscar was a scrounger and a wheeler-dealer, and he always managed to keep his cars on the road. She gave him a couple bottles of good Canadian whisky (she always seemed to be able to get her hands on that), and he'd handed over the keys, saying, "Don't get into too much trouble, now."

Having not driven since she'd moved to Lincoln, the first couple hours behind the wheel were tough, but once you knocked off the rust, it came back easily. The feeling of flat road falling away beneath you. The thrum of the engine, the bump of the wheel. The old Rambler was on its last legs, though, and had been a little tricky to control, especially on slippery patches where loose snow had recently fallen. Luckily, the roads up here had been mostly deserted except for the occasional logging truck.

A couple phone calls to reporter friends had led to the *Courier* as the source of the wire story. A guy on staff by the name of Dan Winters had filed it, she was told. She spent the first night on the road in Casper, Wyoming, and then spent the entire next day and into the night driving to Polson. And now, as morning broke, she'd arrived finally at the *Courier*'s office, right on the shore of Flathead Lake.

Fran knew she might be in trouble the minute she walked into the newsroom. All men. They stared at her, as though she was some kind of rare animal that never ventured this close to town. It was no surprise, then, when the managing editor told her that Dan Winters was out on assignment, and—surprise, surprise—they didn't have a way to get in touch with him. The managing editor was a fat middle-aged man in wire-frame spectacles who didn't try to disguise his leer while he spoke. When she asked if he knew anything about the story, even pulling out the scrap of paper to show him what she was talking about, he played dumb. "No, you'll have to ask Dan about that," he said after barely glancing at the paper in her hands.

"Well, that's not going to be possible—you just said so yourself—so maybe you can try a little harder." She gave him a tight smile, her no-nonsense smile, the one that Richard said could shrivel a man's testicles at a dozen paces. "Maybe there's someone else in town Dan has spoken to? Someone who might have a few details?"

The managing editor stopped leering. Fran had heard, behind them, a few sharp intakes of breath, and she wasn't sure if she'd gone too far, had gotten the man's hackles up. There was nothing she could do, however, but stand her ground.

"Now that you mention it," he said, drawing the words out slowly. "I seem to remember we printed a retraction on that story the day after it came out."

"A retraction?"

His smile was evil. "You didn't catch that, did you? Didn't do your homework. Yeah, Dan told us that he got a call from his eyewitness, saying he had made a mistake. We had to print a retraction. It was a damned embarrassment. So, you see, there's no story."

She leaned over his desk. "What did the witness say? How had he been mistaken?"

He leaned back in his chair, pleased to be back in control of this conversation. "You'll have to talk to Dan about that. Now, if you'll excuse me, I have work to do."

Fran went out and stood on the sidewalk lighting a cigarette, grateful for the cold lake air to cool her down. She considered going back inside and pinning the man's ears back, cursing him out a blue streak in front of his reporters. While it would make her feel better, it wouldn't get her any further.

The *Courier*'s door creaked open timidly. A young man in a plaid jacket stepped out, looking a little sheepish. "I heard you asking about Dan's story? The one about the balloon?"

"Balloon?"

The man started to drift away from the front of the building—obviously he didn't want them to be seen. Fran followed. "Yeah, that's what Dan thought it was. Look, Henry's not giving you the whole story. The story didn't get nixed because of some witness. Dan told me he'd gotten a call from the government. The military. They told him to retract the story. Said it had something to do with national security."

The military. What would a parachute have to do with national security? Fran's pulse quickened. "Is there any way for me to get in touch with Dan?"

The young man frowned. "Henry was telling the truth there—Dan is out of town on assignment. You can try calling back in a couple days." He looked over his shoulder, back at the *Courier*. "Henry can be a real pain in the neck sometimes. He likes to torment reporters for fun. I figure we writers have to stick together."

Fran put out her stub and climbed back in her car, her mind chewing on these latest facts. The peculiar activity had reportedly taken place in Kalispell, about an hour to the north. She hoped the locals there would be more cooperative.

The drive to Kalispell was even lonelier, making Fran worry about what she'd do if Oscar's shaky little car gave up the ghost on the way. She was rewarded at trail's end, however: Kalispell was more beautiful than Polson, if that were possible. The mountains were closer, looming over the town like giants. Signs reminded her that Glacier National Park was well past the city limits—and the temperature was a reminder, too, the frigid air nipping at her nose and earlobes every time she stepped out to refuel the car.

Once in Kalispell, it didn't take too long to locate the sheriff's station, just outside the stretch of Main Street that was home to most of the town's storefronts. The dispatcher at the front desk told Fran she'd have to come back after lunch, as Sheriff Thomas Mc-Carthy was away on a call. Fran found a little restaurant nearby, one that catered to the town's bachelors, judging from the clientele. She ordered vegetable soup and a cup of coffee and ignored the sideways glances she got from the men sitting at nearby tables, men in brown worsted suits who looked like lawyers or accountants, not the farmers and cowboys she'd imagined lived there.

The sheriff agreed to meet with her. Fran sat in a wooden chair opposite his desk. Above Sheriff McCarthy's desk was a huge bass mounted on a plaque. McCarthy was a big man, filling up the space behind the desk. He looked like he might be more comfortable on horseback than behind the wheel of the car parked out front. He studied her for a long time before speaking, though not in the leering way of the *Courier*'s managing editor. He was trying to decide what he was going to tell her. What he could share with a member of the press.

"It was two loggers what found the item," he finally said. He didn't meet her eyes, inspecting his fingernails instead. He could be especially concerned about personal hygiene, or he could be hiding something. "The debris from the balloon has already been spotted and cleared up. No harm done."

"Balloon?" That would be in line with the *Courier* reporter's story. "The wire story said it was a parachute."

Sheriff McCarthy shrugged. "Nope, turns out it's a balloon of some kind."

"It sounds like you now know more details than when this story came out . . ."

He leaned on the back legs of his chair, so far back Fran was afraid he might topple over. "I'm not at liberty to say."

She felt a shiver of excitement. *It was a national security concern.* "Not at liberty? We're talking about something that fell out of the sky, aren't we?"

"That's making it sound quite a bit more dramatic now, isn't it? Could be the work of an amateur balloonist. Could be anything. We're doing our own work to make sure it doesn't happen again. You can rest assured the community is safe."

"Amateur balloonist . . ." Fran suppressed an eye roll. "You get many of those around here?"

"Miss Gurstwold, I don't have whatever salacious media angle you're hoping for. If you're one of these outer space fanatics—"

"You mean flying saucers?" She couldn't keep the sarcasm out of her voice this time. "Get a lot of that out here, too, do you?"

He sighed. "We have a big sky, in case you haven't noticed. Now look—you're asking the wrong guy, I'm afraid. I really shouldn't be speaking to the press about this."

He'd never say such a thing to a male reporter. Fran knew it but she didn't have enough to go on yet—only that percolating, bubbling feeling in her gut. There was a story here. People didn't hide facts when the facts were innocent.

She tingled from head to foot; her throat went dry. She felt, she imagined, the same way a bloodhound did when it was taken out of its handler's truck and given the scrap of an escaped prisoner's clothing to sniff. He was stonewalling her, but that only meant she had to work harder. "Who told you that you couldn't talk to reporters about this?"

He frowned, furrowing a deep crease between his brows. "I didn't say that. Who would put the kibosh on something like that?"

Great question. "I can think of a couple people . . ." The government. Or the military.

"I'm afraid that's all I've got, Miss Gurstwold."

"At least tell me who the two loggers are . . ."

He paused, rubbing the corner of his mouth. "Look here, you seem like a very capable young woman and all, but I want you to listen to me when I tell you, you don't want to mess with the men who found the—object. These aren't city men like you're used to. They aren't practiced in speaking to a lady. I wouldn't want you putting yourself in any sort of *situation*."

Fran swallowed hard. She wasn't threatened by his insinuation, or even shocked by it. But the brush-off was enough to solidify what she already knew. The sheriff here was afraid of what the men might say to her.

She stood up. "Thank you kindly for your advice, Sheriff. Have a good day, now."

Fran went back to the restaurant for another cup of coffee, and this time made a point of chatting up the waitress, an agreeable middle-aged woman. Her name tag read NANCY. Fran always trusted Nancys. Women, Fran had learned from experience, were far more likely to tell her things. And waitresses knew all the scuttlebutt.

"Is this about the balloon?" she asked as soon as Fran opened her mouth. "Half the town went to see it when the sheriff brought it down from the mountain."

So much for the sheriff's attempts to keep things secret. "So, Sheriff McCarthy had been the one to answer the loggers' call?" Fran asked.

"There isn't much of a police force in Kalispell. The sheriff can press anyone he wants into being a deputy, if he needs to. But he's the one who has to answer most of the calls." She ran a damp rag over the counter, wiping crumbs away from Fran's spot. "I tell you, that balloon's the most exciting thing to happen to Kalispell in a long time."

"Oh? How so?"

The woman's eyes shined. "Well, it brought in all these experts from outside. The FBI sent an agent up from Butte. He comes here for his meals. A really nice fellow."

Fran's ears pricked up. "Is he still in town? Could you point him out to me . . . ?"

She nodded absently. "I sure will, if you're both in here at the same time. He comes in every day at the same time, around seven p.m. Then there are those nice guys from the army . . ."

FBI. Army. Fran couldn't wait to toss this in Richard's face. He'd be forced to admit he'd been wrong. He'd beg her to bring him the story, thank her for being mule-headed, for never giving up.

Fran started to gather her things. "I heard a couple local men found it—"

Nancy nodded, giving the counter a final swipe. "Yup. It was Owen and Oscar Hill. Used to be pretty nice fellas, good God-fearing types, but that was before Owen's wife passed. I'd say they're a little rough around the edges these days. All that time in the mountains, ya know. Two toms without much female company and all."

"You wouldn't happen to know where I could find them?"

By the time Fran left the restaurant, she knew where the father and son lived, though the waitress warned her that they spent their days in the forests, cutting up fallen trees to sell as firewood. It might be best to wait until it got dark to pay a call.

The room at the Batavia Motor Lodge was basic. Moth-eaten bedspreads covered the twin beds. Shabby curtains smelled of stale tobacco smoke. An old Bakelite radio squatted on the dresser. A nondescript print of a mountain range hung on the wall—a generic slice of beauty when all you had to do was look out the window and see all the splendor you could want. She'd noticed when she checked in that there was a television set and a phone in a lounge off the lobby, the phone stationed in the far corner of the room in an attempt to appear more private.

She returned there now, after dumping her bag in her room. "Can I make a long-distance call from here?" she asked, pointing to the phone.

The clerk, a thin man in his thirties, looked up from the register. "I gotta charge it to your room."

She waited until the clerk took the hint and wandered into the staff room before dialing. She was momentarily surprised to find that she had to speak to a telephone operator to place the call, then listened to the chirps in the background as it rang.

He picked it up on the fourth ring. "Hanson."

"Richard, it's me."

"Where have you been?" His tone said it all. He was relieved to hear her voice. But he was also exasperated. And something else—his voice sounded thick. Like he was still sick with that flu.

"I'm in Montana."

A knowing sigh. "After I told you not to chase that story." He coughed.

"Richard, you'll be glad I did. Something's going on. It's bigger than we thought. The FBI is here—"

"Fran, I have something to tell you." His tone of voice stopped her dead. He sounded sick, and he was always irritated when he was sick, irritated that his body would let him down by giving into weakness. He hadn't looked good the last time she'd seen him, and worry tumbled over in her gut. What if he was truly unwell?

"There's no easy way to say this, so I'm going to come right out. Winnie found out about us. She's demanded I stop seeing you."

Whatever happened to *It's okay with my wife? Winnie won't mind;*

118

she doesn't like the physical part. She doesn't even like to cuddle. "How did she find out?"

"What difference does that make? Lincoln's not a big town. It was a matter of time, I suppose." Then his tone softened. "I'm really sorry about this but . . . it's got to be over between us. And not just seeing each other . . . I'm afraid I have to let you go. Winnie wouldn't want us to work together. To see each other every day . . . She said it would prey on her mind." His voice shook. She wondered if he was crying. She hoped so. "She's threatened to get a lawyer, Fran. She could take everything: the house, the kids . . . You understand, don't you?" he rasped.

No, I don't.

But of course she did. She had always known this day would come. The truth of that had been baked right into the pie from the start. She had only been renting Richard Hanson, leasing him like a vacation spot. She was never going to keep him. There'd been no endgame. No dream for the future.

He didn't wait for her to answer. "I can give you two weeks' paid leave. It's only fair, of course. And a recommendation. That's the best I can do." He said it like he was being generous, like she should be thanking him. Like this was the standard severance package for a mistress.

Maybe that's why he'd been acting so strangely since the cabin. Snapping at her, scratching guiltily like something was biting at him. Like he had something he couldn't get rid of. He had been planning this.

"Fine. Whatever you say," she croaked, then swallowed back the thing bubbling in her throat. She didn't know if it was sadness or anger. There was no way to fight it. Whatever scenario she thought of, she'd lose.

She heard a noise behind her; was it the clerk? She turned so her back was to the counter, as though that made things any more private. She dropped to a whisper. "But what about the story? I have a couple more people to talk to, but I can get it to you in a couple days. Will you run it? One last story—for me. You owe me that much."

A long silence. "You're not listening to me, Fran. There is no story. There never was a story. Goodbye." The line went dead. He'd hung up on her. She lowered the receiver into the cradle.

A throat cleared behind her. When she turned around, the clerk averted his eyes, pretending to be busy with some paperwork. Even he was embarrassed for her, a night clerk in a run-down motel in a Podunk town. She turned away from him, not wanting to linger a moment longer than necessary.

"Excuse me, miss." It was the clerk.

What now, Fran thought. "If this is about the phone call, just put it on my bill . . ."

He had faded into the background the few times they'd spoken, but now there was something different about him. He studied her eagerly, his fingers twitching against the counter. "I didn't mean to eavesdrop, but did I hear you mention the FBI?"

She put her hands on her hips. "Look now, that was a personal call—"

"This has to do with the balloon they found out in the woods, doesn't it?" He said it matter-of-factly, as though he knew it would get her attention.

He took her into the office behind the front counter. Once he'd closed the door, he pulled out a notebook filled with clippings from newspapers across the region. Mysterious objects falling from the sky . . . and more. "I've been following this for weeks now," he said as she turned the papers. "It's hard because the government is clamping down on it. Sometimes the papers, they get one story out but then it goes quiet. They're being told not to write about it. That's what Dan Winters told me."

"Dan Winters? You spoke to him?"

"He was passing through on his way to California. Told me he was getting out of town for a while. Said everything felt kind of hinky to him."

Fran looked up from the clippings to the clerk's face, shining with intensity. "Who told him not to say anything? Was it the FBI?"

"No, it's the army. I saw them talking to the sheriff myself. Don't you think it's funny that the army is involved in this? I mean, they have a war to fight." Now that the clerk mentioned it, it did seem kinda funny that the army was in the middle of everything, not leaving it to the police.

The clerk pushed his rolled sleeves further up his forearm. "There's something else kinda funny, too . . . The army doesn't know about the FBI man. I caught him watching them here in town. Seemed unusual they weren't working together, both being with the government." He shrugged. "But the agent, he asked me not to tell them."

That was strange. Why did the FBI want to hide their interest? What in the world was going on?

"And look . . ." He dove across the table to rifle through the clippings, pulling some out for her. "It's not just about the balloons. There's something else going on . . . At some of the places where there's been a balloon sighting, they've had these outbreaks. They're trying to keep them out of the papers, these outbreaks, but word always gets out. Nobody knows what's causing them. But it stands to reason that it's the balloons, doncha think? And here's the funny thing: there's outbreaks at the camps, too, and the two sound an awful lot alike."

It depends, she wanted to tell him. The "outbreaks" could be completely dissimilar. Still, she had the feeling there might be something to what he was saying. Her reporter's sense was tingling.

"Theory goes, it all started with some spies from within the camps. An internal attack-like." He shoved a clipping across the table to her. *Mysterious outbreak in Minidoka responsible for three deaths.*

"You mean the internment camps." She remembered a couple similar stories off the wire. The government was pretty tight with news coming out of the camps. It was usually only feel-good stuff, honor students being accepted to college and the like. How had a story like this leaked out?

She looked at the clerk. His name tag read ANDY. He might be all of seventeen, just out of high school. "You think the two are related?"

He tapped the clipping impatiently. "Read the symptoms. They're the same. It can't just be a coincidence."

"Don't get ahead of yourself, Andy. It *could* be a coincidence. Headaches, fever, short tempers caused by pain . . . There are a lot of diseases with these symptoms."

He shrugged but his face was red. He didn't like her putting the brakes on. Shooting him down.

"Pretend you're a reporter, Andy. Follow the clues. What do you think is going on?"

He swallowed hard, maybe surprised to be asked for his opinion. "Well, I don't rightly know but . . . I been toying with the idea that . . . it might be—spacecraft."

"I'm not familiar with that term . . ."

"Aircraft that travel between worlds," he said earnestly. "You know: aliens."

The sheriff had tried to warn her, she remembered with a sinking stomach. *We have a big sky.* The clerk reminded her of someone, but she couldn't think who. Now she remembered: Gary Ry, a boy from her childhood who was obsessed with science fiction stories about life on other planets.

"I mean, these things are falling from the skies. Nobody's seen or heard any planes, so who's dropping them? If it were a plane, you'd hear 'em, but alien ships fly too high for you to hear. And people who come in contact with them are getting sick, like really crazy sick. And then the government's all concerned, sending the military *and* the FBI? It's got to be from something out of this world, don't you think?"

Fran felt her hopes stumble, and then collapse. The country, it seemed, was getting caught up in a craze for little green men, fueled perhaps by all the secret government bases in the deserts doing secret stuff for the war effort. It was starting to be the fodder of radio programs and the funny pages. And this poor boy, stuck in the middle of nowhere with a rich imagination, was one of them. A conspiracy junkie. Desperate for anything to feed his brain.

She patted his hand before bundling up the folder. "Sure, Andy. That's as good a guess as any. Thanks for the research—I'll mail these back to you after I've had a chance to look through them, okay? I'll give you credit in the article, if it comes to anything."

He followed her to the door, wringing his hands. "Well, if it's not UFOs, what do *you* think it is? C'mon, I've got nobody to talk to about this. Something's going on, but I can't get anyone to listen. Nobody believes me."

Me too, kid. Me too.

She stepped outside, into the cold evening. It wasn't a complete waste of time. There was some good information buried in his stories. She wished she'd been able to take notes on the things Andy said, but she'd have to rely on her memory later.

The snow had returned. She followed the open-air pathway back to her room. She had to plan her next interviews, write down questions to ask of people she had to figure out a way to meet. There was still so much to do. She didn't have Richard. She didn't have a *job*. And she was chasing the same story as a seventeen-year-old hotel clerk. But she couldn't let herself be put off by these things. She couldn't look at what her life was becoming—couldn't let the terrible thoughts flood in. There was a whole basement in her head, full of such thoughts, filled with broken detritus, a cellar with no working lightbulb, a dark, dangerous place where you could stumble and fall, cry out and no one would hear you. It was a mess that could take an eternity to make right. In cases like that, what you did was close and lock the basement door.

At least she had two weeks' pay. *Two weeks*, she told herself, pushing back into her room and opening up her notepad. Two weeks, some loggers to interview, mysterious objects falling from the sky, and maybe something going on at the camps.

12

CAMP MINIDOKA, IDAHO

When Aiko had gone to the infirmary three days ago in search of her mother, she'd been told to stay out—that to enter would be risking exposure to the contagion. She'd fretted all the remainder of the day, awaiting news, finally falling asleep alone in her room. When she was shaken awake, at some dark hour before dawn, a man had been crouched down beside the bed. "Hello, Aiko," the man whispered as her eyes flitted open. "Do you remember me? My name is Ken Nishi. I was a friend of your parents."

Was.

"I'm afraid I have bad news, Aiko." The thought of there being any worse news than her mother being sick was so absurd Aiko feared she might burst out in deranged giggles. Instead, she only stared at him, and tried to breathe. "There's no way to say this gently, so I'll just come right out." The man—Ken Nishi—looked at her solemnly. And she understood completely.

His voice broke softly as he continued. "Your mother is . . . is gone now, my girl. I'm so sorry."

Gone? She knew her mother was gone, taken away . . . but she also knew that was not what Mr. Nishi meant.

Her mother.

She couldn't be dead. It was . . . impossible.

Aiko tried to hold on to the thought—*my mother is dead*—but she couldn't.

What was death? She had never seen a dead person. She'd never been taken to a funeral, never seen a body, not even in a movie.

The only thing that she could allow herself to think, the only thing that made sense, was that her mother would be gone. Absent. Missing. Gone from view, but not really gone, not permanently. Aiko would always search for her—she was searching for her now, even as Mr. Nishi was speaking. Looking over his shoulder for her mother to walk into the room, laughing away Aiko's fears, telling this man he was mistaken. *Of course, I'm here. I'll always be here for my daughter.*

And then she was caught up in Mr. Nishi's arms. She had tried to run but he had caught her. He'd let her wail and struggle to get away, but he'd held her, telling her over and over how sorry he was. How, if he'd had his way, everything would be different.

"Let me see her." Aiko knew if she could see her mother as she was now—dead—then it would seem real to her. But without that, she would never believe it was true.

But he wouldn't take her to see her mother.

He'd let her cry in his arms until she was too exhausted to fight him any longer. Then he brought her back to the dormitory rooms and tucked her into the bed next to his own daughters.

That had been two days ago. Each hour, she'd asked him to take her to see her mother. And each time he'd said it wasn't possible. The camp authorities would not allow it. "We must be good. Obedient. Show them that we're loyal Americans. Your mother would want that, Aiko. Don't ever forget that."

And then, on the third day, he told her she had to go away. "I had told the camp administrators that you could live with me and my wife, and our two daughters, but they said that you must go to an orphanage." He shook his head as he spoke, as though he just couldn't believe this was happening.

"An orphanage? At the camp?"

"They are putting the orphans from all the camps into one facility at one of the other camps. They think it would be better. More efficient. That's the military for you," he said bitterly. "They will be taking you to Manzanar, near Los Angeles. That's where they're keeping the orphans."

Los Angeles was even further away from her home. She had been to so many places—Seattle, briefly in that small town in Oregon, and then Minidoka. "How will my father know to look for me there?" Her chin wobbled.

It looked, for a moment, like Mr. Nishi would begin crying, too. "Don't worry, Aiko. I will tell him."

"Why won't they send me to stay with my father's family?" She had a grandmother, a grandfather. Dad's brother—her uncle. They all lived somewhere in Washington State. Her father had told her all about them, even if she'd never met them. He'd said it wasn't a good idea to see them, but he'd never said why. There'd always been a look of pain, or tiredness, in his eyes when it came up.

"I'm sure they'll get word to them and let them know where you are. And once that happens, they'll come for you. But for now, I'm afraid you must go where they tell you," Mr. Nishi said. "They tell us where we must go, and we obey."

A terrible thought struck her. "Can't I stay for the funeral? Isn't there going to be a funeral for my mother?"

Now Mr. Nishi looked terribly ashamed. "I'm afraid not, Aiko. The crematorium . . . They told me they won't be able to take care of your mother for a long while, and the authorities don't want to hold up your transfer . . . They'll make sure your father gets her ashes. Try not to worry about it. You're too young to be worrying about such things . . ."

"Can I . . . can I bring my notebook and pencil?" she asked, a nervous lump rising in her throat.

Mr. Nishi let out a breath, somewhere between a laugh and a sigh. "Yes, I should think that would be alright."

The camp had been dead quiet as Mr. Nishi hurriedly helped her pack her few belongings, sliding it all into her schoolbag. Then he helped her on with her coat, made sure her mittens were pinned to her sleeves so they wouldn't get lost, and walked her down to the front gate, where a truck waited with its engine idling, puffing white exhaust into the dark night. Mr. Nishi insisted that he would ride with them and escort Aiko all the way to the train, that he was not about to leave her with a stranger. The driver didn't argue and let them ride in the cab with him rather than in the cargo area in the back.

Aiko had only been to the train depot once, and that was when she'd arrived at the camp with her mother two years ago. She remembered the day in vivid detail: the sea of people disgorging from the trains, being lost in a jungle of legs. The voices, angry and sad and upset. Soldiers barking orders. She'd clutched her mother's hand for dear life, afraid that if they were separated, she'd never find her again. Tucked under her arm, the book of Japanese folktales her mother had gotten for her from the bookstore in Japantown. It seemed like a lifetime ago, the earliest thing Aiko could remember as her memories of Seattle faded.

Mr. Nishi held her hand as he walked her to the train. A man in uniform stood by the platform with a clipboard. He checked off Aiko's name.

Mr. Nishi looked at the crowd on the platform. It was mostly soldiers but there were a few people in civilian dress. No children. Aiko looked around, too, shivering at the thought of being alone amid all these adults. All these strangers.

"Is she the only one going to Manzanar?" Mr. Nishi asked, surprised. When the soldier nodded, Mr. Nishi got mad. "Then what's the rush? Sending a little girl off by herself in the middle of the night, in the middle of this epidemic . . . It's a disgrace. I'm going to have a talk with the camp administrator about this." The soldier let him rant but said nothing. It's not like anything was going to change. This soldier was not going to let her return to the camp. Even Aiko could see that.

Suddenly, there was a commotion in the station. Through the glass, Aiko saw a man rush through the entrance and the rest of the men gather around him. He spoke in a raised voice, his tone urgent. Most of the men left the station, rushing out the door to a waiting bus.

Nishi noticed something was wrong, too. He grabbed the arm of one of the soldiers rushing by. From what Aiko had seen, everyone knew Mr. Nishi was one of the camp leaders and trusted him, even the soldiers. "What's going on? Has there been news?"

He meant news from the front. That was always what the adults were worried about. News that someone had died.

The soldier shook his head. "Been some kind of accident at the camp. Something got out that shouldn't have . . . That's all they're saying."

Mr. Nishi stood beside Aiko on the train station platform, the rails full of a smoky fog. The sun still hadn't come up—Aiko wondered if it ever would. The wind went right through her coat, but she didn't feel it. She felt nothing. Except, perhaps, the itch to run. Now that they were taking her away, she wanted nothing more than to run right back into the camp, to stay. Her freshly sharpened pencil and notebook were safely tucked into her bag, and she felt a strange tingling in her hands thinking of them. She'd been in the middle of a particularly detailed drawing of a *tengu*, a goblin, but she had not sketched in the face yet.

Now she kept thinking of the faceless monster in her notebook, felt the way it waited for her. The *tengu* was known for kidnapping people, especially travelers—wasn't she a traveler?—and she was suddenly afraid that she'd angered it by leaving it unfinished. It ate at her, pricked her palms, gnawed at her stomach.

For how could she face the demons now, without her mother?

She had cried so much, and so hard, all morning, that her body felt weak and drained now. It was as if her mind had come loose from her body, a kite torn from its string.

A woman came out of the depot dressed for travel in a heavy woolen coat and rubber boots, a valise in one hand. She exchanged a few words with Nishi before turning to Aiko. "I'm Mrs. Abernathy and I'll be escorting you to Manzanar. I'm so sorry to hear about your mother. I know it's sad to be leaving Minidoka, but we're going to get you situated at a place where there will be other boys and girls like you. Won't that be nice?"

She smiled, and Aiko noticed how tiny her teeth were. Straight and tiny, like niblets on the end of the corn cob. It gave her a troubling, unnatural air. A warning for Aiko to be on guard around her.

Mr. Nishi waved as the train pulled out of the station, and soon, darkness filled the windows.

For the first few hours of the trip, Aiko lost track of the time. The woman had made Aiko sit in the window seat next to her, but didn't pay any attention to her, reading a movie magazine instead. Aiko pressed her forehead against the glass, thinking only of the cold burn as it bit into her flesh, and watched the barren countryside roll by as the night drew on, eventually showing nothing back but her own reflection. After a while, she finally opened her bag to pull out her notebook and pencil. She could sketch; that would calm her. But then she saw the other thing she kept in her schoolbag, the clutch of thin, old notebooks with secret writing in them, like a code. It was a puzzle that she enjoyed working at. Maybe she would do that instead. Working on this secret language always distracted her.

It was very late when the train stopped. The sign outside the window read SALT LAKE CITY. Mrs. Abernathy turned to Aiko, scrunching low so they were almost face-to-face. Her coat smelled strongly of mothballs. "Do you need to go to the restroom? Now would be a good time. The restroom in the station is bigger and nicer than the one on the train." She made a face to show what she thought of the toilet on the train. "After this stop, it's ten hours to Los Angeles." She pointed to the building on the other side of the window. "We're going to be at this station for fifteen minutes, then the train will pull out. You can come with me, if you want." She stretched out her hand and wiggled it in invitation.

Aiko ignored it.

"Suit yourself. Wait here. I'll be right back." Then she rose and exited the train, making a beeline for the depot, past a couple soldiers standing on the platform, smoking and chatting.

There were people in the train car, but no one was paying attention to her.

She leaned her forehead against the glass again and sighed, wishing she were back at Minidoka, back in time, with her mother. No, further back than that, before the camps. Before the war.

Wishing she were invisible. Wishing she were like snow, and could float away on the air.

Then she saw, off in the darkness outside the window, a flash of light. No, not a flash, a flicker. She'd never seen anything quite like it. It rose and fell like a butterfly, wobbly and erratic, like a baby goat taking its first steps. *Follow me*, it seemed to say.

She slipped down the steps and climbed over the coupling to get to the other side of the track. She'd seen through the window that the train tracks cut through a big field. She remembered when her parents had brought her to a farm outside Seattle (and now that she thought about it, she was pretty sure it had belonged to Mr. Nishi). This field was beautiful in the moonlight, full of broad, thick leaves that were silvery in the darkness. She'd had fun on that farm, getting to pick vegetables to take home, getting to play in the rich, loamy dirt. Being here now felt like returning to her past, like it was true that everything came around again eventually and nothing was ever really over. Her mother used to tell her the same thing when she was scared, when her father had been working at night and it was just her and her mother in the apartment, and there was a bad thunderstorm and she was frightened. *There's no reason to be worried. It seems scary now but the next day is coming, just like the day before and the day before that. You never have to be worried or afraid because the world was made to change, Aiko. Nothing bad lasts forever.*

What her mother hadn't told her was that nothing good would last forever, either.

There it was again—the flash of something taking shape, calling to her. She moved toward it, walking down one of the rough, darkened rows, bending to touch the cabbage leaves. The vegetables had been harvested a long time ago and only the leaves were left behind, whispering to her. A warning, or encouragement? If only she could understand, the way her grandfather did, at least according to her mother.

But the dirt smelled the same—it reminded Aiko of home. Her mother had had a vegetable garden behind the apartment building where she grew burdock root, a Japanese plant that was unknown to most white people. Her mother would cut the fat white roots into matchsticks to fry with carrots. She put the leaves in soup or dried them like herbs and crumbled them over rice. Burdock root reminded her of Japan, she'd said. It had magical properties, her mother had told her with a wink. It could make sick people better. That was why you always grew a little burdock in your garden.

Her mother had loved folktales. She'd said she got it from her father, that he told her folktales all the time when she was little. Aiko had tried to memorize all the stories her mother had told her, but they were already starting to jumble together in her head. Was she already forgetting her mother? That didn't seem possible. She would fight to hold on to her mother for as long as she could.

There it was again, now a rustle in the leaves just ahead. She stood very quiet and still. A dark dash of fur in the night.

A *fox*, she realized, stunned. It was beautiful, its fur puffed up against the cold. Its triangular head was lifted, nose quivering slightly as it sniffed the night air. Its ears flicked this way and that as it listened. One forepaw was raised, the animal ready to bolt. Aiko longed to touch it, the fur thick and luxurious like the pelts sometimes worn by ladies in church. She'd always wanted one even though the tiny, shrunken faces and little crushed paws frightened her.

She knew what the fox meant, knew it could turn into a human, *kitsune*, a helpful spirit. Her chest tingled with hope. The creature had been sent especially for her.

The tilt of moonlight.

The cold, hard whisper of the air.

The way the fox seemed to have lured her out and waited for her here, in this strange place that was somehow familiar. She wanted to believe.

A ripple of certainty moved through her.

"Mother," Aiko whispered. "Mama."

The fox stood frozen, looking over her shoulder at Aiko, then—in a flash—darted down the row. She moved so purposefully, it was as though she was telling Aiko to keep following her. Aiko did, cautiously at first, but then more quickly. Every time she got almost close enough to touch her, the fox would leap one, two, three steps ahead. She followed the fox halfway across the field, until the train had long disappeared in the darkness, save for the faint twinkle of its lights.

Then the fox dove into the leaves. Aiko ducked under them to see if she could find her. But the fox was gone.

Aiko gasped, a sob rising in her throat. *No, Mama. Don't leave me. Not yet. Not yet. I need you.*

When Aiko stood up, she saw it had started snowing. Very, very lightly. Just a few flakes swirled on the air. Suddenly, she was thirsty and she wanted to taste a snowflake, wanted more than anything else to catch a few snowflakes on her tongue. No matter how she tried, though, she couldn't. The snowflakes danced away at the last minute, maybe blown away by her breath.

Finally, she gave up and held out a hand. A snowflake landed on her mitten. One perfect, round, white snowflake.

She brought the mitten up to her face. She was ready to stick out her tongue and lick it away, when there, frozen in the moonlight, she could see that it wasn't a snowflake at all.

It was a tiny, tiny spider.

Its front two legs wove in the night air like it was knitting. Bowing back and forth, back and forth.

She shook her mitten until it came off her hand. She looked, confused, at the specks of white waltzing on the air.

Her mother had told a scary story about spiders, too. The *jorogumo*. She was not kind like the *kitsune*. She was a spirit who appeared to men as a woman, asking them to hold her baby. Only the baby turned out to be a spider—sometimes a whole swarming sac of her eggs—and while the man was distracted, the woman would return to her true spider form, only giant as a great maple tree. And she'd devour the unsuspecting man.

It is a trick, her mother had said, to make sure she understood this important lesson. *The world is rarely what it shows you.*

Aiko had been so frightened that she couldn't go to sleep after hearing the story, and her mother had told her that she didn't have to worry about the *jorogumo* because she only preyed on men. When Aiko had asked why, her mother had only said maybe she'd understand when she was grown.

There was a noise behind her, the sound of metal against metal. A long, mournful wail. For a moment, she thought it must be her mother, calling to her across the field. A sound somewhere between grief and warning. Then she understood, it was not a human cry but the sound of a whistle.

She squinted through the darkness, watching in shock as the train pulled away from the station. Though she could hardly make out its shape against the blackness of the night, she could hear how the big metal engine rocked side to side as it gathered itself, straining against the weight of all those cars behind it. But it gained speed quickly, hurtling faster, further.

No one had come; no one had called for her. The train had left without her. She stood, trying to comprehend it. She could picture Mrs. Abernathy absorbed in her magazine. Maybe nibbling on a chocolate bar. Assuming Aiko was hiding between the seats. No one had noticed she'd been lost—or had they called and she simply hadn't heard? She looked down at her arms, ghostly wrists, mittened hands barely visible in the dark. She had to make sure she hadn't become invisible. She knew some spirits could and wondered if this magic ever applied to living people, too.

At least she had her bag with her. A voice in her head had told her to grab it, right before she'd left the train. Now it seemed like someone had been watching out for her. She had everything that mattered with her, a piece of everything from her old life. Even a reminder of her grandfather Oishi—a set of his journals. She burned a little with shame to remember how she'd gotten them: her mother had given them to her father for safekeeping. *It's better if you keep them. Who knows what will happen where I'm going?* But even Aiko, a child, could tell her mother had been frightened, hadn't trusted assurances given by the authorities.

But Aiko had seen the neat packet of journals, tied up with a navy blue grosgrain ribbon, and stolen them from her father's duffel bag. There was something about them . . . The promise of secret knowledge, like a book of spells . . . She saw it was silly now, but had been helpless against the journals' pull. She'd itched to possess them. She told herself she would use the books to practice her Japanese, which she had just started to learn. But when she opened the books, she was disappointed to see that they were written in a strange language. No matter: it was a new challenge. She loved having a puzzle to toil over, and worked through the journals, figuring out this language, whenever she had a quiet moment.

She understood what had happened. The spirits had called to her, even the wind had whispered, drawing her forth, into the cold, into the past. The spirits had lured her out here. They wanted her to come to the place where her mother had gone.

She couldn't hear the train anymore. Stillness settled over the valley. Even if she ran, Aiko knew she would be too late. The train was gone, its tiny lights shrinking smaller and smaller until it vanished, leaving in its wake only distance. Distance and darkness.

13

Dawn silvered the mountains as Fran parked her car where the dirt road left off, got out, and tugged up her collar against the brisk wind. She'd have to continue the rest of the way on foot. Nancy the waitress had told her where the two loggers lived, the ones who'd found the balloon. She'd even drawn a map to the Hills' cabin on the back of a paper napkin. Fran trudged up a slight incline, following a set of tire tracks in the mud. Owen and Oscar Hill might've been confident driving this bumpy terrain, but she wasn't going to trust the Rambler—it was her only means of getting home.

She was rewarded at the end of the trail with the sight of a small cabin. Fran took a minute to evaluate the scene, get a sense of what she was walking into. The cabin had definitely seen better days. The porch sagged. The windows were dark with soot. A headless deer carcass hung from a nearby tree. A mangy-looking dog ran to the end of its tether and began barking at her. The Hills' early warning system. Nancy had hinted that the father and son were rough around the edges, but this little homestead was near-feral.

The door swung open, an older man emerging with a rifle resting in the crook of his arm. He must've felt that she wasn't a threat because he started walking toward her.

"Whatcha doing on my property?" he called out from a good thirty feet away. He didn't sound too suspicious—people living in such a remote area probably were guarded whenever a stranger showed up outside their door. No reason to worry—even if he had a weapon.

She took a couple steps in his direction. "Good morning, Mr. Hill. My name is Fran Gurstwold and—"

He cut her off. "You're not from around here."

"No, I'm not. I live in Nebraska but, actually, I came looking for you." She took a few more steps. Now that he was closer, Fran could see what the waitress had meant about rough around the edges. This was not a man who received company very often—if at all. She could smell him and she wasn't even downwind. His gray hair was a bird's nest tangle and there were crumbs embedded in his beard. "I heard you found a big balloon recently—well, I found one, too, in Nebraska. I'd like to ask you a few questions."

He shifted the rifle to his other arm, as though it was a fussy baby. "You came all the way to Montana for that? Well, you should've saved yourself the trouble and stayed home. I'm not gonna tell you anything, little lady."

"Is it because of the government man you spoke to?" Bingo; his eyes glinted. "They told me not to talk to anyone about it, either"—a harmless lie—"but I figure it should be okay to talk to someone who already knows about 'em. I don't know about you but I'm plenty curious. I had a friend with me at the time and now he's sick and I can't get anyone to answer my questions."

Fran wasn't sure he had heard her: he appeared to be scanning the trees, as though he wasn't concerned about her at all. She was just about to ask what he was looking at—a bear or a wolf would be worrying, considering her car was a ways back—when he nodded toward the front door. "I was jes' about to sit down to coffee. Why don't you come in and tell me 'bout what happened to your friend."

She was sorry she'd accepted his invitation once she'd stepped inside; the cabin was even dirtier inside than out, if that were possible. It was dark, with too few windows to let in any of the light that made it through the thick tree canopy. Badly stuffed animal heads hung from the wall—a deer with a bulging forehead, a mangy raccoon. The air was thick with smoke from the fireplace, too, and mixed with a mysterious stink hanging in the air to make breathing nearly impossible.

Owen Hill leaned his rifle against the wall and picked up an enameled tin cup. He threw the contents into a slop bucket and poured a long pull of coffee before setting it down in front of Fran. It was pitch-black and smelled evil and there was no way she was going to drink it, not one sip.

He stood at the counter, eyeing her over the rim of his cup. "So, what were you sayin' about your friend gettin' sick?"

Who knew how long Owen Hill would be willing to talk; she was going to get her questions answered first. "Were you the one who found the balloon? Or was it your son?"

"Oscar seen it first."

"Did you notice anything odd about it? Any markings or labels?"

Owen Hill ran a hand over his long beard like he was stroking a pelt. "There was some writing on it, I recollect, but I couldn't make out what it was. Didn't look like English, though."

Obviously, he wasn't able to identify the language from what he'd seen. She wasn't sure how long she'd be able to get away with asking questions. "Did he touch it? Pick it up? Has he been acting strangely lately?"

"Some people might say that boy's always actin' strange." He shifted so that Fran had to turn in the chair to face him, deliberately steering her away from the window at the front of the house. *Someone is approaching the cabin and he doesn't want me to see.* The hairs rose at the back of her neck.

She thought of Richard and the way he'd changed after they'd seen the balloon. "Your son—does he lose his temper easily? Is he quick to argue?"

Owen Hill started scratching at his neck, a feral scratch at an itch that couldn't be sated. Scratching until he drew blood. That reminded Fran of Richard's neck, how he'd scratched it bloody. "We ain't sick, if that's what you're gettin' at."

"No, no, of course not . . . How about the government men who came to talk to you? Did they identify themselves? Were they with the military?"

"Lemme think . . . There were a couple uniformed men. One guy who said he was with the army, drove out from California. They's the ones who said we shouldn't talk to nobody but the sheriff."

The army had a number of installations in California. "I don't suppose he left a card with you . . . or told you where he was stationed?"

"It was a funny name . . . Alameda, maybe? My cousin Jed's son Tully is stationed there . . . That's why it stuck in my mind."

"And there were feds? Anybody from Washington?"

"That wasn't until a couple days later. An FBI man showed up." Owen narrowed his eyes at her in a way that made Fran's skin crawl. "Why you asking me all these questions? You said they'd talked to you, too. You should already know this."

Her gaze skittered around the hovel, looking for the nearest way out. Owen Hill was closer to the front door than she was, and it didn't appear that there was a back way out. The few windows were small and narrow and would take time to shimmy through if it came to it. Luckily, the shack was full of things that could be used as a weapon: an iron poker, a sledgehammer leaning by the wood-stove, tools strewn all over the house like they used it as a work shed, too.

A long if rusty kitchen knife on the table just out of easy reach.

She was startled by a sudden noise at the front of the house. Through the window, she saw a figure emerge from the woods, a large, hunched figure with an axe resting on his shoulder. It had to be the son. Nancy had said the two men lived alone. She'd also said of the two, Oscar was worse.

"There's my boy now," Owen said, a hint of both pride and malice in his voice. "You can judge for yerself if he's acting strange."

The front door flew back with a bang as Oscar Hill stepped over the threshold. He had a good eight inches and a hundred pounds on his scrawnier father. He hefted the axe off his shoulder and dropped it by the door, making the floor tremble underfoot.

He looked her up and down. Fran had seen that look in his eyes in felons and wild animals. Hungry. Unafraid.

"Who are you?" His voice was so loud it rattled the windows. *Cowards shout*, Fran reminded herself. "I don't believe I've ever seen you before."

The father crossed his arms over his chest, content to let his son take over, like a cat batting around a mouse. "She's come to ask a few questions about the balloon."

The son continued to study Fran. "You're out of luck. The authorities told us we couldn't say nothing to nobody."

"I told her that already, son. But she's a nosy one. She says she found one of them balloons herself and that it made her friend sick."

Oscar Hill took a step closer. He emanated malice, the promise of violence rising from him like heat. He was still checking her out like a wild animal deciding if she was something he could eat. "You know what the army man said: we might get spies coming around, trying to find out what we know."

"Do I look like a spy?"

Oscar started to circle her. "How would we know if you was a spy or not? For all we know, you could be one of them sympathizers tryin' to help the Japs. You know, you *look* like a foreigner . . . Your skin is kinda dark."

That's because everyone here is of Nordic descent. You're all white as sheets. "It's because of my heritage . . . I'm half Jewish. Not many Jews out here, I'm guessing," Fran said, rising uneasily from the chair.

"You know what the pastor says," Oscar said to his father. "You can't trust the Jews."

"We're fighting to free the Jews from concentration camps. Jews aren't the bad guys—Hitler's the bad guy," she said. Like anyone needed to be reminded.

"Not in my book."

They were about three feet away from her, one on each side. She was confident that she could fight off one of them, but not both. The table stood between Fran and freedom.

"She's acting awful suspicious. You know what I think we should do"—Oscar was talking to his father now, Fran reduced to a dumb, mute animal—"we should hold her for the sheriff. Let the sheriff question her."

That wasn't so bad. "Okay," she said, allowing herself a moment of relief. "Let's go down to the sheriff's office together and then you'll see you're wrong."

"We ain't going to town," Owen said to her, starting to scratch behind his neck again. The rasping sound was painful to hear. "We'll hold you here and wait for the sheriff. He comes out here on the bye and bye . . ."

I'm sure he does. Called in by neighbors for drunk and disorderly conduct, thievery, any of a dozen possibilities. Assault. Attempted rape. She wondered if either of the Hills had priors, a rap sheet.

The son squinted at her, a kid with a kitten he was preparing to torture. "I think she's one of them softheaded Jap lovers. Those Japs—they're in the camps because they sold us out to the enemy.

But you city folk don't want to believe it. I seen it in the papers. You feel *sorry* for them. You believe their lies and nonsense, and you want us poor, ignorant dirt farmers to believe it, too. You city people—you *Jews*—you think you're so smart. You think you know better than us." He was talking about the protests in New York and Chicago when the executive order was enacted . . . for all the good it did. "You think we don't know anything, but we know what's *really* going on in this country. There's stuff going on right under your nose you know nothing about. But you'll see. One day."

He was looking at her now, not seeing her as a person but as something he could torment, something that *deserved* to be tormented. Fran took a step backward. Her mind went into instant, rapid calculations. If Oscar got his hands on her, it would be over.

"You're not a real American. You're disloyal, but I bet I could straighten you out real quick." Oscar Hill's face was florid, his eyes crazy. Did he have whatever Richard had or was he merely feral, living in the woods with only his half-insane father for company? She did not plan to find out. She was pretty sure Oscar Hill intended to keep her a prisoner in this cabin for a few days, and what he had in mind would involve the disgusting bed half-hidden under the eaves, rumpled blankets and sweat-stained pillows.

She thought fleetingly of what Richard would say if he could see her now. *You should've listened to me.* But when they'd met, he also said he liked her moxie. *You're not afraid to take matters into your own hands.* That was why he'd given her the job.

When Oscar made his move, she'd only have a split second. No time for second-guessing. *Focus on what you have to do.*

She'd always had great reflexes. *You're twitchy as a cat*, her aunt used to say.

Oscar lurched forward, reaching to grab her arm.

She lunged for the knife and brought it down in one smooth, strong motion. Hard, like her life depended on it.

Oscar's cry rocked the one-room cabin. She'd driven the knife tip through his hand, pinning it to the table.

The father was frozen in surprise, but that would only last a second.

She pushed by Oscar Hill and made for the trail and her car, not looking back.

Fran drove straight to the Batavia Motor Lodge to throw her things into her suitcase. Her heart hammered in her chest. *I stabbed a man.* She could still feel the knife sinking into Oscar Hill's hand, pushing through bone and tendon and sinew. Her stomach flipped at the memory.

She had to get out of town now. The police were sure to show up at any minute, or this mysterious army man Oscar Hill mentioned.

What is wrong with me? I stabbed a man. Maybe Richard was right. Maybe she was too hardheaded. Too independent. That's what came of being an orphan, always needing to look out for yourself because there was no one else looking out for you.

Now that Fran had time to think about it, during the long drive down from the mountain, she was pretty sure she could defend herself against what had happened. Oscar Hill had threatened to hold her in their cabin against her will. That was kidnapping. It would be her word against theirs.

But in a small town like this, there was no telling what the sheriff would do, how he might see things. They were locals; she was from out of town. And she'd stabbed a man. Hurt him good. There was no denying that.

Better safe than sorry.

When she went to settle up at the front counter, the clerk handed her a slip of paper. "Somebody tried to reach you while you were away."

Call Marjorie Elling, it read. Fran's comrade-in-arms at the *Star*. She'd asked Marjorie to keep an eye on the wires in case another story came in about the strange objects falling from the sky. *Look for parachutes or balloons. Sure*, Marjorie had said in her typical wise-cracking way. *Who doesn't like balloons?*

"This isn't about your balloon obsession," Marjorie said when Fran was able to ring through to the newsroom, "but you'd asked me to keep an eye on Ogallala and a strange story came in over-night. Thought you might want to know about it. Turns out some local boy killed his sister before trying to kill his parents."

Fran's palms itched, the way they always did when she heard a good lead. "Did you see an address for the family?"

"The article says they live on Riverdale Drive." The same road as the cabin where she and Richard had stayed.

Fran jerked back from the counter, felt herself plunging back-ward into icy water. Like that time in the fourth grade when she'd fallen into a half-frozen creek.

"Yeah, it sounds like quite the story," Marjorie said, rustle of newsprint audible over the phone line. "Neighbors reported the thirteen-year-old had seemed to change overnight. Went from your typical teenage boy to violent rage."

Her hands shook as she hung up the phone. No one would be able to deny that something was going on, not even Richard.

Lake Ogallala.

This was no coincidence.

The AAA guide put Ogallala fifteen hours away from Kalispell, but that was in a good car with good tires. Fran figured the trip would take her twenty, making stops for gasoline and coffee. She'd drive straight through, not stopping to sleep along the way.

She thought through each piece of information she'd gathered so far. The thing that Andy, the hotel clerk, had brought up stood out in her mind: why was the army involved? That implied that whatever this was, balloon or parachute, it was no harmless civilian toy. The implication was that it had something to do with war, that they were thinking it was an offensive capability. Maybe even had to do with the enemy: Japan. But everyone—from the War Department to the White House—had said that the Japanese would never be able to attack the mainland. No plane could fly that far without refueling in the Pacific. No missile or unmanned warship could reach the West Coast. It was technologically impossible.

Which left spies. Someone operating on Japan's behalf.

She was a little north of Casper when she realized that she was starting to feel a little funny. Sad and anxious all at once. Driving this route again, she felt like she was going home. But there was no home, not really: the life she'd had in Lincoln had been turned upside down. She had no job. She had no man. Even her cat had left her. All she had was a cold, empty apartment and a few hundred dollars in the bank. Right now, she was chasing this mystery, but only because it was a distraction. At some point, she needed to think about what she was going to do with her life.

The sun had gone down hours ago. The highway cut through big empty patches of land with nothing but moonlight to drive by. She found her mind drifting. What would she do if something happened to the car, if she had a blowout or ran out of gas? She tried to remember when she'd last seen a farmhouse, let alone a service station.

Two white pinpricks appeared in the rearview mirror. It was the first car she'd seen in miles and miles. She couldn't check her wristwatch—there was too little light—but she guessed it was two or three a.m. Who'd be out driving at this hour? A deliveryman? Nonetheless, it made her feel a little better to have one more soul on the road with her.

That was, until she noticed it was coming up awfully fast. A crazy hot-rodder. Sure, on these empty roads at this hour, he probably thought he had the highway all to himself. Maybe he couldn't see the Rambler's taillights, not at this distance. The thought of being rear-ended sent a chill up her spine. She repositioned her hands on the steering wheel, her palms growing clammy.

The car roared up on her left side, swinging into the lane for oncoming traffic. Fran swerved to the right instinctively and ended up dipping a tire off the asphalt. The car almost careened off the road and she barely managed to keep it under control. She took her foot off the gas and the Rambler, tank that it was, slowed immediately.

What was the other driver trying to do? Had he tried to run her off the road?

He's past me now. Whatever he was trying to do, he's gone.

To her horror, she saw the speedster, now far ahead, apply his brakes. Taillights like two fiery red eyes in the distance. He seemed to be turning around.

He was heading back toward her.

Her pulse sped. She'd heard of guys who thought it was hilarious to terrorize women driving by themselves.

Then again . . . maybe it was the police finally catching up to her. She had committed a crime back in Kalispell: she'd stabbed Oscar Hill. That was assault. Maybe the Hills had reported her, after all. The authorities could be looking for her and she had no idea.

She should've turned herself in, explained to the police that she'd felt threatened. Anyone who knew Oscar Hill would've understood. But since she'd left town, she looked guilty. Why, the police would have no alternative but to go after her. She had made herself a fugitive.

Or worse, maybe the Hills themselves were after her.

Or . . . someone else. Someone who knew she was trying to track down what was behind those balloons.

The car headed right toward her, blinding her with its head-lights before swerving away at the last minute. The driver was play-ing chicken with her, but Fran had the feeling it was a lot more serious than that. He wanted her to crash.

Who was behind the wheel and what did he want? If the Hills had gone to the sheriff, you had to figure the sheriff would've told the army or the FBI. They could've been watching her at the motel. Whoever was in that car was trying to get her to pull over, but Fran felt in her bones that that was the last thing she should do.

She caught a glimpse of the car as it streaked past. Definitely not a police car. And the tags . . . well, they could've been from California. Alameda ran through her mind.

An FBI agent out of Butte, Montana, wouldn't have tags from the Golden State. Would he?

She stomped on the gas pedal as hard as she could, sending the Rambler lurching forward. It would take this asshole a few minutes to stop and turn around before he came at her again. Fran had ab-solutely no doubt that the car could catch her pretty quickly. She needed to figure out what to do before it ran her off the road because—just like with Oscar Hill—she was pretty sure she didn't want to be alone with whoever was in the car. But what could she do? She couldn't even remember the last time she'd passed a turnoff, let alone someplace safe.

Then she saw it up ahead: a lone light piercing the darkness. It was coming from a farmhouse. There was a truck in the driveway. Somebody was home, probably a farmer up early to milk the cows or whatever they did that got them up at three a.m. Fran hated to think that she might be putting this innocent farmer and his family in danger, but . . . she had no alternative. The presence of other people might be enough to scare this guy away.

Fran pulled into the driveway and raced toward the house, cut-ting her headlights at the same time. With any luck, the crazy guy wouldn't know where she'd gone. She pulled as close to the farm-house as she dared and killed the engine, then crouched low behind the steering wheel.

The other car slowed at the mouth of the driveway. Fran watched the headlights move at a crawl. Whoever sat behind the wheel was looking for her, scanning the unilluminated scrub for a sign of movement. Did he see her car, or had she disappeared completely in the darkness? She held her breath and silently willed him to keep driving, her heart hammering in her chest the entire time.

Eventually, the car pulled away. She watched its taillights disappear and fade in the darkness. Then she waited another fifteen minutes for her teeth to stop chattering before she turned the key in the ignition and continued on her way.

She figured she'd lost time now, on the drive, and there were still nine more hours to go.

She just had to pray that whoever'd been tailing her—whether the FBI or a random lonely psychopath or a deadly Japanese spy—didn't know where she was headed.

There is something on the island with us. We are not alone.

I saw something strange tonight as I went on a walk, alone, my usual evening constitutional. I had the feeling that I was being followed. At first, I was sure it was nonsense and kept walking, ignoring the gnawing in my gut.

By the time I reached the fields near the old man's house, I knew I was not imagining it. <u>Someone</u> or something was following me. I heard the sound of something large moving through the trees. There were no dangerous animals on the island, one of the hunters had told me. Nothing to be concerned about.

There was no doubt, however: I was being followed. Whatever was out there, man or beast, I did not want to lead it back to my family. I walked for hours that night, being extra careful to take note of my path for fear of being lost in the unfamiliar forest. Every time I wanted to rest or give up entirely and head back to my cottage, I would think of my daughter, Meiko. I could not bring danger to her doorstep.

At one point, I caught a glimpse of blood red through the trees. Are there any animals of such a vivid hue? Of course not. A bloodred animal would not be able to hide itself. To blend in.

A bloodred animal would be the most accomplished predator in the forest. Afraid of nothing.

The same would be true of a man. Dressed in red, not afraid of being spotted. Toying with his prey.

That one glimpse kept me walking throughout the entire night. At dawn, when I could see better, I felt secure that I was no longer being followed. I headed back to the cottage, steeling myself for the lecture I was sure to get from Yuriko.

However, I was not too distracted to notice, as I retraced my path, that there were no other prints on the ground. No man's, no animal's.

14

Archie knew he should not go to the meeting in Dutch Talbert's garage. But, after service was over on Sunday and his days stretched empty . . . and Wednesday rolled around, and then the hours inched closer to evening, he knew it was inevitable that he would drive out there. He could not sit alone in the house as eight thirty approached, listening to the ticking of the clock, and so he picked up his keys and headed out to the Nash.

Once he got to Dutch's garage, however, he almost turned around. There were no cars in the parking lot except the ones he always saw, the cars waiting to be serviced or with a FOR SALE sign in the window. He was just about to pull away when he realized there were cars parked out back—probably to avoid being seen from the highway.

He found a group of men inside the old garage, clustered under a couple overhead lights. There were about a dozen, leaning on cars or sitting on the workbenches. More than he'd expected. They eyed Archie warily as he wended through half-disassembled cars toward them.

"Relax," Dutch said to the others. "It's the minister, the one whose wife was killed by the Japs." Archie flinched inside, to think he would be described this way for the rest of his life.

He stayed toward the back and leaned against the wall, listening, with his arms crossed over his chest. He'd decided driving over that he wouldn't speak tonight. It was too upsetting; he hadn't been able to sleep since the visit to the Moose Lodge, visions of Elsie and spiders playing out endlessly before his eyes. *I'm just here to listen to what these guys have to say.* To find out if they knew anything about Japanese spies and if it was tied to the explosion. If anyone else had seen a woman in a kimono in the woods of Gearhart Mountain. If he would know, once and for all, whom to blame for Elsie's death.

The talk at the moment was of some mysterious illness that had survived in town. "Sounds like the Jap flu they've been talking about in the papers," one of the men grumbled. "My Sarah's got it and it's like she's been possessed by the devil. Itching all the time, and mad as hell."

"Do you really think the Japs sent it?" another asked dubiously. "How would they do that?"

"All it takes is to send one or two of 'em over here infected already with the sickness, and then it spreads like any other flu," the first man said, regarding the second as though he was dumber than dirt. *Don't you know how disease spreads?*

A man stood under one of the naked overhead bulbs, making him look like an actor onstage. He was unknown to Archie. Most of the men here were older than Archie, a reminder—as though they needed it—that all the young men were off fighting the war. They were the ones who had been left behind and were always looking for ways to prove themselves. To show that they weren't irrelevant, letting younger men defend the country, protect their wives and homes.

He held an envelope aloft, pinched between thumb and index finger. "We got the next letter ready to go. We sent a letter to the

Yonna Times and Dispatch first of the month telling 'em to stop running those editorials or be prepared to suffer the consequences, signed Loyal Sons of the Republic. But Dell ignored us and ran another one of those bleeding-heart stories, so . . ." The man shrugged. "This'll be his last warning."

Archie had heard rumors that folks all across the county were finding threatening letters left on their doorsteps and stuffed in mailboxes. *You let Japs in your store. Your daughter spoke out in school against the camps. My son died at Pearl Harbor and you're disrespecting his memory. We see you, we know who you are, we know where you live.* It reminded Archie of a story he'd heard in seminary, of letters nailed to the doors of free Blacks in the years following the Civil War. *Toe the line or face vigilante justice.* As Archie listened, he felt chills and aches wash over his body like he had the flu, and he scrubbed fleetingly at the back of his sweaty neck. Anonymous letters delivered under the cover of darkness was the work of cowards, that's what he'd been told in seminary. *The virtuous man does not hide in the shadows.* Weren't these men, fighting a hidden enemy, an enemy who dropped from the sky to kill women and children, also virtuous?

Dutch stood up, signifying that the meeting was over. Was it Archie's imagination, or maybe it was the light, but did he seem different than the last time Archie had seen him? His face was flushed a bright red, like a lobster dropped in a pot of boiling water. "Okay, let's get out there and deliver those letters." The mechanic caught Archie's eye; maybe he'd seen Archie's panic and uncertainty. "Don't worry, Reverend. We're not going to hurt anybody. We're just going to let them know that they're not getting away with anything. Their neighbors are watching."

Should I speak out? Archie thought he was there to testify, to tell others what he had seen and experienced. That was his value. He hadn't pictured doing anything else, not even going along for a car ride.

There could be value in going, though. He could be a witness for them, defend them if they got accused of doing something they hadn't. Go to the police if things got out of hand. Hold them to their word.

He knew he shouldn't go. These days he felt like two people fighting inside his body. One person was the peaceable farm boy who had gone to seminary and loved and respected all people. The other was angry and sad and wanted to see justice served. Who wanted to see Elsie avenged.

Leaving the garage, Archie's hand brushed a neat pile of paper, knocking a few to the ground. Archie stooped to retrieve them— Dutch hustled up behind him, saying, "You don't need to bother with that, padre . . ."—and saw that they were flyers.

Elsie's picture was front and center. He recognized it: it was the one that had run in the church newsletter when they arrived. She looked saintly in that picture. It was his favorite.

Underneath it read in huge letters, *Good Christian men!!! To arms!!! Protect our wives and mothers from the Yellow Menace. This Christian Woman was killed by the godless Japs right in our own backyard. We will not be safe until our land is rid of this dire threat.*

At the bottom, *Loyal Sons of the Republic.*

Archie's heart started to hammer in his chest. The hand holding the flyer was trembling so bad it rattled. "What's this, Dutch?"

The mechanic ducked his head. "I was meaning to talk to you about this . . . Your Elsie is a martyr, padre, and we think people ought to know about it. Make her death *mean* something, you know? They need to hear her story—the *whole* story."

What was her story? Archie looked down at the flyer. What had happened to her at the end was terrible, but that was not the whole story.

Still . . . she was dead, which meant her past was dead, too. She was beyond hurt, beyond pain.

"Don't you think she would want this? To protect her neighbors, to make them aware that there's a danger right in their midst?"

The bomb, he must mean. Bombs falling from the sky.

"People will listen—she was the padre's wife, a godly woman who never did anyone any harm. She's the perfect messenger. A messenger of God." Dutch smiled in appeal, but he was studying Archie, too. "It's what Elsie would want."

How would Dutch know what Else would want? Had his wife ever met Dutch? Archie didn't think so. He rubbed the back of his neck. "I don't know—"

"Don't make your mind up at this minute. You think about it and let me know what you want to do. We won't hand these out until we hear from you."

Outside, the men had split into twos and threes. Dutch steered Archie behind a pair to an old, beat-up sedan and ushered him into the back seat, a hand on the small of Archie's back. One of the men kept up an excited patter as they rattled down the blacktop, even though the other kept telling him to shut up, that it made him nervous. *I got a headache. My head's been killing me all day. For God's sake, stop talking.* Archie had to fight the urge to demand they stop the car and let him out. *This is wrong*, every cell in his body screamed.

They're only letters. No one is going to get hurt.

It took about a half hour to get to Yonna. The roads were empty and dark. Archie drifted into a stupor in the back seat, watching the land unspool out the window, barely illuminated. He'd almost dozed off when he saw it: a woman standing on the side of the road. A blaze of fire-truck red. They passed by her so quickly that Archie couldn't be sure what he'd seen, and his mind put two and two together: the woman in the kimono.

She was here. She knew what they were up to. She was following him.

He spun around and pressed his hands to the rear window, but he saw nothing. No woman. Of course, it was dark out and they were traveling fast.

He turned around. Should he say something to these two men, tell him they'd just passed a Japanese spy? Archie opened his mouth to speak but then caught himself. Surely, if there had been a woman in a kimono on the side of the road, these two would've seen her. Would've *said* something. There was no way they would've missed her, not dressed in flaming red.

She was a hallucination. A figment of his guilty conscience. There was no other explanation for it.

Far from being shaken by it, he was relieved.

They pulled up near a small building on the outskirts of what passed for a town, a half dozen places—Anders Family Hardware, The Pretty Place Beauty Salon, Lords & Ladies Shoes—strung along the highway like beads. One or two of the buildings had left a light burning in front; otherwise, all was dark and quiet.

A weather-beaten sign on the building in front of them read YONNA TIMES AND DISPATCH. The street was dead still, not so much as a piece of trash tumbling down the street.

The man in the passenger seat held the letter in his two hands, staring at it. In the dim light of one interior bulb, his face almost glowed a bright red, like Dutch's. "I keep thinking, what's the point of another letter? We sent one already and he ignored it. I think it's time we showed him we're serious."

Archie could tell by the man's delivery and the calmness of his eye that this was no spur-of-the-moment decision. This had been meant to happen and pretending otherwise was solely for Archie's benefit.

The driver said, "Wouldn't bother me." They reached into their pockets and pulled out bandanas, which they then tied around the lower half of their faces like train robbers in an old-timey movie. *This is wrong. Say something.* But he could do nothing but watch, gaping and paralyzed, as a wave of fire and ice washed over him. Then they got out, leaving Archie in the back seat, and went to the trunk. Archie turned to see what they were doing but the trunk lid blocked most of his view. He could hear things being moved in the trunk and the clink of bottles, and a curt exchange of voices.

Then, around the edges of the trunk lid, there was the sudden flare of light. Of fire.

One of the men skidded into sight, his arm circling overhead like a baseball pitcher, trailing a tail of light arching through the sky like a comet. A crash of glass: one of the windows at the front of the building smashed, jagged edges of glass like teeth.

A second hurling pitch of fire, another window smashed. A frivolous thought—*God, this man has a good arm*—flitted through his head. Flames started to dance inside the building, peeking over the sill like mischievous children.

Archie jumped when the trunk slammed shut behind him. Then the car doors opened—a burst of greasy smoke fed by ink and newsprint—and the two men scrambled inside. They were laughing, flushed with excitement. The driver stomped the gas and they peeled away, sending up a great dusty plume behind them.

"What have you done?" The words tumbled out even though Archie knew it had been planned from the start. Now he was part of it. These men would swear to it. His presence, the grieving widower, would lend legitimacy. "You *knew* you were going to firebomb the newspaper. Why didn't you tell me?"

"Dutch didn't want to take the chance that you'd chicken out. He needed you. Now you're one of us."

The driver turned briefly, pulling down his bandana. "We're helping get the word out, Reverend. You want to stop the Jap sympathizers who killed your wife, don't you? Stop them from killing more Americans. You're okay with that, aren't you?"

Archie fought to stop the spinning in his head. It wasn't panic, he realized: it was excitement. It felt *good* to do something to defend Elsie. To strike back. He'd been taught that violence was never the answer, but now he was seeing that sometimes it might be.

There was something else, too. An unexpected feeling of belonging. In that moment, he felt more a part of the community than he ever had as their minister. Hatred was a powerful common interest.

"Yeah," he admitted. "I guess I am."

That was when he saw it.

The man in the passenger seat turned briefly to Archie, flashing a maniacal grin. The image rippled in front of Archie's eyes, like he was alive with movement—or crawling with tiny spiders. Spiders running in waves across his jacket, making it look as though it was rippling. Hundreds of spiders, flowing seamlessly from one man to the other, and neither of them noticed—because if they did, they'd be screaming, trying to beat them away with their hands.

Archie fought the urge to throw himself out of the car immediately. It had to be a hallucination. *Am I losing my mind? I am going insane.*

Spiders spilled over the seat in front of him. Wave after wave of tiny, near-invisible spiders swarmed toward him. *They're not real*, he tried to assure himself, but he couldn't overcome his revulsion. His fear.

"Stop the car! Let me out!" He pressed as far back into the seat as he could. *Keep them away.*

"You don't want to do that, Reverend. It's a long walk home—"

"I don't care! Let me out." *You're infected, just like Joan Patzke.* He reached for the chrome door handle. He'd jump if he had to.

"For Chrissake, Reverend, take it easy!" The car fishtailed as the driver hit the brakes, slowed enough for Archie to jump out and land on his feet, then skidded away, kicking up dirt and stone. He watched it disappear quickly into the night.

He was shaking from head to toe and breathing hard like he'd just run a race. He slapped at his clothing to rid himself of any spiders that might've landed on him, then rubbed his head vigorously. *They're infected.* The men in the garage, the camp guard at the Moose Lodge. They couldn't see the spiders, but Archie could—even if it was all in his head, if he only saw them because he wanted to.

Where the hell had they come from?

By the time Archie arrived home, he wanted nothing more than to forget the entire night. He'd retrieved his car from Dutch's garage (making sure it was deserted first) and driven home down empty roads. More than once, he almost drove to the sheriff's station to tell him about the firebombing but then he'd have to confess he'd been there, too, and he'd surely lose his position at the church.

Tonight, the Loyal Sons were probably gathered at someone's house, drinking beers and crowing about what they'd done. Others would be patting them on the back, admiring their resolve. They might not walk down Main Avenue bragging about firebombing the newspaper, but they weren't ashamed. Archie wasn't sure that he was ashamed of his part in it. Confused, but not ashamed. Maybe they weren't wrong.

Maybe they weren't in the minority in Bly. Maybe the Loyal Sons had more supporters than he thought.

He ended up talking himself out of it.

Maybe he was still on a wild ride of nightmares and hallucinations since Elsie's death. Maybe he was sick. Maybe he had been injured in the explosion—he couldn't rule that out.

He slammed the car keys on the kitchen counter and staggered to the parlor. It was dark and cheerless, the same as it had been every night since the explosion.

He felt Elsie's gaze bore into his back from the wedding portrait on the shelf.

His wife, a martyr for the cause. Yes, she would like that.

The truth was, she had been no angel.

But neither was he.

Behind the portrait, a second photograph was silently judging him, silently confirming that he deserved every bad thing that happened to him.

15

Meiko was trapped, but not dead—though for stretches at a time, she could almost believe she was and living in purgatory. She reached down to finger the metal rail of her cot where she'd scratched marks into the paint on the frame to count the days she'd been imprisoned.

She'd awoken days ago to find herself not in the infirmary at Camp Minidoka surrounded by groaning patients and harried nurses but locked up by herself in a log cabin in the middle of nowhere. The men who came in and out of the building assured her that she was there for treatment. "You caught that bug that's sweeping through the camp," the orderly named Dave told her. "You're contagious, so we needed to isolate you, that's all," he'd said with a laugh when she demanded to know why they were holding her.

Obviously, this was a lie. It made no sense: if this was a medical facility, there would be more patients. It seemed like half the camp had gotten sick and yet she was the only one there. "Everyone else died," David had told her the first time she asked. "You're the only one who survived. You're our lone hope. We want you to get better." And then he'd given her a not-very-convincing smile.

Could all those people from the camp really be dead? It seemed since the day she had been sent to Minidoka, no one in authority ever told her the truth. She recalled the faces of her neighbors at the barracks, all people she hadn't known before her arrival. They may have been strangers but had generously given her the gift of genuine friendship at a time when she needed it. None of them had deserved to be torn from their lives and their homes and sent to the camps. They had been stripped of their possessions, kept at Minidoka against their will, starved and frozen, and now—if the orderlies were telling the truth—they were gone.

If this really was a medical facility, it was the strangest one she'd ever seen. It was an old hunting cabin, just a couple tiny rooms, but repurposed into a jail for one person. She was given run of the building but, unlike the camp dormitories, here there were bars over the windows and the heavy front door was always locked. Looking through the windows, she could tell she wasn't at Minidoka anymore. The camp had disappeared. She was somewhere on the prairie, surrounded by nothing but scrub brush and unbroken horizon. There were a couple other cabins, but they were widely spaced out and, best she could tell, unoccupied. A trio of caretakers drove out every morning in a big dusty sedan to bring her food, collect blood and urine and swabs of saliva, and check her eyes and ears. Otherwise, they left her alone, like a dog boarded with the neighborhood veterinarian.

"I am better now. Let me go back to camp. My daughter needs me," she'd beg them.

"But you're not better. You don't want to risk making your daughter sick, do you? Just a little longer," was their standard response. If she kept asking, they'd chide her. "Don't be selfish. Think of the others. You don't want to cause another outbreak, do you?" Eventually, she gave up.

The more exhausting part was the unceasing mental struggle. She just could not make sense of what was happening. The last few years were like a nightmare that never ended. If you had asked her during her first years in America if she ever thought they'd imprison their own citizens, seize their property, and make the innocent disappear, she'd have thought you were crazy. That kind of thing happened in vicious dictatorships. Even a benign monarch like the emperor could go astray. But the whole world looked to America for fairness. Even the most ignorant peasant in Mongolia or on the Russian steppe knew the average man could find a good life there. Now she had been separated from her daughter and locked in a prison, with no contact with the outside world, and Americans themselves acted like it was normal.

On the second day, she scoured the rooms over and over, looking for keys or tools she could use to break out. She swept through cupboards and closets, but aside from tins of beans and soup and a box of saltines, there was nothing. There was a desk tucked in the corner of one of the rooms that the minders used, where they jotted notes and packed vials of her blood in a satchel to take back with them. The desk had a couple drawers, but they were always locked. Or maybe they were never unlocked. It bore watching.

On the third day, she had a visitor after the attendants left—a visitor who she knew existed only in her mind. She recognized the old woman crouched in the corner as a *yokai*; in a tattered kimono and with unkempt white hair falling loose around her face, she couldn't be anything else. It was in keeping with what the others who had gotten sick had complained of. Meiko was amazed to find it was true—not that they were real spirits; she was pretty sure that was all in her head—but that this could be part of the disease. It seemed the disease knew to torment that special part of the brain where old anxieties and sad memories were kept. Though she wasn't sure why they were all hallucinating the *jorogumo*.

The spirit kept asking innocently where Meiko's daughter was—strangely enough, in a singsong tone that reminded Meiko of her mother, Yuriko—saying that her daughter seemed to have run away. "Maybe she left you because you are a bad mother," the old woman chided. "Maybe she knows you would choose your gaijin husband over your own daughter, if you had the chance. We know, don't we, Meiko, that the husband is more important than the child."

Meiko thought she recognized the pattern on the faded kimono, the same as one that her mother used to wear. *I didn't run away*, Meiko wanted to tell the spirit. *You sent me to America, you and Father.* Her mother had wanted Meiko to marry well, though the important part had always, Meiko suspected, been more about how Meiko's marriage reflected on *her*. Her rightful place, according to her mother, would otherwise have been to stay in Japan and take care of her parents in their dotage. That job now fell to her brothers' wives.

Still, Meiko knew to remain silent, not to give the spirit the satisfaction of an answer. That was what the *yokai* wanted: to feast on her sadness.

Then, on the fourth day, she saw her chance. Instead of three caretakers, there was only one, Randolph. She was pretty sure he was the most inexperienced one. He was probably no older than twenty but looked even younger with his buckteeth and jug ears.

She was pretty sure he had the illness. He had the same symptoms: beads of sweat on his face, tremors in the hands. Slight impatience. He was probably in the earliest stage.

If it had been one of the other men, Meiko might have been afraid to approach. The illness brought out the worst in people. But Randolph was so gentle and kind, even his worst wouldn't be too bad. Or so she hoped.

Without the other men to worry about, Randolph might be more apt to talk to her.

By now, she knew the routine. She sat in the chair without

being asked. Randolph nervously unpacked the equipment, his trembling hands fumbling with the vials and needles.

He rubbed his palms against his pants. "Well . . . I guess we should get started."

He tied the rubber tubing too tight around her upper arm and jabbed the needle clumsily into the vein, but Meiko didn't cry out. She even managed to force a smile.

"I didn't hurt you, did I?" Randolph asked as the first vial filled.

"No, not at all," she said as sweetly as she could manage. "Are you okay? You seem . . . unwell."

He turned bright red. He knew he had the plague sweeping through the camp. He was probably frightened for himself. "I'm fine. But thank you for asking." Maybe she was the only one who had noticed. The only one who *saw* him.

Five more vials to go, each as big as two of her fingers together. "Usually, there are three of you . . . Did something happen at the camp, to detain the others?"

A look of concern flitted across his gray eyes, Meiko noticed. Something *had* happened, but he was under orders not to talk. She put on a big smile. "Oh, come now, you can tell me. I'm so bored. You won't even give me a newspaper to pass the time. Besides, it's not like I'm going to *tell* anyone."

He felt sorry for her, Meiko could tell. He was a good kid. He might not even agree with his actions; he was just doing it for the money. Jobs were scarce in the middle of nowhere if you didn't want to work on a farm.

He busied himself with changing the vials. Meiko thought she'd lost her opportunity, that he wasn't going to say anything, when he finally spoke. "There was a surprise visit at the camp today. Some high-level muckety-muck—a senator, I think. Getting worried about conditions at the camp, we heard. The director wanted all hands on deck to make sure nothing went wrong, so they kept Dave and Larry."

A senator. Maybe he had heard about the outbreak at Minidoka and wanted to see what was going on for himself. Should she dare hope that they weren't entirely forgotten, that help might still be coming?

Meiko looked up at the boy, who loomed over her. He was alone; could she overpower him and get away? She'd never driven a car . . . but it couldn't be that hard, could it? Still, there were other obstacles . . . She had no money or identification. She didn't know where she was, which direction to go. She might run out of gasoline in the middle of the prairie. And her face would likely get her into trouble.

Then there was the difference in their sizes. He was slender but nearly a foot taller. Besides, he was a young man in the prime of his life, whereas she was as weak as a kitten because they'd been taking a pint of blood out of her every day. Even if she somehow managed to knock him out, she'd probably pass out from the effort. She'd be recaptured, and they'd know to be extra careful around her. There'd be no chance of escape.

She made an expression she'd seen on her mother's face many times, carefully designed to make her seem helpless and yet inno-cent and appealing. "I need your help, Randolph-san. My daughter is in the camp. I am going out of my mind with worry. I need to know if she's safe. I need to know that she hasn't gotten sick like the others."

He looked surprised, but it quickly faded. And then he looked guilty—for separating a mother and her child. For what he was doing.

He wasn't a bad man, not really. He could live with what he was doing, as long as he was surrounded by people who didn't press him. As long as he wasn't forced to confront it. He didn't want to hurt people but at the same time he couldn't find the courage to go against the crowd. His passivity filled her with disgust. Standing on the sidelines, telling yourself that deep down you're a good person, did her and the rest of the inmates no good.

As the vials slowly filled, Randolph answered Meiko's questions. Yes, Aiko was safe. No, she had not caught the illness, not yet. No, everyone who had caught the illness at camp had not died—Dave had exaggerated, though a shocking number of them had died in fits of rage, blood vessels popping in their heads or hearts giving out. But the camp doctor noticed that this tended to happen to the older afflicted or those who were already suffering from high blood pressure or weak hearts. The rest—well, they seemed to linger in an extended state of rage, unable to find peace for more than an hour at a time, constantly throwing themselves at the guards and the administrators, or at each other. He felt sorry for them. Sometimes he thought death would be better than to live in this state of perpetual rage.

And the guards . . . Did they not catch the illness, too? Meiko asked. It seemed odd that a sickness could differentiate between whites and Asians.

Oh no, guards had caught it, the boy confided. Almost every single one of them, though the director didn't want to admit it. It had led to an escalation of violence in the camp, no doubt about it, but the administrators didn't know what to do. They were short-handed as it was. If the army hadn't sent a platoon of observers, now pressed into service as guards, they would've been overwhelmed. They wouldn't have been able to stop the internees from breaking out and then, if they made it to town, who knew what might've happened.

Once Meiko had gotten him started talking, all she had to do was listen. That's all the boy wanted: someone to listen to him. But she had to block out the voices of her family, calling her a traitor and a disgrace.

He's the enemy. You can't trust him to tell you the truth.

"But Dave was right: you are different and that's why you're here," Randolph explained. "You caught the illness and got sick, but then you got better right away. Nobody else has done that. Nobody who catches it gets better. They either die or they . . . well, they seem to lose their mind. The doctors have been really worried about this illness, whatever it is. Afraid what would happen if it got out of the camps and reached the regular population . . ." He trailed off, perhaps aware of how awful that sounded. *It would be okay if it only infected Japanese but if it reaches white cities and towns . . .* "But once the doctors found out about you, they thought maybe there was hope."

Before he left for the day, Meiko decided to press him hard. She would have to be mean, but she had no choice. It might be her last chance. "I don't think you're bad," she said to him, remaining cool to show disapproval. "But what you're doing isn't right and you know it. How are you any different from a guard in a Nazi concentration camp?"

He sucked in his breath hard. The Nazis were the bad guys. Whereas every American believed he was a good guy. Meiko knew she had wounded him.

"I need you to do the right thing and I need you to do it now, not in a month or a year. I need you to help me. If you don't, you're no better than the rest of them, the ones who are killing us. And they *are* killing us. I don't know how or why, but something bad is going on."

He stared at her, stricken.

Meiko stood behind the barred windows and watched the boy leave—the sun starting to go down, which meant he would have to explain his ridiculous lateness—and thought about what would come next. Had her words sunk in? Would he listen to her? The boy was not a born deceiver and they might notice something different about him. It was possible that they would grow suspicious of Randolph and never allow him to come alone again.

But they had a bond now, and he knew what she needed from him. He was her ally, whether he would admit it or not.

For now, all Meiko could do was remind herself to be patient, to watch for her chance.

And to try not to let the memories of the past consume her.

16

"I've just met the girl I'm going to marry." Meiko remembered Jamie repeating to her what Archie had told him, down to the puppy dog eyes and sappy, moonstruck expression. Then Jamie had laughed because he was pleased for his friend, and Meiko knew she could never tell him how her stomach had clenched at his news.

Something bad was coming. Why could men never see it?

Meiko did not want to say anything against Archie to Jamie because Archie was his best friend. They'd been each other's solace for years, both of them estranged from their families. Jamie was well-liked by everyone, that she could see—even if he was married to a Japanese woman—but he always seemed to make time for Archie. To her, Archie Mitchell, who was younger than Jamie by quite a few years, was far too easily led, a little too quick to turn the other cheek, which should have been fitting, she supposed, for a local minister. But there was a cloying weakness in him, which she could feel. A self-hate that caused him to make stupid decisions. And a sweet enough face to earn him forgiveness from others again and again.

She wasn't all that surprised, then, when she finally met Archie's girl-friend. Elsie was also in seminary. From what Meiko saw, Elsie was the more ambitious of the couple. She was always pushing her fiancé to get people to listen to him, to fight for the spotlight. But even though she couldn't fault

Elsie for doing so, she didn't like the lanky blond midwesterner. Behind her guise of obliviousness and sweet temper, there was something cold. Something Meiko couldn't quite put her finger on. She reminded Meiko of a fish— something that glimmers and shines in the water, but once you reel it in and look up close, it's just a strange, pulsing creature with beady eyes, frantic to stay alive.

It used to be that Jamie would let Archie tag along when they went out to the movies or for a malted, but now they double-dated all the time. Meiko couldn't escape from Elsie. She was pretty sure this antipathy was mutual. When Elsie thought Meiko wasn't paying attention, Meiko would catch her looking enviously at Aiko, or note with jealousy when Jamie showed his affection in public. Archie would go no further than holding Elsie's hand. And, though Meiko didn't want to seem paranoid, it seemed to bother Elsie, too, that Meiko was Japanese and Jamie white.

Still, after Archie and Elsie married and the couples became inseparable, the tension between them eased. Elsie was friendlier to Meiko. Once Elsie got pregnant, the two women would sit together and talk babies while the men worked on cars or painted the baby's room in Archie and Elsie's apartment. Meiko promised Elsie Aiko's baby clothes, if she had a girl. If she had a boy, they'd dye everything blue. They'd make it work, Meiko had promised, just relieved that they could be friends.

Then came the Incident.

Meiko didn't want to believe this was the event that ended their friendship, but then, perhaps all that time, Elsie had simply been waiting for an excuse. Elsie was clearly unstable, Meiko had come to believe, and only a fool would try to figure out what she'd done to displease a crazy person. Jamie had begged her not to close the book on Elsie but to give it time. Maybe it was just pre-delivery jitters: "Once the baby's here, it'll work itself out. She'll be begging for your help and advice. You'll see."

That day would never come.

The Incident occurred one afternoon, five months into Elsie's pregnancy. The men were playing sandlot baseball, leaving their wives alone together.

Elsie was having a difficult patch at this point in the pregnancy and didn't want to go anywhere, so Meiko made tea for them.

Elsie was a picky eater. She didn't like to try new things. She preferred the foods she'd grown up with, gelatin salads with marshmallows or cabbage stuffed with ground beef. She never touched the Japanese food Meiko prepared, no matter the dish. Not one bite. She was already convinced that she wouldn't like it.

That afternoon, Meiko was out of the little pouches of store-bought tea that Caucasian people liked, so she substituted wakoucha, a Japanese black tea. It was stale, because Meiko preferred green teas and so had let this canister languish on the shelf, but she thought it had tasted fine and Elsie said nothing at the time. But that evening, Archie had to take Elsie to the hospital with early contractions, and the next morning they heard she'd lost the baby.

It was a very sad time for everyone. How terrible it must be to lose a baby so far along in its term. Meiko could only imagine. She sat up in the evenings, stroking Aiko's fine hair, thanking God over and over that her child was healthy. Elsie stayed in the hospital for a long time, almost two weeks, and Meiko thought it strange that Archie did not come to their apartment anymore and that he turned down every offer to have dinner with them. He must be comforting Elsie in the hospital, *she thought.*

Once Elsie had been released from the hospital, Meiko baked an angel food cake, Elsie's favorite, and brought it to their basement apartment. When Archie answered the door, he seemed shocked to see her and rather than inviting her in, he stepped into the hall and closed the door behind him.

"This is very thoughtful," Archie said, but without his usual warmth, and he didn't accept the cake from her outstretched hands. "I don't think she's much in the mood to eat, though. Maybe you should keep that for Jamie and Aiko to enjoy."

This was all very strange. So strange that Meiko couldn't imagine what might be going on. "Would it be okay to see Elsie for a few minutes? I want to tell her how sorry I am for what's happened . . ."

"Oh no." *The suggestion seemed to alarm him.* "She's asleep right now. She's very tired and I don't want to disturb her—"

He was lying. She could tell by the bright flush creeping over his face. He had never been a good liar. Then, to make matters even worse, he was interrupted by the sound of footsteps coming toward them. Rushed, angry footsteps.

The door flew back and there stood Elsie in her nightgown, her hair uncombed and flyaway, and her face glowing pink and sweaty. She pushed by her husband and knocked the plate from Meiko's hands, sending the cake to the floor, china smashing, crumbs exploding heavenward.

"How dare you show your face here!" *Elsie shrieked, pointing a finger at Meiko.* "I suppose you wanted to see for yourself . . . Are you happy now? How could you do this to me, to Archie, after everything we've done for you?"

Meiko's face went red, too. "I—I don't understand what you mean," *she managed to sputter, but she did understand. She heard it all the time since she had come to America.* You can't trust little yellow men.

Archie tugged at his wife's elbow, trying to get her back into the apartment, but she jerked out of his grasp. She shouted at the top of her lungs in the apartment building stairway, her voice ringing up to the roof for everyone to hear. "The miscarriage is all your fault. The doctor even said so—"

"Now, honey, the doctor said no such thing," *Archie cooed.*

"He did so. He asked me if I'd eaten anything out of the ordinary lately, and the only thing was that tea you gave me"—*she'd whirled on Meiko again, jabbing that finger like she wanted to stab Meiko in the eye*—"that foreign hoodoo tea . . . It's not meant for white people and you gave it to me anyway, you gave it to me deliberately and didn't tell me . . . It's because you wanted me to lose my baby . . ."

This was a nightmare. People had started to come out of their apartments, staring down on them over the railing.

"This makes no sense. Tea doesn't know if you're white or Asian." *Meiko tried to reason with the hysterical, delirious woman.* "Why would I do such a thing? We are friends, Elsie."

The blond woman pulled back haughtily, as though Meiko had spit at her. "Friends? Hah, you were never my friend. I only spent time with you because Archie wanted me to, because it was expected of me."

Archie shook his head vehemently. "Don't say that, Elsie. You know it isn't true . . ."

But his wife continued undeterred. "I knew I couldn't trust you because you're a—" She broke off; she couldn't say the words that Meiko knew were in her head: yellow devil. *Meiko was a yellow devil, conniving, less than human. "You did it because you're jealous of me. Me and Archie. Because we're white and good and God-fearing, and Jesus loves us, and it's something you'll never, ever have."*

The look on Elsie's face—triumphant and gloating and ugly all at once—made Meiko realize this was who the minister's wife had always been. She may have smiled and said nice things about Aiko and the way Meiko kept house but that had all been an act. She had been waiting for the day when she would be proven right, when Meiko would do something that showed her true colors and then Elsie would say smugly, I told you so. You can't trust these Japs.

It was then she realized she would never be friends with Elsie, or anyone like her, again.

And, in a few months, Archie got his first posting in Bly, Oregon. Meiko watched through her apartment window as the moving truck pulled away, and thought, That's that. I'll never have to deal with Elsie or Archie Mitchell again.

17

LAKE OGALLALA, NEBRASKA

It was around noon when Fran rolled into Lake Ogallala. Exhausted, with coffee stains down the front of her dress and cigarette butts overflowing from the ashtray. Bleary-eyed, and her hands stiff from clutching the steering wheel for hours. She'd made decent time in the last quarter of the drive, but as she pulled up in front of the sheriff's station, Fran had to ask herself what she hoped to find. Maybe she was clutching at straws. All she had were isolated incidents that she was stringing together.

Maybe there was no string. Maybe Richard was right—maybe, like Andy the hotel clerk, she was seeing stories where none existed. Maybe the drive she felt inside to get to the bottom of a mystery was a bad thing, the first warning sign of a buried madness. It was a fear she usually smothered, that maybe she had inherited a bad gene from the parents she didn't know, being an orphan. Stories of relatives locked away in asylums that her aunt had hinted at but never told.

Or maybe she was chasing a phantom because it was all she had and the possibility of a delicious story packed with conspiracies and secret government plots was more enticing than a reality where she had no job, no lover, and no prospects.

"The Lassiter boy? He died last night," the dispatcher told her at the police station. Sitting behind a tall counter, the dispatcher snapped her gum as she looked over Fran's press pass from the *Star*, hard with suspicion, like people tried to fool the police in Lake Ogallala with fake press passes all the time. A sign on the counter read NANCY WALDER, DISPATCHER ON DUTY.

Another Nancy. Fran had a good feeling about her.

"Died? What from?" There had been nothing in the wire story about a shoot-out or struggle.

"He was sick. The parents thought he had measles or something, that's why he was home from school. Covered with a rash, going crazy with the itching."

Crazy with the itching. Fran thought of Owen Hill with blood under his fingernails, Richard yelling at her as he scratched furiously behind his ears.

Maybe it was her disheveled appearance that softened the dispatcher's reserve, made her amenable to Fran. Or that Fran had shared that she was going to lose her job if she didn't bring home this story. The dispatcher looked over her shoulder before she slid a manila folder over the counter to Fran.

The woman nodded at a metal stacking chair in the corner. "Go over there, keep your head down, and read this. It's the officer's report. The army man told us to give him all the copies, but the sheriff said to hold one back."

Fran tucked the chair in the corner and sat with her back to the aisle. This had to be the last copy in the carbon copy set, the black typed letters fat and fuzzy.

STATEMENT FROM DONALD AND EUNICE LASSITER REGARDING THE DEATH OF THEIR SON, DONALD JR.

Parents reported that their son began complaining that he was not feeling well Friday evening. Symptoms included fever and headache. Mrs. Lassiter noticed he had broken out in a rash and was scratching. She put a call through to Dr. Whitbey, who said to bring the boy by his office Monday morning but in the meantime to treat him with aspirin and oatmeal baths.

Monday, Whitbey examined Donald Jr. but could not determine the cause of his illness. He ruled out measles and chicken pox, advised keeping him home from school and continued observation. If his condition worsened, parents were to bring him back to Whitbey but in the meantime, they were to apply calamine lotion to the rash.

Parents said Donald Jr.'s temper deteriorated sharply throughout the day. Parents admit he was a difficult boy to begin with, trouble in school, teasing sister, etc., but that he was miserable from rash.

The evening of the homicide: Donald, the father, was working a late shift at the lumberyard. Eunice Lassiter had left the children alone to drop pies off at her sister Joanie Murdock's house in Oshkosh for the church bake sale the next day, and so there was no one present at the time of the killing. Eunice said she left her home at approximately 7:00 p.m. and returned ninety minutes later. She went to check on the children and found her daughter, Susan, unresponsive on the floor of her bedroom and Donald Jr. in a catatonic state in the closet. Eunice's first thought was that someone had broken into the house. She tried to revive Susan but was unable to. She then called the sheriff's office and her husband, in that order, then her neighbors the Falstaffs, who arrived before the dispatched police unit. The Falstaffs attempted unsuccessfully to revive the daughter while Eunice tried to get Donald Jr. to tell her what had happened. She stated that her son told her nothing, except that no one had come to the house.

Deputy Sheriff Sanderson arrived at the scene at the same time as the father. Sanderson determined that the daughter, Susan, was dead and declared the dwelling a crime scene.

How terrible for the mother: to go from taking her son for a routine examination at the family doctor's office to coming home to a murder scene. Fran's eye skimmed down the pages, skipping the procedural stuff, until she found the interview with the dead boy.

Sheriff Clausen interviewed Donald Jr. after he was admitted to the hospital. By that time, the boy had come out of his catatonic state somewhat and had become very agitated. He told the sheriff that he had killed his sister, strangling her before hitting her on the head with a baseball bat. When asked why he had done this (parents reported no untoward animosity between the siblings, no more than could be considered normal in any family), the boy stated that he believed his sister was a "Jap sympathizer" after repeating things she had heard in Sunday school.

Note from Clausen: Donald Lassiter's views on Japanese and Chinese living in the area are well known. It was only a matter of time before the children would start to parrot his opinions.

Fran let the sheet slip from her fingers. A wave of dizziness passed over her. What had gone so horribly wrong in this house, to drive a boy to strangle and bludgeon his own sister? Maybe the father was a monster, spewing invective every day until the boy's head was filled with hatred—but his sister was only eight. Fran could not imagine what an eight-year-old could say that would drive another child to murder, to feel the need to kill her in order to stop the painful words from coming out of her mouth.

It made no sense—or maybe it was just because she didn't want it to be true. Didn't want to acknowledge that such raw hatred could exist in the world.

She read the rest of the report quickly. The doctor hypothesized that the boy might have been allergic to one of the topical medications he'd been given and maybe that was to blame for his psychotic state. Donald Jr. had fallen into a coma shortly after being admitted and never came out of it, according to the report. He never had the chance to fully explain his actions. The parents were devastated, of course. Clausen noted that the father was taking it particularly hard—*as well he should*, Fran thought—and had gotten so bad that he was under a doctor's supervision.

Fran was about to hand the folder back to the dispatcher when she saw a few lines scribbled in the margins of the last page. *Mrs. Lassiter said Donnie had come across remnants of balloon three days before getting sick. Army notified.*

That explained why the army had shown up and confiscated the police report.

Wherever these mysterious balloons appeared, the army was not far behind.

She tried to think of a reason why the army would be interested in a teenage boy killing his sister, why they'd confiscate reports and smother news stories. But she could not.

With great reluctance, Fran returned to the front desk. How she wished she could smuggle the report out in her purse, but she couldn't betray the trust of someone who'd been kind to her. "Say," Fran said as she passed the folder back to the dispatcher. "I don't suppose you knew Donnie Jr.?"

"Sure. Not well, but Ogallala is pretty small." She lingered over the folder. "I know what you're thinking—why didn't the parents see this coming? It wasn't like that, from what I heard. He was normal, you know? Just a normal teenage boy. Liked baseball and fly-fishing and loved his little sister. But, you know, sometimes the tightest ties snap the hardest."

As she turned to leave, Fran remembered one last thing. "I didn't see a medical examiner's report in the file. Is that because the examiner's not finished yet?"

The dispatcher gave her a patient smile. "The army confiscated that, too."

Before Fran left, however, she had the dispatcher show her on a map exactly where the Lassiters lived. With something between dread and certainty gripping her chest, she saw it was close to where she and Richard had found the balloon. Closer than the cabin, even.

Sitting behind the steering wheel, Fran lit a cigarette and pulled her thoughts together. A thirteen-year-old boy, Donnie Lassiter Jr., goes out to the woods, maybe walking a dog, or chasing a lost football, or sneaking a beer. He finds the debris from the balloon—the same debris she'd collected carefully with gloved hands, the same scraps that even now were sitting, bagged, in her suitcase. The kid thinks it's curious and takes a closer look. Or maybe his dog drags one of the scraps to him in its mouth.

He goes home and that night he begins to feel peculiar. At first, the physical signs are minor. But then . . . She counts the days between exposure and . . . *this*, a violent, unprecedented outburst. A normal boy commits *murder*. Within days, he dies and the information that might point to an answer is snapped up by the authorities.

Still think there's no story, Richard? She smirked despite herself. Maybe she wasn't so crazy, after all.

Richard.

She checked into a motor lodge off Route 61, a quiet little place with moose-print café curtains on the windows. The bed looked inviting, and she was exhausted enough to sleep for a week, but there was a phone call she had to make.

Fran went to the lobby. A pay phone hung off the wall next to a rack of brochures for local attractions. She bought a bag of roasted peanuts from the vending machine and sat on the Naugahyde settee, cracking the shells into the wastebasket while she gathered her nerve. Richard wouldn't want to hear from her, but Fran didn't see how she had a choice.

This wasn't just a matter of an unidentified object exploding in the sky. Now it was violence, murder, sickness, death. It was governmental suppression. Nobody in authority would talk to the press.

And what about the car that had tried to run her off the road? Had that been a coincidence or was somebody trying to silence her? She tried to put the incident on the road out of her mind. She was safe now.

The important thing at this moment was Richard. Sure, there might be another reason why Donnie Lassiter did what he did. The similarities between his symptoms and Richard's gave her pause. Add to that the fact that the medical report had been confiscated.

Richard might be in danger. He had to be warned.

Her heart sank when she remembered it was Saturday. That meant Richard wouldn't be at the office. He'd be at home. Fran looked at the phone, hesitating. It wasn't that she didn't have the number. She had it memorized, even though she'd been warned a hundred times never to call there. Never.

But this was different. It was for Richard's own good.

She brushed the peanut skins off her hands before fishing for nickels in her purse. Listened to the *thunk, thunk, thunk* as she fed coins into the pay phone. Recited the phone number to the operator to put her through long-distance.

The phone was answered on the third ring. "May I speak to Richard Hanson?" Fran blurted out before whoever was on the other end could speak. She'd never spoken to either of Richard's children and she didn't want to start today. "I need to speak to your father."

There was a pause. The phone line, connecting her to Lincoln and the home that didn't want her, crackled. "This is Mrs. Hanson."

Winnie.

Fran almost hung up.

There was a pause on the far end. Then the voice again, calmer than Fran imagined. "This is Fran, isn't it? I was wondering if you'd call."

Fran swallowed. This was where she got chewed out. Told off by the wife. *You have your nerve calling here . . .* Well, she deserved it. Fran would put up with anything, as long as she got to talk to Richard afterward. To warn him.

"Yes, Winnie, it is. And I'm sorry to call your home, I really, truly am, but I've got to speak to Richard and it's very, very important . . ."

Another pause. And then—Winnie's voice cracked. It almost sounded like a sob. "I'd let you speak to him, Fran, really I would, but he's not here. You see—he's in the hospital."

Fran wanted to drive straight to the hospital, but sheer exhaustion won. It might've been a mere five or six hours, but she had been driving hard for days now. She was sleep-deprived and famished, jittery from coffee and too many cigarettes. She was intensely aware that her clothes had been worn and reworn several times over and were in bad need of a wash. *Home first,* she told herself. Richard didn't need to see her like this: it would only confirm what he thought about her. Sleep, a good meal from the diner down the street, a fresh set of clothes.

At least, by now, it seemed, she was no longer being tailed.

As she got closer to her apartment building, however, she noticed it was louder than she remembered. There was a palpable tension in the air. Voices spilled from open windows. Two men stood on the sidewalk outside her building, yelling at each other. "You can't trust the Japs. We should line 'em up against a wall and shoot 'em." And when the other man tried to reason with him, the first man pushed his shoulder, sending the man stumbling backward. "You're a dirty Jap lover and anyone who sides with the Japs deserves to have the same thing happen to them."

She hurried up the stairs, listening to fragments of arguments from the apartments as she passed. It was as though someone had stirred a hornets' nest. She couldn't remember her neighbors being so ornery before . . . Could something have happened in Lincoln while she was gone? As she hauled her suitcase over the threshold of her apartment it occurred to her that *she* could be to blame. If this disease—this infection—had come to Lincoln, she might've had a role in bringing it here. But she'd kept the pieces she'd taken bagged up and hadn't taken them out once since she'd returned from the lake trip with Richard. No one had touched them.

Maybe it was all Richard's fault. He had the symptoms, after all. He'd been running around since they'd returned, going to the newsroom and out to lunch and PTA meetings and drinks with neighbors in his home out in the suburbs and who knew where else. If anyone was responsible for spreading it around, it would be Richard.

Except . . . Yes, she remembered now: her cat, Marcel, had gotten into the bag. It was just once, but he'd pulled out the scraps and was chewing on them. She'd taken them away from him promptly, knotted the bag good and tight. But who knew how many times he'd gotten into it before she'd caught him?

And he'd disappeared shortly afterward.

Marcel traveled in and out of the building. He had his ways.

Could he have come back while she was away? She'd found Marcel shacked up with one of the neighbors more than once. His favorite second home was Mr. Martoni's on the second floor, a retired old gentleman who liked to dine on sardines packed in oil, which Marcel loved. Before she headed out to see Richard in the hospital, she'd check quickly with the neighbors—just in case.

As she trotted down the stairs to Mr. Martoni's, she thought she heard Marcel's high, plaintive mewling. So recognizable, she was instantly stabbed with remorse. What a bad owner she was, to abandon him like that. She followed the sound—though she also wondered if she wasn't hearing what she wanted to hear, that it all seemed rather strange and dreamlike.

Funny, Mr. Martoni's door was ajar, though it was dark and quiet within.

The answer could be simple: he'd stepped out and hadn't pulled the door tight behind him.

"Marcel?" A quick check wouldn't hurt. To satisfy her curiosity.

She pushed the door open. The other sounds of the apartment building—the arguments, raised voices, clank of dishes in the sink, clamor of conflicting television programs—all fell away. It was just her and the dark hollow of his apartment.

"Hello, Mr. Martoni? Are you home?" Obviously, there was no one in. She should look for her cat and leave.

She stepped over the threshold and started down the long hall. Martoni's apartment was strangely laid out, making use of odd leftover space on this floor, squeezed between the back staircase and one of the bigger apartments. A perfect place to live if you wanted to be forgotten.

This is where I'll be living in a few years, if I'm not careful. A crazy old lady forgotten by everyone.

"Here, kitty, kitty." She could smell sardines. Fran would bet the last cigarette in her purse that Marcel was here.

There was a second strong odor in the air, like the trash hadn't been taken out in a while.

The kitchen was nothing more than a few cabinets and a hot plate squeezed in a closet between the bedroom and a small sitting area. Sure enough, the trash can had been knocked over and garbage spilled all over the floor.

And there was a large dark shape crouched toward the back of the space, like an animal had made a den in there.

"What the hell . . ." Fran muttered, more to buck up her courage and make herself feel brave, as she reached for the light switch.

Mr. Martoni sat on the floor, slumped against the wall. His face was swollen, and he was white as chalk. His eyes were open and pale like milk glass, his jaw hanging open, like he had something to say.

He wouldn't be talking. He had obviously been dead for a while.

Fran jumped backward but managed not to scream.

There was no telephone in the apartment, so she used hers, then went back to sit with Mr. Martoni to wait for the police to arrive. As she waited, she looked around for clues to the cause of death (occupational hazard for a reporter), but there were only a few.

The window in the sitting room was open about four inches. More than enough space for Marcel to get in, she figured.

There were open sardine cans in the trash and scattered on the floor.

So, maybe Marcel *had* been here, but what did that prove? She didn't see any signs that Mr. Martoni had gone mad with rage, no sign of foul play.

And—most odd—there seemed to be something funny about the corpse itself. Almost like a shimmy of movement. Not that she thought the body was moving—he most definitely was dead—but that, out of the corner of her eye, she'd see a ripple pass over the fabric of his bathrobe or down his cheek.

It had to be a trick of the light.

As for the cause of death, one of the policemen figured it out. "He killed himself," the policeman said after rummaging around the kitchen counter. It was cluttered with open boxes and tins, and Fran had left it as she'd found it, thinking it important not to disturb anything, but the policeman had plucked out the box right away. "Rat poison," he said, sticking the package in Fran's face like she doubted him. He picked up a glass with a little liquid at the bottom and a powdery white sediment streaking the sides, gave it a sniff, put it back. "Yeah, he took rat poison. Shitty way to go."

Fran looked around the messy apartment. She supposed he'd had enough of his lonely life. Poor Mr. Martoni. She should've told him to keep Marcel . . . It was obvious the poor old man needed the cat more than she did.

At least Marcel hadn't been responsible—meaning she, by extension, wasn't responsible.

She was about to walk out the door when the policeman called out, "Bingo." He held up a piece of paper. "The suicide note—that clinches it." He held it out to her, like she wanted to see it.

Well, maybe she did—a little.

It was crinkled, like he'd clenched it in his fist at some point, and she had to hold it between both hands in order to read it.

The handwriting was angry, heavily slanted. Almost like a crazy person had written it.

I hear the shouting all around me nonstop. Neighbor against neighbor. What has become of this country, the perfect country I came to forty years ago?

This madness is not going to turn me into a fascist. I fought fascists in Italy before I came to America.

I would rather die first.

There would be no napping now. Instead, Fran made a pot of coffee and started to get ready to go to the hospital. In the shower, as the hot water streaked over her, she thought about the past couple days. She had to be wanted by the police in Montana for questioning, if not for outright assault. She'd stabbed a man, for goodness' sake. And now here in Lincoln, a sweet, gentle man was dead because of her; maybe she hadn't killed him with her own hands, but she'd brought an unknown disease to the city, one that apparently drove you mad, and that meant she was as guilty as if she'd forced him to take that poison herself.

She'd turn herself in, but to whom? The police here knew her—she was with the biggest paper in the city, after all—but would they believe her? There was a National Guard armory in Lincoln, and an office of the FBI. If what the hotel clerk had told her was true, the FBI already knew something was going on.

Somehow, none of those things felt right. Felt *safe*. The army was going around covering things up. Maybe the FBI was acting separately from the army, but she only had the opinion of one little green man conspiracist for that . . . It could've been the FBI in that car trailing her and until she found out, she didn't feel she could go to any of the authorities.

Instead, she pushed these thoughts from her mind as she walked to her car. As she passed a newsstand, she caught a headline out of the corner of her eye: *Police Provide Additional Details to Mysterious Mountain Explosion in Oregon. Six Dead.* She snatched up the newspaper and threw a nickel on the counter. No time to read it now.

By the time she arrived at the hospital, visiting hours were nearly over. The disease was beginning to touch the hospital, Fran sensed. Doctors walked by in a huff, yelling at nurses and orderlies. Nurses snapped at visitors. Of course, it might be nothing more than the frazzled nerves that come with an increased workload, and it did seem busier than usual. The nurse stationed at the front desk tried to get Fran to go right back to her car and come back another day, and when Fran refused, told her curtly that she had fifteen minutes, no more.

Fran peeked into Richard's room. He lay in a hospital bed, his shiny face as red as a lobster. He appeared to be holding a loud conversation even though there was no one else in the room.

"Winnie told me I'd find you here," Fran said as cheerfully as she could as she entered. He didn't look happy to see her in the least.

"Stopped chasing your important story to see me? Or to ask for your job back?"

Richard could be sharp-tongued, but he'd never used that tone with her before. "I heard you were sick. You're in a hospital, so you obviously are."

"Winnie's a worrier, that's all."

"Will you at least admit there's something going on? You have the exact same symptoms that I've seen in other people who've been around those balloons. One of them is dead. A teenage boy right next to the cabin where we stayed in Ogallala."

"You're jumping to conclusions."

"He touched the remnants, same as you. Then he started scratching, and ranting—and a couple days later he killed his sister. Then he went into a coma and died."

He stopped fidgeting and became solemn.

"Thank goodness that seems to have gotten your attention."

He touched Fran's wrist. "Winnie . . . She contacted the police because I threw a punch at her."

"Richard."

"I'm not like that, you know I'm not. I don't even know why I did it. She was talking—I don't even remember what about—and I suddenly got so damned *mad* . . . It came out of nowhere . . . That's why I let them check me into the hospital. These fits come over me . . . I thought it was just the fever, or the itching—it's enough to drive you crazy!"

Mr. Martoni. *This madness . . . I would rather die first.*

He clenched his fists as though he was fighting an urge right at that moment. "It would be a relief to know that something is to blame for the way I've been acting. That I'm not just losing my mind."

Maybe that was something they had in common. Did it mean she might have it, too?

He tilted his head toward her. "You should know . . . the FBI are looking for you. They stopped by the newsroom. Told me you'd been asking questions in Montana but you were gone before they could talk to you. I was to let them know if I heard from you."

"I'd appreciate if you didn't tell them I'd been by. Strange things have been happening to people on the periphery of these balloon sightings and I'm not sure whom to trust."

He gave her a grin, the kind she'd always liked. Like the old Richard. "Do you know how paranoid that sounds?"

Fran checked her watch. "I have to leave. That battle-axe at the front desk gave me fifteen minutes, no more."

"Here's the part I don't understand," he continued as he watched

190

her gather her things. "You were out at the cabin, same as I. Why didn't you get sick?"

"I didn't handle those remnants with my bare hands, dummy."

"But you were with me the rest of the day. We swapped spit—and other bodily fluids—and then we were closed up together in a car for hours. If we were talking about the common cold, you'd have the sniffles."

He was right. "Maybe that means it's not contagious? At least not in the usual ways."

"Then how did I catch it? Or that kid in Ogallala?"

"I wish I had the answer. You should've been a detective, Richard. Now, you take care of yourself. Listen to the doctors."

But he wasn't listening. He had stiffened and was shaking like he was having some kind of episode, his face turning bright red and breaking out in a heavy sweat.

A fine line of blood trickled from his ear.

"Dear God—Richard!" Fran wasted no time but sprinted toward the nurse's desk at the top of the ward, shouting for help. She dashed back with the nurse but was told to wait at the door to Richard's room. By then, Richard was thrashing against the bed, his eyes and teeth clenched tightly.

The nurse looked over her shoulder at Fran. There was fear in her eyes. "Go to the waiting room. I'm going to get the doctor but—you don't want to watch."

Fran gulped. Should she be saying goodbye to him? There was nothing she could do at that moment but listen to the nurse . . . However, as she turned away, she thought she saw the same weird ripple run along Richard's hospital gown that she'd seen in Mr. Martoni's apartment, a shimmer of refracted light just along the surface.

I am at my lowest point since coming to Shikotan.

Yuriko is furious with me. Enough is enough, she said. Even I must see that I am being wrongheaded. My work is getting me nowhere. I told her, eventually, why I'd walked all night and now she is sure I have let it put my family in danger, somehow, by coming here. She has given me an ultimatum: when we return to the mainland, I will tell the institute that I will no longer study high-altitude winds and wish to be put on their most pressing project. I will make myself more valuable to them. I will try to advance up the ladder. I should be thinking about becoming a manager and earning more money for the family, she scolds me, not proving some foolish and unnecessary theory. I should stop feeding my ego, let go of my dreams, and be practical.

I cannot refuse her. She is right.

18

CAMP MINIDOKA, IDAHO

The dust settled around the wheels of Fran's car. The cooling engine ticked slowly.

She was tired, even with the overnight stop in Laramie. She'd finally read about the explosion in Oregon and it was a doozy, almost enough to make her change her plans and point the car toward this Bly mentioned in the article.

But no, she'd decided to start with the internment camp. Bly and what had happened at Gearhart Mountain could wait. Luckily, she had a few hours before she could execute her plan. She checked into a hotel, took a hot bath, and even got an hour's nap before getting back in her car and heading toward the camp.

Minidoka, the internment camp.

There was no way she was going to get a straight answer from anyone if she played by their rules, if she came through the front door, filled out a request form in triplicate, which she'd have to do if she were still a reporter at the *Journal Star*. She could get in a lot of trouble if she didn't. But she wasn't. She was a freelancer, and everyone knew that freelancers sometimes had to play a little fast and loose in order to get the story. She justified what she was about to do by remembering she wouldn't get paid if she didn't have a story—which meant no rent, no food. Never mind that she had the makings of a great story here: she felt it in her gut.

She pulled off half a mile early, hidden by a couple overgrown trees at a bend in the road. It was about an hour before shift change at the camp, meaning it was only a matter of time before the day shift started to head home. She poured coffee out of the thermos she'd finagled from the motel clerk and waited for the first cars to motor by.

By quarter past five, Fran began to see a steady stream of cars. Most were occupied by a couple men, some driven by individuals. She threw the coffee in her cup out the window and pulled after them, following them back to town. Most would probably head home to families to spend some time with Junior while waiting for dinner, but she figured at least a couple would lead her to a bar or diner where people who worked at the camp got together to blow off steam.

Sure enough, she saw one car with a few occupants pull up in front of a roadside bar, a weathered brown shack with a couple cars already parked in front. She watched from a corner of the parking lot as three men got out of the car, talking among themselves, and headed inside. They seemed completely wrapped up in conversation; chances were good that they hadn't spotted her following them.

She waited a few more minutes before heading inside. On her way to the front door, she passed a smart-looking car that merited a closer look. It was obviously a late model, which made it extremely rare because car production had been shut down since the start of the war. Fran recalled hearing somewhere that fewer than 150 cars had been made in the past couple years, but that a new B-24 bomber rolled off the Ford Motor Company's production lines every sixty minutes.

It was new alright. The paint job practically still looked wet.

You could smell its newness. Fastened to its shiny chrome bumper was a California license plate. And there was something about its shape that reminded her of the car that had chased her down that lonesome highway.

With gas rationing, there probably weren't many cars from the Golden State slumming it in the prairies, but what were the chances this was the same car that had been in Wyoming? It had been too dark to get a good look that night, and didn't all cars look basically the same?

She shook it off. She was being paranoid.

Still, a little alarm in Fran's head was sounding *danger, danger.*

It wasn't strong enough to stop her from going into the bar, however.

She found them in a booth against the front wall, under a window. They had their jackets off and were sharing a pitcher of beer. She hesitated: three men were a lot to handle on her own. She'd been thinking of one, maybe two. It was risky . . . but this was her chance.

She slid into a booth across the room and ordered a beer when the waitress came over. The room was small, and the men—buoyed by beer—spoke loudly, so it was easy to overhear snippets of their conversation.

"One of those fucking Japs bit my hand today, can you believe it? I'm gonna come down with it, I just know it."

"They tell us it's not contagious, but I don't believe 'em anymore . . ."

". . . worse every day. It's out of control."

"And did you see Mulligan flip out at the guardhouse? . . . Practically foaming at the mouth. They had to sedate him."

Fran could tell they weren't talking about a cold or flu.

This story was big—and important—and worth it.

She glanced around the bar. There were only a handful of people besides the men in the booth. Most were probably locals. Which one was the driver of that new car? The only one who stood out was an older man at the bar, talking to a man in a suit. There was just something about him that made Fran think he might be from California . . . His gestures, the clothes he wore all seemed more sophisticated. And he was dressed a bit too lightly for the area, for one thing, as though he hadn't anticipated how cold it would be.

"Hey, little lady—you here alone?" Fran looked up to find one of the men from the booth standing beside her. He ogled her in a way that he probably thought flattering. Maybe he was one of those guys who thought any woman who went to a bar alone was looking for action and deserved whatever happened to her. There was definitely a hint of aggression about him—*danger, danger*—but she'd come to the bar hoping to talk to someone who worked on the inside. This might be her only chance.

"You're not from around here, are you? You look kind of lonely sitting there by yourself. Mind if I join you?" He slid into the booth across from her, his beer sloshing over the rim of his glass. "Whatcha doing in Jerome?"

She feigned nervousness. "I came in for an interview out at the camp. I got family in town—they said they were hiring. You work out there? You mind telling me what it's like?"

He took a gulp of beer, leaving a line of foam on his upper lip. "The guard work pays pretty well, better than anything else around here. And it gives you a chance to do your part for the war, you know, if you weren't able to sign up." He explained how he was exempted being his parents' only son and needed to help on the farm. "Only my sisters are able to handle most all of it, so my folks thought it better if I worked at the camp and brought in some cash."

"And is it rough?"

"The Japs, you mean? It's not like people think. They're pretty docile. They just go about their day."

"What about the illness I heard about?" She played dumb. She was never good at this act, but she'd try her best if it meant finding out what was going on.

"You don't need to worry about that. Only the Japs can catch it on account of their weak constitutions. Makes 'em cranky as hell, though. We've had to shoot a couple of them. It's not what you think—they tried to attack us. They didn't give us a choice . . . but whites are safe."

Did he really believe it? Fran suppressed the urge to roll her eyes. "Is that what they told you?"

He slouched, glancing left and right to see if anyone was listening. "Well . . . that's not strictly true. It's just what the administrators tell us to say. Guards have gotten sick. But"—his eyes flicked over her face, *I'm doing you a favor*—"we're not supposed to be talking about it."

She took a sip of beer. A martini sure would hit the spot right now but that would certainly blow her cover. Farm girls in Idaho probably didn't drink cocktails unless they were pastel-colored and sweet. "You know, when I was there for the interview, I barely had any time to see for myself what it was like. I don't suppose you could sneak me into the camp so I could look around?" She looked up at him coyly, the way girls did in magazines and in the movies. "You gotta understand—this is a big decision for me. It means moving away from my parents and brothers and sisters. I'd be by myself for the first time in my life—"

His head jerked up. "I thought you said you had family in town?"

Oh, right. "Yeah, I do, but we're not close. This is the first time I've seen them in years."

He shrugged and nodded. Made sense.

"I need to know for *sure* before I pack up and move. It's asking a lot, but it would really help me out." Fran leaned forward and let her hand graze his on the table. A tickle of electricity passed between them. That touch was a promise, and he perked up. He stopped by the booth to say good night to his buddies—winks and smiles all around—and met Fran at the front door.

He decided she should hide in the back seat of his car, crouched in the footwell and covered with a blanket, until he got past the guardhouse. He'd park behind one of the outbuildings, so no one would see his car since he was supposed to have left for the day. It was dark and he would feel it would be safe to carefully show her around the camp, as long as they kept to the shadows. "Just a few minutes, okay?" he said as he tucked her in the back. "Then maybe we can take a little drive . . . I can show you around town." He meant a trip to lover's lane. She'd talk her way out of it when the time came.

Fran wasn't crazy about being chaperoned around camp but at least she'd get to see it for herself and be able to judge conditions there. Maybe she'd get to talk to one or two of the residents.

The car jostled as it passed over railroad tracks, signaling they were close to the camp. She heard the gentle scrape of the driver's-side window rolling down as the young man made small talk with the guard—"Yeah, I forgot my thermos and my dad'll kill me if I lose his good one"—before pulling away. Fran couldn't remember the last time she'd felt so relieved, and almost laughed softly to herself. The government was big and powerful and scary, but here she was about to slip past them and find out about this hush-hush project using nothing but her wits.

When the car finally parked, she resisted the urge to throw off the blanket and jump up, too warm and itchy from the wool. They weren't exactly alone, she realized. There were faint sounds off to the side. Muffled talking and movement.

Finally, after what seemed like a long time, the door beside her creaked open. With no streetlight overhead, she could see nothing in the darkness. There was just a small puddle of light at her feet from the dome light inside the car.

But then the blanket was yanked from overhead and the back seat was flooded with pale yellow light. Fran's heart leapt in her throat: why had he pulled the blanket away so quickly? Was he teasing her or trying to scare her?

Someone was standing outside the door. It was the man from the bar, the one she was sure was driving the car with California plates. The young man stood behind him, hands in pockets and drop-shouldered, looking guiltily at Fran.

The California man reached out to her to help her up. She stared at his hand; there was something cold and hard about it. She should expect no mercy.

He almost smiled. "Now, now, miss, don't be like that. You tried to fool us—tried to fool this fine young boy over here—and you were caught. You're not as good at this game as you like to think. Did you think we wouldn't expect you to try again? It would've been much better if you'd listened when the sheriffs told you to walk away. But you're a stubborn one, aren't you? Now, I'm afraid you're going to have to come with us."

19

One day, a new minder showed up at Meiko's cabin prison with the others. Meiko could tell right away that something was up. He was different: he dressed differently, acted differently, even wore his hair differently. He was talkative and bossy, like a city boy. Whereas the other minders were taciturn and apt to turn things over in their minds, like the farmers Meiko had come to know in Oregon and Idaho.

Randolph came out nearly every day. She had questions she wanted to ask him as well as wanting to cultivate this new bond with him, but it was difficult for them to be alone together. If they found out what she was up to, Randolph would be relieved of duty, she was sure of it. The other attendants would be on their guard, knowing she had corrupted one of them. There would be no second chance. Randolph was her only hope.

He remained inside when the others went on a smoke break. As soon as the door closed, he'd want to talk, his big eyes begging for her attention. *See me.*

She listened to his concerns—a bit of sadistic teasing from one of the other guards, his fear that the camp director didn't like him, an argument with his father at the dinner table. She listened patiently but didn't offer suggestions for how he might fix the situation. That wasn't what he wanted from her.

He needed a friend.

She waited until he'd finished before speaking. "Can you think of any way to help me get out of here?"

"They haven't said anything about bringing you back to camp. The whole camp's been taken over by these military men, out from the Army Air Forces command office in Alameda. The new guy's one of them, by the way. He brings the vials into the lab, gets his orders from them. They don't tell us nothing anymore."

Men from command headquarters, observers and doctors . . . She looked at him sharply. "Why would they be interested in this illness at the camp, but not try to make everyone better?" Those weren't medical doctors; she'd spent enough time around her father to recognize researchers. To researchers, everyone was merely a test subject.

This was not just a passing illness. A cold, the flu, or even cholera. "Something is going on. You need to find out. This affects you, too. You have the disease. You're not going to get better." He turned his head; he didn't want to be reminded, but he knew she was right. "But you are more than a victim. You can help prevent others from catching this disease. I'm depending on you, Randolph. As a friend. There must be a way. Be resourceful."

The new man, Duncan, talked incessantly, with a prodding edge to his voice. He was careful when she was around, limiting topics of conversation to baseball or last night's supper, but when they were outside taking a smoke break, huddled against a prairie wind that lifted collars and ruffled short hair, he jabbed a finger angrily toward the cabin as he spoke. He reminded her of the rabble-rousers in Minidoka, trying to convince the others to push back. His eyes always burned when he looked at her, as though she had personally done something to hurt him.

Her inability to figure out what was going on was frustrating. *You have a fine mind*, Meiko's father had told her more than once. It needed to be occupied, however, or else her fine mind would get her into trouble one day. He peppered her with riddles or sent her into the forest on scavenger hunts so he could get his work done. Today, however, her inability to think, to concentrate, was due to lack of blood: lately, they were taking two or three times as much blood as they had at first, far more than she thought safe. But she was also irritated because the information she had was insufficient to solve the problem at hand. She vowed to figure it out, however.

As the sun went down, she watched the attendants climb into the sedan. Duncan took the front seat next to the driver, talking the whole time. He would know what was going on, and from what Meiko could see, the man never shut up. Maybe she would not need to rely on Randolph. Maybe, if she was patient and clever, she could get what she needed to know from Duncan.

She saw what she had to do: she must be like a patient prospector, panning through that incessant stream of chatter, mining for gold nuggets.

I mustn't let him see me listening, she realized, *or he will feed me false information.*

She started by listening with her ear pressed to the door when the attendants went into the back room for their lunch, or to pack up for the day. They talked in whispers about happenings at camp, whether there had been a fight among the residents (they used the word "inmates," confirming for Meiko that the internees were considered nothing more than prisoners), or which of the guards had caught the illness. They called the disease "the fervor" and they always said it with a chuckle, like it was an inside joke.

We are nothing but guinea pigs to them. Test subjects.

It was clear from the way Duncan spoke about the military men that what they were doing was a program of sorts. It sounded uncomfortably like they were developing some kind of germ warfare to use on their enemies. They might've selected an internment camp to test it because the residents were expendable, or because they wanted to see if it would work on their enemies' physiology, though that seemed, to Meiko, especially warped. There were no significant differences between the physiologies of the races, nothing beside the cosmetic. Only a hard-core racist would believe otherwise.

Trying to read the attendants' lips when they went outside for a break proved fruitless; she could make guesses as to what Duncan might be saying but there was no way to know if she'd guessed right. Better to eavesdrop on them inside the cabin. Meiko pretended to be asleep or lingered around corners, listening for scraps. Mining nuggets. In this way, she learned that a dozen residents of the camp had died and there were over a hundred in the hospital tent, with more joining them every day. So far, none of the guards who'd caught the fervor had died—"Goes to show the superiority of the Caucasian race," Duncan crowed in an unguarded moment—but several "had gotten pretty squirrelly," he'd admitted.

"It's frightening," David said quietly one evening as they donned their jackets, readying to leave. "I don't want to catch it. Who knows if you'll be able to come back from it?"

"What are you—a chicken?" Duncan teased.

"Of a disease like that? You're darn tooting. They don't even know if you can carry it home to your family."

"There hasn't been one case yet where that's happened—not that's been proven, anyway. It's always been traced back to a bite," Duncan said as they headed out the door, punctuated by the scrape of the key in the lock.

A bite? From what?

Meiko could not remember being bitten by anything, not even a flea. She knew why she had gotten sick: it was because of whatever she'd been forced to swallow.

It had been inanimate. Hard, pebbly—like sand. Sand could not bite.

But how could sand make you sick?

There had to be a connection, but she couldn't find it.

She had come to a dead end.

Take this and hide it," Randolph hissed at her. He reached under his clothing and pulled out a wad of folded papers, shoving it in her hands. She quickly shoved it down the front of her blouse, trying to wedge it under the waistband of her skirt.

"Those are classified reports. I managed to sneak 'em out of the office. If they find out they're missing, they're going to go apeshit. If they find out I'm the one who took them, well, I'll go to jail. We can't chance them being found, so burn 'em after you've read 'em. Do you understand? There's no telling what they'll do if they find out you have them."

It was then she noticed Randolph looked worse. The disease was progressing, and he knew it, and that was why he was taking this risk. He searched her face. He wanted a sign that he'd done well, that she understood the risk he'd taken for her and was grateful. She squeezed his hand, hoping it would be enough.

Somehow, for the rest of the time the attendants were there, she managed to act as though nothing had happened. Her every movement was careful, lest she cause the papers to pop or crinkle. She thought she would explode with anticipation and couldn't imagine why they were taking so long today of all days—though in reality, it was probably no longer than every other day. With every passing minute she just wanted to scream, *Get out!*

Even after they'd piled into the sedan and driven away, Meiko waited with her back to the door a few extra minutes in case they returned for some reason—it would be uncommon, but it had happened before. She thought of Randolph in the car, sweating, gaining confidence with each mile that took him farther from the purloined papers, that put distance between himself and his crime.

After fifteen minutes, she felt fairly sure that they were not coming back. She unbuttoned her blouse and pulled out the crumpled, damp papers.

There were only a few sheets. They didn't look like regular stationery. Each page had a red-striped banner that clearly implied importance and danger. She took the pages to the window to read by the day's last rays of sunlight.

TOP SECRET APOGEE

To: Army Air Forces Regional Headquarters, Alameda
From: William Miller, director, Project APOGEE

The first intact alien object was recovered on 30 AUG 1944 in the vicinity of Chico, California, enabling the team to make great strides in understanding its origin and purpose. In a bit of good luck, the sheriff who made the discovery is a reservist at Benton Field, who knew to phone directly to Army Air Forces Regional Headquarters, bypassing the usual army chain of command as well as the FBI. This has enabled us to keep the specimen to ourselves.

It is imperative that the following details be kept strictly within the APOGEE channel.

We are now able to confirm and disprove various assumptions made on the partial specimens retrieved to date. **The origin is Japanese** and intended as an incendiary weapon. Our findings thus far indicate that it is in all likelihood unmanned. It appears that the balloon was intended to set a fire wherever it landed with the purpose of sowing terror among the American public. No indication yet of the launch site, though our analysts believe they are being launched from a Japanese submarine surfacing off the coast of the western U.S.

Examination of the balloons led to an interesting discovery. Some of the balloons were found to be covered with a gritty substance that appears to be biological in nature.

Because this substance was not found on all the balloon remnants recovered so far, we assess that the Japanese military did not intentionally send this to the United States, whatever it is, but that some of the balloons merely had been contaminated while in transit.

Interestingly, the Japanese appear to have a sensitivity to this substance and so we are investigating whether it can be used in an offensive capability. **It must not be forgotten that Project APOGEE exists to conduct offensive operations.** We are readying Phase Two of our work: to test the Japanese weapon against a control group.

Meiko's stomach sank. It seemed unreal. She flipped through the pages again; it was a very official-looking report. Her sense was that it was real, that it wasn't some kind of propaganda deliberately fed to her.

There was a second report under the first. Whereas the first one had been written months earlier, this one was from a week ago. It was almost sunset now, and Meiko strained hard to be able to make out the words.

TOP SECRET APOGEE

To: Army Air Forces Regional Headquarters, Alameda
From: William Miller, director, Project APOGEE

I am writing to report an unforeseen development in our work. We have discovered an individual at Camp Minidoka who seems to have a natural resistance to the disease. This is the first such individual we have found and represents a huge potential gain for the program.

We have been trying to produce an antidote using traditional means, by inoculating typical donor animals to produce antibodies to be used in an antidote. However, none of the donor animals were able to overcome the effects of the toxin. The toxin is too strong. This left the men in our program at considerable risk: if one of them were to become infected, we had no way to cure him, and typically the end stage of the infection is death.

We are currently trying to develop an antiserum from this individual's blood. Once an antiserum has been successfully developed and can be produced at scale, we will begin Phase Two of APOGEE: exposing and infecting inmates at camps that are farther from population centers, such as Wyoming (Heart Mountain) and Utah (Topaz), before undertaking California and Arizona (Tule Lake, Manzanar, Poston, and Gila River).

It made sense now: her isolation, the endless siphoning of her blood. Why she didn't descend into raving, ranting madness like the others at Minidoka.

The attendants hadn't been lying. There *was* something special about her.

So, the authorities had messed around with a substance they didn't understand, hoping that it would make an effective weapon against their enemy, only to find out they'd put themselves in danger, too? She'd seen the terrors of the disease up close and didn't wish it on anyone, not even the people who'd hurt her and the other residents of the camp—and yet she couldn't deny there was a sense of poetic justice about it.

Why was she able to withstand this toxin? What made her different from the other internees? There had to be other possibilities, none of which this APOGEE team seemed to be pursuing. Had they tested all the residents at Minidoka, seen if anyone else had this immunity? If so, and they'd come up empty, there had to be something in her background or her environment that made her different, that gave her immunity. To find the answer, they'd have to ask her, but no, they treated her like a dumb lab animal. They'd stuck her in isolation when what she needed to do was ask the others where they'd come from, where they'd grown up, what they'd been exposed to. Without this, there wasn't a snowball's chance in hell that Meiko would be able to find the answer.

The best she could do was to cast her mind back and try to remember what had happened to make her special.

One thing was for certain, Meiko thought as she carefully folded up the pages again: she was not going to destroy these documents, as Randolph had told her. These reports were proof that the military was involved in something bad.

Proof that, God willing, she would be able to use against them one day.

20

Three dollars and seventy-eight cents.

It was all the money Aiko had, all of it found. Coins dropped on the side of the road. Change tossed into a well along with a wish. A dollar bill handed to her by a kindly old woman.

Was it enough to get her a bus ticket? She looked at the dirty money in her hand and then up at the board at the bus depot. Three dollars and seventy-eight cents probably would not get her very far. Surely there were more coins to be found here: the floor was a mess, dotted with candy wrappers, receipts, and discarded timetables. Mysterious brown dots scattered here and there that could be either old food or maybe, if she was lucky, coins.

She shoved the money in her deepest pocket and began wandering the depot, eyes trained on the floor as she moved from dot to dot. Most were, disappointingly, not coins but old gum or blobs of chewed-up tobacco or other bits she couldn't identify. She almost gave up, but then she found a nickel and this buoyed her hopes and she kept moving.

But, looking at the ground so intently, she didn't see the demon. Not until she had practically run into his legs.

He leaned over her, studying her. "Are you here alone?"

She stepped back, clutching her bag. When she looked up, she saw he was no demon but a police officer. She should have felt better, but she did not. "No, I'm here with my mother." She didn't like to lie, especially to a police officer. She wanted to trust him—her father had told her she could always go to a policeman if she were in trouble—but felt instinctively that under the circumstances, she couldn't.

"Here with your mother, are you? Where is she?"

"She's getting our luggage." Aiko thought of the *shinigami*, a demon of death who could take human form and was said to possess you through questions, making it easier and easier to tell falsehoods, until you discovered you'd become a demon, too, and begged to die.

The policeman was clearly losing his patience. "Is that so? Well, we have a rule against children wandering by themselves in the terminal. Why don't we go find her together, shall we?" He placed a hand squarely on her shoulder. The cold of his hand radiated through her and she wondered if it was the cold of winter, or the cold of the dead. "Lead the way," he said.

Aiko turned and started walking, not sure what to do next. Confess? Try to run? There wasn't much of a crowd; surely, he wouldn't have a hard time chasing her down. Still . . . she was small and quick, and he was big and heavy and, undoubtedly, slow. She tightened her grip on her bag. She might have a chance. A slim one, but a chance . . .

Suddenly, cutting through the low rumble of the crowd, three sharp barks rang out. Was someone traveling with a dog? No, that wasn't a dog's bark, not quite. A few people around her stopped and looked around. She looked around, too.

Then she saw it: a fox. Certainly not the same fox that had led her away from the train and through the desert, though she wanted to believe that it was. A big red fox had run into the bus depot and was now in the middle of the floor, unbothered by all the people swirling around it. Time seemed to stop as she took in the magnificent animal. It was beautiful, with a lush red coat and silvery white whiskers, and smart black points on its feet and ears. It seemed to be looking at her, just like her mother's *kitsune*, trying to tell her something.

It tipped its head back and barked again, sharply. This time the policeman noticed. "What the— How did that thing get in here?"

Aiko was relieved. There really was a fox in the bus terminal. For a minute, she was afraid she was only seeing what she wanted to see.

Then, swift as a hound, the fox headed straight for them. It wove in and out of the policeman's feet. It was big and forced the police officer to hop from foot to foot, waving his arms and shouting, trying to get away from it. It was then Aiko saw the revolver hanging from the officer's belt. *This fox is risking her life for me. He can pull out that gun and shoot her at any second.*

After that, she didn't need to think twice. Aiko took off, sprinting into the crowd.

She wasn't going to be able to disappear among the passengers. She needed to find a place to hide, but the depot was mostly open, just a seating area with benches where people waited for their bus to be called out over the loudspeaker. There were restrooms, one for men and one for women, but she knew better than to run in there: that would be the first place the policeman would look for her.

She followed a couple who rose from their seats when a bus was called, staying close enough so it looked like she was with them, but not so close that they would notice. It was hard to move so slowly, her heart pounding in her chest as every second she expected the policeman to grab her by the shoulder again. Once they were through the doors and in the big lot where the buses idled, waiting to board, she veered off, away from the crowds.

She headed to a dark corner. It seemed to be a place where luggage and cargo were held. She climbed onto one of the shelves and pulled some boxes in front of her. It would be only a matter of time before a porter took these boxes away, but hopefully it would buy her enough time to lose the policeman.

She sat in the darkness, knees hugged to her chest. At least she hadn't heard any gunshots. That brave fox! It *had* to be the same fox that had led her away from the train. Her heart hammered, and an ache rose in her throat. It must be her mother, watching out for her. There could be no other explanation.

But that would mean her mother was dead, and Aiko didn't want to believe this was true. There'd not been any kind of service or burial. She hadn't said goodbye. But there was something deeper, too. It didn't *feel* true, though she knew that could be wishful thinking.

She thought she would know if her mother were really gone, that she'd know it in her heart.

Minutes passed. The noise beyond the suitcases rose and fell. She heard buses come and go. It was stuffy in her tight space and she didn't think she'd be able to stay there much longer. Finally, she decided to risk it, and pushed the boxes out of the way. Under one, she found a long white envelope. It was too dark to read, so she put it in her pocket—maybe there was money inside—and crawled out on her hands and knees. She pulled her bag out after her and walked away as quickly as she could, before someone noticed. She thought a porter might have seen her, but he just gave her an odd look and let her pass.

Once she was back inside the waiting area, she brushed the grit and gravel off her hands and looked at the envelope. It held a ticket inside—at least, she was pretty sure it was a ticket. It said, printed in big block letters, DEP 1725 DEST YAKIMA WA.

"WA" probably meant Washington. That had to be in the right direction. It would, at least, take her closer to Bly, Oregon, than she was now. Bly was the last place where she'd seen her father. If he knew she was missing, he'd go to the places they'd lived before, Bly or Seattle, to look for her. She went over to the big map on the wall near the ticket window and searched for Yakima. She found it. It looked very far away.

She pulled out the ticket and looked it over, front and back. She checked the date. It looked good, but her stomach twisted: this meant someone had dropped it. Surely that person would come looking for it. There were four ten-dollar bills inside, too. A fortune. It felt wrong to keep it, like stealing. But there was no name on it: she couldn't give it back. She was in desperate need, or else she wouldn't even consider keeping it. She said a silent prayer for forgiveness, wondering if this was another sign that the *shinigami* had gotten to her, had made her more demon-like herself, just by his touch.

She was finishing her prayer when an elderly man came up to her. "Are you looking for the bus to Yakima? That's my bus, too. They just called it. We need to go to the boarding line." He was short and small, with white hair and a white beard. It might've been just because she wanted it to be true, but she thought he looked Asian. Maybe a little like the elderly men she'd gotten to know in camp. He spoke so gently and kindly that she felt she could trust him.

"Are you traveling by yourself?" he asked, his brows wrinkling toward each other.

"Yes. My mother is going to meet me at the bus depot in Yakima." She hated lying to someone who was being so nice to her.

"Aren't you afraid to travel alone?"

"A little," she admitted.

He looked her over, then smiled, the brows unknitted. "I'm

traveling alone, too. Why don't you sit next to me on the bus and we can travel alone together."

She shuffled alongside him in the queue to get on the bus, ashamed to admit even to herself that she did so because it would be easier if people assumed she was traveling with her grandfather. Besides, it was a comfort to be able to talk to someone else, to know someone was watching out for you.

"How are these seats? Do you like them?" he said, stopping at an open pair toward the back of the bus. He took the seat closest to the window and Aiko took the one on the aisle. They stuffed their bags in the space under their seats, and then the old man gave her a couple wrapped caramels from his pocket. As the bus pulled out of the station, he told her that his name was Thomas Chun and that he was of Chinese descent. He had been visiting an old friend in Utah but was heading home to Yakima, where he lived with his daughter and her family. "I have a granddaughter about your age. Her name is Emily. I suppose you have an American name, too," he said, sounding a little sad. "That seems to be what they do these days. Give the kids American names."

"No. My mother named me after her aunt. My name is—" and then she caught herself. If she told him her name, he would know she was Japanese. He would probably tell the bus driver and the bus driver would call the police.

He patted her arm. "Don't worry. I understand. You don't have to tell me your name. Let's just say for the duration of this trip, you're my granddaughter, Emily. You came with me on a trip to Salt Lake City and now we're going home."

She let out a sigh of relief.

"Don't forget: if anyone asks, your name is Emily. And I'm Grandpa Tommy."

He began to tell her about his life. "I didn't always live in Yakima. Until very recently, I lived in Seattle."

"I used to live in Seattle, too!" Aiko said, happy for the connection.

"Before they found out that I had a bad ticker, I worked at the Boeing plant outside the city. It was huge. As big as some towns. You probably don't know about them, but Boeing is the biggest employer in the whole state. They make airplanes for the military."

"My dad is a pilot. He's stationed in the Pacific, but he's on his way home to see me."

The old man gave her an encouraging smile. "I bet he can't wait to see you. Being a pilot in the war, that's a dangerous job, you know. But he must be very good. The military trains their pilots well, gives them the best equipment. I used to help build them, you know. Bombers, the real big planes. It was really something, working there. Sometimes, they'd bring pilots in to visit and they'd tell us stories—it was to help the designers make the planes better, you see. Tell us what had gone wrong, so we could correct it."

Aiko imagined her father talking to men in an airplane factory. He was good at explaining things.

"We were always trying to improve the planes. Make them safer or faster. Better." He was obviously very proud of his work. "We were always thinking of the men who flew them. We wanted them to survive the war and come home to their families. Like yours."

Aiko wanted to have something to say. She wanted to impress him. "My grandfather is a scientist. He discovered air currents very high above the earth. His name is Wasaburo Oishi, but my mother says no one in America has heard of him or his discoveries."

There was a slight frown on the old man's face. "Wasaburo, eh? He's Japanese, then?"

Aiko understood she probably shouldn't have mentioned her grandfather. *Japan is the enemy.* "Yes."

"Your mother is right. I've never heard of these currents."

"She says they're not well-known in America because Grandfather is Japanese. She says it would've been better for his discoveries if he was German or French."

Tommy Chun chuckled dryly. "She's probably right. The Japanese are pretty smart, like your grandfather, but you have nothing to worry about. Their planes and such aren't as good as ours. They could never make it all the way to the West Coast of America."

"They flew to Pearl Harbor, didn't they?"

"Yes, they did, but even to make it to Pearl Harbor is very difficult, very complicated. The West Coast is even farther still. The men in charge are sure they can't hurt the U.S., but just in case, they have special patrols off the coast at Seattle to look for Japanese submarines. They figure that's the only way they could hurt us, by launching off a submarine."

Aiko fell silent. She hoped no one on the bus had overheard them, or they might turn her in to the driver. She decided not to say anything else.

"Oh, I get it," Tommy Chun said. "You're right—we shouldn't say any more. Mum's the word." He dug into his pocket and fished out a couple more caramels, one for Aiko and one for himself.

An hour had passed when Aiko noticed the old man was not dressed very warmly. The temperature seemed to have plummeted once the sun went down. There was a drop of mucus hanging from his nose, and his lips and fingertips seemed to be turning blue.

Aiko undid the scarf around her neck and handed it to him. "Why don't you put this on? You seem cold."

He looked at it like it was a delicious piece of food that he longed to eat but knew he shouldn't. "I can't take that from you, my dear. You must be cold, too."

"I'm not. I'm dressed very heavily." She pressed it to his chest. "It would make me happy if you would wear this."

With a smile, he looped the scarf around his neck and tucked the ends into his coat.

THE FERVOR

A iko woke when the bus lurched to a stop. Where were they? It certainly couldn't be their destination, not yet. She'd overheard the driver tell one of the passengers that it would be sunrise when they arrived in Yakima. It was still pitch-black out.

Outside the window, she saw a sign: KLAMATH FALLS, OREGON. They were in Oregon! She had to get off the bus and check the map, to see if this was close to Bly. Her heart started to beat faster. Suddenly, she couldn't wait to get there and was impatient with the road. She turned to Grandpa Tommy, eager to tell him everything: what she was running to, what she was running from, how badly she wanted her father, how sure she was that he would be waiting for her.

But when she turned to the old man, she saw right away that something wasn't right. His head was tilted to the side and his mouth hung slack in a way that seemed unnatural. His eyes were partially open and his expression—blank, vacant—was terrifying.

What was more terrifying, however, was that he was crawling with spiders. Small white spiders, almost transparent. Like the spiders she had seen in the field outside the train station in Salt Lake City. They were here, too. Had they been on the bus or had the old man been carrying them, unawares? Her heart sank even as her throat tightened with dread. These spiders . . . were they magical, creatures sent by Japanese gods to avenge their country? Or maybe they were apparitions, like the spirits that had spoken to her in Minidoka.

She *hoped* they were apparitions, but she didn't think that was the case.

She jumped out of her seat, then caught herself. She couldn't draw attention to herself.

It looked like the passengers who wanted to stretch their legs or get something to eat had already left. Everyone on the bus—only about twenty people—was asleep. Still, she couldn't chance making any of them suspicious.

Aiko looked back at Grandpa Tommy. The spiders, she saw, weren't coming from the old man but from her scarf. They were crawling out of the folds of her scarf. *She* had brought them on board, probably picking them up in the field. She had given them to the old man when she gave him her scarf. It was *her* fault he was dead. She nearly broke out in sobs but managed to control herself. She was sorry, so very sorry, and beginning to panic. Who could she go to? Any authority would detain her again. They wouldn't let her go to Bly, and then she'd miss her father. And he wouldn't know what happened to her or her mother. And there'd be no one to help, then . . .

Shaking with panic, she pulled her bag out from under her seat. As much as it frightened her to go near the spiders, she very carefully lifted the scarf from around Grandpa Tommy's neck. Aiko tiptoed down the aisle, holding the scarf ahead at arm's length, careful not to let it brush any passengers. Once outside, she headed off alone for the dark woods.

21

IDAHO PRAIRIE

How many days had Meiko been confined in this prison? The scratches on the bed frame told her thirteen, but she wasn't sure that was right. She might've slept straight through some days; they'd drained so much blood from her that her days were spent in a stupor. Or they might've drugged her outright, keeping her in a twilight state. Hours seemed out of kilter, days as fluid as water.

Things had changed with her minders, too. Dave, the one who had acted like the team's supervisor, was gone. Duncan, the new man, seemed to be the leader now, openly bossing the others around and holding court in the back room behind a closed door. It didn't bode well.

At least he was chatty. He liked to talk while she was strapped down to the chair where they drew her blood—in ever increasing amounts, it seemed lately. Maybe he thought she wouldn't remember what he said since she seemed depleted and weak, and she wasn't about to give herself away. She slumped against her restraints, motionless, as he talked about what was going on in camp. He laughed at the violence, as though it was comical, and dropped names of the dead. He never mentioned Aiko, thank goodness, though she would've given anything for news of her daughter.

But the hardest time to keep still was when he told the others that the front office had been informed that Meiko's husband, Jamie, was missing in action, his plane shot down over the Philippines during a dogfight.

"Why would a guy who's a pilot and in the navy marry one of these slant-eyes?" he said as he tossed the vials in a satchel. "Fuck 'em, sure, but marry 'em? You'd think they had him figured for a sympathizer and kept him out . . ."

It was hard not to weep, to scream, to swoon. To freeze the expression on her face and keep all her fear bottled up inside.

Jamie is a patriot. He loves his country. She could barely keep from breaking cover, she wanted so badly to say something, to tell this monster that he was wrong.

Instead, she fought to disbelieve him. *Duncan doesn't know what he's talking about. He might not be telling the truth. He might be passing on hearsay.* She wouldn't listen to him.

If Jamie was gone, what was left for her in America?

If Jamie was gone, then she was truly alone.

That didn't matter. There was no going back to Japan. Not with the war.

Don't be afraid. The U.S. military would be looking for Jamie; they needed pilots. There were many small, unexplored islands near the Philippines where a man might go undiscovered for a long time; she had learned that from her father. The odds were high that he was alive and waiting to be rescued. She couldn't believe that he was gone. She *wouldn't* believe it, not until they delivered his body to her. Until then, she would keep believing her husband was alive.

Which meant it was her duty to stay alive, too, for him and for Aiko. Maybe that was doubly true for Aiko, now that there was a chance she'd lost one parent . . .

I won't believe that Jamie could be lost. They will find him, and we'll be together again.

After this fright, Meiko spent her days trying to figure out how to escape. *Aiko needs me more than ever. They will have told her that her father is gone, too. I can't let them keep me here.* But there didn't seem to be a way.

She lay on her cot, trying to conserve energy, and thought about the secret report she'd read. Giant paper balloons unintentionally carrying a weapon of some kind to America . . . The strange thing was, there was something familiar to this. Fantastical but familiar. Could she have read it in a book, heard it in a grandmother's tale? No, it felt more personal than that, more like something she had experienced. But she couldn't think clearly, probably due to blood loss, stress, and too little sleep. This sense of familiarity hovered outside her grasp like a ghost, begging her to see it. *Remember me. You know this is true, Meiko. Remember me.*

And then she did.

At first, she thought it was a story her father had told her, one of his folktales. Then, the more she remembered, she was sure that it was a long shot. After all, there probably were many kinds of poisonous spiders in Japan.

But there *was* a chance.

It had to do with a small, obscure remote island where her father had once inexplicably done something very strange to try to save her life.

And maybe this was why she was immune.

I'll only tell the man in charge," Meiko told Duncan. There was no way she would entrust her one precious shot at freedom to an underling, and an untrustworthy brute at that.

He threatened her but she didn't budge. He threatened her with starvation, beatings, the works—but what was left that hadn't been taken away from her already? "Take me to see the man in charge and I'll tell him. Only him." She bet that someone that important wouldn't want to make the long drive across a sunbaked, barren prairie to her cabin prison. If that was the case, he'd have been coming to see her all this time and not relied on low-level attendants to draw her blood and carry out his orders.

The next day, Duncan came alone to the cabin. He didn't even bother to take off his jacket but stood over her bed, jingling the car keys. "Get your coat. You got your wish. We're taking you to meet the doctor."

She did as he directed, silently buttoning her coat, following him to the car. Her wish, of course, would be to see Aiko and to be reunited with her husband, but she knew they were not going to let that happen. She thought of her daughter the whole long, bumpy ride to Minidoka. Her cabin prison was farther from the camp than she imagined. Her heart leapt when she saw the road that led to the front gate, but she was then surprised when they didn't take it.

Instead, Duncan steered the car down another road, one just beyond the camp road. They passed through the familiar barbed-wire fence and past a guardhouse—not one she'd seen before, though not unlike the one that stood at the entrance to Minidoka—that brought her to a completely unfamiliar place. It was mind-boggling to think they couldn't be far from the rest of the camp, from the vegetable garden and dormitory blocks, and this place was entirely unknown to her. She was pretty sure that she knew where the rest of the camp was—which direction it lay in, anyway. She would follow her instincts, if she got the chance to run away.

Duncan brought her to a building that looked newer than the rest of the camp. It was built better than the dormitories and kitchen and the other buildings used by the residents. She could tell it was less than a year old because the boards weren't yet worn by the brutal prairie weather. Nearby was a second building that looked like a barracks. That meant there were more army men at Minidoka than she'd thought.

As she was being escorted down a hallway, she heard a woman's voice raised in anger. They turned a corner and she saw two guards wrestling the young woman through a doorway. She didn't look like she belonged here in the middle of nowhere: she was white and well-dressed in city clothes and heels. The guards were obviously forcing her into the room: *She is a prisoner, too.* Strange.

Duncan brought Meiko to a room that looked like a laboratory, though not a well-appointed one like the one her father had taken her to see, occasionally, at the meteorological agency. This one seemed rudimentary by comparison. There were just a couple tables holding scientific equipment, beakers, flasks, Bunsen burners, and the like. To the side, there was a metal cabinet with glass doors, and behind those doors stood racks with row after row of labeled, stoppered vials. Vials full of red fluid.

She would've recognized those vials anywhere. They were the vials they'd collected from her at her cabin prison.

Her blood.

"I'm going to tell the doc you're here. I'll be right back. Don't do anything stupid," Duncan said before he left.

At length, a man came in. He was older, rather nondescript with white hair and glasses and a white lab coat. It struck Meiko that he seemed almost as exhausted as her. She didn't care for his expression, looking her over without an ounce of warmth, as though she was nothing more than a mouse in a cage.

He sat on a stool and wheeled over to her just like a family doctor, like he was planning to examine her. She drew away from him, as far from his reach as possible.

He smiled, but there was nothing reassuring about it. "Now, now, Mrs. Briggs, you've nothing to fear from me. My name is Dr. Barrett and I'm the head of this program."

"I didn't volunteer to be part of any program."

The smile faded. "You know as well as I that there's a terrible disease running unchecked through this camp, Mrs. Briggs. We've been studying you to help us understand what's going on. I wouldn't think that we'd need your permission to try to cure your friends and neighbors. I would expect that anyone would be happy to participate."

"And maybe I would have, if you'd asked me instead of locking me up against my will." She wanted to tell him he didn't fool her, that she knew about their classified program and that they were trying to weaponize the disease. Anything to wipe that smug look off his face.

"We had to isolate you from the rest of the camp for your own good." That didn't make sense, and he was obviously saying it in order to shut her up. "The attendants tell me that you *think* you know why you've been able to recover from the disease and that you want to share that with me."

She held her breath. This knowledge—her story, her past, her history—was the only bit of leverage she had. Once she gave it away, she had nothing. "Before I tell you, you must promise to reunite me with my daughter. That's all I ask."

Barrett exchanged a glance with Duncan, who stood by the door. Duncan frowned and gave a curt shake of his head. "I promise that we'll do that, Mrs. Briggs, but it will take a few days to make that happen. We had to send your daughter to another camp for her own safety, since there was no one to care for her here when you were hospitalized."

Meiko closed her eyes, fighting to remain calm. Everything he'd just said was a lie. They'd made her ill, in the first place. Second, she hadn't been hospitalized. And third, they could've easily found someone to take Aiko in temporarily—if they'd had any intention of returning Meiko to the camp.

"You have our word." *Worthless.* "Now tell me what you know."

She could think of no way to stall this man any longer, so she told him everything. How her father had taken her and her mother to Shikotan Island, and there was a terrible disease there, a disease that had plagued villagers for generations. How, in desperation for something to save them, her father concocted a tincture from something indigenous to the island and made her and her mother drink it every day. At the time, she'd been appalled and frightened—it had seemed as though her father had gone crazy—and the potion had tasted terrible. She thought he'd been brainwashed by the locals—he'd been charmed by one old man in particular—and given in to their eccentric ways. But she had never thought until now that maybe her father had been right, and that his tincture had worked.

That perhaps it was her father's tincture that had saved her now.

"And what was the cause of the disease? Did your father tell you that?"

Had he? A thought, a word hovered in the back of her mind, hidden, just out of reach. She had only been four at the time. Her memories would be slivers, at best.

"I'm afraid not. But it was something that only grew on Shikotan."

Barrett didn't say a word as she spoke, rubbing his chin, forming questions in the back of his mind, just as her father might.

"So, the balloons came from Shikotan," Duncan said. "At least some of them."

"Quiet." The doctor glared at the guard, apparently thinking it important to continue to hide the existence of the balloons from Meiko. Then he turned to her, his expression cool. "What you've told me is all well and good, but without knowing where the toxin came from, and how he produced the antidote . . ." He shrugged. "I don't suppose there are any records from that time, notes he might've taken of the process?"

There had been notes, however: her father's journals. The answers to all this man's questions could undoubtedly be found in those journals. Only, they were no longer in her possession. Her father had given them to her as a memento to remember him by when she'd left for America—perhaps knowing they would never see each other again—but she had insisted that Jamie take them, that they'd be safer with him. She hadn't any idea what conditions would be like at camp, if something as innocuous as a book with Japanese writing would be confiscated.

And now the possible solution to this terrible problem was gone. There was a slight chance they could be found among Jamie's belongings at whichever base he'd last been stationed, left behind when he went out on that day's mission. But there was just as good a chance he'd had them with him when his plane went down and, if that were the case, her father's journals were lost.

"Can you figure out how to make the tincture without his notes?" she asked.

Barrett wheeled away from her. "Your information, while giving us insight into why you're so special"—the last part said sarcastically, as though she was nothing of the sort—"is useless in every other way. We can try to find out what plants and animals are unique to this island you talk about . . . but that will take time, a lot of trial and error. And we might never find what we're looking for . . . No, I think we have no choice but to try to continue to develop an antidote from your blood. That's the only lead we have. The only course of action."

Or you could stop trying to develop this deadly weapon. Didn't the world have enough poisons?

This Dr. Barrett had no compunction about hiding things from her, lying to her. Though she felt, instinctively, that he'd probably told her the truth about sending Aiko away. Meiko had a hollow, sinking feeling that her daughter was gone.

She walked to the window and looked at the scrubby pines that stood between where she was and, in all likelihood, the rest of the camp. Not far away, the long, low buildings where everyone would be huddled, kept inside in the vain hope that it would save them from catching the disease. Children hugging their parents, hungry for comfort. Where was Aiko, and was she wishing Meiko was with her? She searched over the pines, the spare prairie, for the presence of her daughter, using her mother's sense. But there was nothing.

"Meiko!"

A voice called from below. She looked down to see Ken Nishi pointing up at her. He was completely frozen in surprise, his mouth hanging open.

"Ken!" She slammed her palms against the window, rattling the glass. She seemed to have broken Ken from his trance because he started running toward the building, yelling her name. She beat her fists against the window again, trying to smash it. When that didn't work, she searched all around for a latch, some way to open the window. She wanted to warn him, to tell him she was being held against her will.

Two passing soldiers were on him in an instant. The more they tried to quiet him, however, the louder he shouted. He jabbed an outstretched hand toward the laboratory. "That's Meiko Briggs! You told me she was dead . . ."

"You've got to calm down, sir . . ."

The soldiers wrestled with him, trying to get him to walk away, but he was having none of it. "Don't tell me to calm down. That's Meiko! We were engaged to be married. I'd know her anywhere . . ."

She kept pounding the glass. She didn't expect they'd allow any Japanese in this part of the camp, this secret part, but maybe it was because Ken was one of the leaders. He worked with the administrators . . . Maybe he had been given freer rein to move about the camp and he'd slipped through before anyone realized what he'd done.

Or maybe—and she didn't want to believe this—he knew what was going on.

Maybe they didn't keep him out because he was part of it.

He believed strongly that the residents should cooperate with the government, to show that they were "good" Japanese by being obedient. Good Japanese were obedient, that was how they were raised. It wasn't a hard message to sell. There were a few who wanted to protest, to rebel, to fight what was happening to them, but they were in the minority.

All this time, could Ken have been complicit? A sheep leading the rest of the herd to slaughter?

There was a scramble next to her as Duncan, seeing what was happening outside, rushed away to help. That left her with Dr. Barrett. He stood at a second window, watching the struggle unfolding below.

This was her chance. She did not need to wait for Ken to rescue her. She was familiar with this area; she could make her way to the camp, if not to town. She had a chance of survival.

But there was Dr. Barrett. He didn't look very strong but, more important, he didn't seem like the kind of man who did his own fighting, or that he would deign to grapple with someone he considered his inferior. He'd just call for help and watch as someone else subdued her.

That would be his undoing, she decided.

She picked up the heaviest thing within reach, a big bottle filled with some kind of liquid. It was easier to hit him over the head with it than she'd imagined. She wasn't raised to fight back, but months and months of rage had been building up inside her and this latest incident was enough to push her over the edge. The doctor didn't understand until it was too late, until she was right beside him with the bottle raised over his head. So fragile, his skull. She didn't see how egg-like it was until the last moment. It almost stayed her hand: she might kill him.

But she did it anyway, smashing the bottle against his head with all the strength she could muster. The glass shattered and he was awash in liquid, like a bucket of water had been poured over him. She didn't even know what was in it, it had happened so quickly. She hoped it wasn't harmful.

He fell to the ground like a puppet whose strings had been cut, like a man put under by a hypnotist. He was completely inanimate. For a fleeting second, she was afraid he was dead. But she didn't have time to worry about that.

As she ran to the door, she passed the metal cabinet, saw the bright vials of blood. Something twitched in her chest. It was their only chance of an antidote. *Well, they belong to me anyway*, she thought as she grabbed two of the vials and slipped them in her pocket. She wasn't sure why she took them, only that it seemed like a prudent thing to do. If they had wanted her blood bad enough to keep her a prisoner, then it must be worth something.

The halls were deserted at that moment. Perhaps everyone had rushed outside to subdue Ken, to see to the disturbance. As she sprinted past the room where they'd taken that woman, Meiko saw she was looking through the little window set in the door. "Let me out!" she shouted, rattling the doorknob.

Meiko hesitated. Obviously, this woman needed her help, but she didn't know anything about her. She might be trouble, or crazy. She could be a help or a hindrance. The guards could come back at any moment, however, and Meiko had to decide in this split second.

The fact that they considered her a threat was good enough for Meiko. She twisted the knob and flung the door open.

All the guards were with Ken in front of the building, so Meiko ran in the opposite direction, the other woman close on her heels.

After turning down a couple halls, Meiko found a door that led outside. There was a row of cars parked behind the building, all shiny and new. Meiko was about to sprint for the woods, but the other woman was running from car to car, looking through the driver's-side window. "Aha!" she finally said, opening the door. "This one has the keys. Get in."

A car meant they could drive away from the camp.

After a second's hesitation, Meiko realized she had no alternative. Even if she went to the camp to warn the others, they'd only drag her away. These insidious men were in complete control of Minidoka. She had to regroup and, somehow, find someone in a position of power who would help her.

She looked dubiously at the other woman as she fumbled with the ignition. In Meiko's experience, not many women had a driver's license. "Do you know how to drive?"

The engine roared to life, as loud as an airplane. The woman grinned at her. "Hang on," she said before stomping on the gas.

Her name was Fran Gurstwold, the woman explained as she sped down the highway. She was a reporter from Lincoln, Nebraska, who was following a story about the balloons and what was happening in the camps. She had pieced together that the balloons were probably Japanese weapons but the government had been hiding the story because it didn't want the public to know about it. Meiko listened in amazement, surprised that there had been newspaper stories on the outbreak, and that anything similar was going on in the other camps.

"That proves the army is up to something, don't you see?" Fran said. "Otherwise, how could the same disease break out in different camps?"

She had more pieces to the puzzle, but Meiko still wasn't sure she knew exactly what was going on. Her nature, and how she had been raised, made her want to trust those in authority. "It seems the army is trying to make a biological weapon out of whatever is on these balloons. A weapon to use against us, in the camps"—like the military was trying to exterminate them—"before using it on Japan."

"That's what it looks like to me. Only from what you said, what you read in those reports, it seems like this is only the first stage. A testing phase. Which makes you wonder what they plan to do if they can figure out how to control it. If they develop a serum from your blood . . . it seems pretty clear that they'll only give it to certain people."

Meiko watched the prairie outside the window, an unspooling of darkly ominous shapes. This area was isolated, and that was why the army thought it safe to run their tests here. She thought of Shikotan and what the islanders there had endured for centuries because they were isolated from the rest of the country.

The folly and arrogance of deliberately inflicting that disease on others . . . others who did not have to suffer. It was appalling. "We must stop them," Meiko said finally.

Fran nodded.

The question was how to do it.

As wolf song rose from the valley, they debated whether to keep driving. With the car being brand-new and with those California license plates, it seemed unlikely that they could go undetected for long. They would need to stop for gasoline, for food, to rest, and then someone would see the car, and they would be reported to the police.

The alternative was to take a bus, but Meiko couldn't make herself face what would certainly be an ordeal. At the least, she'd be stared at; she might even be accosted by white passengers. It had been so long since she had been in a place where the majority would be white that she wasn't sure how she felt about it. Would she jump every time someone turned in her direction? Would she feel the urge to run away and hide if someone spoke to her?

They decided to take their chances with the car and continued driving. Not that they knew where they were going. Fran just pointed the nose of the car west. Every mile they put between themselves and Minidoka pained Meiko, however. She couldn't help but feel that she was deserting Aiko, even though she was pretty certain that her daughter wasn't there. Those who *did* know where Aiko was were back there. She wanted answers. She wanted her daughter.

Be smart. Like Father always said you were.

"We must find somewhere we'll be safe. We need to think about what to do with what we know," Meiko said. She had Fran's well-worn AAA map open on her lap. They seemed to be in the literal middle of nowhere, with nothing but empty miles stretching in all directions. The only place where she really knew people, more than a nodding acquaintance, was Seattle, a full day's drive. It didn't seem likely they could drive for that long without being stopped by authorities, and then it was just a matter of time before the army showed up. And that was assuming any of the people she knew in Seattle—shopkeepers, her doctor—would be inclined to help her. You always think the people you know are good at heart; Meiko wasn't sure she wanted to test that. To see the extent of how much her people were hated.

Fran craned her neck for a sideways glimpse at the map. "Hey, that's where I want to go. Bly, Oregon."

It seemed a strange coincidence. Meiko knew Bly, but that place held very unhappy memories. "Why do you want to go there?" she asked uneasily.

"That's where one of those balloons exploded. It killed six people. The only deaths on U.S. soil from the war."

A cold tingle ran down Meiko's spine.

Fran kept talking. "This preacher and his wife took these children out for a Sunday school picnic and they found a balloon in the woods, and it exploded. It killed everyone except for the preacher. The wife was pregnant, too. Real tragic."

Meiko let the news soak in, saying nothing. She hoped it wasn't Archie and Elsie Mitchell, but how many preachers could there be in Bly? And Elsie had always wanted to have children. Her desire for children was, Meiko thought, the basis of the trouble between them. It had seemed that Elsie had always been jealous that Meiko had Aiko, had thought it unfair that her God had given Meiko a child when he wouldn't give one to her.

"What do you expect to find there?" she blurted out, her hardness surprising the reporter.

Fran swerved slightly. "It just makes sense, doesn't it? Every place where there's been one of these balloon sightings, the army has beat me to it and sewn everything up tight. But somebody's gotta know something. I gotta keep trying . . . I gotta believe that eventually I'm going to get a break."

Bly was where everything had gone bad. It was where Elsie had turned Archie against her and convinced him to break his promise to Jamie. But what good would it do to tell this woman? If this newspaper story was correct, Archie and Elsie had been punished. At no point had Meiko hated Archie Mitchell; she was merely disappointed that he had been so weak. That her husband had trusted the lives of his wife and child to such a weak man.

She didn't want to go to Bly, but it seemed fate was pushing her in that direction. Maybe it meant Archie Mitchell was ready to repay his debt to her, that he would help her out of this predicament. But for that to happen, he would've needed to have regained his conscience and she couldn't see that happening.

Fran drove straight through the night, a seemingly impossible thing to do as far as Meiko was concerned, but it didn't bother Fran in the least. The reporter seemed fine as long as she had coffee and cigarettes. When they stopped for gas, Meiko hid in the back seat while Fran got out to distract the attendant. Sometimes, she talked them into filling up a thermos for her. They stopped at a small grocery store in a sleepy town and picked up a loaf of bread, a hunk of cheese, and a jar of pickled eggs.

Luckily Fran had her purse with her and had enough money. Everything else was still at Jerome, she'd explained: the car a friend had loaned her, her suitcase, the tattered remnants of the balloon that started her whole mad search. "I bet it's all been destroyed. It would be evidence and they wouldn't want it around. It's going to sound a little melodramatic, but I think those guards were planning to kill me." Meiko didn't tell her that it didn't sound far-fetched at all.

Finally, the car rolled into Bly. As Meiko watched the town pass by outside her window, she marveled that it had only been a few years since she'd last been here. It felt like another lifetime. She directed Fran down the narrow streets to Archie's house. The entire way, bad memories of when she'd briefly lived here bubbled through her mind. The people here didn't like Japanese, though Jamie hadn't known that. She didn't want to go to the Mitchell house, either. She'd have been happy to live the rest of her life without seeing Archie Mitchell again.

But she didn't have a choice.

Last night, I went out to Fujin's plain, the place that the old grandfather showed me, and released the last of the balloons carrying my measuring instruments. As the night winds whipped and howled all around me, I caught the heated air in the tiny balloons that would carry my delicate instruments up into the sky. I stood alone, the sole witness, as my dutiful sentries rose higher and higher and finally disappeared in the darkness, on this final, important trip. I stood and watched them rise, watching until the last one blinked from view.

Carrying all my hope with them.

22

"I don't care if he's your best friend, he's asking too much of you." The left corner of Elsie's mouth hooked downward in a little sneer. "It's not your responsibility to take care of another man's wife."

"I gave my word—"

"It's not your fault Jamie Briggs rushed off and volunteered. And then left you to handle what he let drop to the floor. No one could have predicted what would happen"—he knew what she meant: the camps—"and you can hardly be expected to honor such an unreasonable request." She had her back to him as she folded clothes. "How would it look to the congregation if we sponsor them and then something bad happens?"

"What's going to happen? We know Meiko. She's not spying for the Japanese . . ."

"It doesn't have to be that. It could be anything. One Japanese in America could do one bad thing and then all Japanese are going to be judged." She was right enough there, he had to concede. "And then they'll be looking at you. At us."

"It's precisely because I am a religious leader that I should sponsor them. Set a good example."

"Except if things go bad, then they'll be questioning why they should *follow you. They'll be asking the church to send a new minister."* She jutted out her lower jaw, the way she always did when she had her mind made up. *"It's an unnecessary risk. If Jamie were really your friend, he wouldn't ask you. He shoulda asked his parents. They're family. It's their responsibility,"* she said. Then softening her tone, *"Besides . . . I'm sure the camps won't be that bad. They're camps. Fresh air and sunshine. They're building housing new—that's better than what we have—and let's face it, they'll be safer there."* She was thinking of the protests, the signs. JAPS GO HOME. People hadn't forgotten Pearl Harbor. *"Safer with their own kind."*

Her arguments exhausted him. Besides, he knew the truth.

It's because you don't like Meiko. Because you still blame her. Because you need someone to blame for what happened to us.

Though Archie understood. He still remembered the horror of that night, seeing the half-formed baby pulled out of Elsie's body. Hastily wrapped up and ferried away. Elsie weeping in her hospital room for days afterward, begging to be allowed to see the baby, railing against the unfairness that God gave babies to foreign devils but not to her.

He had tried hard to accommodate Elsie. Got one of the congregants to let Meiko and Aiko stay in one of their worker cabins across town so they didn't have to live under the same roof. Asked congregants to send some sewing and mending her way, to make a little money. It was Aiko he missed the most, such a smart kid, picked up anything you showed her lickety-split. He'd taught her to cut folded paper to make snowflakes, then trees, and before long she'd made a whole panorama of the mountains. Archie suspected it was Aiko whom Elsie resented the most.

This arrangement was barely working, and he didn't know how long it would last, but then the sheriff said there had been complaints and the government would send Meiko and her daughter to the camps if Archie didn't take them back under his roof.

He knew what he should do. What he'd promised Jamie, what he knew in his heart was the right thing to do.

In the end, however, he couldn't go against his wife. That would be wrong in God's eyes, in the eyes of his congregation. He let the sheriff take his best friend's wife and daughter away to keep peace in his household. Word would get back to Jamie, wherever he was in the Pacific theater. He just hoped Jamie would be able to forgive him, one day.

He hadn't thought about asking for God's forgiveness.

23

Archie woke to a dark house.

He thought he heard someone calling him—was this what had woken him? He kept still for a moment, quieting his breathing, his ears almost hurting from the strain of listening. But it was silent, nothing except the occasional chirp from a cricket or rustle in the bushes outside the window. Just his guilty conscience, then, dragging him back to reality.

He sat up and rubbed his head with both hands, messing his hair, but darnit—it felt good. Elsie was the only one who touched him. It was the privilege of matrimony, the pleasure and comfort of physical contact. How long had it been since he'd been touched by another human being?

He made his way to the kitchen. What would the day have in store for him? He might be contacted by Dutch or one of the Loyal Sons. They might drop by for coffee or to drop off more flyers to be slipped inside hymnals. They were coming up with new schemes every day now. They organized "spontaneous" protests, got people to gather at the crossroads that was the downtown and listen to Dutch or someone else shouting from a soapbox. They liked to stew with righteous indignation and feign punches at anyone who looked at them sideways. To crow about beating up Jap lovers and woe be to any Chinaman who showed his face around there. Dutch and the Loyal Sons liked to keep the fires stoked, to keep the townspeople past the boiling point of outrage.

It was exhausting. And wrong—he knew this by the prickling of his flesh at the very thought. He knew which half of his divided self was winning, though.

He poured leftover coffee into a pan and set it on the stove to warm, then stood staring across the yard at the shadows cast by the trees. The scene outside his window was bleak. Fitting, because Bly was in the grip of a terrible disease, one that was likely to claim a good many more victims. *That's the Japs' fault.* He worried for his neighbors, but he no longer cared about himself. He deserved to die, for what he had done to Meiko and Aiko, for betraying the trust of his good friend Jamie. He'd made a promise and he broke it.

And there was something else for which he would never be able to forgive himself.

A frightening dissonance was growing inside him, this hatred of the Japs and this guilt he carried, one he knew he'd have to reconcile one day. He would no longer be able to be a minister if he let it continue.

He knew in his heart, under the vestments and away from the altar, Archie Mitchell wasn't a good person. That would shock the people in Bly. None of these people really knew him. Certainly didn't know him beyond when he showed up in Bly as the new minister. They didn't know that he'd elected to study Christ's teachings in order to get away from his family in Franklin. They'd always been disappointed in him for reasons he knew only too well. In order to escape his parents' silent judgment, he dreamed of traveling the world, going to exotic places like Morocco and China and Argentina, strange places that only firmed his parents' suspicions.

The only way to travel like that, he figured out, was to become a missionary. He learned about it from a preacher who came to his church for a year—part of their training, the young man explained. You went to the school to become a missionary and after you graduated, you spent a year or two in America learning how to lead a congregation, and then they sent you abroad. Archie was encouraged to meet someone with the same dreams and aspirations, but the young man himself was disappointing. A one-trick pony, he only wanted to talk about religion and Christ and godliness but seemed to know nothing about baseball or music, which made Archie wonder what inner demons the man worked so hard to hide. There were always inner demons to be fought.

Archie decided he would find a way to become a missionary and leave Franklin, Nebraska, behind forever.

What Archie wouldn't give to have those carefree days at seminary back. When he thought of seminary, however, he thought less of the hours spent in classrooms than he did of his time at the boardinghouse on Pratt Street. The boardinghouse meant Jamie Briggs, the pilot who lived on the floor above him. A friendship blossomed until Jamie was more like an older brother, kind and smart and funny, and unlike Archie's real brothers in every way. It was as though, with Jamie and Meiko, Archie had found the family he wished he'd had instead of the dour midwestern clan he'd left behind.

Archie's classmates were for discussions about God and missionary work, and scuttlebutt on good postings. He turned to Jamie for everything else. The best music: Jamie listened to Ella Fitzgerald ("A-Tisket, A-Tasket") and Billie Holiday ("I'm Gonna Lock My Heart") but thought Mary Martin was sappy. He knew how to change the oil in an automobile (his father had owned a garage and made sure his sons weren't afraid to scuff their knuckles). He knew how to dress: Archie's classmates all wore old-fashioned wool suits, castoffs from their fathers and uncles, while Jamie wore pleated trousers and a canvas workman's jacket, and had his hair styled jauntily like a movie star. Jamie took him up in his two-seater crop duster, the one he'd bought with a bank loan. Sitting next to Jamie, for whom anything seemed possible, looking down at the lush green farmland outside Seattle, Archie felt free for the first time in his life.

He would always think of Jamie like that, a demigod who was able to fly, not bound by the same concerns as mortals. A man destined to be freer, happier, luckier.

It had sometimes rankled Meiko, Archie had seen, how her husband drew admirers to him like flies to honey. Every man has only so much attention to go around, which means someone gets shortchanged. Too often, that person is the wife.

Even a demigod has problems, Archie knew. He had read about Greek gods, after all. He knew of the travails in the Old Testament. He caught hints of a secret past that haunted Jamie. There were parts of his life that Jamie didn't want to talk about, those parts having to do with his family. All Archie knew was that Jamie was on his own in Seattle and hadn't spoken to his parents in years. They didn't even know their son had wed a Japanese woman; they'd never met her or their grandchild, an unthinkable snub as far as Archie was concerned. Whatever had come between Jamie and his parents had to be deadly serious.

Then, one day, Archie found out.

They were at the farm where Jamie kept his crop duster. It was a beautiful, sunny Saturday afternoon. Archie should've been studying—midterms were only a couple weeks away—but he could not resist the opportunity to keep Jamie company as he tinkered with the airplane. It was a little two-seater biplane Jamie kept in a barn in Ragnar, southeast of the city. A Stearman Kaydet, a tough little former navy training aircraft modified for agricultural work. Summers he used it to dust crops on farms all over the valley. Other times of the year, he used it to make deliveries, take businessmen to meetings in Vancouver or down in Portland.

It was just the two of them in the shade of the big red barn, Archie lolling on a couple bales of hay and Jamie leaning over the open engine compartment. That's when Archie made an impromptu confession. He told him about the silo fire that had taken his uncle's life—and then he told Jamie something else, something he'd never shared with anyone besides his parents. How he'd always suspected *he* was the reason his uncle had died that day. He hadn't known his uncle was in the silo, see, when he parked the tractor in front of the silo door. No one ever went inside; how was he to know that his uncle had ducked in? Or to know that his uncle had carelessly gone in with a lit cigar clamped between his teeth?

His parents had told him that it wasn't his fault, but Archie had never thought their reassurances sincere. From that day forward, his parents always seemed cool to him. From that day forward, he wasn't treated like his brothers, especially when it came to managing the farm. He was almost treated like a hired hand.

Eventually, he turned his back on his family, planning to make his life elsewhere. It was what had driven him to go to seminary, why he resolved—once he'd left—that he'd never see his family again. But the decision, even for being his own, had never sat easy.

Jamie could see that Archie was looking for reassurance. There was a long silence.

To reveal a confidence of this magnitude required a confidence in kind, Archie knew. If none was forthcoming from Jamie, it would mean that they were not as close as Archie had assumed. During the silence, Jamie stubbornly keeping his head buried in the engine bay, Archie worried that he had made a mistake, had presumed too much, and things might change between them forever. He was about to apologize when Jamie stepped back from the airplane, staring at the ground as he wiped his greasy hands on a rag.

And then he shared his darkest, innermost secret. A secret Archie never would've guessed.

"If my family knew what my life was like now—married to Meiko, with a half-breed child, working with Japanese farmers—they'd do worse than disown me. They'd want to see me strung up. They might even put the noose around my neck themselves." As he spoke, he refused to meet Archie's eyes and his face flamed bright red.

His parents, he said, were worse than mere bigots. His father was a member of the Ku Klux Klan. The Klan had started making political inroads in Washington State in the 1920s, and his father had been part of this, working to get politicians elected who were friendly to Klan values. In particular, his father hated the Asian immigrants who had come to Washington to farm. Their corner of the state had seen a sizable influx of Chinese, not Japanese. His father hated the Chinese with a passion. He refused to deal with any of the neighboring Chinese farms, to fix their tractors or automobiles, to sell them gasoline or parts. Under the cover of his Klan garb, he participated in night raids. He came home afterward and told his wife and sons how he had sent Chinese to the hospital, set fire to crops, killed livestock, even beaten whites who had been bold enough to show their sympathy for the Chinese. Jamie never had the nerve to ask his father if he'd killed any Chinese but he knew his father *wanted* to, and that was good enough.

Jamie's brothers fell in line, but Jamie could not. His father's behavior sickened him. There wasn't room for differing opinions in the Briggs household. His father did not know the meaning of the word "tolerance." There were fights, Jamie going to bed with a black eye or cracked ribs more than once. As soon as he graduated from high school, he went to live with a relative on his mother's side of the family in Seattle. "My family is dead to me," Jamie said, stuffing the rag in his back pocket. "And I'm dead to them, and that's fine with me."

If Jamie could see him today, practically a member of the Loyal Sons, what would he think? Archie's cheeks flamed with shame.

The coffee hissed like a rattlesnake in the pan. Archie looked down in shock: he'd gotten completely lost in his train of thought and the pan was nearly scorched. He snapped off the flame and dropped the pan into a tub of cold wash water, sending a plume of angry steam into the air.

He really should turn on a light, he told himself as he stood in the kitchen. But he didn't: there was something comforting about staring out at the world while hidden in darkness.

When he saw something move out in his yard, he assumed it was a tumbleweed. He'd seen more than usual lately, a bad sign since they weren't all that common in Bly. Those ghostly bundles made him think of animated cadavers rolling through town. But the movement in his yard—low to the ground, wavering in the wind—kept coming closer and closer, and it wasn't much like a tumbleweed, and he started to get apprehensive. It could be a wild animal approaching his house, a fox or a coyote. Could wild animals get infected with whatever was tearing through the town? He could think of no reason why an animal couldn't catch it. It seemed close enough to rabies. It was only a matter of time before one of them would get infected and then all hell would break loose.

Then he saw it clearly, the cause of the movement. It wasn't an animal. It was a human.

It was a child.

A girl with long dark hair.

Why would a child be standing in his yard, all alone, at this hour?

It had to be an illusion. Or a ghost.

God knew he deserved to be visited by a ghost. He had sent that woman on the mountain, hadn't he, the floating woman with the knowing smile. He and Elsie had had two miscarriages. Then there were the kids killed on Gearhart Mountain. Jay Gifford, Edward Engen, Sherman Shoemaker. Dick and Joanie Patzke. Any one of these innocent dead children would have good reason to haunt him.

He shook his head hard, willing the figure to go away, but when he opened his eyes, she was still there. She was closer now, close enough for him to make out her face.

He knew her. He recognized those features.

It was Aiko Briggs.

Or it *looked* like Aiko, and surely it had to be a hallucination because Aiko was a guest of the U.S. government, securely locked up in a facility several states away. There was no way she could be standing in his yard.

She was coming toward the house.

The sight of the little girl walking solemnly toward him suddenly filled Archie with panic. He was losing his mind, there was no other explanation for it. He'd like nothing more than to see Aiko again—he dreamed about seeing the girl, closest thing he'd ever had to a daughter—but Aiko was in Idaho.

He'd as good as sent her there himself, hadn't he?

He was having a psychotic break, succumbing to the disease or to guilt. He needed to go to the hospital, have himself checked out or locked up. But . . . the hospital was filled with sick people ranting and foaming at the mouth with hate. People he was afraid to be around. He couldn't go there.

She climbed the steps and stood outside his door.

She looked so real that, for the first time, he doubted what he knew to be true. *It's not a ghost, it's a real girl. Maybe not Aiko, maybe my mind is only making me think it's her, but whoever she is, I can't ignore her. She may need my help. Why else would she be here?*

He opened the door. Closer now, he could see the poor thing

was a wreck, her clothes dirty and torn, her shoes nearly falling apart.

She looked up at him with big brown eyes. "Mr. Mitchell? It's me, Aiko Briggs. Do you remember me?"

Of course, he did. How could she think he would ever forget her?

He went down on one knee and opened his arms. She fell into them.

For the longest time, he just held her, feeling her heart beating through her rib cage. When was the last time he had held her? She had been so much smaller. He almost broke into a sob for all the time that had passed. "I—I can't believe you're here, Aiko. It's a miracle."

"It's not a miracle," she said into his shoulder. "I walked."

She hadn't changed; she was the same forthright little girl he'd known in Seattle. He ushered her into the house, closing the door before someone saw her. "Really? You walked all this way? That's hundreds of miles. How did you know which roads to take?" The one thing he *wouldn't* ask her was where her mother was. He could only think of one reason Meiko was not at her daughter's side.

Aiko looked up, deep into Archie's eyes. "The *kitsune*—the spirit fox—led me here. She knew this was where I needed to be."

He heated up a tin of chicken noodle soup and used the last of his milk for cocoa. While she took a hot bath, he made up the couch for her: fluffed up a nice big pillow, got out two down-stuffed quilts. He gave her some of Elsie's clothes to wear even though they were way too big for her, rolling up the sleeves and tying the billowing fabric tight to her tiny waist.

It had come out as he fed her that the camp authorities had told her that Meiko was dead, but Aiko insisted this wasn't true. Well, that was natural: no child would truly believe a parent was dead unless they saw them with their own eyes.

"How did she die?" Archie asked, thinking it would help her confront her fears.

"They said she caught the illness. But she wasn't acting like the others." Aiko stopped eating and put down her spoon. "They took her away and three days later told me she was dead."

Archie thought of the scenes he'd witnessed in Bly. There were subtle differences in how the disease manifested in people that had to be incomprehensible to a child. He decided to try a different topic.

"Did you really walk all the way here from Minidoka? That's a long trip."

She toyed with the carrots floating in the soup, but it all came out, eventually. How she'd slipped off the train, the mad scramble after that to make her way home. Hiding on cargo trucks, walking for miles through the plains, then a bus ride through the night . . . She was a brave girl and lucky, no doubt about it, and the thought of such a young child traveling by herself through this madness— and the things that could've happened to her—gave him chills.

Through it all, she insisted, she was led by a spirit fox. The fox knew which way she needed to travel, whom to trust, what to do next. Aiko was grounded, Archie knew, not prone to embellishment. Meiko had been an adherent of another religion, Shintoism, which he didn't understand as well as he should. Jamie had assured him that there would be no conflict with the church: Meiko had agreed to raise their children as Christians. Perhaps this meant Meiko had stepped away from Christianity once Jamie had left. He sometimes wondered if she had converted out of convenience, to make Jamie happy.

He tucked Aiko under the quilts and gave her damp hair a caress. "Try to go to sleep, Aiko. You're safe now."

She looked directly into his eyes. "It's the same here as it was in the camp. People angry and fighting with each other. It's not their fault, you know. It's because of the demons. Demons are responsible," Aiko said, leaning over for her bag. She pulled out a notebook—Archie remembered well how she always had a notebook with her, no matter where she was, and how she was always drawing—and opened to a pencil drawing of a huge, scary monster with the long nose and exaggerated grimace Archie had seen in Japanese block prints and illustrations. He took the notebook from her and flipped through the pages. Every page held a Japanese monster. Floating ghosts in kimonos; samurai warriors with hideous heads; spooky monks bleeding from their eyes; indescribable, disembodied demon heads. Why would a child want to draw pictures of such frightening things? She was copying them from memory, no doubt about it, mimicking drawings she'd seen in her parents' books. Children excel in magical thinking, he knew. At this age, it was hard to separate reality from stories, especially beloved stories.

"You think the disease is being caused by these monsters?" he asked dubiously.

She took the book from him and began searching furiously through the pages. "No, the illness unleashed these demons. Anger. Fear. Unhappiness. These demons are here in Bly. They were in Minidoka." She stopped searching and handed the notebook back to him. "*This* is what's *causing* the illness."

Spiders. Lord help him, she'd drawn an exact likeness of the spiders he had seen from the day of the explosion, the spiders crawling all over this town. Tiny and large. Floating on the wind, crawling up a pant leg, dangling by a thread from the ceiling. Swarms of them crawling up a wall or dropping from trees. Their fiddler's arms waving manically. Their seemingly collective intelligence. She'd captured it all on these pages.

He gave the notebook back to her. "These spiders—you can see them?"

She looked at him as though he'd lost his mind. *Of course* she could see them: she was saying they were *real*. "I saw them at camp and I've seen them here. More here. They're everywhere." She gave her full attention to returning the notebook to her bag, tucking it among the other things she kept there (toys and such, he imagined, precious treasures after the tumultuous last couple years), and looked back at him. "You're not going to tell the camp officials I'm here, are you? I don't want to go back. I'm afraid to go back without my mother."

That broke his heart. He hadn't counted on how it would feel to have a child in the house after wanting one for so long. He and Elsie had tried time after time, once the pain of the miscarriages had worn away. He'd always told himself they were trying for Elsie, because she was the one who wanted children, but now he knew that was an excuse.

Once you let children into your life, it was hard to let them go. Aiko had come here for a reason, he saw now.

God had sent her.

He touched her damp hair again. "Don't worry, Aiko. You're safe here and you'll stay with me until your parents come back for you. I won't let anyone take you away."

I could scarcely believe the radio signals that came back from the balloons I sent out a few nights ago. At first, I thought something had gone wrong with the instruments or that someone was playing a trick on me. But after eliminating every other possible explanation, I must accept that they are genuine. The new wind measurements prove conclusively that there are patterns going on in the higher altitudes that could change the course of travel over the Pacific. It could be possible to travel farther and faster than we ever dreamed. Even polar travel may be possible as well. I told my superiors that I will write a new paper based on my findings.

24

Archie Mitchell's house stood in front of Meiko as though to say, *Here I am. You thought you were done with me, but you can never get away. Not really.*

It stood like a dirtied sugar cube on the side of the road. Besmudged white clapboard, black shutters. Sagging porch. A crumbling brick chimney running up the back of the house like a diseased spine. The yard was weedy, the trees overgrown and wild. Could it be that he didn't live there any longer, that the congregation had let the house go to seed?

There were signs of life, however. Empty milk bottles standing on the front steps. A shirt hanging off the clothesline, flapping in the breeze. Archie's Nash sitting in the driveway like a tired old man.

When was the last time Meiko had been in this house? The memories were so unpleasant she had banished them a long time ago. Elsie yelling at her husband, *I won't have that woman in my house.* Being sent to live in a dilapidated little shack down the road owned by one of the church families. Little more than a shed, no better than the dormitories at Minidoka. Like she was an animal and deserved no better.

It had been bad enough coming to live here without her husband but at least she'd had Aiko then. To come back now without her daughter, it seemed to portend what the future held for her. No husband, if what she'd overheard was true. No family. Her world shrinking, getting uglier and lonelier.

Meiko wasn't sure she could bear it.

She'd been thinking while in the car what she would do next. Fran would want to stay here to talk to Archie if he would allow it, to see what she could find out about the explosion that had taken Elsie's life, but Meiko did not want to stay in Bly. She would leave as soon as possible for California to search for Aiko. She would find out how many camps were in the state and where they were located. Perhaps Archie would lend her money for the trip. If not . . . well, she'd figure out something. This newspaperwoman would undoubtedly say that Meiko should remain with them, to deal with the authorities to find out where the girl had been taken, but Meiko felt in her heart that this would be useless. Why would the government help her when they were the ones behind this terrible scheme?

Only white people trusted the government. Thought you could take your problems to them and that you could expect to be helped. After years in an internment camp, Meiko knew differently. They were heartless, these people who claimed to be acting in your best interest, smiling the whole time but lying to your face.

She would be better off without this reporter and Archie Mitchell.

Nothing would stop her from finding her daughter.

Fran squinted at the dilapidated house, clearly disappointed. "This is where the preacher lives?"

"The house is owned by the church." Apparently, the church didn't believe in spending one more penny than was necessary to make its pastor comfortable. She remembered the groaning pipes and squeaky stairs, the roof that leaked in heavy downpours. Maybe the little shed had been better. At least it had afforded them privacy and shielded her from Elsie's rants and snowballing paranoia.

All she had to do was go up the walk and knock on the door, but she was having a hard time making herself go back to Archie Mitchell, asking for his help.

Suddenly, there was movement ahead. The screen door flapped open, and someone stepped onto the porch. A small woman—the housekeeper? Someone come in to take care of things now that the wife was gone?

No. It was a child.

"Mama!"

The voice was unmistakable but she was hesitant to believe. *My mind is playing tricks on me because I am weak and tired.*

A figure flew down the walk, hurtling toward her.

She felt her daughter's presence with her entire body, this little creature who was almost a part of her. She started to run toward Aiko but her knees buckled—exhaustion, starvation, blood loss— but it made no difference because Aiko was in her arms, face buried on Meiko's shoulder. "Mommy, Mommy, Mommy." The tiny voice she thought she'd never hear again. Meiko was crying so hard she could almost not hear what her daughter was trying to tell her, something about being told Meiko had died and being sent to an orphanage like the little girls in books she had read.

And how frightened she had been, how she had escaped from the camp administrators and followed a *kitsune* across the cold desert. Folktales and real life blended into one story. Could the child not tell make-believe from reality?

She'd even told a story about an old Chinese man she'd met on a bus who'd been killed by spiders. She'd been terribly upset when she got to the last part. "It's my fault, Mommy. I gave him my scarf to wear, but it was covered with spiders. I brought them with me from camp."

Meiko had no idea what she was talking about but tried to comfort her daughter all the same. "You are not to blame," she told Aiko. "If the man died peacefully, it was because his time had come. Back at the camp, none of the afflicted had died in their sleep. That was not the way it happened."

"I knew you weren't dead. I could feel in my heart that you were alive," Aiko said proudly, fiercely.

Without her husband, Meiko felt half-dead. Maybe that was how she knew that Jamie Briggs was no more: she felt it in her heart. She'd resolved on the long journey to Bly that she wouldn't tell her daughter about Jamie, not yet. Not until she received official notification. Why swamp the girl with more terrible news, after everything she'd been through?

For now, the fact that they had each other would be enough.

25

"We've got to figure out what to do next," Fran said to Archie as they sat at the kitchen table, hunched over cups of coffee. Meiko had left the two classified reports with them.

He pushed the sheets away from him. "I didn't want to believe her, but you can't refute these reports. She's right. Whatever is going on, the military is obviously behind it."

The two were alone. Meiko had gone with Aiko to another room, as though there was something contaminating about Archie's presence. She'd extended her condolences for Elsie's death, Fran witnessed, but in the stiffest way possible. And this preacher was no more comfortable around the Japanese woman.

Archie lifted his cup but didn't drink, like he was in a daze. "And you're saying we're on our own."

"I'm not sure who we can trust. The military is involved. Whether or not other parts of the government are, too, I don't know . . . I keep running into the FBI at all these places where the balloons have been found, but what their role is in all this . . ." She shrugged.

"What about the sheriff—can we go to him? Because otherwise, I don't know what we're going to do. We can't fix this on our own."

"Most of the sheriffs I've run into have been co-opted. They're doing what the army asks of them, shutting down anyone who has questions. Freezing out reporters."

Archie exhaled shakily. "What do you think is going on? Are they trying to wipe out people in the camps?"

"I think they found out those Japanese balloons brought something dangerous with them—though how those balloons got here, I have no idea." Fran shrugged again.

"Probably snuck ships in off the coast of Seattle and launched from there. That's the scuttlebutt, anyway: if there's another sneak attack, that's how the generals think it'll happen."

Fran rubbed her weary eyes. "Well, it appears the military is using whatever was on those balloons to make a weapon, and they're trying it out in the camps. Why not? They're a captive population, just sitting there. Who's going to know? Who's going to raise the alarm when they start dying? Only . . . things got out of hand. They can't control the disease, the prison guards get infected, and it starts to spread to town."

Archie frowned. "I can't believe that it was deliberate . . ."

"What's not to believe? That one report clearly shows they're trying to weaponize it."

"But it's so dangerous. If they did do this on purpose, well . . . they obviously didn't fully understand what they have."

"Obviously." Did this preacher think his government always knew what it was doing? That it always did the right thing?

The preacher shook his head. "How could someone in a position of authority get away with such . . . recklessness? To put the entire U.S. population at risk . . . It's madness."

Fran leaned back. Maybe he was starting to see the truth. "They were deluded, is more like it. Meiko said they had a lab where they were trying to develop an antidote from her blood. Once they had that, they could infect the people they wanted eradicated and keep the rest of the population safe. And it makes the people it infects look like they're violent and crazy. Even better for their purposes."

"They pretend to be the firemen when in reality they're the arsonists." Archie rubbed his face in frustration.

The two vials sat on the table in front of them.

"This is the antidote?" Archie asked, picking one up.

"We don't know. It could just be untreated blood. We have to test it on somebody who has the disease and see if it cures them."

Archie stared at the red liquid a long time. "Let me try it."

His offer struck her funny, out of the blue. "Are you infected?"

He got a strangled look. "I—I've been seeing things I can't explain. I feel like I'm losing my mind. To be able to blame it on this disease . . . that would be a blessing, honestly."

"I don't want to disappoint you, Archie, but I don't think that's the case. From what you told us, you've been exposed to it a long time, maybe longer than anyone in this town, and yet you haven't gotten worse." She remembered Richard in the hospital and how quickly he'd deteriorated. "The people I've seen or heard about start bleeding when it gets really bad. And they get—kind of crazy."

He set his jaw stubbornly. "I heard it affects everybody differently."

"Even if you did catch it, it doesn't seem to have progressed far. We don't have a lot of this serum—if that's what it is. We can't waste it."

He looked out the window to his parked car, seemingly turning something over in his head. "Well . . . if we need someone to test it on, there's no shortage of people in this town who seem to be infected. I can think of one guy in particular . . . He's pretty far gone. We could give it to him." But then he turned to her. "It's not going to be easy, though. Last time I saw him, he was completely rabid already. Are you sure you want to do this?"

The ordeal at Minidoka had been sobering. After she had been arrested and found herself being hustled to an unknown destination and unknown punishment, she had to take a long hard look at herself, at what she was doing. Had Richard been right? Was she in over her head?

She was exhausted. It was tempting to let Meiko and this preacher handle it from here. After all, she'd just been chasing a story. She could go back to Lincoln with her tail between her legs and try to put her life back together. As sensible as this sounded, however, she couldn't make herself do it. It was plain to see that, given the enormity of what they'd discovered, two people alone wouldn't have much of a chance. It was dubious that three would be any more successful, but the principle was the same: *everyone* would need to stand up to stop what was happening.

She plucked the vial from Archie's hand, then pushed back from the table. "It's for the good of our country. We have to try to save this country. We have to do what's right." Fran put the vials in her purse. Then, after a second's thought, she pulled out one and tucked it behind the coffee canister. It was good midwestern common sense not to put all your eggs in one basket.

Archie drove them to a farm far outside of town. By then, the sun was going down. They sat in his car, watching a small cabin. It sat down a dirt road from the main farmhouse, brooding in its isolation. A finger of smoke rose from the chimney, a sign that someone was inside.

Archie nodded at the cabin. "His name is Gus Wallaby."

"I know that name from Minidoka," Meiko said from the back

seat. Aiko sat next to her, drawing and humming to herself. As little as Fran or Archie had wanted to bring a child with them, Meiko refused to leave her at home by herself.

"The story I heard was that he was a guard at Minidoka but came down to help his family with the farm. He's the most rabid one I've seen yet."

"Do you have a plan?" Meiko asked.

Fran's proposal was simple. They'd found a hypodermic needle in the church's well-stocked medicine kit. Fran knew how to draw the medicine out of the vial and into the hypodermic, but she had no idea how they were going to get the serum into Wallaby. Could they overpower him? She hoped so. They'd brought rope but the idea of a minister tying a man to a chair seemed . . . well, unlikely.

"We'll try to talk sense into him. He knows you, Archie."

"He's *met* me," Archie corrected.

"Still, you're a minister. People around here respect the church. He should at least give you a chance to speak your piece . . . It's your job to get him to listen." Fran wished she believed this would work. "Meiko, you should wait in the car. The sight of you will only set him off."

She nodded, reluctant to have anything to do with someone from the camp.

As they walked together to the front door of the ramshackle dwelling, Archie asked, "What are we going to do if he doesn't listen to us?"

"Let's think positive. I'm sure you can be a lot more persuasive than you give yourself credit for. You're a preacher—you talk to people all the time." She knocked on the door before Archie had a chance to reply. She trusted her instincts and didn't want him to have too much time to worry. She wanted to get it over with.

"Are you sure we're doing the right thing? We're taking the law into our own hands—"

The door swung open. The man who stood in front of them looked like he'd been on a bender. His face was pale and sweaty, his eyes red-rimmed and bloodshot. He stood shakily in the doorway, gripping the frame to keep upright. Yet, he didn't smell of alcohol. And beneath the shakiness, he was obviously in good physical condition. Who knew what he was capable of? Fran thought of Oscar Hill, how the disease had made him like a baited bear.

"Mr. Wallaby? We need to have a word with you." She brushed by him with an air of self-importance, but Wallaby managed to stick his hand out in time to catch Archie in the chest. He looked confused. "Hey, I know you . . . We've met before. You're the minister in town. You're one of Dutch Talbot's men." He made a little hand signal that Fran didn't recognize, but neither did the preacher by the confused look on his face.

Fran nodded to Archie to close the door behind him. She dropped her purse on the table. "I understand you were a guard at Camp Minidoka, Mr. Wallaby."

He narrowed his eyes. "That's right. What's this about? You're not some Jap lover here to give me grief for doing my job—"

She drew herself up, shoulders back. People tended to obey you if you acted authoritative. A quick glance around the room told her that Gus Wallaby wasn't doing so well. He was living in nothing more than an old shed fixed up to give him a place to sleep, but it was a mess, with his clothing and belongings thrown about, newspapers on the floor, dirty dishes piled up in a corner. The windows were coated with soot from the little woodstove.

And the smell. Musky and acrid. Like something was molting. Like he was changing into something else. He knew he was sick and was in hiding. *He's sick and you're bringing him the cure.*

She turned to him. "You probably heard there's been an outbreak at Minidoka of a very contagious disease."

He edged away from them. "How do *you* know about it? There's been a news embargo on the camps . . . Who are you, anyway?"

She ignored his questions but was annoyed that Archie wasn't helping. Why wasn't he saying anything? He looked confused and stressed. Maybe he was a coward. Maybe he really sympathized with Wallaby and the rabid nationalists. Maybe that was why he was uncomfortable around Meiko and why he was vacillating right now. "Mr. Wallaby, we want to give you an inoculation. They developed it after you left the camp, but we heard you were pretty sick. As I said, the disease is highly contagious, and we need to keep this from spreading to the general population." Fran opened her purse and withdrew the vial and the needle.

The sight of the needle snapped Wallaby out of his stupor. "This doesn't make any sense . . . And I don't remember seeing you. If you're with the project, then you must know the code name."

Archie, do something. She tried to appear calm as she drew the fluid into the syringe. "We're not here to argue with you, Mr. Wallaby. Just take the injection—"

"If you don't tell me the secret password, I'm not going to let you stick that needle in my arm," Wallaby roared. He was as twitchy as a frightened horse and she was worried about getting within arm's reach of him, but there was no way to avoid it.

The classified report. She tried to picture the banner at the top of the page, but the word floated in and out of focus in her mind. It began with an "A," and it was short. At least she remembered that much . . .

The words snapped into place. Big black letters. "Apogee. It's Apogee."

He blinked at her, uncomprehending. That was the name of the project but apparently not the code word he expected. Damn, she'd guessed wrong.

"You're not with the camp . . ."

"We didn't say we were." Archie, at last, had found his voice. He took a step toward Wallaby, holding his hands out like he was trying to soothe a nervous animal. "We're here as Good Samaritans, Gus. You're not well. We're here to help you."

"Save all that Good Samaritan talk for Sunday, preacher. What's gotten into you? I thought you were one of us but you're helping this Jap lover. You're a race traitor."

Fran looked at Archie. *He is one of them?* No wonder Meiko didn't like him.

Taking Fran completely by surprise, Archie leapt at Wallaby. He managed to grab him from behind, pinning his arms back. Wallaby seemed as strong as a horse, though, and Archie wasn't able to hold him for long. He broke free, then spun around and grabbed Archie, powerful hands closing on his throat. *I have a few seconds, tops,* Fran thought, holding the needle upright. But when she was about to plunge the needle into his arm, he released Archie and turned on her.

"You're not sticking me with that. There's nothing wrong with me. I signed up for this. I'm proud of what I've done, of what *we've* done. You're the ones who are sick," he sneered, eyes wild. He knocked the needle out of her grip, sending it to the floor.

He lunged at Fran, grabbing her wrist. With a twist of her arm, she managed to slip out of his grasp, though his grip had been strong. She couldn't let him get hold of her again. She needed to keep the table between them. It was like being chased by a bull.

Where's Archie? If he wasn't coming to help her, he must've been hurt. Wallaby could've snapped his neck but there was no way to check on him.

Wallaby scrambled over the table and managed to hook Fran's

sleeve as she tried to evade him, throwing her off balance. The two tumbled to the floor. He had a good fifty pounds on her, dead-weight pinning her down. She tried to push him off, tried slapping and kicking and clawing, but nothing she did seemed to have any effect. It was like he was possessed. He wrapped his hands around her throat and started squeezing, cutting off her oxygen immediately. *This is what he did to Archie. He knows how to kill people. He's not just some camp guard—he's got training.* With instant clarity, she knew she wouldn't last long.

Did she feel the commotion behind her, the rush of footfall on the floor? She certainly felt the zing of impact, a tremor that traveled from Wallaby to Fran like a seismic quake.

Suddenly, the hands at her throat went slack and the weight lifted off her chest. She opened her eyes to see Wallaby lying beside her. There was blood everywhere: splattered across the floor, pooling under him. There was also a huge gash to the side of his skull.

Meiko stood behind him, holding a poker, shaking from head to toe. She dropped the iron to the floor with a thud. "This man isn't Wallaby. I knew Wallaby in Minidoka. This man isn't one of the camp guards. He's one of *them.* The ones from California who brought the disease to Minidoka. I saw him spreading spider eggs throughout the camp one night."

Rubbing her throat, Fran looked from Meiko—chest heaving—to the still body on the floor, to the bloody poker. "I think you might have killed him." Across the room, Archie sputtered as he rose from where he'd fallen.

There was a look of sheer determination on Meiko's face. "I'm not sorry. He deliberately infected me. He tried to kill me. He's not a man, he's a monster. When I saw him on top of you . . . I know what he's capable of."

They found piles of printed leaflets stacked by the door.

AMERICA IS BEING OVERRUN BY YELLOW DEVILS!

DON'T LET THE JAPS STEAL OUR COUNTRY.

AMERICA BELONGS TO WHITE PEOPLE.

At the bottom of the handbill: *Loyal Sons of the Republic* and a drawing of the American flag adorned with skull and crossbones.

Meiko held another flyer with shaking hands, this one with Elsie's picture. She waved it at Archie. "How could you let them make Elsie into a martyr for their cause? I knew Elsie didn't like us . . . But you? Do you really think we are out to hurt you? Did you hate us the whole time we knew you?"

The preacher hung his head. "Of course not. You know I don't agree with this. I'm a Christian. I know this isn't right. But after Elsie's death, I don't know what happened . . . Everybody around me seemed to believe in this. They were *so sure* and . . . I just got caught up and it got away from me . . ."

Fran sifted through the stacks of handbills. Sheet after sheet of hatred. One flyer urged people to get more guns. *The Japs will be on U.S. soil any day! Arm yourself against the Yellow Menace. Teach your children to shoot before it's too late.* Another advertised a gathering at a nearby armory.

There was a handwritten note on top of that last stack. *Rally*, it read. Underneath, a checklist of names. Fran shoved it under Archie's nose. "That's a lot of people. Recognize any of them?"

Archie squinted, looking it over. "Practically every man in town is on that list." He pointed to one name. "That's the sheriff. The next three are his deputies."

Fran whistled. "So, law enforcement doesn't just know about the Loyal Sons—they're members."

Once they were back in the car, they drove away from the farm down a lonely road. Meiko made Aiko stay in the car and the three adults walked into a field to talk.

It was a lonely, bleak patch. The vegetation was brown and brittle, already killed by frost, and the ground was muddy in some places, hard as rock in others. Cold seemed to rise from the earth, particularly now that the sun was setting. Cows lowed in the distance, demanding to be fed.

Meiko crouched by a stream to wash the blood from her hands. *How can she be so calm? It's because she's in shock; we're all in shock*, Fran told herself. Meiko had saved her life, hadn't she? She had acted in their self-defense. This wasn't murder. The man was obviously a trained killer. Fran knew she should be grateful to Meiko, but the whole thing still left her rattled.

Archie rubbed his upper arms; he, too, was apparently having a hard time dispelling the chill. "It's only a matter of time before someone finds the body. He's one of the leaders of the Loyal Sons . . ."

"He was part of the army unit at the camp, the unit that was spreading the disease," Meiko said. "That proves there's a connection between the Loyal Sons and the military."

"They're going to get suspicious when they find out he's dead," Archie said. "They'll start looking for who did it—"

"How will they know it's us?" At that moment, after everything Fran had been through in the last couple days, she couldn't stand for it to get any worse. The army and law enforcement working with a hateful group like the Loyal Sons, the Ku Klux Klan by another name. The fact that Bly, a little piece of the American heartland, was literally crawling with men and women as bigoted as any Nazi made her nauseous. Did this mean America was secretly riddled through with racists? Had they been silently judging her—a Jew, an orphan, a woman trying to make her way in a man's world—her whole life and she just hadn't seen them?

Maybe she hadn't seen them because she didn't want to. It was easier to pretend they weren't there. That everything was fine.

Archie thought for a moment. "Someone might've been watching from the farmhouse. Or recognized my car. The other thing that makes me nervous is that they know I know about them . . ."

"We should probably take precautions. Hide out. They'll only become more suspicious when they find out I'm back in town with my daughter," Meiko said.

Archie looked from face to face. "I know a place we can hide for a while. A cabin close to where we found the bomb. For obvious reasons, people have been told to avoid the area. We shouldn't be bothered there."

They walked toward the car. "We'll need to go back to the house to get a few necessities," Archie continued as they took their seats. "Clothing, blankets. Food and water. That won't take too long. Then we'll head up to the cabin."

"Cabin?" Aiko spoke up for the first time since they'd set out for Wallaby's shack. "Are we going camping?"

"Yes," Meiko answered. "We're going camping for a few days." If the child thought this was strange, to go camping in the midst of everything, she didn't say anything.

Fran knew this plan was sound and that it should bring her some peace of mind. But all she could think about was the sight of Wallaby's body on the floor and his blood seeping into the old floorboards, and the pile of handbills and placards waiting for distribution.

There had been a lot of handbills, probably more than enough for every man, woman, and child in Bly several times over. Who were all those handbills for, really?

Things were undoubtedly going to get a lot worse quickly. Her teeth started to chatter. For a second time, she wondered if she should leave them and head back to Lincoln. Pick up the tattered remains of her life. Once word of the affair with Richard got out—and it seemed this inevitably happened once the wife knew—she would need to move to another city, one that was far away enough that her reputation wouldn't follow her. She needed a paycheck and, with the war rumored to be winding down, to find a job before all those men came back from the Pacific.

But . . . no. She knew she'd never be able to turn her back on *this* fight. Fran Gurstwold was never one to walk away from a challenge, especially one as ugly and dirty and pervasive as this.

After all, America was her country, too.

They were not out of the woods yet. Not by a long shot.

26

It was strange for Meiko being back at the Mitchells' house.

Every minute she was there, all she could think about was Elsie's betrayal. It felt like that woman's strong, capable hands were at her throat the entire time, keeping her from breathing. She had to force herself to calm down, to ignore the sour wash gurgling up her esophagus or fear tightening her chest. But it was more than just Elsie's betrayal; the visit to Wallaby's shack proved that.

This town—where Jamie had once expected her to live, to raise her daughter—was riddled with white nationalists. Archie had been blind to it because he wanted to believe the best of everyone. Or maybe it was fear buried deep inside that made him ignore what was happening all around him. Maybe he was afraid of the hateful nature of his fellow whites—well, he could afford to pretend it didn't exist because he was white, too. They wouldn't come for him in the middle of the night with a noose and a can of kerosene. Pretending didn't cost *him* anything.

Clearly, he had let himself be drawn into their crowd. Been part of that world—the fact that he knew of Wallaby's involvement, the flyers and posters of Elsie were proof. He had blinded himself to it, pretended he could hate Asians and still be a good person. That he was good enough to take to the pulpit every Sunday and tell his fellow racists that they were good, God-loving people, too.

She couldn't afford to live in a pretend world, however.

We must get out of here. Our lives are in danger.

She didn't want Aiko to pick up on her fear. As long as they hurried, they were safe enough for the moment. Elsie—who had hated her for no good reason that Meiko could see—was gone. Soon, they would be miles and miles away from town.

Fran was frowning when she came out of the kitchen. "Archie, there's nothing in your refrigerator except moldy casseroles and sour milk." And a whole lot of empty beer bottles in the trash, Meiko had noticed.

"There's tinned soup in the cupboard. Should be a jar of peanut butter, too."

"That's not enough for four people to live on." Fran picked up her purse and started for the door. "I saw a corner store, just down the street. I'm going to get a few things."

"We shouldn't separate," Archie said. "It's not safe."

"We can't go traipsing off into the woods without food. I'm a city girl: I wouldn't know how to cook a squirrel even if I caught one. I'll only be a minute," Fran said.

Archie stood dumbfounded as she walked out the front door. Maybe he was used to women doing what he said? Elsie had been obedient, even if she'd had a way of making Archie believe her ideas were his. He heaved a sigh before turning to Meiko. "Alright, looks like it's up to you and me. Whaddya say we go upstairs to pack a bag? You need something to wear. You can have your pick of Elsie's things . . ."

She didn't want to wear Elsie's clothes or be close to anything she had touched. But what choice did she have? Meiko's own clothes were in tatters. She was filthy and longed for a bath—but there was no time for that, not even a damp washcloth. Resigned, she followed

Archie upstairs to the closet in his bedroom. She picked out the pieces that were closest to her size and to Aiko's, and put them in a suitcase. She made a pile of blankets and quilts.

She lugged the suitcase and blankets downstairs to find Archie in the kitchen, filling jugs with tap water. "This is ready to go to the car," she told him. She could hardly take it out there herself, not when she might be seen. It would be safer if Archie did it.

A noise came from the front door, a loud knock. Before Archie could put down the jug he was filling or Meiko could hustle Aiko out of view, the door flew open with a bang. A man Meiko didn't recognize barged in, a big white man much older than Archie. He pointed at Meiko and her daughter, his face contorted with anger and fear.

"Lisa said she saw you bringing Japanese into your house, Reverend, but I didn't want to believe her. I wanted to think it was just hen talk. I had to see the proof with my own eyes," he bellowed. His outstretched finger trembled.

Archie stepped between them and the man, holding his hands up. "Take it easy, Charlie. You met these two a couple years ago, don't you remember? They were members of our church. We gave them sanctuary."

"That was before this outbreak . . . Now everybody in town's sick and it's their fault."

Meiko tried to assess the shaking hands, the fiery eyes. Was this man infected, too? Was this illness talking or plain hatred?

"Now, Charlie, use your head. Follow the *facts*. People were sick before they arrived. You can't blame them."

"They came from the camp where the sickness started. That's what Dutch Talbert says . . ."

Archie dropped his hands in disgust. "You can't listen to Dutch. He's got another agenda. You gotta believe me."

Meiko had no sympathy for this distraught man; they had

whipped themselves into a frenzy over what one person told them. Were their lives so empty that they would believe anything? Tell them any stupid lie and they would swallow it like it was medicine and ask for more.

"You sold out your race," Charlie said. "They're gonna string you up right next to 'em." Those words went through Meiko like electricity. The people in this town were fearful and it sounded like they had a plan. Her daughter's life was in danger.

"Charlie, if they were bad, would *I* be helping them? I took a vow to minister to my flock. Your neighbors. I wouldn't do anything to hurt them—or you. Do you trust me, Charlie?"

Archie was still a fool, Meiko thought with disgust. He put such faith in his powers of persuasion, but it wasn't *his* life on the line. She didn't trust him to save her or Aiko.

She knew she was capable of stopping this man. She thought of the army agent, how it had felt when the poker connected with his skull, the sickening way it had yielded under the blow. The unnatural crack, the fountain of blood. It had been the same with Dr. Barrett, the same gut-wrenching, dizzying feeling.

What was happening to her? What was she turning into? If you had asked her even a few years ago, before Minidoka, when she still had Jamie at her side, if she would ever hurt another person, she would've thought you were mad.

She might've had immunity, but it looked like she hadn't escaped this disease unscathed.

But she knew she would do it again to protect her daughter.

Archie took a step toward the farmer. "Charlie, you can't say anything about this to anyone. Do you understand? The way things are in town right now, our lives would be in danger if anyone knew we were here. You wouldn't want that on your conscience, would you? I know you're a good man."

But the old man was heading toward the door, moving fast. "I'm sorry, Archie, but I can't let you get away. None of you."

Meiko looked around but there was nothing suitable at hand. How would she stop him? He was big, a heavy man. She could hardly stop him by herself.

The next thing she knew there was a loud crack, and Charlie the neighbor was lying on the floor with Archie standing over him, the remnants of a chair in his hands. Splintered wood lay scattered at their feet. The old man appeared to be breathing, but he was out cold.

"Golly, Mr. Mitchell!" Aiko said loudly. Meiko wished her daughter hadn't seen that, of course, but aside from that she was amazed.

Archie Mitchell had stood up for them.

They rushed now. They ran to the car—thank goodness Archie had thought to pull it behind the house where they had a bit more privacy. As they carried out the bags and jugs of water, Meiko thought she heard the sound of a crowd coming up the street. Maybe it was the wife, alarmed when the old man hadn't returned. She pushed Aiko into the back seat while Archie latched the trunk. He started the car and stomped on the gas.

"What about Fran?" Archie asked, swinging the car into the street. "Should we wait for her?"

Meiko was pretty sure the mob stood between them and the corner store. "She'll be okay. She's resourceful. We can come back when things have quieted down." Meiko wasn't sure that she believed her own words but could see no choice. Fran's face was white. She wasn't in immediate danger, not like Aiko.

Out the back window, she watched the neighborhood shrink as

they pulled away. As the jumble of angry voices died, she scanned the sidewalks for a sign of Fran, but there was none. A plume of black smoke started to rise in the air, and it seemed to be rising from the area of Archie's house. If the minister noticed it, he didn't say a word.

It took a long time to get to Gearhart Mountain, but that was because Archie got turned around once it got dark and they ended up getting lost on the endless unmarked access roads. The minister was tired, Meiko suspected, slumped over the steering wheel and constantly rubbing his eyes. He didn't say one word about what he had done. His nerves were undoubtedly as frayed as hers. But he hadn't abandoned them when he could have walked away and left her to a mob of rabid racists. She gave him credit for that.

Arriving at their destination, Meiko saw that their worries weren't entirely over. The cabin was worse than the dormitories at Camp Minidoka, old and weatherworn and dirty. Plus, it was deep in the woods: they'd had to leave the car and walk in the dark, toting jugs of water and blankets, Archie hauling their suitcase. It didn't seem smart to be so far from their sole means of escape, but she supposed they had no alternative, other than for the three of them to sleep in the car.

Once inside, she saw how truly ramshackle it was. A thick coat of dust covered every surface, some sporting a trail of animal prints. There was the absolute minimum of furniture: two war-surplus cots, a few camp stools, a small table. There was a fireplace but no stove. And no toilet, not even an outhouse. "It's a shelter for hikers. It's meant to provide the barest necessities," Archie explained apologetically.

While he gathered firewood, Meiko tried to get them settled.

She made up a cot for Aiko, wrapped her in a blanket and told her to try to sleep. Once Archie got a fire going, Meiko felt her spirits lift a little. Light and warmth worked wonders. She set a pan of water over the fire for washing, eager to wipe away several days' grime.

"There's a day I don't ever want to experience again." Archie sat on the floor and pitched pinecones into the flames. "The part that I can't stop wondering about is why *I* haven't come down with the disease. You, I understand. Fran showed me those intelligence reports. She explained that they hoped to use you to make something to combat the illness. But I've been around plenty of people who caught it, right? So why haven't I gotten sick?"

Meiko dipped a cloth into the warm water and pressed it against her neck. "I can't answer that. Only, it seems in every outbreak there are some people who don't get sick, either through sheer luck or some factor we don't know about." She thought of her father the scientist, who had spent many an hour explaining how the world worked to Meiko. Oh, her mother had objected, wanting Meiko to learn, instead, all the things expected of a good wife and mother. Her mother's training had been put to use over the years, Meiko had to admit, but it was her father's knowledge that would save everyone now. "You may have some other kind of immunity that we don't know about. Or, for some reason, the spiders chose not to bite you."

He hung his head. "You don't understand . . . I wanted to think that my anger, this terrible anger like nothing I've ever felt before, was because I'd caught this disease. If I hadn't, then it means this hatred, this weakness . . . it's all me. It came from inside me."

And it's up to you to take responsibility for it. But she couldn't say that to him. He had to realize it for himself.

To change the subject, she told him her immunity was probably a result of something her father had learned on Shikotan Island.

"The doctor at the camp said if we had his journals, we could figure out what it was he'd done and make the tincture more quickly . . . otherwise, it's trial and error, and might take a very long time. He would've made a record in his journals, I'm sure of it, he was diligent that way, but . . . No use in wishing for them. They're gone." Meiko pressed the hot cloth against her face. She regretted the stupid thing she'd done, insisting that her husband take her father's precious journals with him when he shipped out. She'd let go of the last thing she had of her father's, the last tie that had bound them together, and now she was being punished for being so careless with his memory.

Aiko sat up in her cot across the room, disheveled hair falling in her eyes. "They're not gone, Mama—I have them." Before Meiko could ask what she was talking about, Aiko climbed out of bed and dove under the cot, pulling out her bag. She trotted across the room, clutching something to her chest. With a wince of apprehension, she handed them to her mother: there were Wasaburo's journals, tied up with a navy blue ribbon.

"Where did you get these?" Meiko asked, incredulous.

She shrank back a step, uncertain how her mother was going to react. "Don't be mad at me. I took them out of Daddy's duffel bag. "I saw them and thought of Grandfather and . . . I wanted something of him for myself. I couldn't let them go."

She'd never been so happy that Aiko had disobeyed her.

Meiko flipped through the pages. They weren't quite as she'd expected. That's right: her father didn't keep his journals in Japanese. They were written in blocky roman letters: Esperanto. He'd been a firm believer in internationalism. Japan had been isolated from the rest of the world for most of its history, and he thought language was mostly to blame. The world would be forever ignorant of Japanese achievements because they were written in a language few outsiders understood, he'd insisted. He wrote about all his studies and experiments in Esperanto so—in case anything happened to him—his ideas would still be available to the global scientific community.

"I'll have to learn Esperanto," Meiko said, a little deflated. Without her father to teach her, how long would it take to learn on her own? She squinted at the pages. Roman letters were still unfamiliar to her, despite years of living in the United States. Could she even do it?

"Don't worry, Mama. I'll teach you. Or I can read it to you," Aiko said brightly.

"You taught yourself Esperanto?" The girl had always been good with language.

Aiko nodded. "It wasn't hard. It's like figuring out a code. It was kind of fun."

Then Meiko saw it: Aiko was just like Wasaburo. The kind eyes, the firm mouth. Even her expression, both open and wise at the same time. So full of curiosity and confidence. Blessed with the same gifts. Her father would be proud of Aiko. There was so much of him in the little girl—thank goodness.

27

Meiko and Aiko had finally fallen asleep, Archie saw from across the cabin floor. He'd watched them labor for hours over the notebooks, Aiko showing her mother how the language worked, explaining what the words on the page meant. *What a smart little girl.* She'd changed so much from the shy and frightened girl he'd known a few years earlier, afraid to make friends with anyone in Bly Sunday school. He was glad to see—as terrifying as it must have been in the camps—her experience hadn't crushed her spirit completely.

It had to be well past midnight, but Archie couldn't sleep. He put another log on the fire and then crept outside for fresh air. Or, if he were being honest with himself, the real reason was so he could escape Meiko's and Aiko's presence. He still felt terrible for how he'd failed them—perhaps because he hadn't found the courage to speak to Meiko yet about the guilt that hung over his head.

He walked slowly through the woods, trying not to crush any branches. He didn't want any noise to intrude on his thoughts. He knew why he hadn't apologized to Meiko yet: because, weirdly, it felt like he would be repudiating his wife. Elsie had been wrong—he'd known it at the time as surely as he knew it now—but he'd been raised to believe that a husband took his wife's side, no matter what. That's what his father had taught him, maybe because Archie's mother had been a hard woman, disliked by many of the other wives. His father had stood by his mother no matter whether she criticized another woman's child-rearing skills or threatened to shoot a neighbor's dog for trespassing on their land. It was one of the things Elsie had said she liked most about *him*. He was a loyal son, always respectful of his mother, and she knew he would always defend her.

Even when she was wrong.

And it was more than that anyway, he knew. He'd been *too* enchanted with her. Too struck by her beauty, too awed by her attention, too weak, too ready to succumb. He'd been tempted by the bright, shimmering lie of her, the desperate belief that God had chosen her for him, to come and make clean the sin in his past.

The woods were dark, but his eyes started to adjust. Whereas at first he kept catching his feet on stumps and downed branches and had nearly fallen to the ground multiple times, now he was able to pick a path in the moonlight. It was a relief to walk more freely. Here in the crisp air and quiet, he could leave all his troubles behind, if only momentarily. He could pretend he was camping and that Elsie was back in the cabin, sleeping like an angel. Pretend nothing had happened and he was back before everything started.

Something white and glowing surfaced ahead on the trail. *Dear Lord, not another balloon.* But this was luminous in a way that the bedraggled balloon hadn't been. Whatever it was, it was lean and pure, all light. Would the Lord send a messenger to comfort him in his most desperate hour? His heart started to race; it was immodest to think the Lord would find a sinner like him deserving, but he couldn't help hoping.

Instead, he came face-to-face with his wife.

Elsie stood in the path, wearing a flowing white gown. Her skin was glowing, her bright yellow hair almost too brilliant to take in.

She was almost painful to look at. She was majestic—which, if Archie was truthful, was not what you would've said about her in life. This was not as he'd imagined any ghost. Did that mean she was an angel now? Had God made her an angel?

Even though Elsie had her failings? Even though she had hated Meiko, and made her suffer?

Or was his mind feeding him what he *wanted* to believe?

Had he just been *conditioned* to believe in miracles?

"Husband." Her smile made his heart ache. It was even lovelier in death. Everything about her was overwhelming, her eyes more sparkling, her voice more melodious. It was glorious—and it couldn't be real. He knew she was dead. This had to be a dream. "I've missed you. All this time apart . . . Did you miss me?"

"Of course." He ached to hold her the way he had in their marital bed. Would God be displeased with him—here he'd delivered his dead wife like a miracle, and all Archie wanted was to be intimate with her one more time.

"Wonderful news, husband. I delivered our baby. It's a girl." As if struck by something heavy, Archie's breath vanished. "Do you want to see her?"

There were tears running down his face as he gasped to breathe.

And just like that, there was now a bundle in her arms, a package made of the same dazzling white light. Elsie smiled with such love and devotion, and held the baby out, her arms so close now he swore he could feel her warmth. Maybe she *was* alive. Maybe God had brought her back. Maybe God was rewarding Archie because he was so, so sorry. Couldn't prayer work like that?

The luminous white of her gown was changing. Getting darker, brighter. Redder. The red of the kimono of the woman in the woods at the beginning of this ordeal.

Elsie's sly smile was the same as that woman's. "Hold her. She is your daughter. You must want to hold her."

Of course he did. If it was only a dream, what harm would it do—besides to break his heart, give him a taste of what he could never have.

He took the bundle from Elsie; it was light as gossamer, silky to the touch. It squirmed gently in his hands.

He brought the bundle close to his chest and lifted the corner of the blanket to see her face. To see his daughter's face this one and only time.

He was sure she was as beautiful as her mother.

Elsie was beaming at him. So happy.

He looked down.

But it was no baby in his arms. He wasn't sure at first what it was. Something baby-shaped but covered in shimmering white. A cloth? Skin? Could the baby breathe? It was stirring, but why wasn't it making any noise? Was she suffocating? Should he tear this white veil from her? This shroud?

He looked to Elsie for guidance, but she continued to smile, as though nothing was amiss.

It wasn't a cloth, or a skin, he realized as he struggled with it.

It was a sac.

Suddenly, it split open in his hands and thousands of tiny white spiders came spilling out. Just like Joan Patzke in the hospital. There were so many, they looked like froth bobbing on the tide. Wave after wave of spiders swarming all over him.

His daughters.

Father, Father, Father . . . Like they'd been waiting to see him. To embrace him.

He dropped the bundle, and a gargled scream emerged from his throat. The white blanket fluttered to the ground as he slapped furiously at his arms, his clothing, to get the spiders off.

He thrashed himself awake—found he was not out in the woods but in his cot in the cabin.

A dream. A nightmare. His subconscious lecturing him. None of that had happened, even though it had felt so, so real.

A figure stood over him, looking down on him. Aiko.

And in her hands—something white.

The white blanket from his dream?

Impossible. He jolted upright.

She was holding it out to him, just like Elsie. But this couldn't be . . .

Wake up, Archie. Wake up.

"Mr. Mitchell, I found this outside. It's—"

He snatched it out of her hands and started for the door. He was shaking so hard that he thought he might fall down. But he had to take it away from her. Even if it killed him. He'd give the spiders their chance to bite him. He'd take that chance if it meant protecting her.

"What are you doing? This is dangerous, very dangerous! Don't you know what that is? That's a sac of spider—"

She looked at him as though he'd lost his mind. "Spider eggs. I know. But it's made of the spider's *silk* and that's what we need to make the antidote. It was in my grandfather's journal. The key to all this. My grandfather knew."

It was then he realized his fever had broken. His anger had dissipated.

He fell to his knees before Aiko. "I'm so sorry. I'm so sorry. Never again." The words poured out of him, on repeat, like a soft chant.

Tuesday—My friend at Meiji University wrote back to say that he has never seen this species and asked me to send more samples. He confirmed that they are poisonous and might even be responsible for what has been happening to the patients at the local hospital, but needs to run more tests. In the meantime, we should avoid them, he says. If only it were that easy.

I have decided, while I wait to hear back from him, to make my own antidote. I read of the procedure to make antivenom. It is done by injecting small amounts of poisonous venom into a host animal. The host animal's body will naturally produce antibodies. You then use those antibodies to create the antivenom, which would be given to anyone bitten by the poisonous animal to counteract the effects of the poison.

We need antivenom for these spiders, but I cannot see how to produce it. The spiders are so tiny. How would I collect the venom? How would I know how much to give the host animal without killing it?

But there is nothing I can do but try . . .

Monday—All my attempts to develop an antivenom have ended in failure.

The gamekeeper has helped me trap badgers, chipmunks, and weasels. I leave the cages under the heaviest spiderwebs and watch as the spiders swarm over the helpless beasts. Those are the worst moments and I almost relent and free the animals, but without sacrifice there would be no science. So, I let the spiders attack the poor creatures and silently pray for forgiveness.

So far, I have not been able to proceed to the next step. The animals become rabid so quickly that I am afraid to approach them to draw blood, and within hours they are dead so surely their blood is too virulent to use to develop antivenom.

What I find very strange is that we do not see rabid animals roaming freely on the island, which leads me to believe that when left to themselves, the spiders avoid biting mammals.

What's worse is that the gamekeeper, frightened by the rabid-like specimens, notified authorities on the mainland. They have shut down the ferry to Hokkaido until they are able to investigate the situation.

We are trapped here.

*S*unday—It is the child who may have brought me the answer.

Several days ago, I found Meiko playing with what at first appeared to be a large sac of spider eggs. In a panic, I struck the gauzy substance out of her little hands, only to realize it was not a full sac but an empty web. In the days since, I have monitored her closely, dread keeping me awake all hours, wondering if she will become plagued by the venom and go as mad as the patients at the hospital. But to the contrary, she has given no signs of infection, and it got me wondering.

As of yesterday morning, I have taken some of the spiderweb myself, soaked it in water, and distilled the liquid down to a tincture. My reasoning—my hope—is that there might be a protective agent in the silk, which is produced by the spiders. After all, merely touching the silk doesn't lead to madness, showing that there might be some protection there.

THE FERVOR

I gave some of this tincture to one of my test animals, one that was just beginning to show signs of agitation, and in mere hours it seems to have halted its progress, though more time is needed to test this theory.

I know I may be imagining this result because I want it to succeed so badly.

28

Meiko opened her eyes. A muted early-morning light illuminated the cabin, revealing that last night had been even more hurried, more desperate than she remembered. Clothes abandoned on the floor next to a small pile of food. Dust and smoke swirled on the air.

She rose from the rickety cot, careful not to step on her father's journals. She had stayed up late reading and left them where they had fallen from her hands when she got too sleepy to continue.

Before she'd fallen asleep, however, she'd come across what they were looking for, the information that would save them. The spiders did seem to be responsible for the madness that had spread through the camps and to the guards and townspeople, but the spiders also provided the cure—as so often happened in nature.

She was pretty sure, too, that she'd come across something else important, something she'd never heard her father mention. It seemed his research on Shikotan had led to a startling discovery about Wasaburo's Winds.

The jet stream, his jet stream, would make it possible to travel from Japan to the United States in far less time than anyone imagined:

If my calculations are correct, it seems some of the balloons carrying my instruments made it close to the coast of the United States! The winds off Shikotan appear to have made all the difference.

The Meteorological Institute is understandably excited. It is not yet possible to know, based on my limited research, what the implications are. Does this mean we could fly a plane from Tokyo all the way to America without refueling? It is doubtful that a plane could make it, but perhaps something smaller and lighter. A kite. Or even a balloon, like the ones I use to make measurements. If the object were light enough, I am sure it is possible. Wasaburo's Winds may be a significant discovery, after all.

After she'd read this, it all clicked into place. The washi remnants she'd seen in the army truck. How the gritty substance—spiders' eggs, she knew that now—had gotten from a remote part of Japan to the western United States, picked up at a launch site where the spiders were present, perhaps even Shikotan itself. The Japanese military knew it could fly balloons to strike its enemy, thanks to the work of dogged scientist Wasaburo Oishi.

It was her father's fault. Not that he'd had an inkling of what his research would one day enable.

The realization had made her sick, made her stomach churn and her head spin.

Everything she'd seen . . . the outbreak in the camp, people at each other's throats . . . the army men's diabolical program, the madness of the Loyal Sons of the Republic and their supporters . . . all of it was due to her father's discovery of those high-altitude winds. He was responsible for everything that had happened.

Which meant, in the Japanese tradition, that his family was responsible.

She was responsible.

Her stomach lurched and she feared, for a moment, that she was going to be sick. She couldn't think about this, not now. She had more immediate concerns. They also had the remedy—her father was responsible for that, too—and she had to figure out how to get this to the right people, to responsible people. But they also were being hunted by a rabid, unreasonable crowd right now. She had lives to protect.

Her gaze went to the cot she had made up for Aiko last night. It was empty.

She looked across the room to Archie's spot on the floor, a heap of coats by the fire. He, too, was gone.

That eased her worry, a little. Aiko was probably with him, the two looking for firewood or a second trail that would take them down to the road, or something else useful. Maybe they'd hiked down to the car to make sure it hadn't been disturbed.

She smoothed her dress and fished her coat from the pile on the floor, then stood at the window at the front of the cabin to look for them. She'd half expected to see them right outside the front door, but no. There was no one in sight. She'd need to go look for Aiko, then. Even if she was with Archie, she still felt uneasy.

It was rough going on the trail. She wished they'd brought coffee or tea, but in their rush, they'd overlooked it. She felt very groggy. It was hard to wake up, as though she'd been drugged in the night by an enchanted fog. Her head still hurt from straining over the journals, slowly and deliberately translating her father's pages word by word from Esperanto. It amazed her how well Aiko had picked it up. Her daughter could read much more quickly than Meiko, but the problem was she didn't always understand what she was reading. She wanted to rush ahead, to paraphrase rather than go word by word, and Meiko couldn't shake the nagging feeling that she might be skipping something. That meant Meiko needed to read the journals, too. There was no shortcut.

Meiko slowed, looking and listening for signs of Aiko and Archie. It had surprised her last night how her father's personality came through in his journals. Even some of his favorite little phrases had survived translation. It had filled her with longing and regret, made her forgive him for sending her away. She missed him more fiercely than she had in years.

Those journals. After reading what had happened on Shikotan and the revelation of the new wind measurements, she could only thank goodness her father had managed to hold on to them, that he hadn't allowed the officious little man from the ministry to confiscate all his notes. That was her father, cleverer than most.

Meiko remembered their time on Shikotan vividly. She had been four years old, so they were among her earliest memories. It was the only time she'd been alone with her parents, just the three of them. Her brothers, all older, remained in Tokyo, placed in a boarding school. But her mother had thought Meiko too young to be separated from them and insisted she come with them. It wasn't until many years later that Meiko understood that her mother knew her husband would ignore her, and she'd wanted a child to fill her lonely days.

She'd tried not to be unhappy on the island, but it had been hard. There hadn't been any other children, at least none that she had seen. Only fishermen and their wives. The hospital was at the far end of the island. Her father had warned her to stay away from it. Her mother had hated the island, Meiko was sure of it. She wouldn't associate with fishermen's wives. She'd insisted on accompanying her husband on the trip, saying he wouldn't be able to take care of himself while working. There would be a housekeeper at the cottage, they had been assured, but she didn't trust anyone from the island to take adequate care of her husband. She would leave her other children behind, her aging parents, her friends and diversions, to show what a dutiful wife she was. That Wasaburo was lucky to have her.

She remembered the tincture, too. Every day, he measured teaspoons of it into teacups, then made her and her mother drink it under his watchful eye. She no longer remembered how it tasted or anything else about it. Her mother complained that it gave her headaches, but her father had remained adamant: *As long as we are on this island, you will take it.* Then after a week or so, the authorities said they could leave, and they returned to Tokyo.

She remembered, too, the night he had sent up the last of his instruments. It had been a fierce night, so wild that Yuriko had begged him not to go out. He insisted. He packed a bag with his tools and slung it over his back, giving Meiko a sly wink as he opened the door. *I'm going to converse with my old friend Fujin*, he said before he left.

She couldn't wait to tell Archie and Fran—*where are you, Fran*—of her discovery of the secret behind the tincture hidden in the pages of her father's journals. *We have the solution.* Even the government wouldn't be able to produce enough of the antidote from her blood to take care of everyone who had contracted the disease, but now that they knew they could use spiders' silk, this wouldn't be an issue. The problem she hadn't figured out yet was who to go to with this information? The military was untrustworthy, as well as law enforcement. So were the officials running the camps. Obviously, they were in on what was happening, since they had infected the camp residents. To her, the government seemed like one big entity. If one piece of it was bad, surely that meant the whole thing was.

It seemed all of America was against them.

She needed to keep the secret she'd discovered. At least for now.

She pushed aside those troubling thoughts. They would find a way to get the right people in government to help. They would find someone to listen to them. This would be Fran's job (they needed Fran, but where was she?), and Archie's. She had to trust that they would take care of this. They were white. They would be listened to. No one would listen to her. No white person had listened to her for the whole time she'd lived in America—no one except her husband. She expected, now that he was likely gone, for the rest of her life she would fade into the background like a spring flower in sum-mer. Aiko would be the only person she'd talk with, eat meals with, go shopping with. Aiko would become her whole life—much like the way her mother had ceased to live except through her children. The fate of Asian mothers.

She wiped at tears. Enough. She didn't have the luxury of feeling sorry for herself. She had to find her daughter.

Meiko wrapped her coat more tightly around her as she scram-bled down the trail. It worried her that the reporter was still missing. When Archie had laid out his plan, he'd told them about Gearhart Mountain and described where they were going. It wasn't too strange that Fran hadn't found the cabin yet, since she didn't know the area and even Archie, who'd been there, had a difficult time finding it. Fran would have to be careful about asking for help with everyone in town suspicious. In all likelihood, she was still hiding out, waiting for things to calm down before figuring a way to join them. It didn't necessarily mean that Fran had been caught.

There was a noise ahead, in the woods.

"Aiko?" She strained to listen. *Let it be a little girl's laugh.*

More noise, the snapping of twigs and rustling of leaves. It sounded like more than just an animal picking its way through the woods, more than one man and a little girl. Whoever it was, they weren't making any attempt to be quiet. A bad feeling washed over Meiko.

She heard the rumbling of a car engine trickle up from the val-ley. Every nerve in her body told her to flee back to the cabin. But her daughter was out here so she couldn't turn back. Meiko dashed from tree to tree, looking for Aiko. She didn't dare call out, though she strained with the effort to keep the words bottled up inside. *Where are you, where are you?*

There was a flash of red up ahead. She froze. Focused. It was the nose of a car, inching up the access road. It would get to the end soon and whoever was inside would have to park and walk the rest of the way. They'd see Archie's Nash.

Their pursuers were here. They'd been found out. Maybe it had been a mistake to flee to the woods, where there would be no witnesses to see what was going to happen to them.

Meiko knew she had to go back. Maybe Aiko was waiting for her in the cabin. If not, she didn't know what she would do.

She ran uphill through the woods. Once those men found Archie's car, it was just a matter of following the trail to the cabin. It was faster but harder to cut through the woods, bypassing the switchbacks on the trail. She ran faster than she thought possible, not thinking about her burning lungs and aching calves.

There was the cabin, just ahead. And there were Aiko and Archie on the porch, Archie pointing at a bird in a tree. The two were unaware of the danger headed directly toward them.

She leapt onto the porch and grabbed them by their coat sleeves, pulling them along. "Get inside now!"

She bent over double once inside, gasping for breath, her back to the door.

"What's the matter?" Archie asked. How could he be so innocent? *He should've guessed.*

"Cars coming up the road," she managed between gasps. Aiko rushed to a window, like she was watching for a parade. "Get away from there!" Meiko ordered.

"What are we going to do?" Archie sounded dismayed.

"We must run. Leave everything."

Archie was rooting through his things. "Where are my car keys? We could circle around for the car . . ."

"Someone will be watching the car. We must leave it."

Archie's face fell. "Without the car, we'd be sitting ducks. We're a long way from anywhere . . . There aren't even any farmhouses nearby. No shelter."

"They're here!" Aiko shouted, pointing.

Meiko ran to the window: men were emerging from the trees, rifles in hand, heading toward the cabin. They had to be locals, dressed in flannel jackets and overalls, called off their tractors and out of their barns to hunt them down.

They didn't bother to hide their faces. They didn't plan to leave witnesses.

"Loyal Sons of the Republic." Archie nodded. He stood behind her. "I recognize most of them."

They were headed for the porch, grimly determined expressions on their faces. Meiko pulled Aiko away from the window, toward the back of the cabin. "We need to run now. I'm going to boost you through this window," Meiko whispered to her.

"How do we know there aren't more in the woods?" her daughter asked.

She was right. "We don't. We'll have to take our chances. I need you to be a brave girl. As brave as your grandfather Wasaburo. Can you do that for me?"

Aiko nodded.

Meiko looked back at Archie; he waved at her to keep going. She raised the window as quietly as she could.

Archie squared himself behind the front door. "Don't come in here!" he yelled out. "You'll be breaking the law if you do. This is still America—we have rights."

"Don't lecture me about rights, padre. We're exercising our rights as citizens," a man yelled back. "You're harboring a public menace in there."

"Which one do you mean? The wife of a soldier off fighting in the war, or his daughter?" Archie shouted back.

They were on the porch now; you could hear the rumble of their boots on boards, feel the structure move under their weight. The mob had come to their doorstep, just as Meiko had always feared. And now it was going to kill them. She had never thought this would happen to her in America, a country her father had sent her to. He—she—had always believed they would be safe here.

"Enough with that malarkey," a different man shouted. "You killed Gus Wallaby."

"He tried to kill us," Archie shouted back. "Tried to choke me with his bare hands."

"Bullshit. You're a murderer, and those Japs escaped from a quarantined government camp. Carrying a deadly disease. You're all outlaws. We're taking you in."

Meiko lifted her daughter to the sill, steadying her as she climbed through the opening. The window was high and Meiko couldn't look over it. There was a drop on the other side, but she only heard the soft thud of her daughter's landing and the crunch of dead leaves. She hadn't cried out, good girl. She hadn't hurt herself.

Meiko took one last look at Archie. He stood firm behind the door, holding off the men . . . This was a side of him she hadn't seen before. He was willing to put himself in harm's way to save her and Aiko. Maybe he had been changed by everything that had happened.

Maybe she could find it in her heart to forgive him for his betrayal, for sending them to the camps. For abandoning Aiko when she needed him.

Just as she reached for the sill to pull herself up, a shot rang out overhead. Were they shooting at the house now? Surely, they knew the occupants—a minster, a woman, and a child—would be unarmed. What sort of bloodthirsty monsters would shoot blindly into a house?

A second shot rang out, a blast that boomed over the roof. A blast that dwarfed the first, one that thundered like the voice of God.

"Stay right where you are! This is the Federal Bureau of

Investigation and we order you to put down your weapons and step away from the house," a voice called out.

Meiko froze. Could that be true? Could the FBI have followed these farmers up from the valley? Did they know what had been going on in Bly, been watching as the fires of hate leapt from house to house?

Someone on the porch snorted. Feet shifted restlessly. "How do we know it's who they say they are?" someone muttered.

"No one's going to come up here pretending to be the FBI," Archie shouted at them through the door. "Don't be foolish. Let's not make this any more dangerous than it already is. Nobody has to die today."

Before anyone could say another word, another shot rang out. Meiko could tell it had been fired from the porch. Were these men so foolish or deluded that they would shoot at federal officers? Or maybe having the military on their side had emboldened them. It was quickly answered by more shots from farther away, the blast so sudden and loud that Meiko and Archie instinctively ducked and cringed.

"Get down!" Archie hissed as he dropped to his belly. She followed, and not a second too soon, as both sides began shooting. Bullets ripped through the wooden walls, sending slivers of wood flying. They shattered windows, raining down shards of glass. The air was thick with the smell of gunpowder. Meiko breathed a silent prayer of thanks that Aiko had not been trapped inside with them. *Run*, she silently urged her daughter. *Run to safety.*

There were groans from the other side of the door, thuds shaking the porch. Some of the Loyal Sons had been shot, without a doubt. "Hold your fire," someone on the porch shouted reluctantly.

"Drop your weapons and hands up in the air where we can see 'em!"

Meiko went to the window to see five federal officers emerge from the woods with their rifles trained on the cabin. They looked out of place in their suits and hats and long wool overcoats, like they'd just come from an office. The men on the porch were immobile, clutching bloodied wounds. One lay glassy-eyed while another man pressed down on a bloody patch on his chest. Archie had opened the front door and stepped out, peering through the smoky haze to survey the carnage.

Then he dropped to one knee next to the most grievously injured man and, without reservation, joined in putting pressure on the wound. "Is there a medic?" Archie called to the approaching officers. "This man is badly hurt."

"We're lucky these country boys aren't better organized," one of the FBI agents said to another with a bit of a nervous laugh, "or this could've ended a whole lot worse."

They will learn from today, Meiko thought. *And next time, it will be.*

29

Meiko sat by the fireplace wrapped in a blanket, watching Aiko eat cider donuts given to them by one of the FBI agents. She was happy to escape the pandemonium outside.

The sheriff from Beatty had to be called in to help with arrests since the Bly sheriff and one of his deputies had been part of the mob. The Beatty sheriff grudgingly agreed to come up the mountain but refused to do anything more than escort an ambulance from Lakeview. "These men are my neighbors," Meiko overheard him say to the FBI. "If I arrest them, their kin will burn down my house. And they certainly won't vote me into office next election." Medics were tending to the wounded while FBI agents questioned the rest or marched them down the trail to waiting vehicles. A pile of hunting rifles taken from the Loyal Sons lay on the ground next to an old campfire pit. A deputy from Beatty—who didn't look all that different from the men who were being arrested—stood by the weapons, smoking and eyeing the FBI agents coolly. Meiko couldn't help but wonder if Beatty's police were members of the Loyal Sons, too. An organization like that couldn't operate without some cooperation from the police.

The urge for a cup of tea came back to her, strong. *I want to go home.* But where was that?

What a relief it had been to see Fran rush up to the cabin after the shooting had stopped, the FBI agents unable to hold her back. Fran told her what had happened in Bly once she learned Meiko and Archie had left without her. It had all been a blur, she said, from when the FBI agents plucked her off the street in Bly and hustled her away from the mob converging on Archie's house. The lead FBI agent, Matthew Curtis, had explained that he was part of a special FBI task force looking into a white nationalist group growing in the area—the Loyal Sons—and stumbled into a suspected secret army program. The Loyal Sons, it appeared, fed members into the pipeline of farmhands getting hired to work in the internment camps. Fran had nearly crossed paths with Curtis back in Kalispell. He'd heard there was a reporter looking into the story and tried to intercept her, eager to learn what she knew as well as keep her out of harm's way, but she'd left before he was able to find her.

Meiko was appalled by the FBI's admission that it had not known of APOGEE. "I don't understand how the army could keep this program secret from the FBI."

"It's easier than you might think. Every agency has a program to classify information within its own channels. Especially-close-hold programs get special compartments that restrict access to information." For obvious reasons, the army didn't want everyone in Washington to know what they were doing with APOGEE.

"This is no wild, rogue operation," Curtis continued. "The men running this program are powerful and have top cover from someone in the highest reaches of government. You have to understand: with the war, the Defense Department has a lot of leeway in D.C. right now, and that also means its senior leaders are under tremendous pressure to deliver results. A lot of money gets thrown at them. You start to think you're not accountable, not like 'regular' people. That's how you get programs like APOGEE."

Curtis turned to Meiko. "Washington headquarters had a hunch something funny was going on at Alameda. Now, whenever a new fire balloon was found on U.S. soil, Alameda wouldn't let the locals talk to anyone, not even us. They stopped sharing the information they'd gathered, too. I assume one of their people got sick after handling some fragments and that prompted the army to look into what was happening more closely. That's probably how they found the spiders' eggs—without having any idea how deadly they were. What a dangerous game they were playing."

He explained how they found Fran in Bly trapped behind the mob of townspeople heading toward Archie's house.

"We convinced her it was safer with us. We had to wait for the arrival of agents we'd called in from regional offices before we could move, though." He'd sent a man to watch the cabin overnight but had assured Fran the Loyal Sons wouldn't move until morning. "It's just too dark on the mountain at night. Even people who know the terrain well wouldn't risk it. We knew you'd be safe enough until daybreak."

Earlier, Curtis had taken Meiko aside for a private moment. He told her he'd spoken with Arlington Hall and they confirmed that Jamie Briggs's plane had been shot down over the Pacific Ocean. Neither pilot nor plane had been recovered. Of course, Meiko already knew this, but it wasn't easy hearing it a second time, to have all doubt removed. She appreciated the quiet way he broke the news. She didn't cry, only stared into the flames. She would cry later, she knew, after the shock of their near-miss with the Loyal Sons had worn off.

"You might be the most valuable woman in the country right now," Agent Curtis said after he'd drawn up a chair. "We have scientists who are going to want a little more of your blood for testing— if you agree, of course. It'll be the basis for an antidote."

"The spiderwebs won't be enough?" Fran asked. She'd been filled in on Wasaburo's journal entries. "Only the webs of those specific spiders will do the trick, right?"

"We have agents in the field gathering as many spiderwebs as they can find," Curtis said, swiveling in his seat, "but we probably won't find enough to make as much of your father's medicine as we need."

Through the front window, Meiko saw Archie with Aiko. He'd taken her for a walk in the woods so Meiko could speak to the FBI. She looked back at Curtis. She was too tired to be tactful. "How do I know I can trust you? I thought I could trust the U.S. government and look what happened."

Her abruptness didn't seem to bother him. "I completely understand. Operations like APOGEE upset me, too. All I can say is that most of us who work for the government understand our responsibility to uphold the law, but there are always some who take it too far. Those who are too zealous, or want to impress their superiors. They begin to believe that the ends justify the means, and they forget that we answer to the American people, not just whoever sits behind the desk and gives the orders. Mrs. Briggs, the bureau is working to get it shut down. I can't promise you it's going to happen—this kind of thing can be as hard to bring to heel as an epidemic, and the men behind it will fight to keep from being brought to justice—but we'd stand a much better chance if we had your cooperation. We want you to come with us to Washington, D.C. We'd like for you to talk to our director, and to our leaders in the Senate about what happened at Minidoka. We think it all points to an important threat to the nation, one we can't afford not to address."

Meiko scoffed. "Will they listen to me? A Japanese woman?"

"I understand your anger. But after everything you've been through, you would make a powerful witness. And you're the widow of a war hero—those congressmen would have to be monsters not to listen to you."

"They were monsters to put us in the camps in the first place."

"You're right. But I want to believe the tide is turning in America. I think Americans realize we let a lot of terrible things happen. There are people who want to right that wrong, but they can't do it alone. It's not right that we have to ask you to take this risk after everything you've been through—but we do. There's no other way, except to do it together. And the one thing I can promise you is if we don't fight it today, it will continue. This scourge won't go away on its own. It'll plague America for a long time."

Meiko threaded a strand of hair behind her ear. She was looking not at the FBI agent but at the stack of her father's slim journals and the pile of Aiko's drawings. "My father always thought it wrong that Japan did not open up more to the West. Japan can be arrogant; we are raised to believe our country is the greatest in the world and that we Japanese are somehow better than everyone else. I think it is one of the things that Americans hate most about Japan, is it not?" She said the last part with an ironic smile. "We are raised to believe the emperor is a god who always knows what is best. We are raised to follow orders. To submit, even when we have misgivings. Even when we know that no mortal man can be a god and should not be treated like one.

"My father wanted to share his discoveries with the rest of the world, but the government wouldn't let him. When he found out about the spiders, they took away his notes and told him not to tell anyone, and because he was a loyal citizen, he obeyed. Even though he knew better, he obeyed. Maybe if he hadn't, we would not be where we are today. All those people would not be dead." She bowed her head. "That is my father's legacy, too."

Now she turned to Curtis. "I will go with you to Washington. It is my familial obligation. I will do this because my father did not.

And in doing so, I will prove our critics wrong: Japanese do not choose their country over their obligation to *all* people. That may have been who we *were*, but we can change. And because Aiko and I are loyal citizens who want what's best for all Americans. There is no greater example I could set than that."

They gathered their things and Agent Curtis escorted them down the path to the last of the waiting cars. Along the way, it was decided that Fran would go to Washington with Meiko to watch Aiko. Archie wished them well. He had a congregation to rebuild in Bly, he said. Lots of grieving and angry people would need help healing.

"What about the threat to the Pacific Northwest? There are probably more balloons carrying these spiders out there, ones we haven't found yet," Fran asked Curtis. "They'll need to come up with a way to find them and destroy them. Otherwise, they'll continue to be a threat."

Curtis held the rear car door open as Meiko shepherded Aiko into the back seat. "We're already in the process of conveying this information to law enforcement throughout the region, to make sure they're aware of the danger."

As the car headed down the access road, Meiko watched out the rear window as the wild beauty of the mountain receded. The road smoothed out, dirt became asphalt. Telephone poles appeared, the line of poles keeping a steady rhythm as the car whizzed by. Fences marked the boundary of a farm, barns began to dot distant hillsides. They were passed by a truck hauling a load of freshly felled timber. They were heading back to town, to familiar whitewashed houses and storefronts with peeling paint, children playing stickball in a field. Bly offered a veneer of civilization, of typical Americana, but beneath that façade was a town she knew hated her, a town that wanted her and Aiko dead. The only thing keeping this from happening was the presence of armed FBI agents.

Was all of America like Bly? Was she a fool to risk her life, and possibly her daughter's life, trying to save a nation that would never accept her? That would never be satisfied, no matter how much they conceded and appeased, how many sacrifices were made?

She looked through the back window and watched the forest recede. The quietness of those woods was deceptive, too, as deceptive as the quietness of the town. There could still be spiders in the forest, spiders hidden in forests all over the Midwest and Pacific Northwest with no way to detect them. All it took was one person carrying the tiny, deadly spiders on them to infect an entire city. Imagine what would happen if someone figured out what was going on and decided to weaponize it for themselves? Would the victims ever know, ever figure it out?

And besides, she'd seen now, firsthand, that the real demons they should be worried about didn't live in the venom of spiders. The fervor—that's what she had begun to think of the disease as—had for its symptom the most powerful of contagious elements: fear. It seemed to spread from host to host faster than a spider could and caused violence and cruelty far deadlier than any weapon.

For that reason, the antidote alone, she knew, would never save them. The fervor would ebb and flow, but it would never fully die. It had been here since long before the first explosion.

She knew, someday, the fervor would be back.

And when it came, they'd be no readier for it than they were today.

She wanted to give in to despair, to the overwhelming unknown, but she knew that wasn't the way.

The only way ahead was to fight. And to do it together.

AFTERWORD

The Fervor requires a few words of explanation, I feel, even for readers of my previous two works of historical horror, *The Hunger* and *The Deep*.

It won't take long for readers to see that *The Fervor* is a very different book from those two, and that was by design. What I learned from writing those two earlier books is that every great disaster occurs for a reason that we're doomed to relive it if we don't make the effort to learn from it.

As I write this, America is experiencing a wave of senseless violence against Asian Americans that can't help but remind one of the internment of Japanese Americans following the attack on Pearl Harbor, when policy makers moved to deny tens of thousands of American citizens their rights and caused massive loss of freedom and property. Countless lives were wrecked because those in charge caved to a popular pressure without basis in fact, that was driven purely by emotion. Because policy makers and civic leaders didn't do what they knew in their hearts and heads was right.

I know the story of the internment well because it's part of my history. My mother is Japanese, and my in-laws' entire family were interned during the war. I grew up listening to stories of how my mother was ill-treated when she came to live in America with my father. She had been a child during the war and could hardly be blamed for decisions made by the men in charge, but that didn't make any difference to the people who called her names, mistreated and threatened her. The ugly brutality she suffered at their hands scarred her for life.

As for the internment camps, not only did I hear many stories from my husband's family but, like many Japanese Americans not far removed from that period in history, we watched documentaries and read books, and generally learned everything we could. It is a fascinating, many-sided, and emotional episode in America's history and one that should be studied in more depth in civics classes across the country. There's a long history of violence against Asians in America. If you're unaware of this, it's not surprising: it doesn't make the history books; it's not taught in classrooms in America. But lest you think I'm being histrionic with the white nationalism depicted in *The Fervor*, here's an abbreviated list of violent attacks on Asians on U.S. soil:

- In 1871, in one of the largest mass lynchings in U.S. history, a mob in Los Angeles attacked and killed nineteen Chinese residents, part of a growing wave of sentiment against Asians, who were seen as taking jobs that belonged to white laborers. This led to passage of the Chinese Exclusion Act of 1882, which banned Chinese laborers from immigrating to the U.S.
- In the U.S. in the 1940s, 120,000 people of Japanese heritage were forced to relocate to internment camps due to fears of espionage, following the bombing of Pearl Harbor. Over 60 percent of internees were U.S. citizens. No spies were ever found.
- In 1979, the Ku Klux Klan arrived in Seadrift, Texas, to intimidate Vietnamese crab fishermen, following an incident between

local white and Vietnamese fishermen in which a white fisherman was killed. The Vietnamese involved in the shooting were
acquitted on the grounds of self-defense, but the acquittal
prompted the Ku Klux Klan to descend on Seadrift and main-
tain a long campaign of violence and intimidation against the
Asian community there.

· Vincent Chin, a Chinese American, was beaten to death in 1982
by two American autoworkers who had mistakenly believed
he was Japanese. The incident took place during a recession that
was blamed, in part, on the increased share of Japanese auto
imports in U.S. markets.

· In 1989, Patrick Purdy, a drifter with a criminal record, fired
on a school in Stockton, California, predominantly attended by
Southeast Asian refugee children, killing five and wounding
thirty-two others. This event marked the largest number of
school-age victims in the U.S. until the tragedy at Columbine
High School in 1999.

· Violent crime against Asians in America rose by nearly 200 percent from 2019 to 2020, after political factions implied that
China was responsible for the deliberate release of coronavirus.
There was a swift upsurge in attacks on Asians across the country, with twice as many of these crimes directed against women
than men, possibly because they were seen as easier targets.

One reason the current wave of hate against Asian Americans
strikes a deep chord with me is because for many years during my
career as an analyst for the federal government, I followed civil
wars, genocides, and mass atrocities. For years I watched other
countries weaken and fall apart under waves of baseless propaganda,
generally campaigns run by authoritarian thugs who sought to un-
dermine a society by generating an irrational fear of a scapegoat, an
"other." The playbook is the same, again and again. Lies, lies, and

the willingness of a large part of a population to channel their fear into senseless hatred.

While studying what was happening in other countries—Bosnia and Herzegovina, Liberia, and Rwanda, to name a few familiar in the annals of infamy—I was almost smug in my belief that this systematic dissolution of a country's common sense may have been possible elsewhere but would never happen in America. We had institutions to protect against this: freedom of the press, most importantly, but also safeguards built into our governing laws and principles. It went against our very nature as Americans. We were raised to believe in truth, justice, and opportunity for all.

We all know what's happened in recent years in this country.

Like *The Hunger* and *The Deep*, *The Fervor* is based on two real historical incidents, one being the internment, as already mentioned. The second is the fire balloons, or Fu-Go, which did manage to make it to the American West Coast during the last months of the war. The actual story of the Fu-Go is barely scratched here, and for those who are interested in learning more, I recommend *Fu-go: The Curious History of Japan's Balloon Bomb Attack on America* by Ross Coen. It provides a thorough exploration of the history behind the balloons, as well as a timeline of events.

Unlike my previous two books, which adhered to historical timelines, *The Fervor* deviates from actual events, and I want to be clear about this. This book was written to hold the mirror of history up to the reality of today, to show that the self-deception we were guilty of in the past is back with a sickening vengeance. The timeline in *The Fervor*, particularly the balloon events, does not reflect the sequence in which they actually happened, and while there are a few characters based on real people—Archie and Elsie Mitchell, the children who died on Gearhart Mountain, and a few others—the characters in the book are not meant to be representative of these people. *The Fervor* is a work of fiction, meant to tell a specific cautionary tale, and I've massaged the historical events and characters in order to tell that tale. There are plenty of fine nonfiction books that will give you the full and complete story of the internment, if that's what you're looking for. Just be aware that it's not what you're getting here.

I would like to thank my in-laws, the Katsus, and all the aunts, uncles, and cousins who shared their stories of the internment. I am especially grateful to my former neighbor Kathy Kamo, who let me use her family's invaluable collection of written records from their time in Minidoka. And of course, I thank my mother for not shielding her children from the truth of the world by sharing the sad stories from her first years in America.

This book would not exist if not for the following people, to whom I'd like to express my deepest thanks. To the folks at Putnam for their support: my editor and publisher, Sally Kim; president, Ivan Held; director of publicity, Alexis Welby; director of marketing, Ashley McClay; publicists Katie Grinch and Sydney Cohen; and associate editor Gabriella Mongelli. As always, thanks to Lexa Hillyer and the team at Glasstown Entertainment for their support. Special thanks to my ever-patient agents at Inkwell Management, Richard Pine and Eliza Rothstein, and my film rights agent, Angela Cheng Caplan.

Mostly, I'd like to thank everyone who has read one of my books. I can only hope that you get as much out of reading them as I get from writing them.